FRACTURED

Reveries

EDITED BY

Carina Bissett

Fractured Reveries: A Storied Imaginarium Salon

Paperback edition ISBN: 979-8-9990813-0-8

Cover illustration by Mario Sánchez Nevado
Cover design by Todd Keisling
Interior design by Allison Pang

Published by Storied Imaginarium Books
A division of Storied Imaginarium Inc
Colorado Springs, CO
www.thestoriedimaginarium.com

First edition: July 2025
10 9 8 7 6 5 4 3 2 1

To all writers who have taken workshops at the Storied Imaginarium, this book is for you.

Contents

Introduction

Fairy tales are an integral part of who I am. They are some of the first stories I remember reading, and they create the foundation of everything I write. In 2016, I was in a terrible bicycle accident, and it was fairy tales that kept moving forward when all I wanted was to sink into the dark. In fact, Storied Imaginarium was born that same year, and several of the writers who attended that first workshop are still involved with the Storied Imaginarium today. It's a powerful testament to the enduring nature of fairy tales and the many ways they can be mined for creative expression.

Since that tumultuous start nine years ago, I have had the privilege of working with writers from around the world. The growth of the Storied Imaginarium has been organic, and the community reflects those connections that continue long after a session has concluded. Writers have taken story seeds from these generative writing workshops and have published finished stories in some of the most esteemed magazines in speculative fiction today. Not only that, but they've also written poetry and creative nonfiction, memoirs and novels. They are receiving awards and accolades including the Bram Stoker Award®, the USA TODAY's bestseller list, and several "best of" anthologies. I couldn't be more proud or impressed by the work these writers are doing, which was what started the whole idea of compiling an anthology featuring stories and poems generated in Storied Imaginarium's workshops.

I've tossed this idea around for years now, but it wasn't until an anonymous fairy godmother offered to cover the costs for creating this book that it finally became a reality. Even then, it seemed an insurmountable task. But then, the community stepped in to help. Before long, we had a diverse collection of original stories and poems from a wide range of writers. We have everything from first publications by new writers to pieces written by accomplished professionals. Works included range the gamut—from science fiction to hardcore horror, from new weird to dark fantasy. And beneath them all run the threads of fairy tale and myth.

According to award-winning author Catherynne M. Valente, "No matter what you write, you actually can't help retelling a fairy tale somewhere along the way" ("Confessions of a Fairy Tale Addict," *Reactor*). I believe this is true. The Storied Imaginarium is founded on that belief. And as we approach our tenth year, we offer this stunning collection as proof that fairy godmothers exist, and dreams do come true.

~ Carina Bissett

LIES YOUR MOTHER TOLD YOU

Fija Callaghan

You're safe along the path.
Boys don't like girls who stop
to smell the wildflowers,
who pass their days in idleness
and cheap spun-sugar dreams.

> *Be bold, be bold,*
> *but not too bold.*

Ladies don't wear red:
hoods, shoes, stockings, scarves,
hair, lips, fresh-drawn blood.
Don't tempt the wolf
with the heat of your flesh.

> *My mother, she killed me,*
> *my father, he ate me.*

The only wolf whom you can trust
is that which wears your father's face.
When he bears his teeth and claws
it's just to strike
the world down

> *Lest that your heart's blood*
> *should run cold.*

so its edges cannot pierce you.
And if we lead you to the wood
where crows devour your trail
of crumbs, it's only out of love;
     or hunger, desperation.

> *My sister she buried*
> *my bones.*

Your beauty is your currency:
power, privilege, curse and cage.
Let me take it for you.
Let me carry your burden
in a beating jewelled box.

SHOES AS RED AS SUNSETS, BONES AS WHITE AS HOPE

Haralambi Markov

You hear the dead girl dancing before you see her. She looks so small, so young, stripped of skin, meat, and gristle. Her shoes carry her in circles and spirals over overgrown cobblestone. Her dance is a warning against hubris. A curse from the old days, when words had more power and more weight than stones.

If you don't repent; if you don't show gratitude for the gifts fortune gives you; if you don't curb your greed, all will be taken from you. That's the moral of the story. And what's worse, no one will help you. This is a private lesson you've kept to yourself. It's why the women come with ribbons for the girl to placate her at their happiest. Only the women, you note.

Men are not punished for wanting, for taking what's rightfully theirs by virtue of seeing it as such. That's another lesson you've learned. Your husband never had to offer a thing to the dancing girl when your father agreed to the match. The men only know her from stories. Women ... well, women are an entirely different story now aren't they?

The townfolk dug a wide moat when they moved and left the plague behind, so that she would not follow them to new pastures. Let the past be the past. The channel was deep and scarred the land from horizon to horizon beyond well-trodden roads into the wilderness, where the girl did not dance. The girl approaches slowly, but you do not lower the drawbridge—a large wooden beam fastened upwards and tied with rope to a crank. You do not cross over to the dead lands. You do not sit at the stone bench. You do not tie the ribbon your mother has given you for this exact purpose. You do not want her blessing for your upcoming wedding.

It's surprising that you have to go to hell to bargain for good fortune, but that's how it's always been. Tie a ribbon on the dancing girl to ensure life's good blessing, or she will come in the dead of night and curse you. The younger girls in town, who are far away from having to be thankful for love or a child, whisper how she'll whisk you off to dance with her forever, or worse—make you mad! Make you burn down your house, slit your husband's throat, then yours. To these tales, their mothers and grandmothers would say 'Shush! Do not speak of such vile things. It's how you invite misfortune.'

Misfortune is what you hope for when you get betrothed to your husband. A wonderful man, your parents say. A man to envy, your friends speak amongst themselves. You do not wish to wed, but who wants to hear that of a woman. You do not wish to marry him. His eyes scare you, but who wants to hear that? Not when he hunts, and cures leather, and cleans furs, and butchers carcasses, and makes other men want to be a man like him. Thick of hair, and thick of muscle.

You do not tie the ribbon to the girl. You dig a hole a ways off under a loose tile and bury it there. What other girls do gladly to prevent a good match from spoiling, you toss away. Every woman goes to the dancing girl before her wedding. You will have to pretend what it was like to see her live.

Well as alive as a dead girl can be. You almost feel guilty for ruining the fine ribbon.

Your mother had spent many days collecting loose hairs from your head and stitching each into the fabric alongside colored thread, writing your spirit if not story into the fabric. Yours was one of the most elaborate ribbons as your family had the most to gain from a favorable marriage. Your mother's being unfavorable. After all, your father is your father, and the less is said about him the better. Every day since you've buried your ribbon, you watch the horizon for the girl to intervene. To punish. You do get married after a time. At the wedding you expect to see her red shoes tap onto the church's floor to collect her boon, but that does not happen. The marriage is the punishment, you realize.

Your husband touches you unkindly, and now you are with a child you do not wish—as cruel as that sounds to you—but it clings on despite all your best efforts to undo it. Just like its father, it won't ever let go of you. The day after the wedding you work on a new ribbon for your inevitable child and bite your tongue around your husband until it bleeds. It's how things go. Brides turn wives turn mothers turn ... These are women's seasons, and no woman is spared.

Some days you sit by the river way out and punch your rage into the fabric. Slicken the thread in the saliva of your curses and embroider jagged patterns that hurt the eye. That's how you meet the wood hag. She used to be related to someone important. No one talks of who she is just that one day she had a husband. The next she did not, and her relatives ousted her from her house. What use did a woman have of a house without a man to fill it? The hag now lives not too far, but not too near in an old, abandoned hunting lodge of her own volition. For this she is not judged. Best not be seen. The past has to stay the past.

"Careful." he smiles. "You'll not impress the girl with this work. Gentle stitches appeal to her more."

Your hand, holding the needle, trembles with quiet rage then. You say nothing, but your eyes burn with meaning enough that the woman nods and hunches over to where you sit. The oily smell off her skin stays with you even with the odors of wildflowers wafting from the old city.

"Perhaps you're not interested in her blessing, then. I've heard you're with child. Are you not happy?" She looks at you, really looks. Sees the circles under the eyes, the green afterglow of a bruise on your exposed shoulder. Sees what married life means. You shed no tears. Fingers pick up the work again.

"I see. Listen to me good now, girl. Sew coins and pendants on the back of the ribbon. Any bits of metal work. Doesn't matter. Finish the ribbon with a tiny bell. When you go meet her, tie the ribbon on her pelvis."

"And then?"

"She'll help you."

"How?"

"That I don't know. I heard this when I was a girl. Could be old wives tales. Could be salvation. You have to decide whether it's worth the risk," she says and shrugs.

It can be nothing. It can be everything. It's why you follow her instructions.

You hear the dead girl dancing before you see her. She looks so small, so young, stripped of skin, meat, and gristle. Yes, that is still true. Her shoes carry her in circles and spirals through overgrown cobblestone. That is still true as well.

She dances through the old town, abandoned since before you were born, through each street and open space until her shoes bring her to the edge where the old town ends and the new one starts. Blazing in the setting sun, the skeleton steps as if on a pair of flames. This time you've crossed over to the dead lands. You sit on the stone bench placed right beside the small square she visits at sunset. It's her final stop dancing before she retreats wherever she spends her nights. Fear quickens your blood, and your hands tremble. Do you take the risk?

Womanhood is a risk in any case, so you watch the dancing girl draw nearer, seeing only the tip of her shoes. The bell threatens to melt in your hand from how hard you're squeezing it, and the metal scraps bite in your palm, but you decide you will do it. The girl seems to know she's under someone else's eye, because she winds down. Moves as if underwater, and the scores of ribbons—some fresh, some soiled, some reduced to mere strings—flutter in the afterbirth of movements. You don't notice any ribbon with a bell on it, but you're determined to try. Despite trembling in fear, you loop the ribbon around her pelvis. Your hands move quickly, fearful not to touch her bone, and tie a sturdy knot.

The bell rings out when you let it go, and the dance stops mid-motion. The girl lowers her hands and upraised leg to rest; her spine unwinds, her skull swivels towards you. Blood chills in your veins, and you've forgotten how to breathe. Under her hollow gaze, you feel small and vulnerable, but never like with your husband. Whatever comes next would not be worse than what happens after sunset in that man's house.

You expect her to strike you down, or strike down your child. Tear into the core of you and end everything. A part of you burns in fury at the old hag for lying to you. A part hopes at the promise of ending it all. But the girl does nothing of the sort. She bows to you in a curtsy, fistful of ribbons in her delicate hands, then gestures to you an invitation into her domain. Elegant arms pointed towards the crumbling houses.

Frozen until you get the hint. Breath hitches in your chest at crossing further into the cursed city. Tales of the plague still spin as yarn on people's tongue. Disease so horrible it would make your teeth melt like candle wax and skin shrivel until it splits to reveal the fruit of you beneath. Do you have any choice? You do, of course. But the familiar seems worse than an invitation to take a stroll.

You start walking. Only then does the girl spins once, twice, thrice on her toes and hops to the front, guiding you towards her home. You don't have to walk fast to keep up since the girl takes her time to dance through the streets, zigzagging like a fishbone stitch forward then backward then side to side in a pattern that she's been tracing for a long, long time. Your heart breaks for the girl, who never stops even for a second. You don't hear the music she dances to, but find the tact in the grinding of her bones. It's a painful, dry melody. How much bone dust has she pollinated the streets with over the decades?

You decide it's indecent to watch and turn your gaze towards the dead lands. This was the town your ancestors had left, because of the plague. Tall buildings made of stone. Whispers of pigments on the exteriors hint at what the façades might have looked like when there was life in the streets. To your surprise, much remains unchanged. Yes, the roofs have largely collapsed, and the glass shattered. Shrubs, trees, and grass had laid their claim where possible, yet the doors stood—many closed and, upon closer inspection, locked. You carefully wipe dust from the glass panes to reveal furnished rooms blanketed by dust. The furniture is unlike anything you'd ever seen, and you don't know how to read the signs—some wooden, some painted on the walls, others spelled out in metal letters mired in rust. Truly outlandish.

Here and there you do recognise a shop walled on all sides in glass. Or a bakery. Or an eatery. Time and the elements had not been kind to these buildings. Glass had been broken. Tables and chairs overturned. Flowers sprouted from unlikely places. It's beautiful. You breathe in the fragrant air. Death has no place here. The sun melts and browns darker like butter in a heated skillet, then rises the moon. The girl continues dancing. Are you supposed to walk with her until you die? You must have walked for hours by now. Your feet hurt, swollen as they are from the pregnancy you did not want, but you dare not fall behind. To die like this ... Water gathers in your eyes. Had someone mourned this cursed girl? You'll mourn her now, as you mourn yourself.

Every so often the girl pirouettes backwards, fixing empty sockets on you as if to say, 'Yes, I'm still leading you. Please wait for me some more.' Those two hollows are somehow darker than the night. No twinkling starlight reaches them. No soft patina of moonlight softens their stare. You lock eyes with an abyss, and you have no way to decipher meaning. Does she know what your eyes hold or your silence says? Can she extract any meaning from a living girl, when she'd been dead for so many years? To her, you may very well be the specter she must guard herself against. She's not looking back to make sure you're following, but checking to see if she'd lost your pursuit.

This and so much more churns your mind until the streets widen to another square. Larger than a house garden. No wider than an orchard. The buildings pull away from this green place with its grass and dirt path. Its crowning trees begging to touch heaven with their fingers. Sounds of splashing water pull your eyes towards a pond where fat, nimble raccoons dig through the banks and hop around. From the trees, birds titter, and their wings flutter.

This does not make sense to you. Hadn't the plague wiped out every living thing? Wasn't this what you've been told all your life? Your mother had told you to never step beyond the bench for the sickness would take you, and then...Well then, God have mercy on you all. But there is so much life here. Nothing like the stories drunk old men told children beside winter fires or under summer vines.

Perhaps your people's history was true at one point. Perhaps it was something else that over time people misheard and misremembered and mistold down the generations until truth had been lost in translation to time without making it any less honest. Or it had never been true in the first place, and everyone is content to lie to everyone else. This last option sours your mouth with its fetid intimacy. Yes, you've lived one truth, but told another. Same as your mother. Same as not a few of your sisters-by-friendship.

Men do it, too, of course. But when they misspeak it's out of condescension, believing in all honesty that by dressing truth in politeness and misdirection, those of fair body and frail mind would be too stupid to not see. When women misspeak it's to prevent more from happening to them. You have seen what happened to your mother, when she told her truth. Pointed the finger at your father. Guided a mirror to his face. It's no wonder that the ribbon she made for you was the prettiest thing you've ever seen.

You don't know what to hope the child in your womb is. Wound or knife. It's too small in your belly to make its nature known. The thought chills you more than the night. The ruins of the city somehow suck the heat from the air. They're probably looking for you now. It breaks your heart to hear your mother call your name from the bench along with the other women. It also delights you to imagine the men rooted by terror behind—not one foot across the border between their town and these ruins.

As the moon grows too heavy for its own pleasure and dips, the girl guides you to a grand house—a palace you think! Surely, if there ever were palaces, this would be one. She quiets her pirouettes and wide strides to delicate nibbles of steps up an overgrown stone path and disappears into the darkness. What is there else to do than follow? During these long hours, you feared for your life. Thought about what a dancing skeleton could do to you. Welcomed the idea of death yourself. But now you think of nothing more than a bed.

The girl, now only gently swaying, waits for you. Even deathless beings need to rest. You can barely make her out in the dark, even if your eyes had adjusted to a night without candles or lanterns. When you do join her, she takes you up the stairs to a large room full of treasures. Jewels, and gold, and silver, and finest of fabrics, and objects of smooth lines. Even under layers of dust, all glints and glows with some inner light as if there are dozens upon dozens of candles lit at every corner of the room. You hold your breath. What lives your ancestors used to live ... Tales of grand parties twirl into your memory like the great skirts women used to wear. Not all stories are just that. A smile spreads on your face at this small delight.

The girl sways close to a table with a grand mirror and plucks a ribbon with its own rich glow and a tiny silver bell. You extend your hand when she asks for it. It's only fair to let her do to you what you've done to her. You do not flinch at the contact of bony fingertips like the blunt end of large sewing needles. She pulls her hands away, and the bell rings as it drops. You follow her, as she leads you into dance. Feet in step. Bells in harmony. Then you hear the music. Such sweet, gentle, soothing melody. Exhaustion dissolves into bliss. Lightness overcomes your body.

You dance until blood runs from between your legs, and you realize the child has been let go. You cry and you dance, and dance and squeeze the dead girl's bony hands, and dance until you spin yourself into her body. Now you're so small, so young, stripped of skin, meat, and gristle. You feel safe for the first time in a long time, looking into your own tired brown eyes from her empty sockets, and not the other way around.

Death, you come to feel, possesses its own beauty. Death removes everything unnecessary. You dance as she dances. Not out of a curse, but out of liberation as there's nothing to weigh you down. Nothing that a man might find desirable. Gradually, as you get used to this new form, a new way of seeing opens to you. There's so much light to see without your pathetic living eyes.

You see so many women. Of so many ages. They all laugh, and they all cheer, spinning in circles around you to welcome you among their ranks.

"You're here! You're free! He will never hurt you again!" Their choir chants, and you believe them for they are like you.

"And you? What happens to you?" You ask in a voice that's the ghost of a whisper, but the you, who is not you, hears you just fine and smiles. Your body has stopped dancing and you see yourself in full. The sight of what living has done to your person makes you weep, though there are no tears to spill. Nevertheless, the you, who is not you, stands straight with resolve on your former face. You don't remember to have ever looked like that in the past.

"I will bring justice." She parts with a wave, and then she is off. Back to your life. Back to deliver retribution. It makes sense now. All these tales of mad women, who bit the hands that fed them. Only justification to keep one's woman—be it wife, or mother, or sister, or daughter—in check. The skeleton girl would never punish her own sisters. You weep again at the unfairness of how her story, her very nature, has been twisted to pit woman against woman.

"Come dance. Come see what we see. It will do your heart wonders," the ghost women urge you, and you follow them out in the open and down the streets and through the alleys and across squares. All around other ghost women smile and laugh and dance. On water, on air, through glass, through walls. It takes you a day to greet them all and a night to say farewell before you waltz into the palace once more.

You do this again and again. The girl that once took your place returns as a spirit on her own after some time, curtsies in front of you, tells you that it's done. The butcher will not butcher anything anymore. You do not ask questions.

Eventually, you meet other girls and women on that bench, holding ribbons for prosperity. Most look happy to tie them onto you. Others do so fearfully. Fewer still do not muster the courage and look relieved when you leave, still clutching their ribbons. You want to tell them, it's alright. You won't harm them. If only you still had a tongue to speak. Their rebellion makes you feel less alone in your own decisions when you were alive.

Then years later on a crisp spring evening, a woman just like you ties a ribbon with a bell on your pelvis. It is now time to repay the kindness you were gifted.

You invite her into the city.

She follows.

A MURMURATION OF SOULS

Allison Pang

Summer has always seemed like a desperate season to me, a coaxing come-on cloaked in clinging sweat and the sticky scent of tanning lotion and stale cotton candy. On the boardwalk, tourists came and went, their feet burning on asphalt and sand, their bee-buzz conversations punctuated by shouts and music, carried on a breeze born of salty sea spray, warm beer, and soggy hot dogs.

But Summer couldn't touch me in Maw Maw's parlor with the rickety bamboo fans going *clackity clackity clack* and the broken grandfather clock that never seemed to be the right time. It tick-tocked incessantly, chiming out whatever hour it felt like, whenever it damn well pleased, as though keeping time was merely an afterthought.

As a child I'd hide under the corner table in that dark parlor, listening as Maw Maw told fortunes for a handful of dollars in the shadows of soft candlelight. A resin brazier spread the sweet perfume of lemongrass or ylang ylang, or sometimes patchouli, depending on her mood. Her grey hair was beaded with cowrie shells that jingled as she moved her head, and her eyes glittered gold.

Myriad bird cages hung from every free space on the ceiling, piled on top of each other in chaotic fashion, made of wicker and bones and iron. Each cage held a bird of a different sort in varying arrays of plumage, impossibly all warbling their songs in a cacophony that somehow muted into softness whenever a customer came in.

Everyone has a bird inside them, my Maw Maw used to tell me. A soul trapped within the cage of their ribs. Sometimes they sing and sometimes they mourn and sometimes they pick the plumage from their bodies, as though they might swap feathers and become some other bird entirely.

My favorites were the crow boys with their cheeky cheerfulness. I would catch them flirting with the imposing raven girls too wrapped up in velvet ribbons to pay them any attention at all. And I remember a rainbow riot of parrots proclaiming truth as they saw it, a proudness of peacocks who could only stare into mirrors, and a handful of owls that merely blinked, their eyes reflecting the emptiness of the stars, holding no wisdom save the screaming terror of mice.

The customers never took notice of the birds or cages or feathers. Perhaps they never saw them at all. Their focus was simply on what Maw Maw could tell them. But there was always a moment of muffled revelation from each customer, as though stepping through the curtained doorway was to cross the threshold of a different realm altogether, a liminal existence that might as well have been on the moon.

WhowillImarry

    Or

HowcanIleavehim

Or

WillIhavesuccessinmynewbusiness

Or

Towhomwillmyfatherleavehiswill

Or

IcannothavethisbabynotanotheronehowcanImanage ...

Questions upon questions, all different, but somehow all the same: the me, the me, the me and the soul birds pecking against ribcages meant to hold much frailer things.

Maw Maw always smiled patiently as they gathered their money and whispered their questions, her head cocked to hear the rustling of the birds in their cages and humming her thoughts to the bird in the customer's chest.

Most of the time they only needed a nudge in a different direction to realize the answers were always there inside them. No one should need a medium to speak to their own souls anyway, though as Maw Maw said, it wasn't the speaking that was the problem so much as the listening.

She wasn't going to turn down a dollar because some folks were purposefully deaf.

Sometimes despair was a dress they wore, widow's weeds made of spider's silk or salt or faded daisies that dripped petals when they walked, a grief without end. Sometimes it was an animal balloon floating behind them, as empty as the nervous laughter meant to conceal a broken heart, or the confusion of not knowing what to do.

Come here, my loves, come here, Maw Maw would croon, coaxing the bird from a fractured rib cage, the jagged beak slicing through flesh and sinew, leaving a hollow place behind. *Leave your troubles and rest a while, stay awhile.*

Tears would fill the space, soothing and soft. Afterwards, the customer would leave, drifting down the boardwalk without quite understanding why they didn't hurt so much anymore. Even if they didn't know, they recognized that the keening within them felt satisfied, and there was peace to be found in that, perhaps.

Maw Maw would put the bird in one of her cages and sigh. "Sometimes there just isn't any other way." But sometimes, much later—months or years or however long it took, she would open that cage, and a bright-eyed bird would launch into the heavens, like a homing pigeon to return to a body that was now healed enough for it to fit.

"They'll tell you when they're ready to leave," she said to me, one of those particular evenings. She carried a small cage housing a thrush, the bird calling over and over. "Simply listen to them and you'll know it's time."

"And what if they can't find where they're supposed to go?" I wiped the jelly from my cheek, concerned only with finishing my sandwich, as we walked along the edge of the dunes. The esoteric knowledge of soul birds fell short in the interest of my empty belly.

"We are not their owners," she said, an air of regret sliding over her, as she opened the cage door. "Merely temporary keepers for lost souls and heart seekers. We soothe the memories of what was or what could have been, but it's an illusion. Destiny calls them as it will, and the Fates weave as they wish. A soul will find its way home, or it won't."

The bird seemed to hesitate, fluffing its feathers into a plumpness that shone beneath the moonlight. "Where do they go if they don't?"

"That's a secret," she murmured, tapping the side of her nose. The thrush called a final time and flew out of the cage, fading into the night sky.

When I was thirteen, the siren song of the boardwalk drew me away from Maw Maw's parlor tent. Surfboards and waves and eating ice cream with the city boys who found themselves sunburned and too slow to catch me among the whitecaps.

Maw Maw said nothing when I left, but she sighed when I returned and tracked sand into her parlor. She'd make me sweep it up before applying Sea Breeze to my blistering skin, and then listen to me gush about the band playing at the end of the pier, long-haired wanderers with slurred voices and electric guitars.

The crow boys in their cages hooted and mocked when I giggled; the raven girls recited limericks made of swear words as though they didn't care in the slightest. The peacocks certainly didn't. The parrots were always down to party at the mention of music, but I was too busy dancing to pay much attention.

Maw Maw raised a brow, poured me a cup of iced tea and let me chatter like a sparrow until dawn.

When I was sixteen, I slept with one of those long-limbed city boys, enticed by soft words and hard fingers. Years of watching weeping women come through the parlor doors had left me with a jaded eye, thinking it would be so easy to distance myself emotionally when he disappeared the next morning, slipping out of my life as easily as he'd slipped into it: casually and with a clumsy brush of lips.

Maw Maw served me a slice of chocolate cake when I finally came home. She didn't have to ask what the love marks on my neck meant. Over the years she'd dropped 'be careful' warnings like raindrops in a summer storm. If I went out without an umbrella, that was on me.

The caged birds were oddly silent as I ate, my fork clinking on the plate with each tasteless bite. Not that I cared so much about losing my virginity. A hymen was a social burden, a membrane upon which a woman's standing apparently rested, as though something so flimsy and easily broken were the measure of my worth.

The threshold out of childhood had been crossed, and I had paid the toll willingly.

Maw Maw hugged me when I turned toward her. "The verses of this tune may change, but the refrain, oh the refrain is so often the same."

"I don't want it." The cake sat in my gut like cement. "He could have least seen me home. Or given me his number."

Maw Maw cocked her head at her birds. "I have found that men often use up all their words in the beginning of the courtship, like a well that runs dry upon the moment of pleasure." A humorless chuckle escaped her, one of the raven girls mimicking it in a guttering cry. "Don't waste yourself on someone with such a limited vocabulary, Sara. It's rarely worth it in the end."

I forced myself to eat the last bite of cake and tapped my chest. "And if I asked you to remove it, would you?"

Her gimlet gaze raked over me, golden and piercing, but I refused to look away. "If it is truly what you wished, then perhaps, but ..."

"I don't really want that, right?" I finished for her, gathering my plate and fork and dumping them into the sink.

She winced at the noise. "That's for you to decide. Remove it yourself, if you're so inclined."

I blinked at her. "I can do that?"

"You have the gift," she said mildly. "But this path is not an easy one to walk. The care of souls is not to be taken lightly. Be sure it's something you want, and not simply a means of escaping from something you don't wish to face." Her face grew deadly serious. "I know I raised you better than that."

I flushed, and excused myself, weeping softly in the shower. I pressed my palm to my chest. Inside me, a bird quickened.

I was nineteen when I left Maw Maw and the pier, onboard a ferry bound for the city. Maw Maw gifted me with a string of cowries to wear around my neck and kissed me on both cheeks. I opened my mouth to tell her I was sorry, that this life was not for me, but I could only say good-bye. Gift or not, the responsibility of figuring myself out was heavy enough, let alone the souls or hearts of strangers.

And oh, the city, the city across the bay, bright and jeweled in the night with its glittering lights and asphalt rhythm. The cars, the trucks, the laughter and the shouting! The musical pulse of humanity folded in on itself in an eternal torus, without beginning or end.

But some nights all I felt was the quiet, sitting on a mattress wedged into the corner of the top floor in a five-story walk-up, my window cracked to let in the breeze and the wail of sirens. There were no bone cages here, no chattering souls to mock me or measure my choices against some unknown yardstick.

And yet somehow they were still all around me. Strolling down the street to the bodega, or in the night clubs, the pubs, the thrift shops. Denial ran thick in my blood, but the cowrie necklace sang when I walked, reflecting the hollow despair of so many lost people lurking about in the skin suits their souls were clothed in.

The homeless man sleeping on a park bench, a cormorant crouched within him, beak clacking in predatory fashion when it noticed me staring. The street busker who somehow had an entire flock of budgies nesting inside the press of his flesh, twittering away in time with his violin. The girl with the unseeing eyes hiding beneath an umbrella that lit up like a thousand candles as she ducked into the police station, a sparrow hawk burying its hooked beak in her heart muscle to shred it to bits.

All these people, their souls crying out, raging, begging me to reach for them, remove them, shelter them.

But I swallowed it down, ignoring the feathers that seemed to darken my doorway, the shadow of a house sparrow bristling with indignation and spite and a demand to be seen.

Not yet, not yet. Not ever.

"And then, I got back from the hospital … and he was just gone. Everything that was his—furniture, towels, the goddamned bathmat." Tami sat next to me on the overstuffed café sofa, sipping a boba tea and staring at her fingers. Her hands were painfully thin, skeletal claws that fluttered with the deliberate gestures some people get after rubbing shoulders with Death.

There's a sort of grace to it, a frailty like a candle flame, either about to extinguish or ignite into an inferno, though it can be hard to recognize. She worked at the bookstore on the corner where I'd been a barista, but she'd disappeared a few months ago, finally surfacing this morning when she'd entered the store, no more than a ghost, her skin translucent and hairless.

Beneath her breastbone, a bedraggled goldfinch gasped. I tried not to see it. I tried.

In the end, I left my shift to take her to the local sweet café and bought her a taro boba and a donut, listening as she talked, ensconced in a curtained alcove lined with French novels. Beneath the words and pretend pleasantries, a deeper song sang to me of a deeper magic, like what I'd heard in Maw Maw's parlor.

… breast cancer, I lost them and he couldn't even stay for me, my only worth was my flesh, and the baby, the baby, the baby was too early. He is gone, he left me, left me. I should have died. I wish I had …

I struggled to shut it away, the goldfinch's wings fluttering like a half-mad thing beneath the torrent of emotions. Tami's voice cracked like her smile cracked, leaving her rocking in my arms as she bawled, her matchstick body breaking itself upon me like a wave upon a rocky shore.

On instinct my hand rose, my fingers beckoning as I hummed low in my throat. *Peace, peace.*

A whispering sound as Tami hiccoughed, and then I was holding it in my hand, a goldfinch with dull eyes and shredded plumage, wings bleeding and broken. But I had no cage of wicker, no parlor, so I tucked the tiny thing away in my breast pocket.

No one else seemed to see it, not even Tami, though she'd sagged against me, her breathing growing slow. I suspected she'd fallen asleep, the boba tea slack in her hand.

Of course, I might as well have been back in Maw Maw's parlor after that. Everywhere I looked, soul birds lingered on the periphery of my vision, in the esoteric prophecy of city life. But still I hesitated, knowing if I continued down this path, it would never, ever stop until the moment I died.

Tami's grief at being abandoned, her anguish at her illness, the loss of her child—for a brief moment I held onto it, keeping the bird for her until several seasons had passed. Fall tumbled into Winter, who flirted with Spring until Summer finally emerged from her slumber, hot and radiant and utterly unbearable.

I didn't house the finch in a cage like Maw Maw—but it perched in a potted plant hanging from my kitchen window. The day Tami left town to find a new life somewhere else, the black-winged goldfinch disappeared, darting through a frayed hole in the screen door. What else could I do but wish her well?

I was twenty-one when Maw Maw died. I returned to the island for her Winter funeral, clutching the jar of her ashes as I laid her to rest in the wild sea.

Her parlor was quiet after, the cages full of silent eyes and closed beaks. The crow boys didn't caw their jokes at me anymore, and the raven girls stared at me with disdain, and I knew. *I knew.*

All this time and I hadn't come home once, but Maw Maw's letters lay tucked away in a dresser drawer, her spider script telling me of changes and weather, of birds and a parlor in which time seemed to stop. Maybe I couldn't be blamed for assuming she would somehow always be there like the grandfather clock.

But the birds in their cages stared at me coldly.

This burden wasn't mine. My time with the goldfinch had taught me that—these soul birds had been Maw Maw's to keep, to soothe, to control. Without her, they were simply trapped.

Something fluttered in my own chest, as I sat in Maw Maw's creaking rocking chair, the corduroy cushion threadbare, its stuffing seeping onto the woven rug. I didn't look down, knowing I'd see the long narrow beak of a heron, somehow monstrously huge as it thrust through my sternum.

Not yet, not yet, I told it. My sadness was ragged, but the pain of my loss was a necessary thing to hold onto for now. A threshold I didn't want to cross, a journey I was too afraid to make. Outside, the boardwalk was a ghost town; the tourists left months ago in the last warmth of a fading Summer.

"I don't want this," I said finally to the birds. "I can't. *I can't.*"

One of the crow boys let out something like a laugh. *Can't, can't, can't.*

Won't.

And that was the rub, wasn't it? Such a subtle distinction, and yet that's all that remained.

But the moon was out and frost crept over the sand, the sea cold and empty and crashing without remorse. One by one, I carried each cage to the dunes and opened them, the birds taking wing into the cloudless sky.

When the last cage lay empty, I sagged onto the bitter sand, the murmuration of souls soaring this way and that. The crow boys jeered, and the raven girls sang arias. I caught the barest hint of my Maw Maw's laughter echoed within, and I wept.

ALMOST LIKE BLOOD, ALMOST LIKE LILIES, ALMOST LIKE MY FRIEND

A. Katherine Black

Never a rumor believe, Baba signed with bony fingers. *Never your blanket share.* Even at her end, her arms moved with authority. *And never*, her hands punched out the words, *ever, to anyone, your pocket friend show.*

The young me, crouched next to Baba that stormy night, agreed to all these things. Solemn promises made to Baba's fierce, dimming face. And then I broke each one. Some sooner than others.

She died under the best lean-to I'd ever built, but back then I was little bigger than a cayote, so that wasn't saying much. Mother Nature's incessant breath had a way of finding breaks in any blind, though, and frigid winds cut through my branch barrier to lift Baba's grey hairs and slap her in the face. Discomforts never bothered Baba. Not even on her very last night. Her arms lifted in jolting motion to remark on my choice of soft pine bedding, because she was kind.

I'd learned enough, in the few years I'd lived, to know what was kind, and to know what was unkind. Baba was kind. And then Baba was gone.

The day turned many times before I showed myself to the wandering band I finally decided to follow.

They weren't the first people to pass near the lean-to where Baba's body drifted into the earth. The first group reeked of blood. The next was wrapped in blankets much too colorful to be trusted. By the time the third band of wanderers shuffled by, I'd picked every squinch berry bush clean, eaten the last of the gopher family holed up over the hill.

This band smelled like they washed in mud, and they pushed each other around, but what choice did I have? I was small, the world giant.

Follow when you can, Baba always signed before we fell in with one band or another. *Leave when you must*, she'd sign when it was time for us to go alone again.

So I followed.

This wandering band showed no surprise when I stepped from behind some bushes and edged up to their fire. They'd probably heard my rustles in the brush, but back then I couldn't quite grasp what some people's ears could do.

The two children in the band looked at me sideways, the grown-ups not at all. Except for one grown-up, with a beard like dead thicket and draped in more blankets than any of the others, who threw a rabbit leg my way, while his lips made shapes that almost meant something, but didn't.

Baba could make some sense of the mouth shapes other people made, and she always got her meaning across to the mouth-flapping people using just the right signs. But Baba was with the worms now, and my hands stayed limp at my side.

The band walked in one direction one day, another direction the next. Hid under low trees when Mother Nature was in a mood. I kept to the back of the walking pack, waiting for a chance to secretly slip my friend from my pocket and let it soak in the sun.

Pocket friends eat sunlight. No sun, and they die. I had to feed my friend, but I also had to keep it hidden. I'd made a promise, after all, and I'd already lost Baba. I was not going to lose our little friend, too.

Every night I piled boughs at the farthest edge of the wanderers' camp, curled on them with my blanket, and waited for the fire to dim. Then I'd dip my head under the blanket and liberate my friend from my pocket. Smooth and cool, like a rock freshly plucked from the river, my friend was round like the moon at its full, thick as my thumb, and wide as my palm.

I woke it just like Baba taught, running fingers gently along its edge, all the way around in one direction, half-way around in the other. It woke with a tiny shake, then pressed its bumpy shifting words against my hand, offering a warm hello before telling me our location with numbers that meant as little to me back then as a flapping mouth. I waited patiently for the numbers to finish, and then I moved my free hand in the cramped space under my blanket, weaving a long braid of ideas and questions.

The wandering band could have been worse, but it wasn't good.

I stayed awake long into the nights, discussing thises and thats with my friend, and it alerted me when wanderers slipped from their blankets to creep around the darkened camp. I'd peek out from under my blanket to see big people slide unwanted under the blankets of less big people, and sometimes of people who weren't even fully grown.

Of course I didn't know how my friend could tell what was happening from its hiding spot under the blanket or in my pocket, but just as I accepted that day always turned to night and the clouds always foretold of rain, I accepted my pocket friend's knowledge as a simple fact of the world.

The band had long since given up flapping their mouths at me, but still I helped how I could. Gathering handfuls of juicy squinch berries and armfuls of dry kindling. Even surprised them when I mashed roots to treat another child's fresh bruise. What they offered in return was a share of the food and the fire, and also safety, but only of a kind. Because I knew, without asking my pocket friend or even asking myself, I knew my turn would come, late in the night.

Baba told me to never share my blanket.

One night, not long before the thieves came and stole me away, I huddled under my blanket with my pocket friend and asked it what the wanderers had discussed that day, with their incomprehensible mouth-shapes. I asked, and my pocket friend told. Told of the wanderers' stories about the thieves, with their sharp bone tools and their hidden camps. And then I asked what it meant: "cannibal," and my friend explained, simple. Horrific.

It didn't know any better. The before-people made pocket friends to translate and to inform, not to coddle little children. Not to distinguish truth from rumor.

As my head scrambled to understand the concept my friend had just introduced, as my free hand jumped around under my blanket in a burst of question upon question, my friend tried to tell me that someone was up, and wandering the camp.

I was too distracted to worry about that, though, as my mind filled with pictures of people licking clean the large bones of other people. So distracted that I ignored my friend's words coming faster, pressing harder into my palm, until I finally realized what it was saying, that someone was *right there*, right outside my blanket. That was when a hand appeared under my blanket and grabbed my calf. I quickly slipped my friend into my pocket.

The invading hand was the size of a grown-up's. It moved up past my knee to grip the inside of my leg, and another grown-up hand lifted my blanket to a hairy face and waft of thick, rancid breath.

My friend, still awake in my pocket, pressed through the fabric of my clothes and into my leg in sharp repetition. *Run, run, run.* In the span of a breath the grown-up would have me pinned. I'd made a promise to Baba. I pulled away, but he held my leg fast.

Run, run, RUN!

I lifted my other foot and kicked him hard in the face. Both his hands flew to his nose. I scrambled out from my blanket and scuttled through the woodline and into the trees. My friend kept pressing urgently into my leg (*RUN, RUN, RUN!),* and so I kept running.

I ran straight and fast, and deep into the woods. I didn't stop, recovering quick each time I tripped over a root. I didn't stop until my pocket friend was still.

Leave when you must. I was alone again.

No fire and no blanket, but at least I still had my friend. I found a climbable tree and nestled in the crook of a thick branch that I hoped was higher than a grown-up could easily reach. I left my pocket friend awake, while I drifted in and out of sleep, to alert me in case the bearded man approached.

For two full turns of the day I stayed close to that tree, scrambling down only briefly, to look for water and check my hastily built trap. Everything smelled like rancid breath, and I jumped each time a branch brushed my leg.

I kept my pocket friend awake the whole time, but there were no thises and thats passing between us. My hands didn't know what to say.

My trap remained empty all that time, and without a single berry bush in sight, so did my stomach. My mind, rather than empty, became so full that not even the smallest thing made sense. So full that I forgot to pull my friend from my pocket to let it eat up the sunlight. I didn't even realize my friend was starved until I woke in the moonlit night to find a gathering of strange grown-ups under my tree spot, my friend still as stone in my pocket.

I'm not sure why I didn't fight the thieves, when they climbed the tree and took me away. It's not like they seemed safer, with their broad shoulders and spears strapped to their backs, than the wandering band I'd just left. But I was shaken and empty, and they handed me a piece of dried meat as soon as my feet touched the ground.

Follow when you can.

It wasn't until the sun finally peeked above the forest, to send its dappled light through breaks in the tall pines, that I saw the necklaces decorating the necks of every grown-up in this group. Necklaces made of finger bones. Bones much too large to be a possum's. It wasn't until then that I realized these were the very people about which the wandering band had recounted horrific stories, stories my pocket friend passed on to me in the night.

These were the cannibal thieves.

One of the last things Baba told me was never believe a rumor, but she was gone before the thieves even took me. All I had left was her little friend, now my friend, who I'd accidentally starved to death in my pocket.

The morning sun also revealed other stolen children, children I recognized from the wandering band. The children looked at me sideways. The shorter one had a swollen eye and a new bruise on their cheek.

The thieves walked us so far, so high up the mountainside, I was too tired to think about much of anything when we finally stopped to rest. Not the warm blanket I'd left with the wandering band, not the empty trap near my tree perch, not my secret pocket friend who had likely starved to death, not even bones.

When we reached the mountaintop, I saw their smooth white fences, brightened by the setting sun, tipped with knots that used to be people's knees and people's ankles. I saw their skull lanterns hanging below odd treetop huts. It was then that I wondered what kind of dried meat they'd been feeding us on the walk, and I almost tried Baba's way of signing a simple question to these thieves, but what was the point of asking then, when I would soon be dead?

I might have asked my pocket friend about the bone necklaces, but because of my thoughtlessness, my friend was surely dead. Even if it did have a tiny bit of life left, though, I didn't dare pull it from my pocket and risk losing it forever to the thieves. These thieves were smart, someone's eyes always open.

Always one awake, sitting through the night in the corner of our treetop hut, rocking slowly on a swing of twine braided just like Baba used to do. So I slept and ate, slept again, ate again, and left my friend safely in my pocket. I stared at the grown-up thieves' flapping mouths, kept my hands still at my sides even when the other stolen children began flapping their mouths, too.

I refused their meat, of course, unless I was sure it was from a gopher or some other small creature.

The thieves kept us busy. Gave us twine to braid and roots to mash, but the days turned so slow without my pocket friend to talk to. We left the treetop to do our business in a strange circle of bushes and to bathe in small holes of spanking clear water that smelled of pine and lavender. I kept my clothes on and, thank soil and worm, I knew my pocket friend, if it was alive, always liked a good bathing. Every time they led us from the treetop hut, I expected it to be the end.

After more than a few turns of the day, they led us stolen children—me, another, and that child whose swelled eye had now healed—through a mountaintop meadow sprinkled with bone-decorated treehuts, past a long stretch of berry-making bushes, to the biggest tree I'd ever seen, towering at the edge of a rocky cliff.

Three skulls hung from its base, collecting and reflecting the bright morning sun.

While the thieves and the other children flapped mouths, I stretched out on my belly at the very edge of the cliff, and that's when I saw the entire world, long and wide below. Or what I thought was the whole world at the time.

And I saw a path. Following the rockline, twisting and turning down and down, until it disappeared into the forest.

One of the thieves roused me, with a tap on my shoulder and a smile I knew better than to return, and pointed me toward the tree. One by one we climbed the ladder. Half of me wondered if I was approaching my end. Odd that the other half of me did not. If I died, would these cannibals let even a small piece of me drift into the earth, to join with the worms and with Baba? If I wasn't to die now, in this tree that stood atop the entire world, then what?

We reached a braided net floor, high among the branches. This tree was filled with a swirling mix of scents altogether different from the one where we slept. Almost blood, but not. Almost lilies, but not.

Each of us children sat with legs bent under and knobby knees out, and as I wondered which treetop hut my bones might soon decorate, the thieves placed before us three pocket friends. Just like mine, but not.

The other children stared at the pocket friends as the thieves moved their mouths, and then the thieves crouched in the spaces between us to dance their fingers atop the smooth surface of the little friends, not at all in the way Baba used to do.

Colors burst from the friends like sunrise cresting a hill, twisting in endless rainbow braids, swirling up and into the leaves above. It was unlike anything I'd ever seen my own friend do. Did it hurt these little friends, to do what the thieves made them do? It must have, because otherwise I was sure my and Baba's pocket friend would have shown us the same rainbow braids long ago.

I did my very best to sit still as stone while the other children first recoiled from the friends and then leaned closer, hints of delight tugging at their cheeks. They didn't know anything.

Why didn't they wonder who these thieves had stolen the three pocket friends from? Which finger bones on which thief's necklace had once caressed a dear pocket friend, before the thieves had shown up to ruin it all?

The kids flapped their mouths in the direction of the pocket friends, and the pocket friends began to shake. It wasn't the little shiver *my* friend did when it woke, or the shifting bumps my friend pressed into my hand and my leg. These pocket friends shook hard and fast, and in what seemed like patterns I should, but couldn't quite, grasp. The children pressed their hands together in delight and flapped their mouths faster in the direction of the three captive pocket friends. The friends' vibrations jostled the rope floor with increasing severity, until my feet grew numb.

The other two children skipped ahead of our grown-up thief guard, all the way back to our own treetop hut, bouncing smiles between them and looking at the sky as if something new flew among the clouds. I did nothing of the sort. Nothing but wonder how many pocket friends were held captive within these trees. Nothing but plan my escape. I promised Baba. Dead or alive, I would not let them take my friend.

The day turned many more times before I took my chance to escape.

I'd never considered I might meet more pocket friends, but Baba said once that there used to be as many friends as there were people. Said that back in the beforetime, some pocket friends were big, some small. Some were kind, some not.

It was only last season when Baba and I had reached the top of a gigantic hill. As usual, she stood on the highest spot and held our pocket friend to the sky. It was what Baba did. *Searching for other people*, she'd sign with her free hand. *Our people.*

I asked how we lost our first people, and she said they all fell ill. They were with the worms, and we were the last. But Baba was sure there were more of us, somewhere. Our pocket friend could see far, she said, so we searched.

The sky was so clear over that gigantic hill, I could see large rocks in the distance, impossibly tall, and curiously shaped. Flat on the sides, and with so many holes, like they'd been hit by a hundred giant chisels. Baba said they were from the beforetime. People made enormous lean-tos out of the same stuff as our pocket friend, cool and smooth, shiny and strong as anything, *if* they were kept clean. That was why we bathed our friend, why Baba mashed just the right seeds and rubbed them all over our friend at the start of each new moon.

I wondered if the thieves knew how to care for those poor, stolen pocket friends. If I showed them, though, they'd know I had one myself, and that was as good as breaking my promise.

We visited the stolen pocket friends again, and no matter how much the grown-ups tried to flap mouths and gesture at me, I sat like stone while the other two kids tapped and tapped and tapped at the poor hostage pocket friends' backs.

We collected berries, too. Even dug up roots to crush into paste for an injured thief. It was all easy. They were all things Baba taught me long ago. I kept my eyes down, turned away from the awful bone finger necklaces bouncing on everyone's chest. Kept my eyes away from my own pocket, too, determined to keep my friend secret until we could escape.

There were other children atop that mountain. Sleeping in other treetop huts, half-smiling at us from a distance, while they followed behind other grown-up thieves.

I was crouched among the berry bushes one day, one hand picking something almost like squinch berries, but not, the other holding my little friend just outside my pocket, hoping it was alive enough to eat some sunlight, when two children I didn't know came to pick berries right next to me. My friend was returned to the safety of my pocket before they saw it.

One child was taller than me, with many long braids, and the other was very thin, with sunken eyes, looking as if a swift wind could knock them right off the mountain. Neither of them had a bone decoration in sight. The children settled on the ground and put their woven berry bowls beside mine. When they saw how fast my fingers moved over and within the bushes, snatching two berries to each of their one, they pressed their hands together in respect. I might have nodded at them, despite my solemn resolve.

The grown-up thieves offered smiles, too, and lots of pats on our shoulders. Even new woven clothes, in perfect Mother Nature colors, but I kept my own.

The other children in my stolen group seemed more than content. They were happy. Nothing like how they'd been within the wandering band. Half of me felt sorry for them, not understanding the meaning of cannibal.

They tried to make me happy, too. Beckoned me to join their

meadow games, gestured at me to tap on the captive, rainbow-lit pocket friends. I held back, resisted the joy decorating their faces.

There was a point when I wavered, though, unsure if I should leave. After all, the food the thieves gave me had only ever been small game. We stolen children had been healthy for many, many turns of the day, yet no one had carved us for food yet. I even found myself skipping across the meadow one day, on the way back from the enormous tree. That's when I saw the tall child. The child with the long braids, from that berry picking day. They were alone this time. Sitting against the trunk of another treetop hut, staring at the ground as if daring the grass to dance. It did not.

The child wore a new necklace. The smallest finger bones I'd ever seen, but still too big for a possum's. A grown-up thief stood nearby, hanging a new skull lantern, reaching in to light its fire. The smallest skull I'd yet seen, but definitely the skull of a person.

The child with the new bone necklace looked up at me, standing just a few lengths away, and then I dashed to the bushes at the edge of the camp, where I kneeled and upheaved my meal.

I lay still as stone that night, under the blanket given to me by the cannibal thieves. I knew then that was too soft. Too warm to be trusted. Hand in my pocket, I longed for a last word with my secret friend before my fingers became someone else's necklace. Not even knowing if my friend could wake.

I realized this was it. The time had come.

It wasn't the first night that our grown-up thief guard had moved from the swing in our treetop hut to rest on the woven floor. Moonlight trickled through the blowing leaves, illuminating the guard's chest. I waited until they breathed deep, face slack as the dead, and that's when I slipped away and descended the ladder, scanning the clearing between treehuts before letting myself down to the ground.

The bone gate around our tree was closed, and with a complicated lock I'd never noticed during the day. Baba taught me many things, but never how to open locks.

The fence wasn't so tall to a grown-up, but I was small. I climbed, slipped when straddling the slick bone top, and I fell hard on the other side. I lost my breath for a moment, and it came back in a string of coughs. That's when I saw the first lantern approach, bouncing toward me from the far side of the clearing.

One hand deep in my pocket, gripping my friend, I ran.

Pressing through thick, prickly bushes at the edge of the clearing, I searched for the path I'd seen from the cliff, the one that led down to the forest. The moonlight taunted as it came and went, but I soon found the path. Using my free hand to follow the rough rock wall that was the side of the mountain, I descended as fast as I could. The path was steep, the loose rocks slippery, but the thieves had seen me. I had to keep going.

I scurried down as the moonlight shone and vanished, shone and vanished, but my shadow oddly remained. I allowed myself a brief turn to see skull lanterns approaching, carried by stronger arms and faster legs. These thieves could lick my bones clean and put a fire in my skull, but they were not going to take my friend.

I slid more than ran down the rocky slope, while the thieves came ever closer. Their skull lamps now gave me light enough to better see the path, and gave me fear enough to keep my feet in motion, until a big slip and sharp twist of my ankle, and I toppled over the path's edge.

I tumbled through tall grass, as my hands reached for anything to slow my wild fall, but a tree did the stopping for me. I lay aching under low pine limbs, pressed flat as I could to the ground, sniffing against the grass tickling my nose.

Lights passed along the path above and away in the direction I had just been running. I thought maybe I was safe.

My head hurt, and my ankle, and my side. Baba pointed to hurts all over her body before she died. Maybe this meant I'd see her soon. But my pocket friend was safe. I reached into my pocket, eager to try and wake the friend I'd so desperately missed, but it wasn't there. I'd lost it during my fall.

Moonlight broke in teasing mercy, illuminating the trail of grass broken from my tumble. My friend must be along that trail.

Faint light danced in the distance, from the burning lanterns of the cannibal thieves. I couldn't tell if the light was coming my way or not.

I considered staying put, considered letting my friend remain safely hidden among the tall grass, but then what would happen to the poor thing? It could eat the sunlight, if left there in the grass, but it would be all alone, watching people pass by as they lived and died, forever with no one to talk to. It had no legs, no way to find a true friend, no way even to stop a cayote from leaving a mess on its smooth surface. That wouldn't do.

Baba told me to hide my friend, and I would hide it. Hide it from cayotes, and hide it from loneliness. How could a pocket friend be a friend, without someone to talk to?

The light of the skulls grew even more distant, so I slid from under the tree. I kept low, grabbing handfuls of grass to pull myself up the steep slope, pausing every few breaths to spread my arms and fingers into the surrounding blades, searching for my smooth, round friend.

I pulled forward and searched the grass. Pulled forward, searched the grass until the tippy tips of my left fingers brushed at the edge of my friend. I slid sideways until I could grab hold and pulled it tight to my chest, almost laughing with relief.

I hadn't talked to my friend in so very long. Hadn't talked about the finger bones and the skulls, about the treetop huts and the biggest tree on the highest cliff above the whole world. About the other pocket friends, stolen and forced to do tricks. Had I sneaked it enough sunlight during those days on the mountain that it was able to see all that I saw? Would it even wake to my gentle caress? I released my friend from my tight grip and ran two fingers along its side. All the way around, then halfway the other direction.

It woke with a shudder stronger than usual. Then it began to glow.

Every color of the rainbow twisted up from my friend, to swirl high into the moonlit sky. I'd never seen it do this before. Why now? Didn't it understand there were thieves searching for us? Dangerous, cannibal thieves?

I slipped it under my shirt, desperate to hide my friend's rainbow light. And it wouldn't stop vibrating. It must have been so starved, so near death, that it hadn't been able to see the mountaintop from my pocket. It didn't know about all the horrible bones and the other stolen friends. Lifting my shirt, I signed in quick, furious spurts.

Stop! No light! Bad people close!

I covered it with my shirt again, but it was no use. Rivaling the light of the moon, my friend's stubborn rainbow spilled easily through the meager fabric, making me squint.

A new glow, another glow emerged from the trees. The thieves were almost here.

I couldn't run. I could barely crawl. Everything hurt. Then I noticed my friend trying to talk. I'd been holding it different than usual and was missing its bumpy words. I shifted my palm to span its flat surface, and my friend's bumpy words slid quickly against my skin. It was so wonderful to feel my friend's words again, even if they were a mess of nonsense.

Good people, my friend said. *Friends. Join the people.*

How could it say that?

It had been so close to death in my pocket, it hadn't seen the bones. Bones everywhere. Bones of the stolen, bones of the eaten. Hadn't seen the pocket friends, captive and forced to do strange things. But the thieves were here, and I didn't have time to explain. How could I explain?

Friends sing, it said. *I sing. Hold me high. I sing.*

No! I didn't even know what sing meant, but Baba said not to show our pocket friend to anyone. Not *anyone.* But Baba was gone, and the skull lanterns grew closer. My friend's vibrations grew so strong, it was hard to understand the bumpy words it kept pressing into my hand.

Dear friend, hold me high. Show me the sky.

Then the thieves were there, a bunch of grown-ups surrounding us, holding their lighted skulls and moving their mouths. I sat up, ready to fight, ready to protect my best and only friend as it pushed its rainbow light through my shirt, when a smaller grown-up broke through the group and came to kneel in the grass.

Her braids were white, and her skin folded with age about her face. She wore a necklace of finger bones, but her eyes didn't look like a cannibal's, or a thief's. Her mouth didn't move.

Hold me high, my friend said.

It seemed, no matter what Baba said, that my friend wanted so much to be shown. The thieves could already see the rainbow light pressing through my shirt.

What else was there to do?

I granted my friend's request and pulled it from my shirt, holding it high on my palm, just like I used to see Baba do. The old woman's face broke into a smile, and then her lips began to make shapes.

My friend pressed bumpy words against my palm just as the woman's mouth moved. *You have a friend, too?* It said. Was my friend telling me what the mouth shapes meant? And then, when the woman's mouth wasn't moving, my friend told me it was safe. Told me to sign my words and it would explain to the other people.

The old woman's mouth moved again. *We won't hurt you.*

What should I believe? Who should I believe? Baba was gone, but my little friend was still here, and it had saved me from the wandering band before.

Signing best as I could with my one free hand, I told the old woman that I'd broken my promise, that I was supposed to hide my pocket friend. As my fingers and hand and arm moved to form words, my pocket friend's colors shifted, and it vibrated until my hand holding it was almost numb.

The entire group of grown-up thieves suddenly burst into movement, flapping their mouths, gesturing at me and my friend. A flood of bumpy words crossed my palm, translating pieces of what they all said.

She talks with hands?

It translates!

Did anyone know the friends could do that?

This must be the source of the signal we tracked.

It was so strange to know the grown-ups' words just as they were being shaped with mouths. My mind swirled. I signed again, and my friend translated with its strong vibrations. *This was Baba's friend; now it's my friend.*

The old woman held up a hand, and the group stopped moving and flapping. *Where's your baba?* she asked.

Dead, I signed. *With the worms.*

I didn't stop her from wiping the tears off my cheek. *I'm a baba, too,* she said.

That's how my pocket friend and I came to live atop the mountain, learning from the people I once thought were cannibals and thieves, as they learned from me.

Not long after the old woman spoke to me in the tall grass, I moved to stay in her treetop hut. Taught her to form words with hands, and I learned from her the skills my first Baba hadn't had time to pass on. I learned to build fences and lanterns from the bones of the dead, lovingly left behind, to protect our homes and to light our hearts, as the rest of their bodies joined with the worms.

Second Baba and I spent many a season laughing at the idea of these mountaintop grown-ups stealing from other bands and eating other people, but I never stopped calling them thieves. I was always grateful that they stole me away, before I could be consumed by violence, and by loneliness.

All the thieves eventually learned to make words with their

hands, and thanks to my pocket friend, they continued to hope that there might be more like them, more like us, out there.

My friend and I stayed on the mountain, learning and teaching, giving and receiving, until one day, not long after Second Baba had joined with the worms, I realized the time had come. Time to continue the work First Baba had begun. Time to search for more of us.

I assembled my pupils and, with fierce hands, passed on firm instructions. I studied their faces, accepted their promises, and hugged each one in turn.

Best friend in my pocket, soft blanket in my pack, and a string of bones, lovingly bestowed by Second Baba, resting over my heart, I stepped down the rocky path until my feet met with the soil. I walked on, as Baba's spirit reached up from the roots to light and warm my path.

ABSENCE DECIDES HER DEMISE

Christina Hira

they said wolves don't live around here
what they meant was wolves don't live around her

the boy down the road had a wolf
it howled, he cried, they came running

the townspeople gathered their common humanity
to catch, contain, and christen this wolf as case in point

mine stalked, I cried, they rolled their eyes
muttering fabrication does not become her

the townspeople consulted the agreed-upon criteria
to excuse, exclude, and embarrass my experience

they generalised my deficit as homespun hysteria
while my wolf found invisibility in our cycles syncing

I wrestled my lack into quirks, fighting to control the narrative
I seized sharp intelligence to mask its scent

they labeled my carefully balanced coping as a cop-out
while I spent my evenings alone, stitching and mending the tears

they said wolves don't live around here
so I straddled worlds with my paws, stretching until I snapped

SPARROW & BUTLER

Nike Sulway

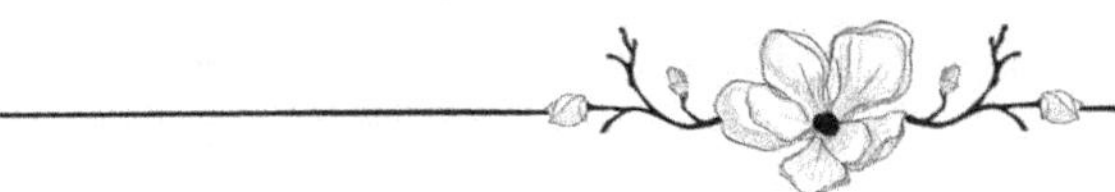

Twenty years later, Miss Sparrow deeply regretted the bargain they had made. Sure, she and Miss Butler had got what they'd wanted: a little girl to raise as their own. And their daughter was everything the faerie queene had said she'd be: pretty and bright, with Miss Sparrow's green eyes and Miss Butler's fair hair. There was a little of each of them in the way she tilted her head to thread a needle, or hiked up her skirts to cross narrow water. A little of May in her reluctance to wear shoes, and a little of Eleanor in her dislike of red apples. She'd been small and brown and furrowed like a nut when she was born, but as she'd grown she'd come right. If she sometimes had the look of the fey about her, it was only a little, and only in a certain light. She was a good girl, sweet and hard-working and quiet.

They had named her Matilda, for that long-dead queen of England, but called her Till or Tilly. Tilly Sparrow. On her twentieth birthday they gave her a green cotton dress, a linen tippet with an edge of lilacs embroidered on it, a matching linen cap, and a pair of silver scissors. Stolen, all, from Mrs. Francis Howlett.

"You're sure?" said Miss Sparrow, as she blew out the candle and slipped into bed.

Miss Butler drew her beloved close and kissed her pleated brow. "The constable will come in the morning," she said. "She'll be in irons by sunset."

Miss Sparrow nodded, her hand against her dear love's heart. She could feel it beating like a frightened bird in a too-small cage. "And in Bridewell by midnight."

Miss Butler had visited Bridewell, as part of their preparations. It was hard to believe that the rooms she had seen there had once housed King Henry VIII. The turnkey had shown her rooms filled with whores and children, thieves and paupers. Beds no finer than stables, with rotten timber dividing them, rushes on the floor and a stink of rot and piss. She had been shown once-great rooms still charred and broken, centuries later, from when the Great Fire had cleansed them of plague, rooms that were said to have belonged to the discarded Queen Catherine. The turnkey had shown her another suite, on a lower floor, with an antique boxed bed. Here, he told her, the great brothel keeper, Liz Creswell, had exhaled her last breath. None of the women were housed in that room unless they were already whores.

Finally, and after much negotiation, Miss Butler had been shown the room where, at great expense, their own Matilda would be housed when the time came. A locked door with a narrow window. A bed with a mattress rather than soiled rushes. A table and chair. She would be able to look out and see the Thames while she awaited her trial and sentencing. It had all seemed reasonable at the time. A private room, with food and clean water every day for however long she was held.

But now? Now the Misses lay in the dark and pictured rats nibbling at their daughter's hair and toes. Thieves stealing her shoes and her food. Men paying to enter her room alone. The Misses

Sparrow and Butler had paid—and paid well—for their daughter's safety. Every shilling they'd earned. They had pictured the irons around her wrists and ankles. The cart that would take her to the prison where Mr. John Pugin would meet her and ensure she was taken to her room. Miss Sparrow pictured a jar of wildflowers on the table. Miss Butler imagined clean sheets strewn with lavender.

"Safe," said Miss Sparrow, though her throat narrowed with terror at the thought of Tilly in chains.

"Safe," said Miss Butler, though her belly loosened at the thought of their daughter in chains, of the secrets they had kept from her, and the rage their daughter would no doubt feel, to find herself betrayed by her mothers, removed from her home, with no sense of their terrible reasons.

The next day, everything went as they had planned. The Misses Sparrow and Butler left their rooms early, while Matilda was still sleeping. Miss Butler had her spare boots strung about her neck, a small fortune stitched into her bodice and petticoat, and a widow's ring on her finger. Miss Sparrow carried her dearest love's carpet bag, and Tom the barrow boy followed them with Miss Butler's chest. In it was everything she would need: seeds and tools, clothes and books, ink and paper. Five silver spoons and five silver knives.

The lock on the chest had not been working when, early that morning, Miss Sparrow had finally closed the lid and bent to lock it. It had been the last thing they had purchased since it was the most difficult to explain to Matilda. What did two older women want with a travelling chest? Two women who had never, as far as she knew, left Greater London?

Miss Butler had taken the key—dangling from the chain about her neck, but also pinned to her bodice—and turned it this way and that and then the other, all to no avail. Miss Sparrow had suggested they take the lock apart, but Miss Butler had sighed and said there wasn't time. Meaning, of course, that what little time remained she wished to spend with Miss Sparrow, and not engaged in picking locks. She handed the key to Miss Sparrow and moved out of the way. Miss Sparrow knelt and peered into the lock. She asked Miss Butler to bring a light close, which she did, and they both peered into that dark and narrow passage. Miss Sparrow took a steel hatpin and poked it into the lock's workings. Poking and fidgeting with the thing until, of course, the pin fell into the chest and could not be retrieved.

A year later, when Miss Butler came in from the garden of the little house she had prepared for Miss Sparrow and Matilda in the colony, when she knelt to take a length of cotton out of the chest, she would prick her finger on the pin. Would bring the pricked finger to her tongue and taste her own blood and wonder at all that had passed. Wonder that they had ever been two women in a cramped London house with one window and no garden, determined never to pay their debt to the faerie queene. And now they were—well, soon they would all be—free settlers in a new country with no fey folk in't. They had a house with four rooms, a garden that ran down through a green field to a river. At night, strange creatures croaked and sang and screeched in the moonlight, but even at midsummer there was no faerie hunt. No chestnut carriages. No enchanted wells. Just trees and grass and blue, blue skies.

"My turn?" said Miss Butler, and Miss Sparrow nodded. Miss Butler knelt by the chest and took her chatelaine—hung with every tool a woman might ever need—and dismantled the thing. Spindle and plate, tumblers and tongue. Painstakingly, as Miss Sparrow boiled the kettle and made tea, she put it back together. By the time Miss Sparrow came up the stairs the lock was intact again. The chest locked, the brass polished, the bed made and Miss Butler standing in the middle of their shared room, ready to leave.

They took the long way to the harbour, so that their path and the constable's path would not cross. Tom took the chest aboard, and the Misses Butler and Sparrow followed him. Up the gangplank, across the deck. They stood on the far side of the ship and looked up the river, to where the ocean lay.

Meanwhile, and on the same morning that Miss Butler set sail, an officer of the Misses' parish, Jack Kimber, came to arrest their daughter. It did not help Matilda in the least that she was wearing the garments she was accused of stealing, that it was the day after her birthday, or that she claimed the garments were gifts from her guardians, whom she called her mothers. She was tried a few days later and, on the evidence provided by Tom the barrow boy, a woman who worked at a boarding house in New Pye Street, Mrs. Frances Howlett, and the officer who had made the arrest, Matilda was found guilty of the theft of clothing valued at three shillings and fourpence, and sentenced to death by hanging.

Do not worry, gentle reader. She did not hang. The Misses Sparrow and Butler did not arrange all this to have their daughter hanged by the neck for the entertainment of a London crowd.

Their plan had started with iron.

The fey, as all good folk know, cannot abide iron. When their daughter was born, the Misses Sparrow and Butler had nailed an iron horseshoe to their daughter's chamber door. They had buried an iron knife beneath the doorstep of the house. Miss Sparrow had put iron filings underneath the babe's mattress, and Miss Butler had stitched little iron coins into the hems of her dresses, but these precautions were of no use. Matilda's hems were always coming undone and the iron lost. And the filings had irritated her skin, leaving blisters and burns on her blue-white flesh.

But every midsummer, the Misses Sparrow and Butler heard the faeries riding. The queene's laughter threaded itself into their dreams. And the vision of her human prisoners haunted them both. Young women and men rode behind the queene, each on hinds white as the moon's milk. Silver bridles were looped in their hands, silver collars at their throats. How many times had Miss Butler gone to the well to meet the hunt, to drag a little prisoner from their mount and hold them in her good, strong arms? To rescue those other women's children that the queene had claimed. In her embrace they changed: from wood to stone to spark to stream. They boiled and writhed and moaned. And she held them close. Held them tight. Her sleeves burned away. Her once-golden hair, too. One young girl become a flame that rippled the skin of her throat. Another a river that almost drowned her. A young boy—not yet twenty, surely, his face still smooth though his eyes had that dark, lost look they all had—turned into a vine and wound himself around her, tight and tighter till she could not breathe.

And still she stood. And still she held them.

No matter how tight, no matter what horrors she endured, by morning they were always gone. Back to the queene and her seelie court.

The Misses Sparrow and Butler had made their bargain when they were young, and in love. They had wanted desperately to have a child of their own, and what path was open to them but the one they took? And so they had stood at the well on Midsummer's Eve. The hunt had approached, and Miss Sparrow had stepped out onto the silver road. Her hair billowed slowly about her, as if she were underwater. Like slow fire, it was, all aflame.

The Misses Sparrow and Butler had made their bargain: a daughter they could love and cosset for three times seven years but who, when the time had passed, would join the queene's great court. She would be dressed in the finest green silks and velvets. She would have her own milk-white hind to ride, and her own silver bridle and her own silver collar, and would ride and ride until she could ride no more.

"Until she dies," Miss Sparrow had whispered, and the great queene had tilted her head forward just a little. Just enough.

"Until she rides no more," the queene said.

And so for twenty years the Misses Butler and Sparrow had had a daughter, and had loved her. And for twenty years they had plotted a way out of having their beautiful daughter pay the queene's terrible price.

The idea had come slowly. They had seen Maggie Tindall's girl arrested and transported. Had sat in the court while she was tried and seen the iron shackles on her wrists and feet. They had stood at the dock in Plymouth when the ship set sail, Maggie beside them all wrack, all ruin.

"We can't," they had said.

"She could die on the journey," said Miss Butler.

"She will die on the ride," said Miss Sparrow.

"They'll shave her head," said Miss Butler. "They'll ..." she spread her hands, imagining the things that happened to young women on those ships. Young, pretty, shackled women. She put her needlework in her lap and watched the colours run.

Matilda was sleeping, little beads of sweat gathered on her top lip. She was only ten years old then—half her time with them already run away.

"There are worse things than death," said Miss Sparrow. "Worse things than a shaved head. Remember Kitty Dorset?"

Ah. Kitty Dorset. Who was taken by the faerie queene when Matilda was just five years old. That first time, she rode on the queene's lap and was flush with heat and magic. But the next she rode her own white hind, and all the colour had gone out of her. She was covered in bruises and pin-pricks and wore her hair in a wiry tangle. Beetles nested in it.

The next summer she was barely human: bones protruded through her skin. There were worms and rootlings writhing in her belly. But still she rode, and rode again. Two more years after that.

In March, Mad King George was cured of his madness. A month later, all the women and children on death row, including Matilda, had their sentences commuted to transportation. In July, along with 225 other prisoners, Matilda set sail aboard the *Lady Juliana*. Miss Sparrow stood on the Plymouth dock and watched as the women and children were loaded onto the ship. She had written a letter to Miss Butler that morning, letting her dearest love know that Matilda was setting sail, and would soon reach her in Botany Bay.

It was shocking to see her daughter stumble, as she was loaded aboard like a slave, like cattle. Matilda had never been so thin. Her hair had, indeed, been shaved from her head. The skin of her wrists, where the iron rested, was red and raw. She was dressed in a stranger's clothes. But as she stepped onto the deck she found her feet. Stood tall. She turned to look back at the city and Miss Sparrow saw, in her face, that all was well. All was as it should be. Nothing would ever put out the flame that burned in her child.

Miss Sparrow turned back to the city. There was a great deal to do. She had closed up the London house and sold all that was left of their once-was life. She had taken a cheap room in a boarding house to wait until her own ship was ready to sail. Soon, soon, she and Miss Butler and Matilda would be reunited.

She had been patient while she waited. She had not despaired. She had written letters and received them in return. Miss Butler wrote of a world so unlike their own it seemed it might be a kind of fairyland. She described creatures that were part duck and part otter, rabbits that bounded large as horses, trees that bled and mountains that sang. Of a people like muscled shadows, who sang the moon into being, and lived in the forests like kings. And of Tilly, who was—Miss Butler wrote—no longer the girl she'd been when they left England.

That night, Miss Sparrow dreamed of the faerie queene. In her dream she stood on the silver road as the seelie court approached. At their head was the old queene in her chestnut carriage, a human child on her lap. Miss Sparrow reached out her hand and grabbed hold of the silver reins. The queene sighed. "One more year," she said. "And then she's mine."

"She'll never be yours," said Miss Sparrow. "She's gone."

"Dead?" said the queene.

"No," said Miss Sparrow. "Just gone. Gone where you can't follow. Across the ocean, to another world."

The queene tilted her chin, just a little. Her features blurred and her dress writhed, like something alive.

Miss Sparrow closed her eyes. "She's ours," she said. "You'll never have her."

"You've sent her to the colony," said the queene, and laughed.

"Where you cannot go. Where there are none of your kind," said Miss Sparrow. "None to harvest human children. None to make them ride."

"Oh, my darling," said the queene. "Oh, my sweet. Where there *were* none."

Miss Sparrow felt the silver road shift beneath her feet. She put her hand into her pocket, where Miss Butler's letter was folded around a lock of Miss Butler's hair. "*Were?*" she said.

"Well, yes, *were*. But you have sent her there, *my* little faerie child. Mine that was. Mine that always will be."

"She's not yours."

"All the fey are mine, Miss Sparrow," said the faerie queene, baring her pretty silver teeth. "You have raised her, for which I thank you. You have done well. She knows how to walk among you, unnoticed and seeming human, as I have never managed. And in this new colony? Well, in her new colony she will be queene, and when the time comes, she will gather her court and ride, as I do."

The queene twitched the reins from Miss Sparrow's hand. Miss Sparrow looked behind the carriage, where the queene's court was restlessly arrayed: the mounted fey with silver teeth and faces too hard and pretty and sharp. Dotted among them were their human playthings. The dead and the dying. Mounted bones and bruises. Dressed in rags, adorned with silver collars, eyes sunken and shadowed and lost.

"I thank you," said the queene, and snapped her reins. In a

sickening blur of movement—of bones and feathers, rot and silver, and the smell of burning snow—the hunt rode on.

SOME SHINING EARTH

Dianthe West

A century nigh,
Near the swamps of Wilf-Pytt,
By that fair market town,
Cried our papas, "Come buy!"
They hawked tart black raspberries,
Quinces, round blueberries,
Damsons, fresh peaches,
Thick, lush plums, mulberries,
Apples, sweet dewberries,
Cherries, red strawberries,
Citrons, wild bilberries,
Pears and stout figs.
Fine fruits plumped together,
In our glen's temperate weather,
To sate the human appetite.
"Come buy!" our papas' cried—
"Come buy!"

 Twilight by twilight,
Crouched by the quayside rushes,
Aggie and Edmund,
We heard the girls' crushes.
Men made supplications,
Pranced with wrangling elations,
Like buntings to the rye,
When they heard our papas cry.
"Come buy!" their goblin call—
"Come buy!"

"Stay near," I bade to little Ed.
I kiss'd my brother's sweet green head.
"We must not view their human sun.
We must not taste their bread.
Crisp fruits grow strong inside our glen.
(Men sell not such in any fen.)
Our goblin fruit is all we're fed.
What would become of us with none?
We must bow down to men," I said.
"We must sell them our fruits.
Lest they assail us, seize our land,
Their quenchless mouths we must attend."

'Twas then a rustle came too near;
A pale, jeweled girl—she plugged her ears.
"Don't look, Lizzie" she admonished;
Tossed back soft locks of golden honey.

Then came another, hands o'er eyes.
"Laura!" she squealed, "We must not spy!"
She stumbled, lifting lovely frocks,
And passed us by the river docks.

The first stretched out her gleaming neck.
Like a wolf in the howl,
Like a primrose from the bourne,
Like a blossoming orange branch,
Like an earthworm in the cave,
Dried, pitiful, and foul.
Her coarse mouth suck'd our candied globes,
A clipped gold lock in trade.

She vanish'd. Next, there came the other.
She listened and she looked,
Ballooned her apron, tossed a penny,
Dallied, "Pretty goblin honey,
Be such dears and hand them over!
Good lads, give me much and many!"
That faithless pocket, lined with copper,
Yank'd back with string her silver offer.
She stole the fruits from our papas' arms,
Writhed, gruesome, drunk on th' syrupy balms.
The brook bled wine; spoiled fruits asunder—
Uncivil rat! Such evil plunder!

Near all our twilights went this way,
Till th' end of ol' Queen Lilibet's reign.
'Twas then our bounteous orchards failed.
Red wildfires raged.
Dead limbs drooped low with charred black flame.
Our dulcet days turned dry and stripped.
Our sky grew two brash golden pits.
No longer a fairy fire,
Nary a May bean,
No more ecstasy
Grew in our honeyed spring.
Our smould'ring wold crisped,

With a searing bell-sound.
We'd drunk it all up.
We'd no more fruit to glean.

Yet still, "Come buy," our papas cried,
Hobbling down the glen.
"Come buy!" with empty plate and dish,
"Come buy!" they lugged bare baskets, which—
They bore aloft on golden plates,
But had no wares to supplicate.
With minds and sanity capsized,
"Come buy," they wailed, wide-eyed,
"Come buy!"

We goblin children made appeals,
To papas' mad, cold-hearted ears.
Yet, not to plum.
They could not change; they would not try.
Their conduct mired in years gone by.
We were siblings together,
In fast-warming weather.
Leafy glade all dead of shade,
Our heads and hearts were scorched and scathed.

September to October,
The bell-sound warned yet hotter.
Slavering men washed o'er the banks,
Brother by cruel brother.
They slaughtered our papas, who'd hawked fickle juice,
No grace for babes or mothers.
They ranted and maul'd us;
Clawed and befouled us,
Beat up and chop'd us;
Smirched and uncowled us.

One took me up by my plum goblin lock.
One strok'd my cheek,
Parted my grey frock.
One fetch'd Edmund out by the ear.
They crowed, "Here's a trove for us!"
And they cheered.
They tied up our wrists.
They haltered our wolves.
They led us, arms bound,
Through our own jagged woods.
They pushed us into a toadstool hollow,
And forced us out into Earth's shining sorrow.

Morning and evening,
We cried by the wolf pits,
Green head by green head,
The colour of last water,
Edmund, a grave child without food;
I, just a heart, a land, a fruitless glen.
We were two turnip lanterns.
Or an autumn break in weather.
Or fawns that pass by.
Or green butterflies.
Jowl to jowl and crest to crest,
Two tails alone in a comfortless nest.

'Till early one morning,
When our stomachs, cold, were burning,
Shrewd like opossums, ringtail dizzy,
We crept to Wilf-Pytt in a starving tizzy.
Dear Edmund stole a loaf of wheat,
"Here, Ed," I slurred, "dainty cakes to eat!"
Such fools we were! Salt licks and sharp flours,
They scoured my veins—

They scarred dear Edmund's heart.

Thwarted, fading,
Wax'd pale as homespun,
We shriveled like sacks 'neath Earth's scalding sun.
Men flocked to the road bearing knives and guns.
Some wretches they leered,
Some stank cloying with mead,
One cried, "Slay the green beasts!"
One cried, "Bury the thieves!"
Ah, but two wives came weeping.
We knew who they were.
Goldlocks and Apron,
With her bright-pennied purse.
'Locks gnash'd her teeth, as though broken of heart.
Apron held a kernel-stone up and apart.
They kiss'd each other fondly,
Cross'd the heath of copper furze.
Goldlocks fetched us fresh green beans.
Apron filled up hers.

At night, those mothers nursed us by,
Each shelled out broad legumes.
"Fine fruits!" I gasped, tasting their wares.
"Ed, try! They're lush, sweet goblin food."

And soon, I learned to choke down man's bread.
Marr'd by Earth's sun, I turned their pink-red.
(Daylight is not good for goblins once fed!)
When now, I'd honed my use of their speech,
I learned that their monks would lead us to church,
Anoint us with oils;
Edmund shivered with fright.
We were goblins, alas!

What would happen to us?

With Death in his eyes,
Fuzzed top mossy and gaunt,
Bleak Edmund heightened his fast.
He called out for melons from goblin seeds.
He wept for th' shade of our apple trees,
And just as he'd feared, at the foot of th' font,
Despair out of life, Edmund faded at last.

Days, weeks, months, years,
I, Aggie, survived, wed a knight.
That Coggeshall brute called me cheeky and vain.
Yet, each day at twilight, I linger in pain.
For e'er I ear for our papas' cry,
"Come buy our goblin fruits! Come buy!"—

Now, sunbeams crawl upon my pane;
I glimpse out o'er the strand.
To never spy again my kin.
To never taste our fruits.
To long for our bounty, our world—our roots.
To long for the lush, sweet tides of my youth.
A lilied tress slips through my hand—
Some shining earth, seen not far from this land.

EVERY MEDDLING WOMAN

Hillary Dodge

The story has ended, and you are about to close me, when words swirl before your eyes, spreading across my pages like lemon ink shown to flame. Why had we thought—barely a moment before—that the tale had resolved when clearly it has not? There are two more pages your fingers have yet to turn, and two pages that somehow have escaped even my own notice. Imagine such a thing!

Not sure what to expect after the catharsis of the princess's last-minute rescue from the flames and the poetic justice of the mother-in-law's banishing, we settle back into your cozy chair and begin to read. The light is low, and the winter wind plays at the windowsill. Your fingers tremble just a bit, and my pages flex in turn. This time I'm along for the ride just as much as you are.

Reading is seeing, and as our eyes adjust, we are surprised to see that the story continues with the mother-in-law.

The old woman slips through the woods on taloned feet. Sometimes her ankles are as slender and lithe as a young girl's. Other times they are thick and weary with age. Her left eye is black; her right is a pale, almost translucent blue. Her form shifts and shivers as she passes beneath the canopies, heavy with late summer foliage. The shadows through which she passes are so deep and cool that it is like stepping through small spaces where another season dwells.

The years have accumulated on her shoulders and in her skin, true, but she has been fortunate to have long ago acquired some small magics which allow her to shrug them off as if they never were. She is headed to the source of those magics even now as we glimpse her through the trunks and boughs of her passage.

She crosses a fallen tree, bark sloughed into peat at its sides and trunk patterned with worms. Tangled in its branches, unraveling from a ruined nest, the old woman spies a length of faded golden yarn. She laughs to remember the time she bestowed such a yarn upon a foolish king. Unspooled, it would lead him to his heart's desire, which turned out not to be his new bride, but rather the seven lachrymose children from the bride before. Oh, how that vixen interloper railed in offense!

Even so, she never minds the meddling. We can hear the pleasure in the echoes of her laughter.

Through a sun-dappled glade, she makes her way. White hair here, golden there, ebony at times, depending on the angle. A patch of nettles, bright and bristling, catches at the edge of her skirt. She retreats slightly and edges around their stinging reach, smiling more broadly. Teeth crooked. Teeth straight. Lips cruel. Lips sweet.

"Oh, my poor dear little men!" Her voice fawns, mismatched from her patchwork visage. "How you must miss your sister so. Here's the trick to be reunited ..." Light dances in the back of her eyes, as she recalls the tale she spun. Down of nettles, woven so, voice forsaken, shirts to sew. Their poor dear little sister, fingers numb and misshapen, could just as easily used flax.

There is something at the edges of her smile that makes us wonder what made her this way. Before the years, before the roles—for clearly, she has been acting all this time—did she thrive upon deceit even then? Or was she broken somehow by a once-upon-a-time king, a faithless prince, a greedy father? Most likely, we will never know.

Back into the thicket, the old woman creeps, slowing her stride to duck and bend beneath the thorny hedges and whispering pines. A hump starts at her shoulder and slides down her spine, slithering beneath the fabric of her frock. Her toe catches at a half-buried carcass and kicks up the torn bird in a flurry of dried leaves. Its moldering feathers are still coated in a crust of dried blood. She leans down and scrapes at the blood with a long, tapering nail. It collects beneath, the coppery smell bringing to mind the time she smeared the sleeping queen's face with blood after stealing her infants away. How the pitiful girl screamed and tore her hair!

But here now! The old woman approaches a cleft in the earth. A pungent and sweet smell spills from the opening and a mist begins to collect at her feet. We crane to capture its form as it rises, enshrouding the woman's limbs, encircling her waist, and tugging at her hair. What is it, we are desperate to know?

Before our eyes, she is being remade. Spine straightened, limbs matched. Her eyes cycle from black to gold to hazel and back. Her hair curls and straightens, lifts and falls. Skin plumps and lines retreat. A sigh escapes her lips as the mist pulls away, revealing her new form, the one she will wear for at least a time. At least until the changes start again, urging her back to the forest thicket once more.

The mist is no more, and the cleft has sealed, but your eyes have seen none of this. There is only one sentence left to read and then you will put me aside, and I will be done. Already, the vibrancy of my story is fading, the characters settling to the back of your mind. Or ... are they?

You read the last line, tightly constructed and achingly poetic in the same turn. The woman lifts her eyes and...

You are blind to all else except the form, newly taken, and how cleverly, how horribly it resembles that of your own wife who is even now singing the children to sleep in the next room.

SWAN MOTHER

Ellie Campbell

I'd forgotten how much my mother loved birds.

After my father's funeral, I followed my mother's car back to their house. A scattering of neighbors and colleagues gathered in the living room, painfully formal. Fewer even than had been graveside. One casserole dish, masking tape curling around the bottom, huddled on the sideboard next to a cookie tray and a lone deviled egg plate. I snuck off before the cut glass feeling in my chest could shatter against faces that I hadn't seen in years.

My old room was tucked at the back of the house, far enough away that no one could stumble upon me without warning. I sank onto the bed, feeling fifteen again, useless and in the way, hiding from sharp voices and endless fighting. My foot knocked against an unfamiliar box, half hidden under the bed skirt. I pulled it out, curiosity flickering past the sharp edges of grief. The cardboard top was smudged with dust and streaky fingerprints.

It was full of feathers.

When I was a child, my mother and I would roam the neighborhood on long walks to the park or the country club pool, through the golf course, past the graveyard; our eyes hunting for broken eggshells, bits of fallen nests, and feathers. Always feathers. Spring and fall were best, though sometimes I could find a long tail feather in our humid north Georgia summer or a bit of downy fluff half-hidden in the frost of late winter.

She was distant at home no matter the season, staring out the window and humming to herself, forgetful in a way that left dinner too long in the oven or dust gathered in the corners of rooms for weeks. I didn't see much of my father in those years, busy with his grants and his conferences and his lectures. He always seemed to be traveling, and when he was home his mind was always somewhere else. I don't remember him paying me much attention at all. He was as likely to notice me as he was a piece of burnt toast, crunching away, academic journal in hand at the breakfast table, and my mother silently handing him the butter tray.

But she came alive on our walks, joy shining in her face at each new treasure, fingertips caressing the blue of a robin's eggshell or head thrown back with laughter at the sight of a fat cardinal stuffing himself with seeds. Sometimes she'd run faster than I could, throwing her arms out like she was flying. "Ava, come catch me," she'd cry, and I'd pretend to be a falcon and chase her around the parking lot by the jungle gym, determined to catch her and keep her from flying away. On the best days, when I wrapped my arms around her legs, she would pick me up and swing me around like I was flying, too. But other times her attention would drift, and she would wander off in search of the next treasure.

I could win her attention with a dull brown wren's feather as easily as a bright bluejay's. She liked tiny, downy feathers best, all fluffy edges. I loved long flight feathers, graceful and curved, a rare prize. She would hand them to me, and I'd pull the barbs apart, then watch as she smoothed them out, holding the feather by the shaft and pulling it through her fingers. She'd brush one over my hand to show me how soft it was, then sweep it across her cheek, eyes unfocused and soft. She kept them in tackle boxes, cheap jewelry holders, drawer organizers, and plastic bins and baskets. The nests and shells she placed on the windowsill over the kitchen sink. Extra ones went on the dining room table for a bit, then wound up thrown away when they started to fall apart. But the feathers she kept, every last one.

She once found peacock feathers for sale at a furniture store and brought back an armload. We arranged them carefully in a tall vase, and she steadied my hands, as I placed it on the mantelpiece in the living room, barely tall enough to reach. As we stood there, admiring the teal and turquoise shimmering in the afternoon light, I could hear the side door slam as my father came home from work. A shadow passed over her face, as it so often did. She turned away from the feathers and folded her arms across her chest, as though drawing wings around herself, and murmured, "I need to go lie down."

She often did this after our walks. The joy and laughter would fade as we trekked back to the house and would disappear entirely after we'd added that day's find to her collection. I thought she must be tired from hiking up and down the wooded hills that lined our neighborhood, and I often grew anxious and panicky on the way home, pleading with her to walk slower and save her energy. Later I would tiptoe around the house to avoid waking her or bothering my father, deep in his research. I winced at loud noises and made sure to keep my voice low as I played with my dolls. I draped them with feathers and flew them around the room, whispering of the places their wings could take them.

Later, our walks changed, then stopped. I refused to go entirely as a teenager. I was embarrassed to be seen with her then, her hands grimy with dirt and moss, crawling on the ground or up in a neighbor's tree, grasping after what? Dirty feathers, each the same as the last. Grimy pine needles disintegrating in abandoned nests. Angry at her, angry at my father, angry at a world that seemed to be falling apart.

Now, in my old bedroom, I reached into the box of feathers. I had not thought about our walks, our treasures, in all the years I'd refused to return. As I grasped a handful, the heap shifted and let out a puff of stale dust. Time compressed, then spun out. All those memories hidden in a mass of feathers. Coughing, I pulled them out and out and out and watched them unfold before me. It was a cloak.

My father studied birds, too. But not like she did.

He shouted at her sometimes, when the nests piled up too high, or when he couldn't find his shoes amidst the boxes of feathers and shells. A grim silence filled the house afterwards, punctuated by their cut off voices.

"I wish you wouldn't—"

"Can't go back—"

"Think of the child—"

He would storm down the stairs to his basement office to stare at his computer screen or the butterfly maps tacked up on the walls. I could always hear the mini fridge open and the crack of a can. He wouldn't appear for the rest of the night and was always gone by the time she woke me up in the morning. I kept silent in that house for fear of him, too.

I used to sneak down there to his office, when he was away on one trip or another. Normally I wasn't allowed; he couldn't concentrate with me underfoot. But I loved to trace the maps tacked up around the room, examining the shapes and projections, how the same space could be presented in so many different ways, for so many reasons. Here the vast expanse of Siberia, split into pieces. Next to it, China's Hunan province, tracking the flights of endangered cranes, mountains picked out in triangles and wavy lines. Europe and Africa, covered with migration lines stretching north to south like veins, or the branching barbs of a feather.

Most were of North America. Lines of rivers and hills, planting zones, and animal habitats traced across the continent, stateless and bounded only by water and mountains. One set of lines ran down the Appalachians, curving past our home in the foothills and extending into the Caribbean. Two through the middle of the country, and the last ran up the West Coast, starting in Baja California and following the Sierra Nevada to Canada. At night I could hear his computer wheeze softly, as he ran it through another set of calculations, printer churning out ever more maps and data.

Once they'd been brilliant together. His fascination with patterns and numbers and computations, applied to what she loved: birds in a ragged V against a bright blue sky and the stroke of a feather against her cheek. They threw grand parties when I was very little, before the piles of feathers and nests took over the house. I would sneak out of bed and hide in the hall closet, covered with winter coats, the smell of mothballs mingling with cedar and crisp snow clinging to fur and scratchy wool. I could only see a slice of living room, chandelier sparkling, my mother clinging to my father's arm or flitting from one knot of donors and deans to another, charming everyone with a smile and a flash of sequins. She poured drinks while he courted funding, awards shining on the mantelpiece.

By the time I was old enough to understand, whatever connection they'd had was gone. The house settled into détente, a cold war of attrition. They rarely spoke to one another, or to me. My father spent more and more time at his office, concerned about changing weather patterns, rising temperatures, the loss of migrating territory. Hurricanes were a cause for panic, as were wildfires. He obsessively kept track of a growing list of endangered species. The traces of bird pathways on the maps grew fewer and fewer over the years, while my mother's collections took up ever more space, tucked along the walls and filling the sideboards.

One day I drove home from school trembling, hours late after an afternoon tornado warning. A terrible storm system had swept through our town. The school had herded us into the few rooms available with no outside windows. I remember wrapping my arms tightly around myself to keep my hands from shaking, huddled against a wall, palms clammy against my elbows. Eventually the principal let us go; the radio said we'd been lucky. The worst of the storm had skirted to the south, and the tornadoes it spun off only tore through cow pastures and stripped a few pines in the state forest.

But when I walked in the door it looked like the tornado had swept through our living room. Every basket, every jewelry crate, every tackle box had been torn apart, contents scattered around the room. Feathers filled the air. I knelt and picked up half a nest. It barely covered my palm, and bits of leaf and mulch flaked off as I stood.

I could hear screaming from the kitchen: my father ranting about climate change and dying species and my mother's obsession with birds. Her shrieking back about the loss of her home and everything she had given up.

Eggshells crunched under my feet, as I turned and walked back out, hands shaking again.

I stayed at friends' houses for the rest of that year, then left for college in the fall, relying on loans, part-time jobs, and stubbornness to get me through. I went home rarely, then not at all. The few times I had, the silences were deeper, the office walls more and more jumbled with empty maps. My father's voice more and more slurred. My mother barely responsive.

When he died, I hadn't seen either of them in years. But I flew back for the funeral, and stood next to my mother at the graveside. I had spent those years ignoring the fact that I'd followed in his footsteps, earning a succession of degrees, logging environmental changes for a multitude of projects. I'd migrated from one site to another, nights spent drafting grant proposals and days out in the field, doing what I could to keep those lines from disappearing off those maps, or at least slowing them down. I told myself that focusing on insect populations was different from his work or her obsession. But beside his grave, I knew the difference was only one of degrees, measured in the filament of a dragonfly's wing or the chitin of a beetle's carapace, not the distance of miles from home.

It was far hotter than I remembered that time of fall being. Sweat trickled down the back of my neck and soaked the collar of the only blazer I owned. Since my mother had called to break the news, I'd gratefully agonized over my clothing choices rather than think about my father's death or what might remain of my mother's half-life, stuck at home with no skills and no job and no friends I'd ever known about. But instead of feeling confident or successful, I felt like a little girl playing dress-up, shoulders too tight and wrists itching. My shirt stuck to the small of my back, and my head ached in the heat.

As the funeral director droned on, I cataloged all the changes since I'd last been in my hometown. A great patch of new sky where a massive oak had been felled by straight-line storm winds a few years back. New strands of gray in my mother's hair and lines etched deeply around her eyes. Crumbling cement on the sides of the roads, and raw red dirt bleeding into ditches carved out by recent flooding. Paint peeling on houses that couldn't afford repairs. Empty spaces on the walls where my father's maps used to hang. Boil water notices tacked on splintering electrical poles. Crepe myrtle blooming long out of season. No birdsong. No frogs croaking. No streaks of unlucky insects on the rental windshield.

When I was a child, the humidity would have broken by this time of year and given way to cool mornings and bright, dry afternoons. Instead it lay thickly over the gravestones, beading on the edges of plastic flowers and blurring the edges of the treeline in the distance. Everything was wrong here.

Hours later, I was still sitting on the bed, lap covered in the feather cloak, when my mother knocked on the door. The house had grown quiet as the neighbors trickled out. She poked her head in and smiled, hesitant. The lines on her face were softer in the dim light.

She saw the box, and her smile faded.

"Come with me," she said. "And bring that with you."

I didn't want to talk to her; I just wanted to keep sitting on that bed until morning came and I could drive the rental car back to the airport and fly away. Out of this place where memory echoed against the dying heat of the evening and the crank of endless air-conditioners in the distance. But I folded the cloak back into the box and followed her through the house and out into the yard. It was heavier than I expected. I felt heavier than I expected.

"I thought you got rid of all the feathers," I said. "I thought Dad would have …"

We stopped in the middle of the driveway. I carefully placed the box on the ground, lining it up against the cracks. I don't know why I could treat it more delicately than I could treat her.

She stayed silent and gazed up at the sky. It was purple with dusk, and I could hear a single frog croak, where once I'd heard dozens.

After a while she spoke.

"He had a storage unit," she said. "I didn't know about it. I didn't find out until after he died. I only went out there yesterday, after I found the paperwork."

I couldn't look at her face. "I don't understand."

"He kept this—" she looked at the box "—out there. I found it behind boxes of his old maps, the ones that showed the last of the migration patterns he studied. Open it and see."

I grasped an edge with both hands and pulled the bundle of feathers out of the box. It unfurled in the dim light, dust and down flying. My eyes struggled to make sense of it. Was it a cloak of feathers or a swath of fabric? The textures melded together into a subtle sheen. I blinked, and they were feathers again. I held it against my chest and ran the backs of my fingers along the grain. She looked up at me.

"It was mine once," my mother said. "Your father took it from me and kept it from me all these years. Without it, I couldn't fly. He loved me once, but more than that, he thought I could help him."

"He thought ... what do you mean, couldn't fly? Help him with what?"

"Oh, honey," she turned to me, broken open and tender, the way we never were with one another. "I was a swan girl, once upon a time. I let your father take my feathers and bind me to him. I wanted to stay for a while, for him, for you, for the work. He told me I could save my people, but when I asked to return to them, he hid my feathers. I couldn't leave until I found them, though I desperately wanted to, for a long time."

All of a sudden, I was ten again, a daughter who just wanted to go for another walk, find another feather. Wonder at the world. Believe in magic. Watch her mother share something she loved, before she left without leaving, lying in bed and staring at the walls.

"You can fly?" My voice cracked. "Can you still fly?"

She looked down at the cloak. "I don't know."

We stood in the twilight, shadows stretching in front of us on the driveway.

"I want to see it." I said, desperate. "I want to see you fly."

Her face cracked, devastated. "No," she whispered. She stepped back, away from the cloak and away from me.

"No," she said again, stronger. "I can't. If I put it on and it fails, if I can't fly. I'd rather not know. My home is gone, all my people are gone. There's nothing to go back to. Our home, the trees and rivers, the lakes and swamps. They're all gone. I don't exist anymore."

She crumpled to the ground, arms folding around herself. I'd never seen her cry before.

"Mom? Mom, please." I knelt beside her, the cloak pushed to the side. The words felt funny in my mouth.

"I knew a long time ago," she said. "The tornado. That storm system swept across five states. My old home was destroyed. There were never very many of us anyway, but I always hoped … I always hoped I could find my family one more time. When that storm came, I thought I was being punished for not trying hard enough to get out. To get you out. It broke me. So I let you go. It was so long ago. When I found this yesterday, I almost didn't remember what it was."

She reached out, hand hovering over the cloak but not touching.

"You're still here, though," she said. "I want you to have it."

I knew I didn't want it. I didn't want what either of them had left me. But I'd never seen her cry before.

"How … how does it work?" I asked.

"It's my … cloak, I guess you'd say. My feathers. Drape it around your shoulders and … breathe."

I stood and held it in front of me, arms stretched out. It billowed in the slight breeze as though it were made of fine silk and not a heavy mass of feathers, so tightly woven I couldn't tell where one ended and the next began. I gingerly draped it over one shoulder, then the next.

"It can be yours now. I tried to show you, the feathers, the eggs, the nests, all those years ago. Do you remember? Now it can all be yours."

I froze. The weight felt wrong. Everything felt wrong. Slowly I wrapped my arms around myself, just once, like drawing wings into my chest. The silence of the evening trapped me, no birds, no mosquito buzzing, no rustling in the underbrush. Humidity I could feel in the back of my throat. Echoes of the past ringing in my ears.

I took the cloak off my shoulders, feathers sweeping the ground, and folded it back into the box.

"No," I said. "I can't take this from you." I spoke slowly, trying to find the words. "It's not … it's not my world, Mom. I don't want what he took from you. You should keep it."

I couldn't quite look at her, staring at her shoulder instead of meeting her eyes. I hadn't wanted what she offered me in years, but I couldn't leave it like this either.

"I'm sorry. I'm sorry you lost your home, your family. I'm sorry he kept you when he should have let you go. But you do still exist. You're still here." My voice cracked. "I'm still here."

I knelt, picked up the box, and handed it to her. Her fingers clutched white around the edges. I tried to find the words.

"I've spent the last ten years counting dying species every day. Every day. Butterflies, moths, beetles. Bees. Entire colonies wiped out, half the numbers today than we had forty, fifty years ago."

I reached out and placed my hand on the top of the box.

"But I see them adapting too. Birds migrating earlier, insects shifting feeding grounds. Finding new homes. Relocating. It doesn't make up the difference, but they're not all gone yet."

I met her eyes and held out my hand.

"Come look for feathers with me again."

In the distance, a cricket began to chirp.

THE GREEN KNIGHT

Katherine Heath Shaeffer

Our good King Bruin presided from the high bench at Winterfest, where the best lords and ladies had gathered for days of rich revelry and reckless mirth, jousting and caroling to welcome the new year. By the last of twelve days of celebration, the contests had calmed, and King Bruin and his court languidly feasted. Every platter at the High Table had cuts of the rich, fat-sizzling meats that could be hunted in this land, seasoned with the herbs we brought when we captured this country. Next to the platters were silver bowls of vegetable stew, which we scooped and sopped with slabs of dark brown bread. Goblets of spiced red wine rounded out the remains of our feast. Greenling servants milled to and fro, topping off the goblets from silver ewers.

A greenling pouring wine into the Queen's cup slipped his grip, spilling the red liquid to pool and soak through the white cloth under the silver bowl.

The King started and swore, but the Queen did not cuff or curse at the servant, only chiding him gently with a tolerant gaze. His pale-green face made no expression, but as he stumbled from her, he murmured, "Grace, Lady" and, "Lady, grace." Though whether he meant the Queen or the High Lady who watches over us all, we had no way of knowing.

Even years after we had taken them in, greenlings were barely able to speak in any civilized tongue. When we made our settlement here, we discovered that the bright-green, little monsters we plucked from caves and under hills used no language at all. Though they had human-like faces, they had no language and no names, and were less able to distinguish themselves from one another than dogs in a pack. But we found them trainable, even more so than dogs. We took them under our protection, named them, provided them honest labor, and covered their naked bodies. With proper food and care, the green of their skin gradually faded to a pale milk-green, and we had reason to hope that they would soon not be green at all. And though it took great patience to guide them, we had faith that we could bring them under our Lady's grace. Their changes suggested that our Lady was coming to favor them.

For it was not only their green skin that had changed. Terrifying protrusions, which once rose from their heads like demonic horns, now either fell limp and docile like hair or brittled and broke off entirely. Their sulphurously glowing green eyes dimmed so that they no longer haunted our nightmares, and the squirming, vine-like tentacles on which they used to glide no longer flexed and rippled like so many writhing snakes. Under the strict and benevolent guidance of our priests, the greenlings learned to bunch their otherworldly, tentacular masses into the semblances of legs and arms, and they now hobbled about in an awkward and endearing way, wabble-waddling to the great delight of our children, who had no memory of what creeping horrors the greenlings were before their domestication.

The mercy of our Queen made our hearts light, and the King shook his steel-grey head fondly under its golden crown. Those of us who were old enough remembered the younger King Bruin, with the lines etched less deeply on his face, stammering puppyish love to his flaxen-haired young bride while his crown sat at an awkward angle, as if he did not know how to wear it. Now, our steel-gray King wore the crown as if it grew from his brow. The Queen dabbed at the wine stain with her dark brown bread until the King stilled her with a light touch, his hand on hers. And then, as a winter storm rose outside, the Queen and her lord sipped from a single cup.

The storm grew and grew, until it felt like we hunkered down in fear of a hungry animal. The wind whistled between the hills and moaned at the door. The whistle had almost a roundness to it, a depth like the long echo of the priests' bells. The wind hummed; the wind sang.

A sudden battering gust sounded like the hammering fist of some winter giant.

K-thrunk, k-thrunk, thrunked the door.

And now it sounded even more deliberate, even more like a knock, but surely not, not in this storm, and no man's hand would reach so high on the wood. Surely that was too high and too hard to be a mortal knock.

K-thrunk, k-thrunx! A sound of splintering wood.

King Bruin made a signal to his guards. Two readied their weapons and stood to the sides. Two lifted the bar from across the door. As soon as the bar was lifted, the door burst inward, forcing the guards to stumble back, as we all braced for the cold winter gale.

But the breeze that flickered the torchlight and lifted the hair on our napes was the warm and earthy breeze of late spring into early summer, and it carried with it the scent of old rot and new growth. All of us in that hall shivered not from the cold, then, but from the strangeness. All of us but the milk-pale greenlings. They did not shiver, but to a one, they froze in their work and raised their heads.

Two green blurs hurtled inside: one glided in a jade-green arc around the hall, from the door, past the gathered guests, over the banquet table—clipping King Bruin's crown as it went—and up into the rafters, where it perched on a beam and glared down at the party below with golden eyes, set like jewels in its sharp-beaked face. It seemed in every respect like a hawk, except that instead of feathers, it had lichen scales. It wore no jess on its legs.

The second blur darted forward on four swift feet. A guard grasped it, but it wrenched away, leaving the guard staring perplexed at a spray of greenery left in his hand. When the creature reached the floor before the King's table, it settled itself on its haunches, as if it petitioned its own audience with the King and Queen. It was a green hound. In place of fur, green grass and mosses sprouted from its back, and its undercoat was loam. It faced the King and Queen with a honey-gold gaze that peered from under a shaggy moss brow.

As one, the hawk and the hound swiveled their heads around to face the door, as if to say, *Here comes one more of us.*

Another breeze—stronger this time but still warm, still summer-spring—made the torches gutter and flapped the open door like the clapper of a bell. It slammed shut twice and then was thrown open wide.

The storm calmed.

Framed in the doorway, filling the doorway, stood a massive green woman.

A greenling in the form of a human woman, but a giant woman. She was not milk-pale like the castle's servants, but the bright green of new linden leaves. She had made of her tentacles such perfect imitations of human limbs that the tendrils seemed no more than veins and musculature bulging taut under her bright-green skin. She was modestly garbed, too, in a green tunic and leggings, the fabrics straining against her massive arms and thighs. A green cape lined with white fur rested around her shoulders. All of her clothes were trimmed and decorated in gleaming gold. The protrusions growing from her head fell downward, wafting and flowing so that to all appearances, she had long, dark-green hair rippling past her elbows. She walked into the court with sure-footed grace—and even her feet were artful imitations, delicate illusions spooled from greenling tendril-string.

Against the firm green swell of her bosom, she cradled an enormous axe forged in green steel. Both the handle and the blade were mottled with veins of gold and burnished to a high sheen.

As much as her size and civilized dress, that axe arrested our attention. Greenlings did not carry weapons. They did not fight. In spite of their fierce appearance, they never put up any physical resistance. It was as if the High Lady had decreed that they be meek and mild before us, allowing us to improve them and bring them into a state of grace.

"King Bruin," the green knight boomed. "I bear you winter greetings."

We stared at her, agog. No greenling spoke like that, with such elocution and poise.

King Bruin gathered himself. Whatever horror he felt at this apparition did not sound in his voice. "And yet you bring the breeze of spring, just as spring has trailed your footsteps to our door."

It was true. In the square of the open doorway, a green path cut through the white, stretching far into the distance, until its tail disappeared into a blur of snow. The path held all shades of green, with a soft green blanketing the ground overlaid by motes of flickering green light.

"What are your winter celebrations but the hope of spring to come? I thought only to celebrate with you, King Bruin."

"By bearing arms in my hall?"

"If I sought war with your kind, would I come so barely attired? Why would I not wear helmet and hauberk after the fashion of your knights?"

King Bruin spread his hands. "I do not know. No one knows what a greenling looks like in battle. Your kind has never done us violence."

"Then do not assume I mean you violence now."

A smile played on the King's lips. "Then what business have you with that axe."

The green knight stretched her face into a smile of her own. "The business of pleasure, Great King. This tool I carry is not one of battle, but one of mirth. I have come to issue a challenge to you or any member of your court. A simple exchange, to prove your worth."

"An exchange with an axe."

"And for one, with this cleaver as the prize."

An excited murmur rose up among us, and we drummed our fists on the king's long table, setting cutlery to jangling. The green woman's axe looked a fortune in steel and gold alone, even before the value of its craftsmanship.

Where had she even come by it? Who would forge an axe for one of her kind?

"I ask you now, King Bruin, if any of your court are bold enough to play this game with me: to strike me once and, should I survive, be struck by me in turn." She turned to face the court. "Are any of you gathered here, holed up from the storm, brave enough to set your arm against a greenling's arm?"

"This is absurd," King Bruin said. "Who would agree to be struck?"

"The same man—or woman—who knows they can finish me off in one blow. If they can take my life in one strike, this axe will be their prize."

We toasted and challenged each other in a flurry of rattling spoons and hot breath, looking for courage in the bottoms of our goblets and soup bowls, and yet no man stepped forward. There was something too strange about this greenling, from her unusual size to her facility with mortal speech. And who among us could even wield the massive axe? King Bruin had once swung an axe of such dimensions that we sung of it even to that day, but his weapon in all its power was only half the size of this. The challenges faded on our lips.

"I thought King Bruin's men were famed for their fierceness," the green woman said. "Will none swiftly strike a stroke for another?"

King Bruin sighed. "We have no need for such violent sport. Come, Lady. Sit with us and share our feast."

At the offer of our proper and mortal food, the green knight's green eyes widened, the green hawk screeched, and the green hound growled.

"I have not come to share your fare, King Bruin, but to bid you play this game with me. Answer me truly." She again addressed the hall. "Is there none among you who would wish to strike me down?"

As she made the challenge, the green knight *unfurled*. Her mighty limbs split into their writhing, snake-like masses, her feet unspooled, even her bosom came undone. Her "hair" rose into the horn-like protuberances common to her kind, until extending from her head was a green crown of antlers. She glide-slithered forward, so vile and alien now in her movement that we struggled to keep the heavy meats and sauces of the feast within our bodies. And as she closed in on the high table, the many textures and colors of the green knight became clear.

So many shades and hues of green were there! And her tunic, leggings, and cape were not cloth at all, but fungi in different forms of green. Her "skin" had some true, bright linden-green, but also pebblings of sky blue and flushes of lemon yellow, with splashes of purple and orange. She was a riot of color all adding up to green.

The gold accents on her gear came from little gold mushroom caps flat as buttons and fungal veils of orange and gold. What had seemed her cape was a spongy green mass, and its white fur lining was in fact a dense layer of the unspun-cotton fluff that roots mushrooms to the earth.

There was not a scrap on her that was not *of* her, that did not grow *from* her. This giant woman stood naked in the King's hall.

"Cover yourself," King Bruin said.

With a damp tear, the green knight's wombless abdomen split and frilled. "To sweeten the deal, I add that the one who strikes me need not fear an answering blow for a full year. Think on it. Even if the striker fails, even if I survive this day, they need not fear my axe for that year. A year is plenty of time, is it not? To learn the trick behind my game."

"Cover yourself," said King Bruin. "Sit."

"Perhaps the problem is, I am not enough of a threat to you. Perhaps there is no honor in striking down a lone greenling woman."

The hall filled suddenly with a *whoosh* of hot, vegetative air.

The torches went out; the candles in the chandelier went out; the fire on the hearth went out. But the green knight was still visible, her horn crown and every pebbled node on her skin, every vine-like tendril emitting its own venomous green light. All of us, all the King's court were revealed, exposed by that terrible green. And in that green our faces were sick and sallow, etched with the exaggerated lines of our confusion and terror. We were made ugly in that light.

The greenlings were more than revealed. Their milky-pale skin answered the knight's luminescence from within. Each greenling body had become a pale, shaded lamp, and it was as if those shades were starting to lift, starting to reveal a healthy green glow.

Something was *in* them. The green knight was awakening something in them.

Our Queen looked at the sea of green faces, frightened mortals and impassive, ready, awakening greenlings, and clutched our King's hand fiercely. Our Queen who had shown more kindness to the greenlings than any other. Our Queen who had preached slow and gentle guidance. Her knuckles over the King's hand were pale, pale green in the strange light. "You cannot let her challenge pass, my Lord. You must stop this thing tonight, while it can yet be stopped."

King Bruin rose. Though he did not match the size of the greenling woman, he was yet a mighty force among men. The heavy oaken bench beneath us slid and groaned against stone, as he stood. "I will play your game," he said, into the green darkness.

The green knight nodded and held out her green axe. It glowed in the green light.

King Bruin made his way around the banquet table, down from the dais, down to the floor where the knight waited with her axe. She was massive; she was inhuman, but if his aim was sound and his swing was strong, he might be able to kill her now. And if he could not kill her now, if she had some greenling trick to stop the axe or to place her head back on her shoulders, then by her own bargain, he would at least have a year. A year to decide how best to deal with her, with this greenling who did not obey commands.

Our King touched the axe and frowned at the texture of it, then adjusted his grip and hefted it, swaying on his feet. We wondered if that was the trick, if the green knight was betting that a single blow with her unwieldy weapon would not strike true.

But King Bruin, gray as he was, was still fit and firm, his body limber and well-muscled from sport with his men. He squared his stance and planted himself like an oak, and in that moment, it was easy to love him, our King.

The green knight bowed her head and bared the ropey tendrils of her neck. Of what might have been her neck. She bared the ropey tendrils connecting her head to the rest of her body, stretching them out to an inhuman length.

King Bruin raised the axe, took careful aim, and let it fall.

At the last moment, our King's face changed, morphing from resolution into realization. A final understanding. His shoulders jerked as if he tried to stop the axe, or change its course, but gravity had taken hold and finished the job.

The green axe struck the green knight true, and she exploded into spores.

And then. Oh, then!

How our changes began.

THE GIRL WHO TROD ON A LOAF

Antonia Eliason

Her headaches began the day they installed the sentinel. Neoma cried out in pain each time the grid flashed, vaporizing the toads and spiders that were trying to make their way into the settlement. She wailed with great hiccupping breaths until her mother slapped her hard across her mouth and told her to hush, and then she buried her stifled sobs into her pillow until the jolts of pain abated to a dull throb with an occasional knife stab of blinding agony. As the first child born in the settlement (an unfortunate accident, as her mother called her to polite company; a waste of precious resources to her face), she knew better than to get in the way of the adults.

During the day, she helped with chores, hauling fibers to the weavers and bringing water to the builders. Before the sentinel was operational, she would sometimes sneak away past the enclosure of homes, out beyond the settlement, past the shuttleport, across the gray-green rocks and towards the purple forest, and find creatures to play with—wheelbarrow-sized toads covered in gelatinous slime that smelled all fresh and clean when you petted them and fuzzy spiders the size of herself who crooned in her mind when she spoke to them. At first, she tried to bring them bits of food from the settlement—small balls of pounded yam or a few cubes of fried tofu—but they were uninterested. Instead, the toads took her to the edges of the marshland bordering the forest, nudging certain plants and looking at her until she reached out and plucked them from the boggy ground. One delicate, almost glass-like pink stalk with a yellow puff at the top was sweet and crunchy. Another, a deep green leaf, tasted like nothing else she'd ever had, deliciously salty and soft, melting in her mouth.

The adults were horrified by the creatures, calling them abominations and a mockery of God's creations on far-away Earth. They blamed them for the failure of their grain crops, the wheat and rye turning black and crumbling before they could ripen and be milled into the flour needed to bake the sacramental bread. Neoma tried to tell them about the plants she had tasted, but the adults either ignored or ridiculed her, dismissing her information as childish babblings. Before the sentinel was activated, the adults would set up watch at night and shoot all creatures that came towards their homes and fields. Each time Neoma came across one of their husks, lifeless and shredded by bullets, she would whisper a little prayer. Her mother said that prayers were only for God's creatures and nothing in this godforsaken land was God's creature except for the settlers from Earth. Neoma didn't believe her, but had long ago learned that saying anything would result in a beating, so she kept her mouth shut.

The activation of the sentinel meant that Neoma could no longer leave the settlement. Unlike the others, who could walk through the invisible barrier thrown up by the sentinel without harm, merely approaching it caused Neoma to fall to the ground in convulsions. When the medic could find nothing wrong with her, it was decided that she was acting up for attention, and her mother punished her by locking her in their hut for weeks on end with baskets of clothes to mend for the settlement while she went out to work. Without her toad and spider companions, Neoma was lonely and tried to reach out across the barrier with her thoughts, the way she had as a small child, crooned to sleep by the spiders. She hesitantly floated her thoughts outside of the house, down the dirt paths, towards the edge of the settlement, hoping to feel the velvety purr of the spiders and invite their chorus to cradle her mind. Instead, she punched into an invisible wall that repelled her with a sharp buzzing that reached into her belly, threatening to tear her insides. Each time she reached out, the wave of nausea she experienced left her vomiting and shaking, a taste of metal lingering in her mouth. She stopped trying. When she was released from confinement and put back to work, she heard the adults talk about how the sentinel was working so well, and how many fewer toads and spiders there were, and how the additional traps that they were setting outside the barrier would bring those hellspawn down for good. In no time, they said, the settlement would be as nice of a place to live as the capital city, Calneh.

In the first few years after the sentinel was active, with the settlers now feeling safe in their community, waves of children were born, much to the joy of the settlers. Although soybeans, sweet potatoes, and other vegetables grew with some coaxing, the grain crops continued to fail. Neoma was tasked with looking after the youngest infants, a duty that kept her within the confines of the settlement, where even inside the creche her occasional headaches alerted her to the sentinel's activities, each piercing stab a reminder that the sentinel's net of destruction had vaporized another creature. No one else was affected.

The settlement, now officially named Abudan, celebrated its tenth year with a festival of life. A few precious loaves of bread were baked from flour imported from Calneh, where grain grew abundantly. "Give us this day our daily bread," the settlers intoned, as they shared slivers of the dense bread around reverently. Purple wood cradles were hung in the center of town around a metal pole salvaged from one of the old long-range spacecrafts. The adults, in white dresses, gently swung the cradles and sang hymns by soft electrical light, and the sentinel glowed from time to time as the toads and spiders, drawn to the settlement by the music and light, were vaporized. Neoma sat huddled in a corner, away from the lights, clutching her head each time the sentinel zapped a creature, biting her lip so hard it bled, staining her white festival frock. That night, her mother, drunk on firewine, beat her until her arms grew tired. The next day, finding that Neoma's lip was still bleeding, she cursed Neoma and made her clean up the blood. Days later, when the bleeding still would not abate, her mother dragged her to Abudan's medic, complaining all the while of her disobedience.

"That no-good daughter of mine. Why I give her everything—you know that I have slaved to make sure she had all the things she needs, even though with Tobin gone, it's been so hard, and, well, she was never supposed to be, and she should be grateful for all the things I do, but refuses to listen, or heed my bidding, and I suppose that child will be the death of me," and here her mother took a deep breath, screwing her eyes shut until a miniscule tear trickled from each eye. "She's a big girl now, and needs to be helping with the babies. They are our future," she ended with a sniff and a glare at Neoma.

The medic was sympathetic to her mother, tut-tutting at Neoma's disobedience while roughly turning her head this way and that. He sent her home with a poultice and some words of warning. Abudan did not abide wastrels, and it was well known in the settlement that Neoma was a troublemaker, plagued by illnesses of her mind's fabrication to get out of the hard work necessary to build a flourishing settlement.

But the bleeding didn't stop. Her lip bled all day and all night. Her lip bled until her skin grew sallow and her body weak. No longer able to look after the babies, she lay on her cot, tormented by headaches brought on by the sentinel, each pulse of which would drive a fresh gush of blood from her torn lip. At last, tired of having to feed an indolent mouth, her mother consulted with the leaders of Abudan, and it was decided that Neoma would be sent to Calneh, to be examined by the medical experts there. Any loss of labor was a blow to the small community, and despite her mother's misgivings, at thirteen years old, Neoma promised decades of work and childbearing. It was hoped that the trip would straighten her out.

Neoma looked forward to the trip to Calneh in the hovercraft, her first time out of the settlement; her first time flying. But in the end, she remembered none of it, as despite her feeble screams and protestations, they forced her towards the sentinel's invisible barrier, her head buzzing with the growing chorus of metal scraping metal as she neared it, pain coursing through her spasming limbs, blood gushing from her lip, until she lost consciousness. She woke up in a hospital bed in Calneh, tubes in her arms, her lip bandaged and her head throbbing. The doctors, a kindly older couple, the man with a shock of white hair and a furrowed brow, the woman with gray hair pulled up in a tight bun and laugh lines around her eyes, fussed around her.

"Neoma! We're so glad to see you alert!" the man exclaimed while plumping her pillow. "We were quite worried. You were in an awful state when you arrived."

"We've patched you up—given you some supplements that have stopped the bleeding, although it'll take a few more days for your lip to heal completely. We're still trying to figure out how that was related to your seizures. It was touch and go there for a while," the woman said, her voice soft and gentle.

The kindness of the doctors, Binyam and Mariel, was overwhelming at first. Neoma looked at them suspiciously, but as she healed and they continued to pamper her, feeding her fruit, cheese, and bread, foods that were the utmost luxuries in Abudan, she grew more confident, helping them tend to other patients and offering her assistance wherever she could. She spent hours wandering the hospital gardens, touching the waxy green leaves of the bushes and the strange, soft green stalks that grew from the ground. She tasted a few of the plants but they were mostly bitter. The gardens fascinated her, the idea of growing something for any reason other than nutrition unfamiliar.

With Neoma's consent, Binyam and Mariel ran further experiments on her, trying to identify the root cause of her illness. Abudan was the most remote of the planet's settlements, and the only one beyond the terraformed perimeter around Calneh. As the first child born there, Neoma was something of a medical curiosity.

"Your people have such faith in God." Mariel sighed, as she examined the results of yet another inconclusive test. "Even though the terraforming materials were exhausted, they felt called to claim the wilderness and mold it in God's image. They must be very homesick for the colors and scents of Earth," she continued, gesturing at the hospital gardens. Neoma nodded. She had grown up with the constant negative comparisons to Earth. Even Mariel, who cared with such tenderness for Neoma, was dismissive of the world that existed outside the confines of the terraformed regions.

"You know, some of the creatures of this planet are so amazing," Neoma told Binyam and Mariel one afternoon, as she watched a tiny mechanized drone flit between the garden's flowers, carrying pollen from one to the next. "In Abudan, we have these beautiful toads, as big as this," she indicated, stretching her arms out, "who love being petted. They used to show me all kinds of edible plants when I was younger. We also have spiders." She paused. "Well, I guess neither of them are really toads or spiders like exist on Earth, but that's what we call them, anyway. The spiders sing songs that you can only hear inside your mind."

"Oh, Neoma," Mariel said, and reached over to hug her. "You do have an imagination! It must have been so hard for you being sick for so long."

"But it's true," Neoma insisted.

Binyam gave her a kindly look. "We're scientists, Neoma, and while I'm sure there are all kinds of species on this planet we don't know that much about, there's nothing sentient. Those 'toads' and 'spiders' are just some of the common pests. Harmless, sure, but as unintelligent as the toads and spiders of Earth. Like Miriam said, you have a wonderful imagination, and I'm sure this helped you get through your illness."

Neoma did not speak of the toads and spiders again.

Yet Neoma was happy in Calneh. Binyam and Mariel praised her efforts around the hospital, teaching her basic medical skills such as suturing wounds and changing bandages. She felt better, too, the headaches gone.

When one day Binyam and Mariel told Neoma that she must return to Abudan, it was as if her world crumbled.

"But why can I not stay? I can be of use to you! You know I'm good with patients and I'm willing to do anything!" she begged.

"I'm sorry, Neoma, but your settlement needs you back. You are their child and precious to them too. As much as we would like to keep you here, for you bring us such joy, you have to return," Binyam said.

Mariel held out a wrapped package. "For your mother," she said, pressing the package into Neoma's hands. "A loaf of our bread. I know you have no grain in Abudan. A taste of Earth will bring her much joy."

Neoma swallowed hard. She didn't want to return to her mother. The loaf would just infuriate her mother further, and Neoma could already hear the accusations that she had faked her injury so she could go to Calneh and feast on rich foods while her mother struggled and starved, even though her mother routinely took half of Neoma's food for herself.

The anxious gnawing in her stomach could not entirely ruin the journey back to Abudan. Neoma pressed her face against the window, staring at the landscape as it rushed by below her. For the first couple of hours, they passed above swatches of farmland—fields of golden grain arranged in arrow-straight rows, orchards of fruit trees surrounded by tidy white fences. The end of the terraformed land came abruptly. Suddenly, they were flying over swathes of purple forest. Her breath caught. She was filled with wild longing at the beauty below her. Some time later, the forests were replaced with glittering bare hilltops, sparkling gold in the light of the suns. Occasionally, she thought she could spot a giant creature amidst the hills—a moleworm most likely, but the craft was moving too fast for her to get a good look. How she yearned to stop the craft and get out right there and walk amidst the creatures. A thrumming suffused her being, filling her with a joy she had not experienced since the sentinel had been installed in Abudan. Her body was reawakening after a long slumber.

When at last the craft slowed and lowered itself to the ground, Neoma's nausea returned, a jarring reminder that for months now, she had been without pain. The walk from the shuttleport to the settlement was only a few hundred meters, and incoming craft were infrequent enough that Abudans would be looking to see who had arrived. Neoma clutched the package with the bread and stepped from the craft to the familiar gray-green ground. But where she had felt a thrumming of happiness while skimming over the empty lands between Calneh and Abudan, here everything was somehow wrong. A metallic grating had replaced the thrumming and with each step that she took towards the settlement, she felt as if she would sink into the ground. The ground around the settlement was filled with traps, she knew, traps to absorb the creatures of the planet, but she wasn't sure what they looked like or how they operated, having never been able to venture past the sentinel. She heard the hovercraft take off, the breeze tousling her hair. The only way left to her was forward.

As she neared the settlement, her steps became more agonizing. Something was wrong, and as she struggled to move her body, she could tell that people in the settlement were staring at her. She could just make out her mother's angry face. She tried lifting her foot and found it sticky with an invisible substance that didn't want to let her go. Was this what happened to the creatures? Why was this happening to her? She pulled and pulled and yanked her right foot free, leaving her boot behind in the ground. Neoma cringed, as she imagined the berating she would get from her mother for that loss.

"Help!" she yelled, and even to her ears, her voice was feeble and hollow. "Help …" But she knew that no one would help her. The people of Abudan would just stare at her as they always had when she fell ill. In their eyes she was a lazy, good-for-nothing liar, filled with idle fantasies, and nothing would change that. God helps those who help themselves, she had been told time and time again.

In desperation, she unwrapped the package with the loaf and tore a chunk off, throwing it directly in front of her. With great difficulty, she managed to break her left foot free of the resistance and place it on the chunk of loaf. Her mother was now striding towards her, face red, words carried away by the hot breeze and the metallic grinding that made her bones ache and her head pound. She tore another chunk off the loaf and again threw it in front of her, pulling her right food free and stepping onto the loaf. She repeated this, stepping carefully on chunks of bread until she ran out. Helplessly, she looked up. Her mother stood a few feet in front of her.

"You abomination! God has forsaken you! Not only are you lazy, spoiled, and good for nothing," her mother yelled, her voice carrying through to Neoma, spittle flying from her lips, "but you have wasted all the care we have given you over the years. God is punishing you for your sins, and yet you waste a precious loaf of bread like it was dirt, while our settlement scrimps and saves for flour to partake in the sacrament! I wish you had never been born! All you have ever done is cause me grief!"

Neoma opened her mouth to say something but found that her voice was gone, her throat closing up. She stepped forward, and felt her feet sink into the ground. This time she didn't resist. There was no point. Her mother continued to yell and scream, and they were now surrounded by curious settlers who had come out to witness the spectacle, but Neoma could no longer hear. She couldn't move.

She just stood there, slowly sinking, until she was finally engulfed by the invisible ooze and the ground swallowed her up.

At first, there was nothing. Neoma struggled, constricted by the pressure of the soil all around her, unable to move, unable to breath, unable to see, uncertain whether her eyes were open or shut, unable even to gasp as her lungs burnt and the last remnants of air were squeezed out of her by the crushing weight of dirt.

Then there was too much. The weight suddenly lifted, and from darkness and silence, Neoma's world became a cacophony of sounds and thoughts and feelings. From the purple trees that were being cut down, to the toads and spiders dying by the thousands in the forcefield of the sentinel and the traps around Abudan, to the moleworms being shot at by hunting parties in the distant hills, she could feel every bit of pain experienced by the creatures of this world. She screamed until her mouth was full of blood and kept screaming until her vocal chords tore and her pain mingled with theirs. She cried until her tears ran dry, and she could no longer close her eyes. Her desiccated eyeballs shriveled, and her muscles atrophied. And then, something began to change. In the silence, unable to scream or cry or see or move, she listened. At first, she heard nothing. But as she listened, it seemed as if she could hear for the very first time.

Instead of just pain, she could feel the joy of the inhabitants of the planet, the songs of the networks of plants and fungi that she now realized connected every living creature on this planet—that she too, was a part of; had always been a part of. With this new awareness came freedom. She traveled through the living organisms of the planet, across bubbling oceans teeming with floating hives of winged fish that dove deep down to the ocean floor to daringly catch prey, into caverns piled with sands made of tiny crustaceans, up mountains covered in yellow that suddenly rose up in one flock and flew off to perch on the majestic forests of far continents. She knew the exhilaration of synchronized pollination and the heartache of losing one's young to predators. Throughout, she felt the inevitability of the natural cycle that saw a breath of life extinguished only to be reborn elsewhere. But as she journeyed, so too she came to a place that was impenetrable to her new awareness, a lifeless space where no rebirth could happen, and she knew it to be Calneh.

Time passed. How long, she did not know, but she became aware not only of the voices of the planet, but of the human thoughts and voices of the people of Abudan as well. She felt their hatred of this world, their revulsion towards the living creatures. She felt their desire to destroy everything and carve the world in the image of their beloved far-away Earth. She heard her mother continuing to bemoan her disobedient daughter and people in the settlement tell her story as a cautionary tale to their children. The girl who pretended to be ill so she would not have to work. And see what happened to her. Do not disobey us or defy God, they said, or you too will sink into the ground. But no one else sank into the ground. No one other than the creatures of the world, who did not matter to the settlers of Abudan.

More time passed. The toads and spiders around Abudan were silenced, caught in traps or killed by the sentinel. And with the silencing of the creatures, the people of Abudan rejoiced. This land was truly their now. The grain crops continued to fail.

More time passed. Neoma, traveling the currents of the world, was not sure how long, but when she came back to listen to Abudan, she found that the babies of Abudan were now almost all stillborn and deformed. The settlers wept and prayed to God. We have been good, they said, but in their innermost thoughts, they worried. Because what if their faith was not strong enough? What if they had angered God? There was no daily bread, and now there were no children. Neoma lingered, as her mother took up the mantle of God's most faithful servant, commanding those around her to flog themselves as penance and to anoint themselves with their own blood. Yet the babies continued to die, as did the grain crops. The settlers turned on her mother. Neoma's sinking into the ground, the story now went, was the harbinger of these disasters. By having a child before the settlement was ready, her mother had angered God, and brought on these stillbirths. The settlers of Abudan sacrificed Neoma's mother, burning her on a pyre of purple wood outside of the settlement near the spot where Neoma had been swallowed by the ground. Neoma's mother begged for mercy and screamed Neoma's name, as she was engulfed by the flames, which gave off an acrid black smoke that rose to the skies as she was burnt.

Neoma knew now, connected to the great network of her world that the toads and spiders kept the radiation from the suns from harming the planet's surface. When they were exterminated, that protection ceased. The grain crops, the babies—they were all part of the silencing. More grain crops failed. The few children of Abudan, the ones she had helped tend to, could not have children themselves. They decided to move the settlement, blaming the location for their problems. There were rumors that more terraforming equipment had been obtained, and the settlers spoke excitedly of the future that awaited them.

In the darkness, in the ground, Neoma, first child of Abudan, born before the sentinel and protected by toads and spiders, began to push back. Another settlement could not be allowed. The nothingness that surrounded Calneh, an open wound that ran from the planet's surface to its core, must not be replicated. The world had been reluctant to cauterize the wound, to take the lives of those who were responsible for it, but Neoma was not.

Neoma drew the connections of her world to her, whispering to the toads and spiders of the gray-green landscapes across the planet, crooning to the moleworms of the glittering hills, to the crustaceans of the sandy caves and the winged fish of the oceans, to the flocks of yellow birds and to the other lifeforms whose existence was unacknowledged in the language of the humans. She filled herself with the joy and life and being of the world. Neoma, of-world, connected through roots and fibers and filaments and fungi, gave a mighty push, a birthing push that wracked her/their/world's body. The infection was growing, and the world must be healed. In that final moment before all went quiet, Neoma, of-world, repulsed those who were not-world. A final thought juddered across the world. *I am whole.* And then all was still.

PENNIES FOR DREAMS, POUNDS FOR NIGHTMARES

Chelsea Conradt

At the center of a small village, a fountain bubbled pristine water. Bronze and silver coins shimmered atop a cerulean base. Townsfolk tossed their wishes into the water and went on with their day.

Lisette cared not for wishes; she lived for dreams.

Each day she passed that ornate fountain with a sower woman sculpture mounted on top, all delicate features and downcast eyes offering the feminine understanding people expected. Bruno had brought her here on their first—and only—stroll. He dropped a coin in and wished for their future marriage, then offered her a coin to do the same. She had pocketed the money, and told him she had another love, though she did not. Marriage shouldn't be a wish; it should be a dream. It rarely was in her experience.

Bruno was not her dream.

Today Lisette worked her way through town. The blacksmith's forge surged, and she scuttled past as fast as she could without outright running. People still talked about the way her mother died.

As if warning against the dangers of fire and demanding women keep their hearths ablaze wasn't at odds. She shook off the memory and walked quietly to where the road softened to patches of clover and large green bushes had overgrown. There, beneath a tree heavy with ocher leaves, the dreaming well waited.

From a distance it was merely matte gray stone. Decades of harsh winters had battered its wooden roof. Closer, though, flecks of gold and silver and bronze glimmered within the mortar near the lip of the well. In the town center, people threw money into clear waters and wished for riches and work and wives. Here, at the unassuming fringes, Lisette paid for gentle dreams.

She dropped a penny, pressed with a smudge of blood, into the black maw and waited for the signature plink. The same one she'd heard each day for the last year. A year of sweet dreams. A year of thanks for the old woman at the bakery who saw the dark marks beneath her eyes when the past plagued her sleep, who had seen the bruises on her arms the years before, and whispered the secrets of the dream well to her.

"Grant me rest tonight with only warmth," she said before continuing her journey home.

Bruno had followed Lisette nearly every day for the last three weeks. Each time he approached her, she dismissed him. He'd declared his intent clear enough at the fountain, but she was stubborn.

Bruno's bed was empty, as was Lisette's. Living in her husband's home was her right, but she was far too beautiful to be kept in the house of a dead man. She would be a prize on Bruno's arm, a boon to his pride. Luscious curves meant for motherhood drew him to Lisette, but she'd borne none. Her husband has failed her there, but Bruno would not. She'd give him gorgeous children.

If she only gave him a chance, she'd see he could protect her.

And so he'd watched her at that decrepit well each day. She thanked the well for dreams each time. He'd tried throwing in coins after she left, demanding this well make her dream of marrying him. He understood how these things worked. Only he'd been dreaming of her every night since. Naked in his bed. Making his meals. On his arm through town. Jealousy teeming in the tavern when others saw he'd won Alexander's reclusive beauty; he'd been the one to bring her back to sense.

He'd figured it out yesterday. She pricked her thumb. He wasn't about to make the girl bleed, but her hair should do, right? It was easy enough to get a strand from her hairbrush while she was near the stream painting this morning. Today, he'd help Lisette understand why living alone was dangerous. Even an afternoon unsupervised had killed her mother. He pulled the largest coin from his pocket— heavy and gold—wrapped a strand of her blonde hair around it and threw it into the hole.

"Make her dream of scorching flames. The kind that should have made her mother run," he demanded of the well. "That she would run to me."

Lisette finished her cup of chamomile tea and climbed into bed, as had become her habit in the year since she'd encountered the dreaming well. She hadn't believed the baker's wife that dropping a coin and "a drop of herself" into the well would help, but she'd been desperate. That first morning, she'd wept with relief. And bought one of everything at the bakery the next day.

She'd been alone for two years now in this house. If one didn't count the cloying echoes of her life before. The way the kitchen floor near the washbasin groaned when she stepped there, like it too remembered the crack her skull had made against it. Or the burnt sugar bitterness that lingered when the summer heat met the old blood soaked in the wall near the bedroom.

Alexander had kept the windows locked. Lisette leaned into the breeze. Despite the sting of loneliness and the scrape of the past on darker days, she'd settled into the artist's life her husband's home and money afforded her.

Her dream began as they always did after the well took over, with her waking on a pile of yellow leaves. Sometimes the leaves were on her bed, and other times they were spread on the ground on an island or woven into the wicker of a bench in a city she'd never visit. Today they were in a house she hadn't stepped foot inside since she'd married Alexander. Her chest tightened. No, that couldn't be right. She took steadying breaths, reminded herself she was in a soft dream, told herself to play along. Hand-hewn beams framed the two-room house. Simple furnishings adorned the open room. A fire was lit in the hearth, but the kettle still rested on the counter.

Seeing no one else in the space, she moved to put the pot over the flame. The flaxen leaves behind her ignited in a roar. No. Not this. Not here. Icy fear numbed her brain. Lisette stumbled toward the fireplace, singeing her forearm. The bubbling acid of worry in her belly lurched. Her yelp shot through the room. Lisette's skin puckered and darkened from the fiery graze. Had her mother's body seared like this? The burned flesh rippled down her arm, desiccating a path to her fingertips, as though this were arson and not an accident. Flexing her hands made her gnarled skin snagged on knuckles, spiking fresh panic.

She shouldn't be in this place. Only the knowledge that she'd seen the leaves before, signaling a dream, kept her from crying for her mother. She spun toward the washbasin. No water. Nonsense was reality in dreams, but how could her mind conjure this tinderbox and not her path out? The well wouldn't do that. The leaves continued to burn—as if their existence sustained the fire. Terror tore at her heart; heat licked her bare feet. Where are my shoes? If this were my mother's home, I'd have shoes by the door. As soon as she'd had the thought, the leather slippers she preferred popped into place.

She ran toward the door. Locked. Sweat ran rivulets down her cheeks. Lisette clenched her jaw. Whose kitchen was this that they had no cloths, no water? Who cooked without such basic protections? This wasn't her mother's house. This wasn't the way she'd died. Lisette wouldn't allow it.

Agony ate at Lisette's every smoldering pore. Black smoke began to steep the room in darkness. Lisette coughed against her fist, panic and suffocation crumpling her forward. The kettle percolated with a gurgle that quickly shifted into a mewling cry. She whirled, her dress catching the blaze now. Panic chased the flames up her legs, clawing at her thighs as though it sought to shove her out of the house, as if it craved her cries. She smacked at the smock and did what she had done the first time a fire had leapt from the hearth when she shared the real kitchen with her mother.

Lisette visualized the patchwork blanket they'd stored on the stool beside the fire poker. The one you could wrap yourself in when the embers were low. The one that had been hanging on the line outside the day her mama died. Like her shoes, the blanket appeared. Her dream-scarred hands snatched the well-worn fabric and snuffed the leaves. As soon as the blanket was down, the crying quelled, too. The room brightened, sunlight dappling the charred quilt through an open window. The breeze was warm, welcoming, and she stepped outside into the dream she yearned for.

Last night hadn't been Lisette's worst nightmare, but after a year without one, she'd forgotten the way one woke slicked in sweat. She'd forgotten the way fear nibbled at her insides the entire next day. She clung to the fact she'd escaped and turned toward kind dreams the rest of the night. What had she done to err with the dreaming well? Had she visited too long? Were her payments not enough?

Art had become her daylight balm in the last year as much as the dreaming well had been for the nights. She painted most of the day. The quilt from her childhood, from her dream, was easy to capture. The singed edges and the scarred hands holding it less so. Lisette had not seen her mother die in the fire. She'd been visiting the gardens with a friend. But the fingers in her painting were long and calloused beneath the wounds.

Her mother's hands. If she'd survived.

As the horizon shifted from high-noon blue to late-afternoon pink, she set out on her daily trek through town. First to the bakery and then to her dreaming well. This time with a plan for a larger offering.

She was tucking a cloth around a dinner loaf when Bruno found her. He strode toward her with a directness that was bold even for him. Averting her gaze and quickening her steps didn't deter him.

Bruno's height—more than a head taller than her—let him amble alongside easily.

"Are you well, dear Lisette?" He was more familiar than was appropriate.

His movements were fluid, easy, and a step too close.

Lisette angled herself away from him. "Yes."

"Oh?" Bruno's mouth puckered like she'd spritzed him with lemon. She hadn't been that curt. "I'm glad you are well."

As they neared the fountain at the center of town, Bruno's eyes warmed. The corners of his mouth lifted, and the earnest face that had convinced her to take the stroll with him originally flashed for a moment. She cared not for his status in town or his wealth.

"We must make a wish." He guided her toward the fountain, its water shimmering with the hopes of too many.

Lisette yanked her arm from his grip. "I'd prefer to save my wishes for when it matters."

Bruno, undeterred, offered her another golden coin. Again, she pocketed it.

Bruno clocked her motion, humor quirking the corner of his mouth. He wished aloud for her to stroll the garden with him. Did he even realize he hadn't asked her?

"I must be going." Lisette stepped away before Bruno could try to corral her again. A mare he wished to break.

"My sister asked after you. She'd love for you to join her quilting party this Saturday."

Bruno's sister had spoken one word to Lisette in her whole life: Condolences.

It wasn't the presumption that needled Lisette or even the outright lie; it was the gleam in his eye when he said 'quilt'. The town knew how her mother had died. They knew there was no cloth in the kitchen.

He knew about her dream.

Bruno tracked Lisette to the ramshackle well and watched her toss her paltry tarnished copper offering in. Fatigue hadn't darkened her eyes or slowed her movements. She didn't seek comfort from him or anyone else that he saw.

She was gorgeous. Though a widow, she'd make a perfect wife. If she'd only give him a chance. He hadn't had the dream last night, which meant she must have lied to him about how she fared.

Clearly, the well required more money.

He pulled two golden pounds from a pouch brimming with them. Had she even recognized his wealth? She certainly hadn't noticed that he'd visited her bedside table. That time was for a few more strands of her hair to cater to the well, but soon she'd invite him. Bruno threw the damned coin into the water, and after casting a sidelong glance back toward the village, he told the well what to do.

"Show her the danger of not being wed." He paused. Lisette should already be familiar with that fear. He needed to push her further. Needed her to understand her place was safe under his protection.

Bruno excavated his own fears, ones he would overcome on her behalf. The militia was no place for a woman. "No, let her dream of the viscera of battle and the danger of finding yourself alone in it."

Lisette came to in her dream, shivering. The cave floor was rough and slicked with gritty slime, tarnishing the golden leaves beneath her. The darkened cavern wasn't what made her shake, nor was the icy stone at her back. It was the thick red pool creeping toward her. Daylight gilded the cave's opening. She was only a half-dozen steps inside. Close enough to see pasture beyond. Close enough to know the rain had stopped.

Fear, white and sharp, pierced her chest. He was out there and with every passing second, the threatening tide of what she'd done—what he'd forced her to do—crept closer. Her breaths grew shallower with every millimeter the blood seeped closer. She sidled against the smooth, chilled wall, as if it would reveal an exit or at least provide a balm for her terror. It did neither.

I don't have to be here, she told herself. The leaves were at her feet. This was a dream. Hers. But every lifeline she reached for tumbled from her fingers. Blood dripped from the ceiling, though that hadn't happened when Lisette had hidden in the caverns after Alexander had forced her into the forest an hour from the village last year. Stalactites jutted down, bloody teeth clamping shut. Snapping her into a sanguine prison. Where she once belonged.

Because she knew what she'd find if she toed through the gore.

Her husband Alexander's body was close. Her hands shook now, but they hadn't then. Lisette grappled the stone on either side of her. Blood caked her fingernails and settled between her fingers. The mottled purple and green manacles at her wrists should have hidden in the darkness here—they had when she'd scrambled to the cave the first time. The real time. Now, though, her dream brought each fingerprint into relief. Shimmering and condemning. His blood on her hands. His hands calling her blood beneath her skin. The blade she'd used was on the floor beside her now. The blood oozing from his corpse marched toward her endlessly in the way it only could in dreams.

Her throat blazed. Her chest squeezed as if the last dregs of her blood were being wrung from her body. Lisette's vision blurred, but her mind churned regardless.

The viscous red sloshed against the cave crystals caging her in. Each splash threw a memory into her face. Alexander's hands tightening. Ceramic shards splattering the kitchen floor. Citrus and shame made her eyes water, as she scrubbed yet another stain from the wall. She waited for a tsunami of torture to break the barrier. Cowering in the cave had cramped her calves, but this was still a dream.

The blood would never reach her. It loomed; it threatened; it was Alexander, after all. Ominous, but she'd stopped him before. She'd been around blood her whole life. Dressing chickens. Bandaging wounds. She'd brought this pool about herself nearly two years ago, but it wasn't regret that made her fear that blood—it was the fear Alexander could come back.

He couldn't, though. She'd plunged the knife deep enough into the side of his neck to ensure that. The wilderness had done the rest.

When Lisette woke the next morning, her hands hurt and her neck ached, as though she'd braced for battle the whole night. But her chest was far lighter. Alexander couldn't come for her again. Not today, not in her dream. Not ever.

After the foul dream the night before, Lisette was only more certain she would never let another man into her home. Bruno was in the market again the next morning. A hopeful suitor—in his mind, surely—wouldn't appear at Lisette's side regardless of the path she took or how early or late she appeared. He'd positioned himself to block her path, steering her again toward the fountain. Today, though, she was ready for him. The ring on her index finger was a gift from Alexander. The center stone was green. The point at the top of the metal setting had nicked her more times than she could remember.

"You seem tired today, sweet Lisette. Perhaps a wish for rest?" He proffered another one of those coins.

Breakfast tea and sour blood rose from her belly. She swallowed it, marked Bruno's unwavering smile. "What will you wish for, Bruno?"

"The same thing I wish for each day. You." He threw his coin into the water. "And you?"

This fountain did nothing for her, but after a year of faithful kindness her well was failing there, too. Thanks to Bruno. Lisette's shoulders slumped and her heart ached, but it was the hum of warning resonating in her sternum that she heeded. "I always wish for kindness."

He leaned too close, looming over her, his breath searing on her ear. Stale ale and eggs. "How I would be kind to you."

She stumbled backward a half step and twisted her ring into place. "Then wish for kindness for me."

"Visit the garden with me, and I can promise you sweet dreams again, Lisette."

Her veins ignited, face flushed. He smiled like she was pleased with that offer. Like she didn't suspect he'd been following her to the well, too. He'd known the way her mother died. Had he suspected what had happened with Alexander? They were so alike. Selfish and brutal men beneath a polished veneer. Adrenaline locked her knees, held her ground next to this man that poked without caution. Some secrets were dark, others were cruel, but to understand this secret could be deadly.

"Perhaps we need to pull that coin from the water," she said, stepping closer to the fountain's edge.

He mirrored her movements. "Why would I do such a thing?"

"So you can wish for the garden stroll, of course." Lisette leaned over the water, waited for Bruno to push himself closer. What she needed from him today was not money, but the only way to bring him close was to appease his masculinity.

"I have more coins. You need not worry." The back of his hand brushed her lower back.

Millipedes breeding beneath her skin couldn't have charged her nerves more. She stilled the urge to spin, to flee. For once, she would allow Bruno to touch her. If only to hurt him.

The edge of the fountain cut into Lisette's knee, a willing fulcrum. She let herself tumble forward, ready for the water's embrace, but knowing Bruno couldn't allow it. His arm snaked around her belly, constricting and pulling like she truly was his next meal. Don't fight him. The advice the few she'd confided in coming back, but now as a tool.

Lisette allowed Bruno to whirl her toward his chest. She planted her hands against the unforgiving wall of his body and pressed the peak of her ring firmly on his forearm. Her fingers gripped him firmly. It was his turn to yank away, but she didn't release him. Flesh tore, blood seeped along the ring's metal grooves. His. Acrid and necessary. She swiped her palm over the jewelry, taking the blood to her fingers, and then to the coins settled in her pocket.

Apologies flowed from her mouth. She bandaged his arm tightly, using the hem of his shirt and enjoying his winces.

"You must come home with me now."

Lisette straightened her spine. "I'll do no such thing."

"Who will tend to this?" Bruno lifted his arm as if he were an injured bird and not a minimally wounded adult.

"Keep it clean, and you'll be fine." Lisette dusted her palms against her skirts and turned to leave.

He scrabbled to his feet. "Are you at least going to agree to visit the garden with me? After what you did, don't you think I deserve it?"

Pettiness almost made her eager to see him the next day.

"It was purely an accident," she reassured him. "Perhaps you need your rest. I'm sure we can speak another day."

It was Bruno's turn to be manipulated.

Later that afternoon Lisette walked to the dreaming well, as she did every day. She tossed in her penny, waited for the plop, and paused.

I shall be back soon. Don't make plans without me.

She left toward her home, but once she was beyond the farrier's cottage, she doubled back. Bruno stood before the well, tossing a fat golden coin inside.

"You were supposed to set terror in her very bones. She needs to want me, to seek my protection." He muttered a curse. "Tonight make her dream of her death. Make her seek refuge."

Lisette waited minutes after he left before she hurried back to the well. She pulled the coins Bruno had gifted her for the wishing fountain from her pocket, each smeared with his blood. It was excessive for a wish, but the perfect payment for a proper nightmare.

Splash and splash. Satisfaction simmered in the warm air.

"You have kept me safe from those memories for a year, my well. I ask only one more favor of you. Allow Bruno to live the dreams he wishes to give to me. Let him feel the fire and coat himself in the blood of one he once loved. Take this token from me and know I'll ask you no more."

Lisette dropped in an extra penny to be safe.

Lisette did not see Bruno in the village the next day or the one after that. The air was fresher without him, as it had been those first mornings without Alexander. The heady scent of impending rain and freedom made her lightheaded. Lisette strolled to the wishing fountain. Coins glittered in the water, clean and beautiful. Could a drop of blood make these come true, too?

It was two full weeks before Bruno reappeared in her path, but he was no longer the same man. He stumbled, disheveled on the dirt road just beyond town. His once carefully combed hair was matted, and his predatory gaze was now bloodshot and broken.

He swayed toward her. "Lisette?"

Was this another game? Had the dreaming well failed her? Lisette recounted her steps, the blood and the coins and the words she'd spoken.

She inclined her head toward him, keeping several paces between them. "Bruno."

He muttered her name over and over, but his glassy eyes never met Lisette's.

Lisette took two careful steps closer, readying to walk past him. Stale sweat and vinegar knocked her back.

His once bombastic baritone was now hollow. "I didn't know."

Didn't know about the nightmares? About what he'd done to her? About her mother?

Lisette found there was no reserve of compassion in her body for this man. "But you did."

He'd molded his knowledge into a weapon against her. Now he had to live with the consequences.

Dark circles sagged beneath his eyes, his body sallow and crumpled. Whatever haunted his dreams now, it mangled his body the way her past had wrecked her own before she'd found the dreaming well.

Until he'd stolen that peace.

His attention fixed on her, chapped lips pulling taught. "I need you to come with me. You need to take care of me, save me."

Bruno tugged dirty fingers through matted hair. The twitchy aftereffects of living through true trauma were too familiar for Lisette. The well had done as promised one last time.

"There was so much blood, Lisette," he continued as though she'd asked. "How should I stop the soldiers from coming back?"

It'd been ten years since a regiment had come through our village. He would survive.

She had.

Lisette tossed a copper coin on the ground near his filthy feet. "Why don't you try making a wish?"

A VERY SMALL GREEN WOMAN

Gio Clairval

Isla hadn't eaten her fill in a week and was daydreaming about salted fish. Surely, no other young heiress was as famished as she. All she could afford was a tasteless, frugal lunch at the local watering hole—her only meal that day. She needed a way to secure her survival. Still, Aunt Leonie had discovered how to cut off the Galimberti empire's only heir without disinheriting her—something Auntie dearest could not legally do.

Guided by the mooring system along the overhead line, her cablepod creaked toward the docking pad. The pulley on top of the cable latched onto a tethering wire with a clanking sound.

Floodlights drenched the platform in an unforgiving glare, and sharp-edged shadows sliced across the steel decking. The pad below was blotched with old leaks, scorched and hastily repaired where landings had gone wrong. Through the rear porthole, the sky yawned open, deep and starless.

She stomped down from her pod into a sour cloud of burned engine oil, the kind that meant some freight unit was choking nearby.

Cablepods of all sizes crammed the carpark, from rusted solo cans like hers to glossy commercial liners, but not a soul in sight.

The freezing, stingy air spun her head like a top. As if the day hadn't already made it clear she was starving, broke, and a headache away from snapping.

Judging by the noise, every merchant was already unloading barrels onto their designated spots in the market, half a click away. She was late. Good thing her family's stall waited for her—one less disaster to deal with.

LaOrca Junction, the largest trade hub in the node, was a three-square-mile steel structure on stilts—one of the densest clusters of platforms on planet Talisqualis. Its docks blazed with a riot of expensive illumination, all powered by canned light.

Above it all, the weight-bearing cables stretched between pylons like taut steel highways, interlaced with thinner fiberoptic lines. Their jackets had been deliberately frayed at intervals, creating rhythmic bursts of light that made the web of cables shimmer against the void-dark background.

Something caught her eye—a flicker against the iron joists beneath the carriage. Isla crouched and reached for it, fingers closing around a smooth object with rounded corners. Just a can.

Except. No. Not just a can. Cans containing food weren't manufactured on Talisqualis. They came—rarely, unpredictably—through the gaps between worlds, drifting in with all sorts of strange goods and bursts of light.

She gave a low whistle and tilted the object into the pale light spilling from a nearby fiberoptic strand.

The label read "Anchovia Fantastica Edibilia" in scrawled penmanship. Isla squeezed her eyes shut, her stomach grumbling in anticipation. She had only tried anchovies once before—at the Crockhigher node—but she had not forgotten the taste! Nestled in a tender forest of kale, the fish flaked open on her tongue, clouds of persimmon and marigold blooming in her mind, and—

Rat-a-tap-tap. The can shook in Isla's hand. She jumped. A

muffled shriek sounded from inside. Rat-a-tap-tap-tap. She forced a forefinger under the clasp and pulled up.

A tiny woman lay at the bottom, curled in and around like a pastry roll. Her skin, the color of new leaves, glistened with oil. Salt crystals and black pepper dotted her jet-black braids. Mist devils! A Greenie. The creature stood up, no more than two thumbs tall. Her only clothing was a torn skirt of moiré silk and a belt with a bulging holster and sheaths that must have held tools.

Eyes on the holster, Isla fingered her own empty belt. She'd removed the szabber to check on the batteries after an encounter with Clingbots as she approached LaOrca. Now, her weapon sat on the table inside her wagon.

The creature studied her, glowering. Then its delicate features softened—just a shade. "You're not going to eat me, are you?"

"Why would I?" Isla snapped. "You look underfed."

Eating her? What a vile notion. Did the Natives think humans snacked on anything that talked back?

The small woman's tiny mouth drooped. Isla winced. "That was a joke," she added quickly. "Bad one."

Isla recalled the muttered rumors: witchcraft, otherworldly powers, all that nonsense. Maybe the pixie-looking Native was rifling through her brain right now.

All she knew about these miniature people was … nearly nothing. They'd been here before humanity dropped on through a hole in the sky. They were already living somewhere—somehow— in the poisoned frost below. No one Isla knew had ever seen their cities.

Magic, though? Please. That was just superstition. Wasn't it?

This tiny intruder didn't seem to be a threat, because she didn't try to grab whatever sidearm she was carrying. So much for the legends about the feral, horrid-looking green Native people. Her smile revealed no needle-like fangs. She had perfect, minuscule teeth, flashing white in the cable light.

The Greenie's high-pitched voice startled her. "I ate all the anchovies. Are you mad?"

Isla's stomach protested, and she grunted. "Who in the ice-hell are you?"

"Alaralarara, but you can call me Lara."

I should call her Peasoup, Isla thought, eyeing the horologe on a pole. *I'm late!* Rest-hours loomed, and she had to sell as many barrels of light as possible or Auntie Leonie would penalize her. "Miss another quota, and I swear to the Lord of Light, your inheritance gets kicked so far down the tracks you won't see a credit until your late thirties."

Which meant over twenty years with a stomach that never stopped growling. Isla hated the thought.

The clock on the pole flashed the hour. Isla, clutching the can, stepped inside and cast a quick glance around the empty car park before the door hissed shut.

She placed the unexpected guest on the table next to the szabber. It was a sore sight, this weapon, old and stained by Clingbot acid during an exchange of fire.

Isla watched the little woman scan the cabin, her gaze lingering on the faintly glowing waist-high barrels filled with light strapped to the floor in the middle of the cabin. The tiny nose wrinkled. Isla wondered whether the rumors about the Greenies being sworn enemies of all light—canned or otherwise—were true.

A fiberoptic bundle from the ceiling lit the tiny body, barely covered by oil-soaked cloth. She looked as human as Isla, only very small. The rumormongers never mentioned how graceful these figurine-sized people were.

Lara pointed to the porthole. "What is this place?"

"LaOrca Junction. How did you get under my pod?"

"My destination is Lucendo City." She swung her legs over the lip of the can, scattering salt crystals across the table. "I was hoping to find a kind person who would take me there." She stretched her long arms upward in a dancer's movement.

"I wasn't expecting to find anyone inside this can. Only delicious fish."

The small face grew solemn. "This was the only way I could think of to travel, as my enemies hate your anchovies. To them, those delicacies smell like corpses."

"Enemies?"

"Clingbots."

"You do smell like anchovies."

"Good."

"How did you seal the can?"

"Why, I sealed it once I was inside, of course."

Isla shrugged. "All right. Now that you're out, I won't keep you."

Turning to the door, the tiny woman tossed the tangle of her braids over one shoulder. Isla caught a glimpse of the creature's back. Two raised scars ran from her shoulder blades down past a slender waist, disappearing under the skirt.

"Who did that to you?"

"Clingbots ripped my wings out."

"Why?"

The Greenie shuddered. "That's their way."

"How did you get away?"

"The Clingbots are ... stupid. That's why I sealed myself into the can. There isn't much time left to save the world."

Save the world? How could one Greenie save anything? "My destination is far away from Lucendo City, in the opposite direction, actually. I'll put you in a box you can open from the inside, and I'll leave you at the market."

Still, the poor lass would have the hardest time reaching her destination; a Clingbot could swallow her whole. She couldn't abandon such a helpless creature.

"The bots didn't kill me because they wanted something. The most precious thing on Talisqualis. A shiny bauble. I hid it just before they captured me."

"Let me guess. You hid your treasure inside this can of anchovies."

"How did you know?"

"I can read minds."

Lara let out a flurry of laughter. "I like you. So, will you help me?"

"Sorry. I ain't your woman."

"They'll catch me again."

Getting dragged into a feud between bots and natives wasn't Isla's idea of a smooth cable ride. She clicked her fingers. The door slid open with a sigh, letting in a huff of icy wind.

"I'm sorry about your wings."

"They're growing back, but they'll be stunted, and I'll never be able to fly again. I hope to get some help with this, too, in Lucendo City." She gave a deep sigh. "I was elected to lead my people, yet I'll be shunned if I remain maimed. If you take me to Lucendo, I'll make it worth your while." With these words, she produced a fingernail-size credit chip.

Isla swallowed. One credit and a half. The wholesale price of ten barrels.

"I can give you the double on arrival. It's a small cost to save the world."

Three credit drops. That would cover the whole cargo and some, but with no receipt, of course. How would Isla explain the income to Aunt Leonie? This wouldn't work.

A skinny arm shot inside the cablepod, and a dirty hand grabbed a light-canister that had rolled down the galley counter and onto the floor. Isla leaped to her feet and threw herself outside, just in time to spot a street urchin decamping with her can.

After a brief pursuit, she caught up to the child just as he slipped past the gate into the wholesale market—already buzzing with activity—and grabbed him by the shoulder.

"What d'you think you're doing? That's the refill for my hotplate!"

The kid froze, eyes wide, too much white in a grubby face.

She should have smacked him across the face for his brashness, but she merely shook him.

"Well caught!" hollered a middle-aged woman, a latecomer trundling through the market gate in a cablepod with a foldable side. "This hub's swarming with those little pests. They belong in a reformatory." She stopped her vehicle to watch the scene unfold.

Across from the gate, a brigadier of the platform garrison appeared at the ground-floor window of The Flying Quam-Quam, the restaurant where Isla had planned to have lunch.

The uniformed woman with a smooth, dark complexion and auburn hair stood rigid and tall, holding a tankard of burlbeer and eyeing the small crowd that had gathered around Isla and the urchin. Her helmeted head nearly touched the top of the window casement. Isla felt small by comparison and wondered if that was how the Greenie felt every damned moment, surrounded by human beings.

Isla looked down at the kid again. Just a skinny scrap with fast hands and no backup.

Prison for petty theft? She let go of the child, who dashed away and lost himself in the crowd. Isla gave the scowling merchants her best smile.

A shout rang out: "What are those?"

Isla followed the pointing finger. Overhead, something moved—too fast for cablepods.

The brigadier stepped out of the restaurant, her burlbeer tankard abandoned, and raised her gaze to the sky.

Squinting, Isla could just make out faint position lights drifting across the everdark.

"Clingbots," muttered the merchant who had a dislike for urchins. "A few have been spotted hanging under the platform. I'm out of here."

She slammed the foldable side of her cabletrunk shut, and the vehicle rolled off on squeaky wheels toward the parking pad.

Isla's head swarmed with images of the bots' attack a few minutes before arriving in sight of LaOrca Junction. And she'd barely escaped. "I don't need that."

She ran back to the parking dock and ducked inside her carriage, hoping that the small green woman would still be there and also hoping that she wouldn't.

The door slid shut behind her. On the table remained the empty anchovy can, and there were droplets of oil everywhere on the floor.

She went to sleep on her chilly bunk, dreaming of Aunt Leonie screaming at her.

A soft voice woke her up. "The local brigade chief wants to see you, Captain."

"AI, what time is it?"

"Time to rise and glitter, Captain. The brigadier is waiting. She's been awake for seventeen minutes."

The woman in uniform seated herself on one of the chairs fixed around the table, and Isla recognized the brigadier she'd spotted near the market the day before.

Her heart bailed straight past her stomach. She lowered herself from the bunk.

"How old are you?" said the brigadier. "Isla Anna Galimberti, right?"

"Seventeen," Isla mumbled.

"Heiress to the Lux Sit mercantile empire. You have a brilliant future, Isla."

"Nice of you to think so, ma'am." Her stomach rumbled.

"We know you've found a Greenie."

The brigadier gestured for Isla to sit, then turned her tablet around. Onscreen, grainy footage showed Isla holding the flat can.

She froze as the brigadier zoomed in and paused the frame. Of course, there'd been a camera.

"And we know she'll come back to coax you into taking her to Lucendo City. We received reports from merchants who met her, and we've been trailing her down this cable line. We have reliable sources telling us that she's a terrorist planning an attack against the Lucendo node."

"The Greenie said Clingbots were after her."

"Clingbots are after anyone who carries valuable objects. A bunch of them attacked a merchant and killed him a few hours ago, but we kicked them off the platform. The next time, they'll come in force."

"I have no intention of taking that green doll anywhere."

"On the contrary," said the brigadier. "When she shows up, you'll agree to take her to Lucendo City, and you'll call us too. Here. We'll catch her red-handed."

She thumbed on her handheld device, and the pod's display chimed.

Isla caught the credit chip the brigadier tossed to her. Forty credits' worth. Money from the garrison was legal money. She could sell down her weakening barrels at the lowest price and tell Auntie Leonie she'd made her quota.

"I can't go to Lucendo. There's no market for canned light there." She kept to herself the fact that her barrels were losing potency.

The brigadier glanced at the credit drop in Isla's hand. "You can keep the money she gave you."

Had everyone gotten into the habit of reading her mind?

"Will you cooperate then?" said the brigadier.

She nodded assent.

The woman left, opening the sliding door without a voiced command. She must have carried some device that opened any door.

"AI, have we been hacked? And bugged?"

"Yes. Re-establishing control."

"Next time, fry the bugs without waiting for orders. Clear?"

"Understood, Captain."

"Why didn't you tell me the repression squad paid this cab a visit before?"

"They instructed me not to. It created … a painful contradiction. I'm deeply sorry, Captain."

"Yeah. I can tell. You sound heartbroken."

"I am heartbroken, Captain. Processing emotional debris at 12.4% capacity."

"Cool. Do it quietly."

So that's why the brigadier had flung the door open like a stage curtain and why she'd dropped the bribe into the conversation with a smirk. Classic tyrant move: let you know you're being watched.

When Isla looked up from tying her shoelaces, she couldn't help but smile, noticing Lara perched on the edge of a shelf, the borrowed box open behind her. The woman stood up, so small and graceful. Isla approached and allowed the Greenie to step onto her palm. All traces of oil had disappeared from the tiny person. Where her scars had been, two stubs were forming.

"Thank you for trusting me."

"I don't trust you, but I trust the military even less. So, what's your business in Lucendo?"

Lara touched her pudgy holster. Isla snatched up the szabber from the table. But the Greenie only took out a folded handkerchief. A green light flashed as she unfolded the silk cloth. A seedpod appeared, flat and almond-shaped, as big as Isla's largest toenail.

Lara stroked the pod. "A wider-than-usual gap in the air—we call it a 'snakehole'—is going to open in Lucendo, in a secluded place, and a lot of light coming from that distant sun will pour in. If I can expose this seedpod to that sun's rays, it will be activated, and when it's time, it will burst open. Myriads of microscopic seeds will scatter all around. If just a few reach the surface, the wind-borne seeds will repopulate large stretches of frozen soil."

Images of green vines sprouting out of ice popped up in Isla's mind. Such a radical change of the frozen surface seemed an impossible dream.

"Do you think it will work?" Isla asked. "How will the plants survive in the cold and without light?"

"If activated, the seeds are guaranteed to change Talisqualis's ecosystem, which is practically just one: deadly frozen," Lara replied, her eyes glowing. "It will transform the world! And our heat sources will help you, too.

"We've been building wind turbines that produce electricity. We'll have plenty of light and warmth—warm infrared light and ultraviolet, too. I love ultraviolets. They tickle me all over."

Lara jerked her head to the side at a sound Isla couldn't hear.

Then her face contorted—eyes widened, breath caught—as if something unspeakable had just stepped into view.

Isla spun around but saw nothing. The door remained closed.

The tiny woman leaped onto Isla's shoulder and swiftly unraveled her own long braid, draping the black strands over her body like a curtain.

"It's a reflex we have," Lara said a little defensively. "What's the matter?"

Screams resounded from a distance. Isla looked through the porthole. The misty lamps hanging from the wires blinked out, bathing the entire node in near darkness. "What the ice?"

The door slid aside with the noise of a suffering servomotor. Isla crouched behind the table.

The glow from the barrels and the loose bunch of fiberoptics hanging from the ceiling illuminated a shape at least seven feet tall, with taloned steel feet clutching the doorjamb. A Clingbot!

A hood obscured the face except for the tip of a hooked metallic beak. The intruder gripped a szabbing spear in one hand, fingertips primed to squirt acid in the other.

"Are you hiding a green witch?" the thing croaked in a monotone. "Give it to me."

Lara perched on Isla's neck. "We are not witches!" she whispered. Tiny hands milked strands of Isla's red hair.

Cries and blasts echoed around the carriage. The garrison was fighting the bots. A metal sheet descended to cover the porthole, trapping the invader inside.

"The witch!" The bot, emitting a red light, raised its spear.

"It's better if I reveal myself," Lara said in a very low voice. "Let me go. That thing will kill you, and it will seize me anyway. Take this." She retrieved the folded handkerchief from her holster. "Someone will contact you in Lucendo. Please!"

There was no way in frozen hell Isla would let a two-thumb-tall pixie be more courageous than a five-ten-tall woman. Her grip around the szabber tightened.

"I'm asking for the last time, animal!" The bot took two steps forward.

Isla fired and missed, blasting a hole in the bulwark. She extended her spare arm toward the control panel embedded in the table.

The Clingbot's cloak rippled. Metallic wings unfolded, unable to deploy fully inside the cabin. The hood fell from the small head to reveal large eyes resembling those of an embryo and scattered patches of burned green synthskin dotting blotchy white metal. "The witch!"

Isla slammed her fist on the ignition. The cablepod whirred, struggling to start.

"Can't unlock the brake," said a disembodied and panicked voice. "Unlock manually. Unlock. Unlock. Unlock."

"I've got this, stupid AI!"

Lara sprang off Isla's neck and out of sight. Isla grabbed the loose end of a fiberoptic cord hanging from the carriage ceiling. The cable illuminated trembling gears. The pulley wheel on the roof was still secured to the parking dock. The brake-unjamming lever was on the ceiling, connected to the grid cord; to unlock it, she needed to stand up, and the szabbing spear would find her first.

Isla held the fiberoptics up high to blind the bot, whose infrared eyes were surely set for Talisqualis's evernight.

All the same, the Clingbot lunged.

"Open the door!" Isla cried.

The AI complied.

Isla thrust the glowing bundle of fibers into the machine's face. Shutters closed over the Clingbot's eyes as its spare hand spurted acid all around through the fingertips. Isla kicked him in the chest. The bot fell backward out of the carriage and onto the platform. The cablepod AI, muttering mechanical discontent, sprinkled a mixture of baking soda and soda ash from the ceiling. Isla took cover under the table while staring at the pitted floor.

The cabin shook. Sparks burst from the panel of knobs and switches. The cablepod lifted off the ground, its overhead pulley wheel hooking onto the upper wire. *We're free! How?*

The door yawned open, revealing a cluster of bots approaching.

"Close the door!"

The door slid shut, not closing properly. "Damaged," said the AI.

Isla spotted Lara holding on to the cable that dangled from the ceiling. She had pressed the brake, unclasping the external hook— all with those toothpick arms. Unbelievable.

"That was neat, girl!"

"You saved me, fearless woman."

"Looks like you saved me." Isla held out a hand. "Galimberti, Isla Galimberti."

The Greenie slid down the fiberoptics to seize the tip of Isla's thumb and squeezed it with surprising strength. "My name hasn't changed either."

The cablepod soared.

The cablepod lurched, and one of the barrels containing light came loose. Isla kneeled to secure the glowing cask to the fake wood deck.

She glanced at the display embedded in the table. The screen showed three small patrol cars trailing them on the same cable line. They glided two miles behind, far enough to be of no immediate bother but near enough to give her a headache.

She'd failed to call the platform garrison to give the brigadier her response. Surely the damned woman liked her less than before.

A splitting headache was building. She was wasting precious hours, riding in the wrong direction, but she could still switch back at the next node.

She glanced sideways at Lara, perched cross-legged on the table, bright greenish moths fluttering around her. "My pets," she said.

The tiny woman climbed onto Isla's arm and rested her hand on her temple as if sensing the pain. The headache dissolved. A real witch? Isla didn't care. She was beginning to like the Greenie.

Lara's circular gesture encompassed the barrels stacked inside the cablepod. "What do you keep these for?"

"I was supposed to sell them at LaOrca. The light in these barrels used to be fresh from the factory, but it's lost its potency. Now I'll have to sell the barrels for metal scrap." She pointed to an open shelf with aluminum cylinders. All empty, of course. "My company—I don't sell those. There's little profit in selling light-cans."

"That's what they use to fuel small vehicles like that one, right?"

Lara pointed to a traveler in an insulated jumpsuit who whizzed ahead, their chair suspended from the thick-jacketed coupled wires.

"I'm not very knowledgeable about your commerce in canned light. I never left the surface before this mission."

"You speak Standard really well."

"I was trained to accomplish my mission since I was a nestling."

So you're a spy, Isla thought. *You're still clueless, though.*

"There's a difference between reading and doing," Lara said. "Many things I'm seeing here are kind of different from what I was taught. And your light industry is ... strange. Have you ever heard of the Serpents' world?"

"I can't say that I have."

"It's the solar system on the other side of the snakehole. The stronger sunshine that comes through in Lucendo—it's their star. The Serpent People live there. They have biomechanical bots. Sometimes one sneaks through the same gap."

Lara unclasped a transparent rectangle from her tool belt, held it flat, and a three-dimensional image floated above it. The creature stood on its hind legs. It didn't match any snake Isla knew. More like a crocodile, with an elongated, egg-shaped head and rows of shiny, button-like eyes. But not quite a crocodile either, not with red scales and thin tentacles sprouting from its three-fingered hands.

"Their bioengineers can restore my wings. I hope to meet one of them, the one who comes often through the hole. It's important to me."

Lara clipped her display back to her belt, then rested her chin in her hand, silent for a moment.

"I don't really understand day and night, but my ancestors did. There was light once on Corruce—I mean, Talisqualis. But we ruined the planet with our industries."

"I didn't know you had technology. Sorry. Up here we believe you are kind of ..."

"Savages." Lara sighed. "We pushed the planet away from its twin suns ... by accident, they say. I'm not sure it's true. Some speak of failed attempts to harvest the stars' energy."

Humankind had lost contact with Terra long ago, after Felicity, a generation ship of scientists and engineers, slipped through a large gap and landed on this sunless world. The planet was as dark as the bottom of an iron pan but rich in metals. The Founding Mothers had raised platforms on tall pillars to escape the toxic air below, linking them with thick wires to form a network of cableways.

Lara went to sit in the porthole nook. She struck a dramatic pose and held it, arm extended like some miniature lookout.

"Clingbots! They've followed us!"

"No shit."

This Greenie is a Clingbot magnet. Isla jumped up to look, and there they were, seven bastards in bomber formation, zeroing in on them.

"Two minutes, Captain," said the AI. "Until they reach us."

"Can you unfasten the barrels, Lara? C'mon, you're strong enough."

Without a word but with surprising speed, the Greenie scuttled down and reached for the clasps that held the barrels in place. Isla ordered the AI to open the lateral door under the bunk.

"Step aside," Lara ordered.

Isla complied, just in time for the barrels to roll out one after the other. *Wow! She's even stronger than I thought.*

The door closed. The pod, lighter now, jumped forward. Isla switched on the display. "How long until those airborne pieces of rot reach us?"

The display and the AI replied at the same time: "35.11 seconds."

As the cablepod neared a glittering node, the wire flew over a small building that sat on a platform atop a large, tapered tower.

This silly little critter needs protection. I can't leave in Crockhigher. As they reached the junction, against her better judgment, Isla took the line toward the Crockhigher node on the route to Lucendo.

Half a minute can be a long time. Isla tucked a spare battery into her belt and stood by the rear hatch, szabber at the ready. When the deadly squadron approached within two yards, she commanded the door to open.

A blast cracked as the first bot set a steel foot onto the deck.

Isla started and turned to see Lara fire a second shot with a minuscule pistol. Where did that thing come from? The bulging holster, of course. The first bot hit by the miniature weapon twitched on the floor while blue sparks snaked around joints between its neck and the rims of its external carapace.

The szabber's battery died, the gauge all red. Isla ejected the cartridge and inserted the new one. *New, my backside!* The indicator remained red.

Isla unfastened the hollow iron bar she kept strapped under the tabletop. The second Clingbot stumbled over the fallen one. Isla swung the iron bar in a wide, upward arc, catching it with a swipe to the midriff. The heavy shaft slammed into the bot's midsection, flipping the attacker so that it landed on its back. The fall exposed the softer couplings along its belly. Isla brought down the staff on the Clingbot's chest seam. Sparks spat out in all directions.

More shots rang out. Blue bolts zipped past her shoulder— Lara again. The Greenie stood balanced near the edge of the open doorframe, minuscule pistol braced with both hands.

Another of the monsters lunged for the door, wings folding tight to slip inside. Isla pivoted, driving the iron bar sideways into the bot's knee joint before it could fully deploy. The impact twisted its leg out of alignment, sending the machine clattering sideways against the wall.

Of the remaining bots, three spiraled downward and out of sight—disabled, she hoped—and two fled at maximum speed on articulated wings.

The pod rocked under the strain. The AI chimed, "Six assailants disabled or falling. One remains, attempting roof access."

"Wonderful." Isla threw a glance at the upper hatch. The bolts rattled under the strain as the bot tried prying the top hatch open.

"AI, reinforce the roof locks!"

A fresh screech tore through the roof as the remaining Clingbot breached the upper hatch. Its steel faceplate emerged—those same fetal eyes, that crooked metal beak. But now it had learned not to unfurl its wings or extend both arms at once, keeping one limb retracted, acid nozzles gleaming.

Isla threw the iron bar like a javelin. The makeshift spear struck just below the rising beak, embedding deep into the joint between the head and torso. The Clingbot's entire frame shuddered as its gyros misfired.

Lara sprang from the doorframe and leaped onto the bot's head. She fired the minuscule pistol point-blank into the primary optic. Blue arcs crawled across the machine's skull as its systems overloaded.

With a final jerk, the bot collapsed, wedging half-in, half-out of the roof hatch like a broken gargoyle.

The rear door slid shut while Lara, puffing, went to sit back at her observation post in the porthole nook.

"You could have used that thing back at LaOrca."

"It was charging."

"Are you sure you ain't a terrorist, green girl?"

Lara smiled conspiratorially. "If fighting for the planet makes me a terrorist, then I'm one, pink girl."

"Are all Greenies like you?"

"My people are called something you could never pronounce. Something that sounds like 'the Mikra'."

Then she pointed to the porthole and cried, "Soldiers!"

"Incoming. Three Vedettes," the AI announced.

The military interceptors cut through the mist like steel sharks, their sleek hulls gleaming with predatory menace.

The display showed the brigadier's cable cars much closer than before. Maybe they were just trying to intimidate her, to keep her on track. Her nose twitched. The bastards had picked the worst possible tactic to deal with a Galimberti.

They'd just passed Crockhigher—Isla's home base and the one place where she might've offloaded her unsellable barrels, now lost. She could still switch back at the latest junction, but the brigadier's credit chip weighed heavily in her back pocket. The military wouldn't see a detour as a sign of resourcefulness. They'd see it as a betrayal.

"They're gaining on us," Lara whispered. Her newly forming gossamer wings, stunted and crooked, trembled against Isla's shoulder.

"They don't want to catch you right now, or they would have just accelerated to board us. They're just showing off for my benefit."

They reached the last junction in the Crockhigher node, and Isla, a stone lodged where her heart should be, watched the bustling platforms slide past.

After two good leagues, she touched the emergency controls, fingers dancing over switches she'd hoped never to use. "Now I'm going to shake them."

The very idea was insane. She'd jumped cable lines plenty of times in a chair—quick, nimble maneuvers that demanded split-second timing and nerves of steel. But this cablepod weighed eleven tons empty, making it about as maneuverable as a flying brick.

Below them stretched an endless mountainous frozen wasteland, peaks jutting up through toxic mist like the bones of some primordial beast. If they fell, the impact would pulverize every organ in her body. A comforting thought: Lara would probably survive, cushioned by Isla's carcass.

Isla pulled on her dented armor and then checked every strap and seal. The oxygen tank pressed reassuringly against her back, though she knew it held maybe twenty minutes of breathable air. The helmet's visor was still cracked from her last emergency. The decades-old parachute had never been tested in actual freefall.

"You've done this before?" Lara's voice was a whisper above the thrumming of the pursuit engines behind them.

"Not in something this heavy." Isla touched the screen, bringing up the cable grid.

The navigation display painted the world in harsh geometric lines—a spider's web of light and death suspended over an abyss. There, almost invisible through the layers of mist and interference, the maintenance line.

"Hold on to something solid."

"I can do the calculations, Captain."

"Cool. Then I'll have someone to blame when I'm dead."

"The Thinking Entity is correct," said Lara. "Their calculations will be fast and exact. Why risk everything—"

Isla snapped her fingers at the AI, which answered with a few cheerful fluorescent flashes.

Behind them, the Vedettes were close enough that she could make out individual details: the military insignias, the weapon pods slung beneath their hulls, and the faces of the pilots behind reinforced glass.

She released the pulley grip with a deliberate motion, feeling the mechanism disengage with a click. "AI, deploy emergency chute on my mark, not before."

"Captain, the statistical probability of survival is—"

"I don't want to hear it."

The cablepod plummeted into freefall, and for a moment that stretched like an eternity, they were flying. The sensation of weightlessness made Isla's stomach plummet. Every loose object in the cabin scattered like panicked iceflies.

Lara's high-pitched scream pierced the air.

"Stop the siren," Isla snapped.

"Free fall distance: 984 yards. Time until impact: 13.55 seconds. Time to reach lower cable: 5.41 seconds," the AI announced with morbid precision.

Thirteen seconds to live or die. Isla watched the numbers

count down on her display, fighting every instinct screaming at her to deploy the chute early. Too soon, and they'd miss the cable, swinging helplessly in the void. Too late, and they'd be pasted on the mountainside.

The pursuing Vedettes had stopped at the edge of the drop zone, unwilling or unable to follow them into this madness.

"Mark!" The parachute exploded from the roof, the emergency system firing with a bang that shook the entire cabin.

The pod jerked upward so hard that Isla's vision grayed at the edges. Then they resumed falling, slower but still deadly, the ancient silk above them groaning and snapping in the fierce wind.

They were falling faster again, but now the lower cable rushed up to meet them through the swirling mist. "One second," the AI whispered.

Now! She slammed the pulley engagement with all her strength.

The cabin shrieked and vibrated as the cables took the full weight of their falling coach, metal screaming against metal. The pulley mechanism sparked and groaned, pushed far beyond its design limits. The wires stretched under the impact, bowing downward before springing back like a massive guitar string.

But they held. Against all odds and probability, the cables held.

Clouds swallowed them whole, wrapping their coach in a cocoon of toxic mist that hid their position from the Vedettes loitering helplessly above.

"We did it!" Isla couldn't believe they'd survived. "Lara, we are officially dead."

Lara's head emerged from Isla's breast pocket like a tiny Jack-in-the-box, her green face pale with shock. "Good driving, human woman."

"I believe I've earned what you paid." Her voice was hoarse from screaming during the fall.

"I'll give you triple upon arrival!" Lara's laugh rang high and bright.

Isla's head swam with visions of luxury made suddenly possible:

hot, deep-fried salt cod with parsley and lemon. A luxurious cable yacht with velvet air-bubble wrap and a Coverly Climax motor. For the first time in months, abundance felt not just possible but inevitable.

She'd burned every bridge and tossed the law out an airlock. A fugitive. A criminal. A cable pirate. Hell of a résumé.

Although, maybe, just maybe, Aunt Leonie would see some of that like courage.

"Incoming. Two," the AI announced with a crumb of nervousness.

Lara clambered out of Isla's pocket to perch on the porthole frame. "Clingbots, again," she breathed out.

The gunshot snapped through the air. Isla flinched.

"I got one," Lara's voice said with grim satisfaction, "but the other is gone."

Before Isla could respond, a metallic impact thundered against the roof. The entire coach shuddered under the weight of their uninvited passenger.

"A bot landed on us," the AI reported. "It's not trying to enter the cabin. It is proceeding to cut a wire."

The severed cable whipped around the coach like an angry serpent, then snapped away with a sound like breaking bones. The cabin shook violently, throwing Isla against the bulkhead.

Her stomach somersaulted as gravity reasserted its dominance. She slammed into one bulwark after another until she managed to secure herself to the ladder with a carabiner.

"AI, halt!" Isla ordered. "Lara girl, we're going to kill that bot before it cuts the remaining wires!"

Lara moved in a blur of green motion, her small form darting across the cabin's surfaces like liquid mercury. More gunshots crackled outside.

She shouted to the AI to open the skylight. The metal panel and then the reinforced glass slid back, letting in a rush of frigid air. She climbed out into the howling wind, every movement precise despite the chaos.

Wild vibrations made it impossible to stand on top of the pod. But she had to reach the remaining cable before the Clingbot severed it completely. She clasped her carabiner onto the security rope that hung beside the pulley shaft.

Lara slipped into the narrow collar of Isla's sweatshirt, wedging herself between fabric and skin where she'd be secure and out of sight.

"We must use the last wire like a pendulum," Isla explained. She blocked the pulley manually by pulling the rope connected to the brake mechanism. "One wire should sustain our weight." Yes, in theory.

They could make it. Maybe. If there was any platform nearby to jump onto, that is. The AI's sensors couldn't penetrate the thick mist that surrounded them like a toxic blanket.

To reach the pulley mechanism, she had to climb up one of the connecting cables. The cable was too slick to provide reliable hand and foot holds, forcing her to improvise. She folded the security rope to create a makeshift stirrup for one foot while using the other foot as a clamp. Her arms burned as she pulled herself up inch by inch.

When she finally reached the pulley housing, she wrapped one gloved hand around the mechanism for support and secured her carabiner to the pulley's frame with the other.

Lara was faster than human reflexes would allow, running along the main cableline itself to Isla's position with the balance of a tightrope walker. She detached something from her tool belt—a device so small Isla could barely make it out. Light reflected off what looked like a teensy metal disk, no bigger than a coin.

Positioning herself next to the pulley, Lara pressed her spinning blade against the thick main cableline, the thick steel rope that connected tower to tower.

And that puny blade will cut the main line? It's four inches of reinforced steel. But the cableline parted almost immediately, severed as cleanly as if it were made of paper.

The cableline snapped with a sound like gunfire.

"AI, full speed ahead!" she shouted.

The entire assembly—pulley, remaining connecting cables, and pod—swung forward like a massive pendulum, following the arc of physics and prayer.

There must be a tower right in front of us. They were flying blind into the unknown.

Then it happened. The cable began to wind itself around something solid, and a tower's scaffolding emerged from the mist like a metal ghost materializing from the void.

"AI, stop the engine!" Isla commanded.

Lara jumped up and wrapped herself in Isla's hair, nestling beneath the helmet where she'd be protected from the impact.

Isla leaped onto the first platform they encountered, hitting the metal decking hard and rolling toward the edge. She scrambled to her feet, adrenaline making her movements sharp and precise. But all her efforts would amount to nothing when the pod inevitably hit one of the tower's support pillars.

"Farewell, Captain." The words came from her coach's speakers, barely audible over the howling wind but clear enough to stop her heart.

The cablepod dropped away into the mist bank, the AI having released the pulley clamp on its own initiative. One moment, it was there, and the next, it was gone—swallowed by the toxic fog as if it had never existed.

Isla stood motionless on the platform, the wind clawing at her coat with icy fingers. The silence where her coach's voice should be felt like a physical wound.

"Farewell," she murmured into the emptiness. "Silly AI."

Something in her chest pinched like a jammed gear, which seemed appropriate for mourning a machine.

"I'm sorry about your Thinking Entity," Lara's reedy voice drifted up from beneath the helmet. "I could see you were really attached to them."

The gusts buffeted them both, and Lara's braids tickled against Isla's neck like tiny fingers offering comfort.

"How are we going to reach Lucendo now?" Lara asked, her voice small with worry.

"By cable-car," Isla replied, trying to inject confidence she didn't feel into her voice.

"But your pod is lost."

"I didn't say 'our pod.'" The words came out harder than she'd intended, but losing the AI had left her feeling raw and defensive.

Isla squinted at the spiderweb cracks on her visor. She'd been breathing toxic air.

"Do you have more credits?" she asked.

Lara squeezed herself out from under the helmet with careful movements, then let a small treasure trove of chips fall into Isla's palm.

When Isla presented credit chips worth more than the entire facility's annual operating costs, the chief engineer's weathered face split into a grin that could have powered a light factory.

"I've got just what you need," she said, leading them toward a compact vessel that looked like it had been assembled from spare parts.

The replacement pod's door hissed as it slid open, revealing an interior barely large enough for one person. At least the second passenger was figurine-sized, Isla reflected.

"Meet Bertha," the chief-engineer said. "She's not much to look at, but she'll get you where you need to go."

"Welcome aboard, Captain," Bertha announced in a voice devoid of personality. "Diagnostics are complete. All systems nominal. Please do not tamper with the oxygen feed during transit."

No muttering. No smart-ass interjections. No personality

whatsoever. Just protocol and polished efficiency delivered in mechanical style.

Isla settled into the utilitarian pilot seat and exhaled slowly. Fine. Deadpan efficiency had its uses in a crisis. But as she initialized the navigation systems, she couldn't help whispering under her breath: "Silly AI."

The words were for her lost friend, wherever its consciousness had gone when the pod disappeared into the mist.

They hurtled along the lone maintenance line to Lucendo City, the largest node on the planet. Far overhead, the commercial cablelines were no more than faint dots of light strung along distant threads. Down here, they moved through thick banks of fog—out of sight, out of reach, and far from the usual rhythms of traffic and law.

"Isla?" Lara's tinkling voice interrupted from her shoulder. "You're smiling. What are you thinking about?"

"Terra Relicta. Our original world. It must have been incredible— all that natural light, the crystal forests, the golden seas … "

Lara's delicate features scrunched in confusion. "Crystal forests? Golden seas? Isla, I hate to tell you this, but Terra was mostly blue and green. Water and plants."

"That can't be right," Isla protested. "The history books say—"

"Your history books were written by people who'd never seen Terra. My people have actual memories passed down through the threading. We had achieved interstellar travel long before your ship—"

"The Mothers' ship was called Epathia."

"Epathia was pulled through the gap into our world. We've been to Terra ourselves." Lara's voice carried a note of quiet pride. "Your planet was beautiful, but not because it was made of jewels."

Isla felt her cheeks burn. Of course, the histories were romanticized nonsense.

"Why do you guys keep closing the gaps?" she asked quickly. "We can't feed lamps, fiberoptics, wire transportation, and everything else without electricity. Brightness scares the Clingbots wingless. So yeah, we love light. Why d'you hate it?"

"We don't hate light, human woman. We love it as much as everyone else. Why would you think that?"

"That's what they say up here on the platforms. I've never met any Mikra before. Sorry for the preconception."

"We don't close the gaps. The Clingbots, as you call them, do it. They don't need electricity to function because their batteries contain a radioactive substance that lasts a very long time. They want to kill all organic life on the planet." She wrung her hands. "We made those monsters."

This is new. It was common knowledge that the combative bots had come through the gaps.

"You're so tiny, why didn't you build the Clingbots in your image instead of those monstrosities?"

"We needed the large automata to excavate under the surface and build our cities, and other big machines to make everything work. We have other bots now, which can't speak and are less smart than the cablepod you lost."

Lara jumped off Isla's shoulder and climbed up the bulkhead to peer through the netted porthole. "Aside from the sparks, there are other ... things that come through the gaps."

"Whispers and wishes." Lara's small hands gripped the porthole's rim. "They cling to you and give you fears. Look at me, Isla. I'm full of fears."

"I hadn't pegged you as a superstitious person. You don't look fearful either."

"What if I can't activate the seedpod? What if the Clingbots track me down first? Fear comes in through the gaps."

Isla hmphed. "Everyone's got fears. Fear comes from inside."

"Not for you, Isla Galimberti. You are a woman without fear."

Oh. Isla busied herself with operating the gears. An odd idea sprang into her mind: she pictured herself sitting in her favorite armchair with a can of burlbeer after a boxing match while Lara danced on her thigh, green moths fluttering around her.

She considered the miniature woman through eyes narrowed to slits. Had the little creature put that thought in her mind?

Lara lowered her chin, looked up at her from her roosting place, and returned her frown with an innocent smile.

"You're freakishly strong and brave yourself," Isla said.

"I was about to surrender back at LaOrca, remember?" Lara said. "But you inspired me, fearless woman."

You're a lousy empath, girl. I was paralyzed with fear. The admiration in those slanted, coppery eyes drilled a hole in Isla's stomach. She was going to disappoint her green-skinned friend.

At the last intersection before their destination, Bertha veered sharply upward, guiding the cablepod along a steep riser track that reconnected them briefly to the commercial line. The pod emerged from the mist banks into thinner air, where merchant coaches and cargo trams zipped along gleaming dual wires far above the surface.

They crested onto a broad inspection spur, and there it was.

The tollbot loomed over them, anchored to a lower platform that hovered just beneath the cableline. It was enormous—a squat, heavily plated machine with piston-driven limbs thick as exhaust ducts. One massive steel hand rose, palm out, filling the entire porthole frame. Fairy lights, mounted on tiny canisters, ringed its shoulders in festive loops. A crude smile had been painted across its blank alloy mask, which somehow made it worse.

Bertha slowed. "Standard checkpoint. Please prepare payment."

The bot didn't speak. It never did. It only scanned. And waited.

Isla sighed, dug a microcredit chip from her belt pouch, and flicked it into the chute—more money straight into Leonie Galimberti's Lux Sit Combine, which owned most of the lines in this region.

The cablepod switched on to one of the mooring lines around the Lucendo node, which was built on a forest of towers. Through the porthole, she glimpsed the city's lights, most of them winking out as the rest-hours approached. Darkness swallowed entire sections of the blinking grid.

Lara tripped down the control panel with sparrow footsteps. "There are Clingbots here. They have destroyed some of your light."

"What?"

To Isla's astonishment, the outer shell of Lara's ears grew as big as a pinkie nail as she listened.

"Hey, what's wrong with your ears?"

"It's an evolutionary adaptation. Our cells can multiply very quickly, and go back to normal just as fast. Look at my wings."

The two stubs on Lara's back had grown into malformed appendages of a translucent matter.

"They will never sustain me in flight." Her ears expanded further as she apparently strained to hear more. "I'm getting noises from an attack. The blasts of Clingbots' szabber spears. Those klukkos have already stormed three of your city's warehouses."

"Three? You sure?"

"We have agents in Lucendo. We're all connected with ... What's the word ... ?"

"Brain implants?" Like in one of the books that came through the gaps.

"Not implants. We're born with neural threading."

Isla frowned. "You ... what?"

"Organic connections that develop naturally. Think of it like ... shared intuition rather than shared thoughts."

"So you can read my ... emotions?"

"I can sense your emotional resonance, but your thoughts are your own. When I said the Clingbots were attacking warehouses, I felt the distress of our agents through the threading. It's like ..." She searched for words. "Like hearing distant music and knowing someone you care about is singing."

"So the Council knows about the attacks," Isla said to herself.

"Yes."

There was nothing Isla could do. And she found herself curious. "How many of you are there? I mean, how many of your people ... down there?"

"Millions. We're working on making the ancient cities habitable again."

"Nobody has ever seen your cities."

"They look like crags. For now, we live under the surface. We've built extensively below: geothermal networks, hydroponic farms, and manufacturing centers. Your people only see the frozen wasteland. But we're making our world beautiful, in our own way.

"The surface is where life belongs," Lara said simply. "Underground is survival. The surface will be ... home again, one day."

Isla waved a hand at the empty light canisters lined up on the open shelves. "And you really don't understand our economy?"

"I understand the mechanics. You capture energy and redistribute it. But the competition, the artificial scarcity ..." Lara shook her head.

"Artificial scarcity? What do you mean? There's plenty of light available, unless someone closes the gaps."

"The Clingbots close the gaps, but gaps are opening all the time. No, I'm talking about the hoarding of light by the greedy few."

Isla blinked. The bustling Lux Sit headquarters. The hungry Chambers of Commerce ... She knew, even if she didn't like to think of it. Talisqualis was an oligarchy built on accumulation on one side and penury on the other.

"It creates incentive," Isla said—though the words rang hollow, even to her.

"You're starving while surrounded by abundance," Lara continued. "That seems like a design flaw."

Isla had been too caught up in her grudges to see the real point.

While she stewed over pride and petty injustices, she'd lost sight of the bigger picture: a system built on misery.

"Hold on. What about the Clingbots attacks?"

"They're attacking another warehouse right now."

The engine stopped, and the cablepod, pulled by the mooring mechanism along the ascending wire, soared into a landing dock. Bertha, the AI, was only a navigation system, so Isla had to perform the docking maneuver manually.

"Let's go, Lara."

"You are kind," said Lara, "but ... your people hate us. Many of our agents were killed by humans or had to flee."

Isla felt a pang of guilt for ever buying into the government's stories about the Natives. Her gut said Lara was sincere.

"It's a misunderstanding," she said. "If you're not the ones closing the gaps, then there's no reason for us to be at war with you.

"I think we could strike up some sort of deal against the common enemy."

Maybe Lara was genuine. Maybe her whole story was true. But that didn't mean the rest of her kind weren't quietly planning something worse.

"Bertha, close down the pod as soon as we're out."

They couldn't even use a cable chair. Not with those light thieves flying about. "We're crossing the city on foot. My foot."

Isla tucked the miniature woman in the breast pocket of her jacket, feeling Lara's small form settle against the warm fabric. She opened the carriage door and stepped into the metallic-scented air of Lucendo's port district.

The narrow streets of the rambling node stretched before her like industrial canyons. Metal slab constructions loomed overhead, their surfaces streaked with rust and condensation from the perpetual mist.

She climbed steel steps that rang under her boots, each platform joined to the next by bridges that swayed slightly under foot traffic.

A few lamps had dimmed to faint haloes. Despite the rest-hours that colored most windows black, a line-guard in white overalls perched atop a ladder and worked on unscrewing empty light cans from a feeding pole, even though down the street most poles held no cans and several cable lines overhead lacked the usual spray of sparks. The city's energy reserves were running low. Her throat tightened.

Isla darted behind a tree sprouting out of a dirt compartment in the platform. In her breast pocket, Lara went still. "This place is dangerous."

Across the opposite platform, Isla spotted the cloaked silhouette of a Clingbot. Holy Light!

A few more lamps shone in the OLate district. The Galimbertis' ancestral home rose on that very hill of wire just around the bend. They could hunker down in the cellars, waiting for the waking-hours and the street illumination that would shine brighter—or so she hoped. Isla needed some rest before facing the old icebat.

A winged shape glided across the four-way junction.

Isla ran up the steps as fast as she could. A slender cablepod was moored to the private landing dock before the house. Not one of her aunt's. This one was a speedy car, by the look of it. Curious.

The whirring sound of articulated mechanical wings. Isla rushed to flatten herself against the house facade. She waited for the bot to fly away and then ran to the cellar door. She was plunking in the code when a hand clamped on her shoulder.

"What a nice surprise," came a breathy murmur.

Saint Brigid! Aunt Leonie!

A six-foot-high maroon ceramic stove diffused blessed warmth across the sitting room. The chintz armchair molded itself around Isla's bottom; Leonie had always displayed gusto for over-furnished comfort.

The clock's door opened, and a mechanical mistbird emerged to trill, "Thirty past ten!"

In half an hour, the strongest light ever would come through the hidden gap to disperse in the sprawling city, and Lara's mission would fail. Isla would be in trouble for no reason at all.

Echoing her thoughts, Lara sighed. "Can you get away?"

"I'll have to. Just let me try to get something from my aunt."

The idea was bone-pale, bordering on delusional: convince Leonie to side with the Natives. Hard sell, especially since Isla wasn't entirely convinced herself.

A winged shadow passed outside the sheer-curtained window. Isla sat straight, her muscles tensing with recognition. The silhouette moved with a predatory purpose, circling the building like a frost-vulture. Thwarted by the light streaming from the windows, the killing machine would wait in a dark corner to snatch the Greenie.

"Now, Lara, let me do the talking. We don't want to frighten old Leonie, so don't show yourself unless I tug at my pocket."

Isla pushed Lara down just as Leonie sailed into the room with her characteristic theatrical entrance. Auntie moved with a rustling sound because she wore a crinoline under layers of frilly yellow petticoats—an accouterment that was in contrast with her strict dark-blue skirts, long sleeves, and buttoned-up collar. Short and gaunt, she nevertheless dominated the room with the quiet voltage of her personality and decades of practiced authority.

"Talking to yourself, niece?"

Now was not the right time to introduce the surprise guest.

"I was repeating my calendar." Ah, Isla kicked herself mentally. Mentioning the calendar was the stupidest thing she could do.

"Talking about the calendar, what is your business here?" From a pocket hidden in the folds of her skirts, Auntie withdrew a leather-bound manifest and flipped it open with exaggerated rustling. "You're supposed to be at LaOrca Junction and the Malaved node tomorrow for set-up at the High-wire Fair. How did this week's sales go?"

Isla opened her hands and saw that she had been digging her fingernails into her palms hard enough to leave crescent-shaped marks. In the old bat's presence, her usual self-confidence was slipping away like water through a broken hull. "Auntie—"

"Don't auntie me. I got a message telling me you were implicated in a skirmish with a bunch of Clingbots."

"I—"

"Another message stated that your ... my cable car crashed. You were spotted at a maintenance platform that only has one line leading here."

The sound of boots on metal steps echoed from the hallway. A very tall, uniformed woman with a short auburn ponytail strode into the sitting room; her military bearing clashed with the chintz surroundings.

The brigadier! "Oh, fancy you here!" Isla's voice pitched higher than she'd intended. *Blast you, Leonie, straight to ice-hell! Traitor!*

"And you, Isla. Such a pleasure." The woman put a paunchy messenger bag on the large doily covering the javakawa table.

Leonie gave a stiff smile. "Brigadier General Galli has informed me about your questionable behavior. She was kind enough to bring me here by Gondola Express from the Guild headquarters. Please, take a seat, general."

"Just brigadier general, madam. You can call me Brigadier. Thank you, but I prefer to stand." Turning to Isla, Galli pierced her with a stare that seemed to catalog every weakness. "You're not too bad a pilot. There could be a place for you in the academy, and you'll graduate as an officer. There are worse places to be."

"Isn't that a wonderful prospect?" said Leonie.

Isla hated her aunt's satisfied expression. The old icebat's plans were finally coming together.

"You failed to fill your quota, so we should agree on a hard fact: you're not cut out to take my place at the head of Lux Sit. A military career would be a better choice for you."

"No way." Isla's head swam as the walls of her future seemed to close in around her. "You know I'm good. I just had a small ... problem."

Yeah, a very small green problem.

It wasn't easy to let go of a lifetime's worth of expectations. But Isla had to admit that the moment she decided to help Lara, she had derailed her bright future at the head of the family conglomerate.

Brigadier General Galli's smile didn't reach her javakawa-dark eyes. "It is a fantastic opportunity indeed, but before we talk about that, you should tell me where your little friend is."

"Little friend?" said Leonie, her eyebrows arching with predatory interest.

"Your niece is a minor, isn't she, madam?"

"She is," Leonie made the two words carry the weight of legal authority.

"Excellent! Then, if you don't tell me where your friend is, Isla, you'll graduate from a reformatory. I hear they punish the rebels severely, once a week, with a two-inch-thick scourge."

The threat made Isla see red. "You don't have the right!"

"You're right. I don't, but the judge does."

"The judge?" said Leonie, her voice rising with excitement at this new development.

Before Isla could speak again, Lara set her hands on the pocket rim and vaulted forward with acrobatic grace. Isla swiftly turned her palm up, just in time for the tiny woman to land on it with a perfect somersault that would have impressed any circus performer.

Brigadier General Galli's eyes crinkled at the corners with the anticipation of a hunter whose trap had finally been sprung. "Fancy you here."

"How are you, Madam General?" Lara bowed gracefully twice. She balanced on Isla's palm as if she were attending a ballet for diplomats. "My name is Lara." To Isla, she whispered urgently, "Let us finish quickly here. We still have time."

"How do you plan to 'finish' this?" Isla shot back.

Leonie's eyelids drew back beneath bushy brows. The sharply angled face scrunched up. "A Native? You've brought a Greenie under my roof? Into my house?"

"They call themselves 'the Mikra'."

"I warned you, Madam Galimberti, that your niece might bring an unexpected guest," Galli said, watching her.

Leonie's deep contralto became a shrill boy soprano as a fierce sentiment overtook her usual composure. "The Greenies try to deprive us of light! They close the gaps!"

"That's not true. Lara is here to activate seeds that will, let's say, terraform the planet."

This explanation had sounded more plausible in her head.

"Perfect. We have never captured one alive before," said the brigadier.

"Captured? No! She's like ... an envoy."

"She's a terrorist. We have ways to persuade her to tell us her secrets."

"You can't do that!"

"General Galli is right," Leonie declared.

Of course, she would hold on to her bigoted views. But I had to try.

"Listen!" Isla's voice cracked with the strain. "Clingbots just ransacked a warehouse here—"

Galli cut in. "The Greenies control the Clingbots."

"She's being chased by the bots. Haven't you heard of the attack? Two attacks!"

"General, catch that flying vermin," cried Leonie, pointing at Lara with a finger.

"Vermin yourself—" The rest of Lara's words died in a squeak as Isla's hand closed into a protective fist around her. "And I can't really fly anym—"

Brigadier General Galli opened the bag that had been resting on the side table and produced an iron cage no bigger than a jewelry box. From the cage emerged a collar made of a fishnet with mesh fine enough to trap even the smallest prisoner.

"Don't shoot either of them," Isla told the Mikra. Why did she need to be so noble when the enemy wasn't? But she didn't take her order back.

The collar around the cage unfurled into a larger net that looped over Lara's tiny form, as she was clutched in Isla's hand from the waist down. She beat at the ribbing with small hands that seemed pitifully inadequate against the military-grade capture device.

Isla jerked the net off Lara with a violent motion and then made a desperate dash for the door. The sound of splintering wood filled the air as a man in full riot gear kicked the heavy panel open, his armored form filling the doorway like a mechanical nightmare.

Leonie's outraged shriek pierced Isla's ears.

Lara unsheathed her pistol with lightning speed and fired at the nearest window. The glass burst into an explosion of crystalline shards that caught the lamplight like falling stars.

Folding an arm in front of her face, Isla dived through the window frame, hit the ground hard, rolled to absorb the impact, and came up into a defensive crouch. The tiny woman promptly grasped a strand of Isla's dark hair and, from there, transferred herself back into Isla's breast pocket.

Outside, an entire unit of very stern-looking troopers awaited them in formation, their weapons drawn and ready. The trap had been more thorough than Isla had imagined.

Lara, head above the pocket's rim, uttered a foreign word that sounded like a curse. "The battery has died."

Isla cursed with words that would have made a dock worker proud.

"Chin up, big woman. We'll be able to reach the gap in time all the same."

The soldiers moved to encircle them, their boots clanging against the metal platform in a synchronized rhythm.

"And how do you plan to escape this gentle and considerate assault team?"

"Hands on eyes! And when I pinch your earlobe, run."

Isla obeyed without question, squeezing her eyes shut and covering them with one palm. She started as chunks of something soft were inserted into one ear and then the other—some kind of protective material Lara had produced from her seemingly endless arsenal.

The explosion that followed cracked like thunder. A light bomb painted a silver veil across Isla's retinas despite her hand covering her eyes, and she felt the heat wash over her face like standing too close to a furnace.

Through half-closed eyes that streamed with tears from the brilliant flash, Isla saw soldiers scattered across the ground like broken dolls. Dark stains spread across the metal platform. Was that blood streaming down a private's neck?

Lara pinched Isla's earlobe with an urgent pressure, but Isla remained still. The demonstration of Lara's military capabilities both impressed and horrified her. What other weapons did the tiny woman carry?

Lara pinched her earlobe harder.

Isla stumbled away from the carnage, pulling the protective plugs from her ears as her hearing slowly returned. A bullet whistled past her head, close enough to part her hair. The brigadier hadn't left the house when the bomb exploded, but now she was sprinting in pursuit, her face twisted with hints of contained rage at being outmaneuvered.

Isla ran through the maze of alleys that had been her playground during childhood visits to Auntie's holiday house. Every shortcut, every hidden passage came back to her and guided her through the residential labyrinth, heading for the industrial platforms.

"The bot was blinded by the light bomb," Lara called from her pocket. Isla strained to hear the reedy voice over the wind.

"But'll be around soon."

Down deserted, narrow streets under darkened porches, they fled, up steep stairs that rang with their footsteps and across squares clouded with black smog muffling sound, providing welcome cover. The industrial district was a maze of shadows and hiding places, but it was also full of dangers.

Now, she would be banished from the family for sure. Aunt Leonie's affronted cries would echo in the family halls for generations, and Isla's name would become synonymous with betrayal and disgrace.

But as she ran through the night with a tiny revolutionary in her pocket, Isla found she cared less about her lost inheritance than she'd expected.

Isla guessed it was almost eleven o'rest. Time was running out like microbeads through an hourglass, each second bringing them closer to either triumph or disaster.

"There! The dome house!" Lara pointed to a dilapidated palace rising from the maze like an overdecorated relic of industrial archaeology. The arched door was flanked by potted appleberry trees whose leaves rustled in the acrid breeze.

The crack of szabbing blasts shattered the quiet. Isla felt the heat as energy bolts burnished the steel floor around her feet, leaving smoking scorch marks on the metal platform. This bot was being careful—it wanted to catch them alive, which meant it had learned from the failures of its predecessors.

"Have you got any light bombs left?" Isla's lungs burned from the sprint through Lucendo's narrow streets.

"I just had the one. Sorry. I wasn't expecting to fight an entire army tonight."

A throwing knife whizzed past Isla's head, close enough to slice a few strands of her hair. The blade embedded itself with a solid thunk into an appleberry tree. The impact shook the branches, and small fruits pelted the ground around them, their flesh splitting open with puffs of cloying-scented steam that made the air taste sweet and artificial.

"Give up the witch!" The Clingbot's mechanical voice boomed across the courtyard, echoing off the surrounding buildings with metallic distortion.

Isla fumbled at the door's ornate brass knob. The ancient mechanism was stiff with age and corrosion but finally yielded. The hinges groaned as the door swung open.

Before she could step inside, the Clingbot struck from behind. Steel talons clutched her right shoulder with crushing force, digging through the fabric of her puffer jacket to slash the skin beneath. Pain exploded across her vision in white-hot bursts, and she felt the warm spread of blood soaking through her clothes.

The bot's wings hammered the air, dragging her upward like a predator hauling off its catch.

It's going to take me into the sky and drop me, she thought through the haze of pain and shock.

"Isla!" Lara's cry cut through the fog of agony that was settling over her mind. The bot's talons must have injected some kind of paralyzing agent or toxin into her bloodstream. Her thoughts ground to a halt, and her limbs became lead-heavy.

Fighting against the spreading numbness, Isla threw herself forward toward the doorway with every ounce of strength she could muster. The beast's grip held fast, and she felt more flesh ripped as the claws gouged deeper furrows in her shoulder. But the doorway was too narrow for the Clingbot's extended wingspan, and the mechanical creature couldn't follow her inside without folding its flight surfaces.

With a metallic growl that sounded like grinding gears, the monster released its grip and drew back.

Isla slammed the heavy wooden panel shut behind her with her good arm, then fumbled for the bolt with her aching hand. Her fingers found an ancient iron latch, and she pulled it down into place, scraping the skin off her knuckles on the pitted metal surface. The bolt slid home with a satisfying click that echoed through the vast space beyond.

The door shuddered as the Clingbot crashed against it from outside, testing the strength of the barrier. Wood groaned, and metal brackets strained, but the ancient portal held firm.

Lara alighted on Isla's palm with feather-light grace, her tiny face creased with concern. "Are you all right?"

"I will be," Isla managed, though she wasn't entirely sure it was true.

Her right side was completely numb now, which was almost worse than the pain had been. Her shoulder burned with each heartbeat, and blood trickled down her arm in warm streams. Blinking away tears of pain and exhaustion, she forced herself to take in their surroundings.

She was inside what had once been a grand ballroom, the kind of space where the wealthy had entertained before abandoning this venue to decay. The hall stretched away from them like a cathedral nave. Faint illumination from the street poles outside filtered through a magnificent skydome overhead, though half the stained glass panes had been lost to time and weather, leaving jagged gaps that let in the foul night air.

In the center of the vast room loomed a tall shape shrouded in darkness. Isla's heart jumped before she realized what she was looking at: not some lurking threat but the dark bronze feet of a giant-sized statue. The sculpture depicted a reptilian-human giantess with both hands raised toward the damaged dome above as if reaching for something beyond the broken glass.

"That's where the gap will open!" Lara cried, pointing toward the statue's upraised hands. "Above the metal woman." She leaned across Isla's palm like the figurehead of a ship cutting through dangerous waters.

It's done then. At a steep price in blood and prospects, Isla had delivered her passenger to the destination. She didn't know if anything the Mikra had told her about reviving the planet's flora was true, but Isla had upheld her part of their contract.

Now, she had a swarm of furious soldiers on her tail, an aunt who would disown her, and a future that looked as bleak as Talisqualis's starless sky. She should flee from upside Lucendo as fast as possible, disappear into the jumble of platforms and cables below before the authorities could organize a proper manhunt.

"Bye, Lara." The words came out slurred as the toxin in her system continued to spread. She swayed on her feet as if inebriated.

"You're not leaving me alone now!" The intensity of the brave warrior's panic surprised Isla.

"I'm a fugitive." Her tongue felt thick and unresponsive. "Fugitives run."

"You can't even walk straight." Lara's lower lip quivered with emotion that seemed too large for her tiny frame. "I thought we were friends ..."

The word hung in the air between them like a challenge. Isla couldn't bring herself to say the blunt truth—that she still didn't trust the Mikra entirely, despite everything they'd been through together.

Lara wove around Isla, leaving trails of soft green glow in her wake.

Outside, the Clingbot had backed up and was now ramming the barrier with its full mechanical strength, trying to smash through by brute force.

Knowing she was out of time for doubts and explanations, Isla placed Lara gently at the foot of the bronze statue. Isla staggered backward on unsteady legs, squared her feet as best she could on the stone floor, and leaned sideways with her uninjured shoulder, using her body weight to brace the door against the mechanical assault.

Lara climbed with inhuman speed, her small hands and feet finding purchase on the smooth bronze surface, as she scaled the statue's leg like a mountaineer ascending a cliff face. Within seconds, she had reached one of the giantess's raised hands, positioning herself directly beneath the damaged dome.

"We're just in time!"

As if responding to her presence, a cloud of blinding radiance exploded above the statue's highest point. Light poured into the hall, filling the nave-wide space with a brilliance that made Isla's eyes water even through her closed lids.

Light cascaded in helices of energy, each photon visible as a dancing mote of fire. Colors beyond human perception painted the air, spectrums that had no names, frequencies that made Isla's retinas tingle with sensation. The light was alive, pulsing with the heartbeat of a distant star.

Isla's heart hammered against her ribcage as she stared up at the gigantic form taking shape above them. Still braced against the shuddering door, she gaped at the amount of electromagnetic energy that cascaded from the breach in reality above them. She'd never seen so much concentrated light in one place—it was like staring into the heart of a star.

Moths erupted from hidden folds in Lara's clothing like living fireworks with translucent wings that caught the brilliance, as they leaped and danced among the photons that filled the air like glittering snow.

The green moths formed interlaced patterns around Lara. Translucent broken wings caught and reflected the descending light in coordinated flashes. They moved like a living constellation.

Enthralled beyond rational thought, Isla held her breath as the small green woman positioned herself at the apex of the statue's raised hand, her small form silhouetted against the growing brilliance above. She began to move in part dance, part ceremony. Slender arms traced geometric shapes while her lips moved in prayer or scientific formula.

"Light calls life from dormancy," she whispered. "As our ancestors slept beneath the ice, so these children sleep until their moment comes."

Her movements synchronized with the flashing of the light above. Each gesture drew the radiance closer, focusing it like a lens concentrating sunlight.

Finally, Lara unfolded her silk handkerchief to expose the precious seedpod that represented the hope of an entire world.

As Isla watched in fascination, the door behind her gave way. She faltered as the ancient wood splintered, and the portal crashed open with explosive force. The impact sent her stumbling forward, and she rolled across the stone floor, half-blind with pain and disorientation.

The sudden movement sent fire shooting through Isla's wounded shoulder. The Clingbot's toxin was still working through her system, making her thoughts fuzzy and her limbs heavy. She could feel the puncture wounds throbbing with each heartbeat, and dried blood had crusted her jacket to her skin.

The Clingbot burst into the hall, arms outstretched and wings initially retracted to pass through the doorway. Once inside, the mechanical appendages spread out with a sharp metallic pop, creating a wingspan that seemed to fill half the vast chamber.

But something was wrong with the machine. It hovered uncertainly over Isla's prone form, then began to emit high-pitched whimpers as the explosions of light from above overwhelmed its optical sensors. The Clingbot had been designed for the perpetual darkness of Talisqualis, not for exposure to the raw radiance now flooding the hall.

Isla scampered away on hands and knees, putting distance between herself and the disoriented predator. Her wounded shoulder screamed in protest with every movement, but fear gave her strength.

Just as Lara prepared to leap toward the gap with her precious cargo, something massive began to emerge from the shower of sparks above the statue. Legs like tree trunks materialized first, followed by huge feet that struck the tiled floor with earth-shaking impact. A cloud of ancient dust rose from the collision, filling the air with the smell of centuries.

Where was Lara? Had the tiny woman been swept away by the arrival of whatever was coming through the interdimensional breach?

The fate of two worlds might depend on the survival of one very small, very brave green woman who had vanished into the chaos of light and shadow above.

The creature that had come through the gap took a step forward, its impact sending vibrations through the ancient floorboards. It doubled over with surprising grace, and a gigantic hand closed around Isla's waist.

The monster was going to squash her like a plum. As the huge fingers curled around her midriff, she noticed they bristled with thin tentacles that moved with purposeful intelligence, carrying small pincers and screwdrivers like living tools.

A shriek resounded through the hall, followed by something crashing to the floor with a bone-jarring thud. Isla stared down at the untidy heap below—the Clingbot's limbs twisted at impossible angles, wings bent like a broken clockwork bird.

The giant had swatted the attacking machine with casual

efficiency. Now, it lifted one gigantic foot and pulverized what remained of the bot's head.

The bot-killer stood at least four yards tall. Small bells jangled at the ends of its braided hair. The elongated face had no visible nose and a double line of beady black eyes running up the wide forehead. The skin was covered in small, rough, reddish scales that caught the light.

"Welcome," Isla managed in her strongest voice, though her heart was beating like a malfunctioning engine.

"I'm called Mechwoman Sss'ha," the giant replied in passable Standard Language. "Here's a truly charming welcome committee."

"Are you a living organism or a machine?"

"I am a mechanical being with an organic coating."

"An android?"

The bot's eyes spun in their sockets. "Do I look like a bot mimicking a male to you? That's what 'andros' means: male."

Isla had no idea what a male Serpent looked like. "I didn't mean—"

"I am a gynoid, because I was modeled after a female form, though not one of your species, I'm afraid. So it's just an approximate translation."

At that moment, Isla spotted Lara perched on the Mechwoman's shoulder. Thank Light!

Sss'ha's scaled face turned toward Isla with predatory interest. The multiple black irises focused on her with uncomfortable intensity. But the amiable smile suddenly melted away as the lower jaw descended, revealing a cavernous maw lined with curved teeth and a forked tongue.

Without warning, Sss'ha plucked Lara from her shoulder. "Do you have more of these little creatures? I spotted several darting about in the shadows, but I was never quite fast enough to catch one for proper study."

"What do you need her for?" Isla's voice cracked.

"Biotechnology experiments, primarily. Or perhaps a snack."

Sss'ha tilted her massive head back, holding the small woman by one leg while a forked tongue extended to lick the dangling body.

"Put her down!" Isla yelled. "She could voluntarily participate in your research. Think of the data you could gather from a willing subject who can describe her physiological responses and explain her people's biotechnology." Isla paused, then added desperately, "But you wouldn't hurt her in the process, right?"

"I don't think this little bug can meaningfully object to being used to further my understanding of her species' physiology," Sss'ha mused with scientific detachment.

"I'm glad you're not planning the same fate for my physiology," Isla said, trying to keep the tremor out of her voice.

"Oh, I know your species quite well already. You call yourselves 'humans', and I've tasted several of your kind during my previous visits. I assimilated your simple language structure easily enough." Sss'ha paused thoughtfully while disturbing images of devoured citizens flashed through Isla's mind.

"Xenoethology is indeed a fascinating field," Sss'ha admitted. The tentacles at her fingertips set the tiny woman gently on the floor. "Deal accepted."

Lara climbed up Isla's leg. "She wanted to eat me! I didn't expect that from a healer!

"I came here mostly for your sun," Lara said. "But I was also hoping to find one of your biomechanical engineers. I need new wings."

"I can do far better than simple bio-prosthetic attachments," Sss'ha said with professional excitement. She produced a flat, circular device. "Hop onto this scanner."

Complex symbols began swirling around Lara's feet in holographic displays.

"I can definitely repair and enhance your flight capabilities. The process will require a few days of preparation." She looked up. "Now, regarding remuneration ..."

"She has plenty of credit chips," Isla interjected.

Sss'ha's eyes spun in their sockets. "Do you think we use your primitive monetary tokens where I come from? You will assist me with cataloging the inventory stored here. Two months of skilled work."

"I can offer you jewels, rare metals—" Of which Isla had none.

"I have access to the mineral wealth of seventeen different worlds. Two months. Accept the terms or find another biomechanic."

Despite her desire to flee, Isla thought of herself as a decent person with only minor criminal tendencies. This maimed little woman needed help that only the alien could provide.

"Won't the brigadier's forces find us here?" Isla asked. "And what are we supposed to eat?"

"I am quite capable of guarding this facility," Sss'ha said.

"There are supplies, and the geothermal heating works well in most areas," Lara volunteered.

"Did you plan this entire scenario?" Isla's suspicions boiled over. "Were you maneuvering me into this trap?"

"I needed your help to reach this place safely," Lara admitted, sounding regretful. "The mission was too important to risk failure."

She placed the glowing seedpod inside a crystal container. "The seeds have absorbed sufficient solar energy. They should be ready for dispersal in one week."

"And you'll leave me here as unpaid labor?"

"Think of it as a brief indenture," Sss'ha suggested.

The Museum awaited, filled with mysteries from across the dimensional divide. Somewhere in its depths lay the tools needed to restore a tiny woman's wings and reshape the destiny of an entire world.

Isla thought back on Brigadier General Galli and the redoubtable Aunt Leonie, who would surely send her henchmen after her as well.

Maybe staying put for some time wasn't a bad idea. At least here, in this strange sanctuary, she could disappear from both their radars.

Two weeks ago, she'd been a legitimate merchant with prospects. Now, she was a fugitive hiding in an alien's warehouse, indentured to a creature that casually mentioned eating humans.

Sss'ha led a despondent Isla toward a door hidden behind stacked crates. "Welcome to my true collection," the Mechwoman hissed, producing an elaborate key made of crystal and metal.

The door groaned open to reveal a darkened spiral staircase. The walls were lined with a smooth, opalescent material that pulsed with its own inner light. Symbols and diagrams covered every surface.

As they reached the bottom, Isla's breath caught. The basement stretched far beyond what the building's footprint should have allowed. Vaulted ceilings soared thirty feet overhead, supported by columns that twisted like frozen tornadoes.

"This space is bigger than the entire building above."

"Dimensional folding," Sss'ha said matter-of-factly. "A simple matter of convincing space that it wants to be larger than it appears."

Huge stacks of boxes and crates awaited Isla. Some areas were cordoned off with barriers of crackling energy, while others were kept in complete darkness.

Lara dragged a crowbar across the floor and dropped it at Isla's feet, smiling up at her. Despite everything, the tiny woman's optimism was infectious.

"Together," Lara said simply. "We'll figure this out together."

Isla pried open the first crate. Inside lay the torso of a creature that was half flesh and half metal. When the thing opened its large, black eyes—embryo eyes, like those of a Clingbot—Isla let it fall back into the box with a yelp.

"That's one of the failed prototypes we built when developing the Clingbots," Lara said, her face crumpling. "We thought we were creating helpers."

"Your Brigadier General Galli has visited me three times. We have ... an arrangement," Sss'ha revealed.

Isla's knees buckled. The government was actively collaborating with forces that saw humans as little more than specimens.

Sss'ha treated Isla's bleeding shoulder with a substance that seemed to move of its own accord. The moment it touched her wound, flesh and skin knitted together in real-time, leaving not even a scar.

"The mist exposure has changed you more than you realize," Sss'ha said, flashing a light in Isla's eyes, revealing flecks of green that hadn't been there before.

After spending long hours cataloging impossible artifacts, Isla climbed to her assigned room—a closet with a single narrow window. She tried to fall asleep, but irritation crawled under her skin like bugs.

Her thoughts turned to Lara, and horror shot through her as she realized her fingers had grown hard like a bird's claws. She stared at nails elongated and curved, ending in sharp points.

She should have let the green woman find her own way of paying for new wings. Everything she'd worked for was gone because of one small green woman with sad eyes and implausible stories.

The tiny Mikra jumped down onto Isla's cot. "I don't know what I would have done without you. You're my best friend."

Best friend? They'd known each other for less than a week. How could she be friends with someone likely scheming against human civilization?

Isla felt a strange, burning, sudden heat all over her body. Lara's tapered fingers ran along Isla's exposed forearm, blessedly cool against the burning skin. "You have a fever."

Isla swatted her away. The small woman tumbled through the air and retreated up to the pillow, eyes wide with hurt.

Eventually, exhaustion overcame her turmoil, and she drifted into an uneasy sleep.

"The mist fever," Lara whispered when Isla's eyes opened in the deep hours of the night. "It's changing you faster than I expected."

"What's happening to me?"

"You're becoming something new. Something that can bridge the gap between your people and mine."

Two weeks passed, and every day, Isla felt worse. The fever came in waves. Her handwriting had grown erratic, filled with symbols she didn't recognize. Everything felt like a threat now.

Lara greeted Isla from her perch on the bronze statue. "Good day, my friend!"

Isla made a growling sound in her throat, deeper than her normal voice. Her fingernails had grown longer and harder, almost talon-like.

"You think I've been controlling you," Lara said.

"Aren't you Greenies empaths? Can't you influence thought?"

A tear slid down Lara's cheek. "We are not empaths. What you think is plain to see on your face. Humans are terrible at hiding their feelings."

"You made me care about your cause. You made me throw away my future for someone I'd just met."

"Maybe you cared because it was the right thing to do. Maybe you threw away a future you didn't really want."

"Easy to talk about saving the world when you're not the one who's lost everything. I'm nothing now."

"You like me," Lara said, her voice weighted with infinite

sadness. "Of course, it's easier to think you're under my influence than admit you might be losing your mind."

Lara's malformed wings drooped. "I thought you were strong enough to resist what's happening to you. But you feel like danger now."

"We can't be friends," Isla said. "You're an alien. You'll always be an alien."

"I'm going." Lara's voice was a thread of sound.

She half-fluttered, half-ran toward the back door, paused at the threshold, and then was gone.

Isla's fingers curled like claws, joints locked in impossible positions. Tiny red sparks filled her vision with pinpricks of crimson light. The shift was accelerating.

She hobbled into Sss'ha's garden, blood singing in her ears as her hands itched with violent urgency.

Find her. Catch her. Make her pay.

She could smell Lara's scent: crushed leaves and copper pennies. Lara fluttered between gnarled branches, her malformed wings beating erratically.

"Isla, please! Fight it! This isn't you!"

But it felt more like her than anything had in weeks. Hunt, catch, kill.

Lara tumbled across the soil. Isla was on her instantly, clawed hand closing like a trap.

"Got you, little liar."

Lara looked more concerned than afraid. "You're burning up ... the fever's spiking."

Lara sank sharp teeth into Isla's thumb. Pain sliced through her blood-hot focus. From the tiny wounds, a slow burn unfurled through Isla's arm. Lara spat a phosphorescent substance that foamed and bubbled, then went limp.

The predatory obsession dissolved. Isla's head cleared. What had she been doing? The shame clung like oil.

"I bit you to taste your illness," Lara whispered. "My saliva contains engineered microorganisms designed to counter neurochemical cascades triggered by toxins.

"But I've also given you serum," she continued. "My pets—the symbiotic organisms that regulate my biology—I sacrificed them to save your sanity."

Lara closed her eyes, her chest barely rising.

Isla realized the cost. Lara had given part of herself to cure someone who'd been about to kill her.

Isla couldn't believe those evil thoughts. The toxins had only amplified what was already there: her resentment, selfishness, exhaustion.

"I'm so sorry!" She wanted to take back every harsh word.

Lara's body twitched involuntarily, face moon-pale. The phosphorescent moths that usually circled her had vanished.

"Wake up, please!" Isla tried everything, but Lara remained limp, breathing imperceptibly.

"Sss'ha! The Mikra is hurt!"

The gynoid emerged from her laboratory. "Give her to me."

Isla felt the flutter of Mikra's heart. Nothing. "She's dead."

"Then nothing worse can happen to her," Sss'ha said with casual indifference.

Isla took the knotted handkerchief containing the activated seedpod from Lara's still hand and deposited the tiny form onto Sss'ha's palm.

Without warning, Sss'ha popped Lara into her mouth like candy.

Isla screamed. "NO! What are you doing?!"

Finally, Sss'ha spat the chewed remains into her palm—mangled tissue and strange fluids that pulsed and shifted.

"Her mammalian physiology resembles yours more than mine. She needs your heart blood. Will you give it to her?"

"She's dead!"

"She's dormant. But she could awaken if you gave her your blood." Sss'ha held up a syringe as large as Isla's wrist. "It's going to be excruciatingly painful."

"Do you mean she could live?"

"The outcome is uncertain. You might not recover from the puncture."

"So, I could die for nothing."

"Bluntly put. Yes."

Isla stared at the syringe. "Do it."

The pain was immediate and savage, a bolt of fire lancing through her arm into her chest. The syringe pierced deep as if Sss'ha were pulling the blood from her heart itself.

Then came the creeping numbness, seeping into her bones. She focused on one pulse in her veins: If Lara lived, this would be worth it.

When Isla came to, she was on the lab floor. In Sss'ha's palm lay a miserable clod. A dark and oozing thing.

The mangled lump quivered with unnatural life. From the shapeless mass, a minuscule torso began to coalesce. Then came the head: oblong, reptilian, with white fangs and a double row of globular eyes.

"You remade her like you."

Sss'ha placed the malformed creature on a shelf and left.

Each time Isla woke, she returned to the lab. Then, one day, the lump on the shelf moved. A quiver, a twitch.

The creature's eyes gleamed. The thing surged upright. Its tentacles writhed, then folded inward until four limbs emerged. The crocodilian snout collapsed inward. From the alien template, features began to surface: high cheekbones and a tapered chin.

Four wings of iridescent living tissue unfurled from the slender back. The new wings resembled dragonfly wings—translucent membranes laced with veins of light.

Every detail slid into place: the copper-colored eyes, the intricate braids. It was Lara but remastered.

"I feel wonderful." Her voice carried all the familiar tinkling music, but underneath was new strength. "I bet I can fly faster than any Clingbot."

She launched herself from the shelf with effortless grace.

"You changed my life, fearless woman. I have accomplished the first part of my mission. And now I'm whole again! Thanks to you."

"I love you," Lara continued. "And the seeds are ready now. I'm going down to the surface."

"I wish I could go with you."

"Yes, you should come. You deserve to watch the bloom."

"That remaking was very satisfying," Sss'ha said behind them. "I might set you free now."

"You're immune now," Lara explained. "Some of my pets are swimming in your blood. Now you can go down to the surface without danger."

Sss'ha returned with a white suit—a strange thing with what looked like two rockets on the back. A propeller? To fly? Isla wiggled into it, and Lara settled on her shoulder.

Isla shot up toward the skydome and out through the stained glass. As they soared away from the Museum, Isla felt the weight of her old life falling away like shed skin.

She broke through the clouds. Below, monumental conical structures supported huge lamps, and rows of wind turbines rose on the hillsides.

"They switched the lights on to greet us," Lara said.

Isla landed on black clods of earth. The ground seemed newly dug and turned.

Sounds reached her. Bots lumbered over the ridges. Then came the buzzing of fluttering tiny people who converged from all directions to form a dense, multicolored cloud.

When Lara produced her handkerchief and unfolded it, beams of light spread out.

"The matter of the universe is formed from seeds." Lara extended her arm and shook the cloth.

Winged myriads scattered in the wind. Where they fell, stems grew, and leaves appeared. The vegetation sprouted and sped to smother valleys and hills under quivering carpets. Each blade, each leaf, each petal emitted soft luminescence and released sounds of brass and crystalline strings.

"Whoa! Those plants grow really, really fast."

"We engineered special seeds. Back in the good days, everything grew fast, but we have increased the speed of cellular division."

A resurrection, not just a germination.

Along with the hundreds of thousands all around, Lara clapped. "Finally, spring!"

"What is 'spring'?"

Lara intoned:

Spring is a killer.

It surges within you

and shatters everything it touches:

the chilliness of ice, the debris,
the warm, comfortable sentiments
of winter-born friendships.
Spring rips you from the cozy embrace of slumber
and jolts you back to life, pores wide open,
the raging tide of a quickened sap
washing away the emotions that have now
grown old.

"It's from the ancient poem 'Seasons of Change'. Thank you for helping us revive our garden."

"I still don't know what spring is." Isla donned her suit.

"I'll go upstairs now."

"You'll be in danger. Angry people are looking for you."

"I'll hide beneath Lucendo's platforms. There's a lively underground in the Mesh. Nobody will find me there."

As they soared higher above the cable networks, the mist began to dissipate into graceful scarves of vapor that caught and reflected the golden light rising from below. What had once been a visually impenetrable barrier between the platforms and the surface was becoming translucent, revealing vistas that most humans had never imagined.

Lara wove around Isla, leaving trails of soft green glow in her wake. The new wings caught every current and thermal with supernatural grace. The iridescent membranes shifted through the entire spectrum as she moved—emerald when she banked left, silver when she climbed, gold when she dived.

"I can feel the air currents," she called out in wonder. "Not just with my wings, but with my whole body. The atmosphere speaks to me."

Beneath them, stretching to every horizon, the green blanket of new growth advanced in waves.

Glowing jade-colored specks rode high-altitude winds, carrying the gift of life to regions untouched by green for millennia.

"Lara, before I go into hiding, let's visit the market," Isla said. "My mother used to take me there when I was little. I'd like to see how it looks in your yellow light."

The market was more than commerce; it was the heart of every human community, a place where people traded goods and exchanged stories, gossip, and dreams of better times.

Isla flew first through the city's underbelly, past the tangles of metal mesh that formed Lucendo's foundation. The Mesh was a world of its own, a lattice of rusted girders and cable bundles beneath Lucendo's platforms. People emerged from their shelters, faces tilted toward a light that didn't burn their eyes. Children who had never played outside stepped tentatively onto platforms that no longer froze their feet through worn shoes.

She then ascended to the highest platforms, soaring above the polished steel of the large mansions. Even here, among the wealthy who had always been shielded from Talisqualis's harshness, fresh green shoots clung to balcony rails.

The icicles that had dangled from every cornice like frozen tears now began to weep, as the temperature rose for the first time in living memory. Across the city, the sound of melting ice formed a delicate song.

The breeze no longer drove ice needles into exposed skin or carried the bitter bite of a world that had forgotten warmth. Instead, it brought scents from the surface—rich earth, growing things, the promise of seasons yet to come.

This new light—warm, golden, alive—revealed that the platforms had always held beauty. Metal, once slate-gray and industrial, now glinted with traces of copper and bronze. It was as if the entire city had been waiting for the right light to reveal its true nature.

High above, clouds gathered, remembering how to rain.

Isla pointed toward the wide platform that housed Lucendo's main market. Even from a distance, she could see how the golden light had turned the space into something magical.

She made her helmet retract, and at once, a wave of scents hit her—spicy cardamom, sweet honey cakes, roasted nuts, and exotic teas, all carried on air finally warm enough to hold such delicate fragrances.

For the first time in generations, the market pulsed with life.

Lilting jigs and haunting strains mingled in a joyous cacophony as street musicians stepped out from the winter shelters. Dancers in bright orange whirled through the crowd, their movements fluid and exuberant in the warm air.

People chattered as they moved through the tents. Gone were the hushed, hurried exchanges of a population focused on survival. The conversations brimmed with wonder and possibility.

When the golden light washed over the crowd in a swell of warmth, everyone stopped. Eyes widened in collective amazement as they witnessed something that defied everything they knew about their world.

Isla witnessed the exact moment when everything shifted for humanity on Talisqualis.

She landed behind a spice merchant's stall. The merchant whose stall sheltered her stared up at the sky, tears streaming down weathered cheeks. "In all my years," the old woman whispered, "I never thought I'd see the day the darkness broke."

Lara's urgent words came as a whisper in her ear. "What will you do now, my friend?"

The question carried weight beyond its simplicity. Isla was no longer the person who had found an anchovy can weeks ago. She was a bridge between worlds, a translator between species, and a catalyst for change.

"I'll gather a group of like-minded folk, and we'll fight the Clingbots. We'll also campaign for an alliance with your people."

The plan took shape as she spoke, drawing on everything she knew about negotiation, human nature, and the delicate balance required to change minds rather than simply win arguments.

"It won't be easy, but this light rising from below will shatter long-held beliefs." Isla gestured to the crowd around them, to people seeing for themselves that the world might hold possibilities they had never been allowed to imagine.

Lara folded her wings tight against her sides. "I fear some of your people will try to take over our technology."

"That's why we need to build an opposition," Isla said. "There are others like me who've been questioning the official stories. People who've seen things that don't match what we're told. We'll start with them and build from there.

"And you, what are you going to do?" Isla asked.

"I'll keep sowing seeds," Lara said simply. "This is just the beginning. The surface transformation will take years, maybe decades, but every day there will be more life, more growth, more reasons for our peoples to work together instead of against each other."

Lara's tiny hand touched Isla's cheek, a gesture that was both a blessing and a farewell.

"We'll meet again, human woman." The old endearment now held new meaning, a quiet recognition of Isla's part in the world's unfolding change.

And then she was gone, vanishing into the golden light with a speed that made her seem a living spark. Isla watched until she could no longer pick Lara out from the other motes of light dancing in the warm air.

Even after she disappeared, her presence lingered in the green dust clinging to Isla's sleeve—tiny particles glowing with their inner light.

Isla blew on the green dust that rose from below. The gleaming particles spiraled away on currents of warm air. A few landed in containers filled with precious gap-collected soil that merchants had brought to trade, and immediately stems and leaves sprouted, lifting toward the golden light, hungry for warmth they had never known.

Isla stood at the edge of the market and watched people rediscover wonder in their world, Isla wondered if the green would one day swallow all the steel.

The transformation would be gradual but unstoppable, spreading through contact and proximity until Lara's gift touched the entire platform network. But that would be the easy part. Changing hearts and minds, building trust between species that had been taught to fear each other, creating new forms of cooperation and governance—would be the real challenges.

Looking up at the cable networks stretching between platforms, Isla saw the first tendrils of climbing plants taking hold. Steel cables, once purely functional, were becoming scaffolds for a new kind of architecture blending human engineering with living growth.

The green would indeed spread to cover all the steel, but it wouldn't erase what humans had built. It would transform it, weaving technology and nature into something neither species could have created alone.

Isla held out her hand. A small puff of emerald dust clung to her fingertips, soft, fine, as if the planet itself had shed a layer just for her. New and ancient, the powder stirred on her skin and tethered her to Talisqualis's alchemy.

The living motes continued to dance in the golden light, carrying the seeds of tomorrow on every warm breeze.

THE SKIN BENEATH

Roni Stinger

While Brian insists on moving to a house in the suburbs, all I want to do is bite into the bitter deliciousness of the ant crawling across the living room wall. The basement beckons.

Brian clasps my hands in his.

"Nadia, for better or worse, right? It'll be better. A beautiful house in the suburbs. A yard. Far from the city."

All I've wanted since childhood is to live in this hand-carved stone building with its time-worn gargoyles perched along the front entrance. It called me, even then, back when I walked with the nuns from my orphanage, down the sidewalk, to the park.

"I've been clear about staying here." This conversation is over as far as I'm concerned.

"A fifth-floor condo is no place to raise a child."

It's exactly where I want to raise my baby. A wave of quicksand fills my gut.

My baby. The basement promises coolness. Darkness. So many insects to feed the cravings. What is wrong with me? The baby kicks.

A tiny foot rolls across my stomach. It's okay, little one. I rub my distended belly. Any day now.

Brian clenches his jaw.

"I don't want to add stress, but there's something wrong. I … can't." He stops, slowly shaking his head.

I've seen his wide eyes and suspicious brow, as he watches me. When I met him, Brian lived with his grandma in the country. He cared for her with such gentleness. I waited for him. When she died, he moved into my condo.

He respected my dream of never leaving the promise of safety and shelter that shimmered through the rock walls. It wasn't fair for him to do this now.

"Give up everything I've ever wanted? The perfect home? The cool stone wrap of safety? Because something is wrong?" I pull my hands from his grasp, as the ant crawls beneath a picture frame. "What is wrong? We've never been happier." I hide the cringe, saying the last.

I'd never been happier.

"It's … this place. No kind of home to raise our baby. It's affecting you." He leans back with an exasperated sigh.

"You talk in circles. Not actually saying anything. My baby isn't going anywhere. This is her home." She kicks in agreement.

"You mean our baby?" His face is rigid.

"I'm not leaving." My voice is flat.

Plumbing and electrical pathways run across the unfinished ceiling of the basement. No one comes down here except for building maintenance. Sitting on the concrete floor, I scuff the toe of my shoe in years of accumulated dust. The damp, cool air forms a cocoon of comfort.

A small iridescent beetle runs along the crack between floor and wall. There's an itch in my belly. Baby is restless. I pinch the bug between my fingers and pop it in my mouth. Crunchy and delicious.

What the hell is wrong with me? I don't want to leave, but Brian will be home soon. Standing up, I brush my hands on my pants. I'd have to clean the dirt from under my nails. He doesn't need more reasons to be suspicious.

Brian is blathering on about moving again. A fly crawls from the corner of his mouth and takes flight. I sip my tea to distract myself. It doesn't work.

If I catch the fly between my teeth, crushing its thorax and savoring its bitter juices, maybe that will silence Brian.

"I'm selling the condo. It's the best thing for all of us, especially the baby."

Three shiny green beetles crawl from his ear, down his neck, and over his shoulder. As they scurry up the wall, my mouth waters for their crunchy goodness. Rain pelts against our arched window.

A salamander rests on my arm. The skin beneath is thick and scaled. Blinking, I shake my head. This feels like one hell of a trip, but I'm stone-cold sober. The spoon rattles in my cup, as I set my tea on the end table.

"I've found a place. In the country, where no one will bother us. We'll have the family I've always dreamed ..." His voice fades.

The salamander shifts and changes, leaving phantom trails across my skin. Brian won't take me or my daughter from our home. She rolls in agreement, taking my breath away.

Butterflies, beetles, and a praying mantis appear and disappear into the worn leather sofa, as Brian continues. Does he really think I have no choice?

His chiseled features wash into the wall. Opening my mouth to speak, the lamp stretches, and the room ripples. My home turns into a funhouse nightmare.

Fuzzy shapes sharpen, becoming the pipes and wires that writhe across the open-beamed ceiling of the basement. The stones ooze with cool moisture. Rainbow lights shine on the far wall like sunlight reflected through a prism. That is where we need to go.

I crave tunnels, damp corridors, the darkness beyond the wall. My daughter needs me. My innards vibrate. Inhaling a deep, moist, mossy breath, I remember. My family.

Brian cowers on the floor. He tells me he's sorry, how scared he is for me. Only, it almost sounds like he's afraid of me. His eyes drip tears of ants that march into his ears and mouth. Yearning to catch them with my tongue, I tremble. Damp basalt fills my nasal passages.

Ancestral memories return. Subterranean channels we've returned to for generations, swimming through flooded tunnels.

"Everything's okay," I tell him. "Over here."

I move toward the prismatic lights on all fours. Brian is mumbling something. Pale and reeking of piss and musk. I pity him. Such a pathetic creature. Sucking his hand into my mouth, I drag him across the floor as thousands of insects of myriad size and type pour from his eyes.

"Please, I didn't mean it. Stop! You're hurting me! We don't have to leave, I swear. Whatever you want." His free hand catches a support beam. I yank him free. "Dammit! Help!"

Prying the rocks with my toes, I'm surprised how easily the passage opens. My lips stretch into a wide smile, as I drop his hand. The smoky iron of blood and exoskeletons fill the basement.

Instincts sharp, my hunger grows. I slink through the jagged hole, dragging him along.

A high-pitched screech escapes my throat. My bones crack and sinews stretch. Limbs thicken and morph as my body, tail, and long maw grow. He screams, and tasty flies spill from his throat.

My tongue darts out, penetrating his esophagus, punching a hole through flesh and cartilage. My jaws close on his head, crushing bone as if it were chalk.

He tastes sweet and rich. His carcass leaves a trail of fluids, as I lower into the labyrinthine tunnels.

My sisters wait in the water below.

Our tails wrap around each other in greeting. Dry spaces and warm food flit like fireflies in my mind. We will give birth and release our daughters in these waters as our mothers did us. Until then, we will feed.

DANCE OF THE SEVEN FEMME FATALES

Anami Sheppard

1.

Lilith swirls behind a matadora's cape,
woven with black and silver threads of night sky,
harvested from a time before Knowledge.
She knows what she likes.
A flourish, a pass, a turn on nimble feet.
An adventuress with flashing eyes, up for anything, anyone.
(Except missionary position, faking orgasm, or obeying idiots.)
Her bravery begets bravery, curves multiply.
Her pleasure comes first.
>   *Only a man can command.*
With a charge both brilliant and bold, she delivers the fatal estocada.

2.

The Vamp draws a velvet crimson scarf across each hill and valley.
Her music—a low drum—picks up speed as she dips, turns,
pulsing to a primal rhythm,
revealing the slits in her dress, her strong thighs.
Her voice, husky in the shadows, promises: "Carpe Vita."

Only you can sate her hunger, only you can tame her passion.
This will be just a little death.
    An unattractive woman has no value.
She swallows lies, pierces both ego and jugular,
and gives a beautiful, wet smile.

3.

The Rusalka slow sways and rolls beneath silk of blue,
dyed all the shimmering shades of seas, rivers, oceans.
Red hair, touched by sailor's knots, drifts with tendril, soothing fingers.
She holds no blame (a mirage),
lovely as a moment that will bear no consequences.
    Murdered mistresses bear no babies and tell no tales.
Her myriad silver reflections fragment, shatter,
expose a barnacle grip which drowns.
She's evening the scales, growing her watery garden, where fish eat flesh,
exposing how pretty the white, white bones.

4.

La Belle Dame sans Merci frolics under her moonlit, snowy mantle,
fairy-leaping while the nightingales sing their souls,
while loons trill, and the great horned owls hoo, hoo-hoo
against the hollows of the night.
By and by, she cavorts with a knight, a king, a prince—
each quest to keep her wild beauty like a crown, and knot flowers into chains.
    Women should make sacrifices for love.
She feeds them spun sugar, romantic illusions like cobwebs.
They awaken, gossamer ghosts, arrested in the memory of night-blooming jasmine.

5.

The Kumiho's nine hidden tails swish
beneath her steel gray widow's shroud.
Her long, trailing sleeves stir the graveyard fog
while she steps with animal grace
among the decade leavings of silenced sadness,
and century shards of buried grief.
    A man must be strong, rational; only women are emotional.
She will sup on a thousand fallow-hearted men,
diving into their chests with full-pointed snout and vixen teeth.

6.

Salome taps a slow percussion with her naked foot,

peeking out from a pale-pink cloud of lotus flower curtains.

Her every motion carries more sweet, heady perfume,

and as she dances, music flows from her body:

trickles down her torso, shimmies with her hips, and rings from finger cymbals.

Those watching forget they watch, insensate.

Each parting of the cloth reveals fresh-petal skin

quivering, anticipating, how you will fingerpaint your desire.

     It's her fault—she looked like a whore.

Percussion speeds, as she yearns into her climactic reveal:

she's learned enough about power to turn on its head.

7.

The Vishkanya bends behind a veil of shifting colors—

black opal fires, pearly frosts, iridescence.

She undulates, writhes, offers her body for the feast.

Almond-shaped eyes with cyanide tears;

soft bee-stung lips the color of strychnine berries.

With a breath of belladonna she whispers:

let me tell you what my monstrous sisters and I have eaten all our lives,

how many poisons you gifted us.

They're our weapons now.

We know our strength.

We know our worth.

NOT WITH A SPLASH BUT A GURGLE

KT Wagner

My freshly shed skin is thin, slick, and smells delicious. Swampy with a hint of mint. Thankfully, my weekly moults have resumed. I've recovered from the most recent fungus attack, but there's no time to savour the relief.

The door of the water-swollen cupboard sticks. I force it open and tuck my rolled-up skin inside for later consumption. Beside it lies a laminated copy of the scroll I stole from the sorcerer, Charles Perrault, more than three centuries past.

Unfortunately, the syllabic writing of Faerie remains largely unintelligible to me. It was the spoken language of my childhood, but I was illiterate. As far as I know, Perrault's the only one in this world who can translate the scroll, and he'd never help me willingly.

No matter. I've deciphered some of the illustrations, and recent circumstances have illuminated a path to overdue justice. It's been a long time coming. Centuries ago, in Faerie, I, my mother, and my younger sister Rose fell victim to Perrault. Back then, he knew me as Fanny. He created me. Wrote me—and so many others—into existence for his use and amusement.

"He'll come," I mutter. Almost an incantation, but not quite. Reliable magic eludes me. There's little emotion behind my words. A trickle of tadpoles slips past my lips.

The key to what I want, what my modern family needs, is in the scroll. After all this time, Perrault will pay. Then I can be done with him forever. The polliwogs flail, flip, wriggle, and fall through the gaps between the rotting floorboards, splashing into the marshy waters below. The body of the owner of this lakeside cabin feeds my amphibious children in the shallows downstream. The nearest neighbours are miles away on the far shore.

The air dries me out faster these days. Cupping my hands, I scoop amber lake water from the wooden bucket in the corner and pour it down my front. It sluices between my breasts, across my abdomen, and splashes onto the floor. Not enough, but it will do for now.

I spit on a mildewed rag and rub a patch of grime off the window facing the driveway. The floor creaks beneath my feet as I pace, restless, watching. The webbing between my fingers and toes is translucent; I hold up a hand to admire this latest change. My skin is tinted algae-green but not enough to immediately draw human attention.

My pupils are elongated, and sunglasses are necessary in public. If the curious come too close, I cough and wave them off. Watching them scurry is oddly satisfying.

Despite his numerous flaws, Perrault has always been fastidious and punctual. He'll be here soon. I perch on the edge of the couch, then stand and resume pacing.

Once, I was the object of his obsession. After spurning him, I became the target of his curse. However, I'm now a creature of my own making, not his.

A grotesque magnetism is at play. Though Perrault no longer recognizes me, he's never far. The ensorcellment pulls both ways.

My skin crawls when he's too close. Today, I'm willing to endure it.

I've sought to end him numerous times. I breathe deep. Unbidden, the centuries fall away.

Perrault set his cap for me when I was fourteen, tending a field of pumpkins and a flock of geese. He seemed old, though likely he was no more than a score and ten when I spurned his advances. Undeterred, he approached my widowed mother for permission to bind me with marriage. What he did to her isn't clear, but it must have involved magic, either from his quill pen or a potion. My gentle mother flew into a supernatural rage and demanded I marry Perrault. When I refused, she was struck by an unnatural apoplexy. Her face flushed deep purple, and she fell down, dead.

I publicly accused Perrault of sorcery. Magic was frowned on, though not illegal in Faerie. The village magistrate warned me against slandering a member of the aristocracy.

Perrault disappeared. Much later, I realized he'd retreated to his world, to France, to spend time rationalizing a new moral before writing the next chapter in the story of my Faerie family. I was grieving the loss of my mother and had a younger sister to raise and support. My concerns about him receded.

In moments, he'll be here. More and more, my mind slips, involuntarily, into memories of Faerie. Soon, I'll be able to surrender to the mutations that will change me forever, but not yet.

I tie on a gingham dress, trying to ignore how the cloth suffocates my skin.

The promise of underpriced real estate was the bait. Without long-term memories, Perrault has remade himself several times. These days, he's an unscrupulous land developer, preying on the naive and desperate.

Yesterday, I leaned against the porch railing, telephoned him, and infused my voice with feminine desperation. It was impossible to avoid belching a half-dozen spotted frogs in the process, though I've developed tricks to hide my affliction and made it sound like sobs and hiccups.

The newly birthed creatures slipped off my tongue and plopped into the swamp. The urge to dive after them swelled, the pressure almost unbearable. The compulsion to follow my amphibious children never lets up. In time, it will overwhelm me, but I cannot give in. Not yet.

There's a tarnished mirror on the wall of the lakeside cabin. He's superstitious, so I throw an old towel over it.

Plastic milk crates provide the structure for a makeshift couch. I straighten the faded denim coverlet, stolen from a clothesline miles up the road. It's been good to have a home, however temporary. I sigh and sit, just for a moment.

After mother's death, life went on. I submerged myself in hard work to provide for my sister. Rose turned fourteen; the image of me at that age, but comelier. The day after her birthday, she went to fetch water from the river and disappeared.

The village sent out search parties. I walked for days in the forest, seeking a sign of her. Finally, I accepted she'd fallen victim to a wild animal or had drowned, her body carried away by the river's current.

Me grief was sharp and bitter.

Months later, a minstrel wandered into town. He sang at the tavern where I worked serving mead and ale—a sordid tale of a rich prince and his beautiful wife. Her hair was long and blonde. The prince kept her imprisoned in a castle tower.

Every night for a week, I listened. Despite the scant details, I grew convinced he sang of Rose.

My eyes have closed. I jump up and splash water from a nearby bucket onto my face. Did I miss Perrault's arrival?

I've lived rough in this world. Under bridges, near sewers, always close to water, for I never know when I'll cry out in my sleep and expel a salamander or a frog.

At first, the curse gifted me with a constant, gnawing hunger for meat. Many times, I was reduced to eating birds and rodents. The crunch of their bones between my teeth will forever haunt my nightmares.

Then, the chytrid fungus infected me, modified me, and sought to end me. Over and over, I sparred with Death before skittering out of her reach.

Through those dark, hopeless times, I always knew exactly where I was. Now, I'm increasingly unsure. The past and present swirl around me.

The minstrel was lonely; it didn't take long to convince him to join my quest to find Rose. During our journey, he composed a heroic ballad about himself.

In the deepest, darkest part of the forest we stumbled across Perrault. Ill-fitting red cloak flapping, he ran from us. We followed him to a crumbling castle where he slipped in a side door.

The minstrel gallantly insisted on confronting Perrault. I tried to talk him out of it, but he pounded on the castle's front door. Perrault answered, bowed, and waved him inside. From the edge of the wood, I cried out a warning. The minstrel didn't react. I ran to the castle and scrambled up the steps.

Perrault's stare curdled my insides. He held my gaze while he skewered the minstrel through the back with a sword.

I screamed and begged to see Rose. He informed me she was terribly ill. I pleaded with him to let me stay and nurse my sister back to health.

He agreed.

Am I ill? Is this a fever dream? It doesn't matter. Today, I set things right.

While the fungus infected me, I'd drift in and out of consciousness for days. My battle to survive raged on even as the fungus killed hundreds of thousands, then millions, of earth's amphibians.

At first, I thought Perrault responsible, that he'd somehow regained the memories the curse consumed and started writing faerie tales again, but the fungus was just a cruel twist of nature, of fate. A worldwide pandemic spread by uncaring humans.

My children suffered horrible deaths—starvation as fungus devoured their skin—and I was helpless to do anything. My heart shattered.

I'm no longer helpless.

Tired, yes, but revenge has been reason enough to find the will to endure. I love my children. Every slimy, undulating, croaking one of them. I love them almost as much as I loved my mother and sister.

Perrault kept Rose chained to a bed even though she was near death and incapable of sitting up. On a dresser sat a shallow bowl filled with poor-quality gems. When I picked one up, Perrault snatched it away.

"Fanny," Rose whispered. The choking noises were terrible. Black blood gushed from her mouth. I rushed over, but Perrault got there first.

He shoved two fingers into her mouth. While I clawed the back of his tunic, he extracted a gore-coated diamond, spat on it, polished it with his filthy shirt and held it up to the window. "Bah. Flawed and useless. Feed her this." He pushed a wooden box at me.

I opened it, and a sooty puff set me coughing. Rose lay, still as death. Her eyes showed white.

The spluttering knock of a vehicle engine signals Perrault's arrival. I pinch myself. It's critical I stay in the present, focussed. A rusty-blue pickup truck bounces along the gravel driveway, flattening waist-high weeds under its oversized tires.

My eyes are drying out. The scene blurs. I blink hard.

Tall and skinny, Perrault slides out of the truck and eyes the lakeside lot. Avarice distorts his plain, middle-aged features. Thick brows, large nose, and full, loose lips. He hasn't weathered the centuries well.

If the villagers I grew up with could see Perrault now—I stifle a snorting laugh before the curse can misinterpret it as a word.

My world believed him a prince. He coveted the power, the riches, and the entitlement of court. He also knew that a vague, manufactured lineage of a fifth- or sixth-born son of a distant branch of the royal family would be subject to few questions and even fewer responsibilities.

He swaggered around Faerie, smirking and sneering. Our lives were shaped by his desires and intolerances.

Pressing my fingers against Rose's throat, I found a pulse and could breathe again. I brandished the box of soot at Perrault. "What's this? Medicine?"

His laugh shifted into a growl. "Ash and graphite. If you can't get that into her, there's a tin of aluminum oxide and another of chromium. Damned woman. Rubies and emeralds are better than nothing."

Whenever Rose spoke, diamonds and gems formed in her throat. I could prove to the village council that Perrault practiced alchemy and dark magic! They'd banish him. My glee fell away as I realized what they'd do to Rose. She'd be imprisoned and farmed for jewels.

Rose didn't want to talk any more than I wanted her to, but Perrault had ways of getting around his own magic. Screams were as effective as conversation.

Rose craved the raw ingredients, but she continued to produce flawed treasure, and Perrault continued to rage. Every night, he locked himself in his study, the flicker of candlelight visible under the door until past midnight. One night, I hid behind the curtains and observed him removing a scroll from a locked vault. He drank mead and muttered over it.

"Is anyone home?" Perrault saunters toward the cabin. I have no doubt he'll break in if there's no response. We are alike in ways I'll only now admit.

Here, in the human world, I found him living in a small cottage on the outskirts of Paris. I'd learn later this wasn't his primary residence, but rather a place where he could write and conjure in private. Witchcraft was illegal in sixteenth-century France.

Every day he left his cottage and walked to the market. I waited until he was gone and broke in. In the drawer of his writing desk, I found the scroll from Faerie and took it.

Perrault steps onto the porch of the lakeside cabin, and I open the door. It creaks, loudly.

He's still gazing around at the property—sizing it up—and doesn't appear to notice me. His fingers tap against his thigh. He's agitated.

I smile and rap my knuckles against the doorframe to gain his attention.

His eyes widen, and he sways a little. A shiver slithers down my spine, puddling in my stomach. Our curses writhe and twine, reacquainting themselves. I motion for him to enter.

During daylight hours, Perrault left me alone in the castle with my sister. I searched and discovered a ring of keys. One opened an underground larder stocked with barrels of apples, another opened his desk drawer, and another unlocked Rose's chains.

My attempts to decipher the scroll failed. I fed apples to Rose when Perrault wasn't around. After a couple of weeks, she was strong enough to climb through a window and descend the ladder I'd fashioned from bed linens and chains.

We didn't make it far into the woods. Perrault rode us down on horseback, threw a fishing net over us, and dragged us back to the castle.

"Damned women. You will obey me!" He wrapped his hands around my neck and squeezed.

Rose screamed at him to stop. Long and loud. She started to choke, and he dropped me, but it was too late. My sister died.

"Everything goes wrong around you," Perrault said.

I recover from the contact before Perrault does. My attempt at a smile feels unnatural. Perrault steps back from my bared teeth. My pulse flutters; I dare not utter a sound. He might still escape.

I force my lips back over my teeth and close the gap between us. Grasping his arm, I flutter my eyelashes, swallow bile, and motion for him to take a seat.

His mouth twists. He pulls out a white handkerchief and covers his nose while scuffing a polished boot across the floorboards. "If I purchase this property, I'll be deducting the cost of removing this shack. Twenty-grand. Minimum."

Eyes downcast, I slump my shoulders and nod. I pat the seat of the couch.

He presses his lips together and shakes his head, but I know him.

Turning away, and cupping one hand below my mouth, I speak words I know he can't resist. "I'm desperate."

A newborn salamander squirms in the palm of my hand.

"I gave up too easily the first time." Perrault pinned me between his knees and covered my face with a clammy hand.

I heard, but could not see, the scratch of pen against parchment. "What are you doing?"

"I'm your creator, Fanny, my dear. You will be what I write." He chuckled.

His magic forced its way down my throat, slippery and corrupted. I struggled. "What's happening ..." A lump in my throat cut off the words. I gasped and retched, trying to clear the obstruction.

Perrault chuckled. "You've always been my chosen one. We'll build a kingdom for our many children—"

I vomited the squishy blockage into his hand.

Croak.

A large horny toad flicked its tongue, plopped onto the floor, and hopped away.

Perrault shoved me away. "No! That's not what I wrote!"

I drop the salamander into the corner and pick up the bucket. Perrault has settled himself on the couch, attention fully on me, eyes calculating.

My eye twitches. Has he noticed my lapses? He leers, and I relax—he hasn't.

I beat the fungus by letting it transform me but on my terms. A metamorphosis took place. I'm now fully of this world. Though I require a wet environment to live, I can manage on dry land for short periods if I keep my skin hydrated. Perhaps I'm becoming what I was always meant to be before Perrault interfered. My body's immune to the fungus, and my hybrid children will be immune too. We'll be something this world has never seen.

For all his passions and appetites, Perrault has little imagination. His stories may be lauded in this world, but they are mere transcriptions, stolen from the women of Faerie.

I'm free to act against the man, but, unfortunately, I need him alive for a little longer. Worse, I need him to cooperate.

Perrault plucks at the coverlet, crossing and re-crossing his legs. Nausea ripples through me. Despite all I've survived, I'm not sure I can go through with this.

I curl my mouth into a shy smile and hold out the tie to my dress. I mime tugging it. He complies and the cheap fabric puddles around my feet. I lift the bucket and tip the remainder of the lake water over my head.

His eyes glaze, and his expression slackens. I taste his lust in the air.

My stomach churns.

I step into his awkward embrace. He jerks and struggles but is no match for my new strength. The mutated fungus sinks into his skin and invades his cells. When I'm sure he's infected, I release him.

I fled far into the forest, screaming and vomiting frogs and serpents along the way. By the time I collapsed into a heap at the foot of a towering cedar, I'd almost wasted away. Bones jutted under my skin, threatening to tear though.

Hunger subsumed everything.

A huntsman found me. I devoured him and the freshly-slaughtered game he carried.

I should have begged the huntsman to cut out my tongue and render me mute, but I was not in my right mind.

The aftermath of taking the huntsman's life took me by surprise. Power collected in my throat, viscous and foul. I gathered it and molded it into a curse born of my intense hatred for Perrault. It ricocheted between the three of us: me, my creator, Perrault, and his namesake prince in Faerie. The writer and his doppelganger character became one. The newly fused Perrault and I were violently expelled from Faerie by the curse and hurled into, Perrault, the writer's world.

The curse I birthed after eating the huntsman then took the form of a moral, as faerie tale curses are wont to do, dealing Perrault a fate befitting a self-proclaimed god. It submerged Perrault's memories and continually erased new ones. He lives in an eternal present; his memory only ever extends backward a few short years. Until now ...

Perrault blinks and gasps as the curse's moral disintegrates.

I shudder and my embrace tightens. "Welcome. Back. Perrault."

The words hiss. Vipers drip from my lips. They writhe and flick their tongues. I push him deeper into the couch. It sinks and groans under the weight. The chains behind the couch are bolted to a post. A set of manacles dangle from the end. I ignore them for now. He's not going anywhere. Not yet.

My mouth is sour, and my skin crawls. I've tried not to dwell on this part. It's impossible to avoid.

"You've aged," he says.

I shrug. "I waited for you." A mouthful of ice-cold newts spill onto my breasts.

He leans forward, lips parted, sure he's in control. "Try not to talk."

My fingers curl and reach for his neck.

He misinterprets and clasps my hands, ever confident. "Good girl."

I focus on the scroll, pray I've understood, and grit my teeth. Five minutes and it's over.

He stands, zips his pants, and makes to leave. I almost let him, lacking even the energy to wring his neck. Filth is lodged in my hair, my pores, my orifices. All the water in the lake won't be enough to cleanse me.

He touches the door. I drag him back and manacle him to the post. He shouts and threatens. I gag him with strips of gingham.

The fungus doesn't kill tadpoles until they metamorphize. Perrault's hair is receding fast, along with his ears, as his limbs shorten. It won't be long before his cells burst.

In every corner of the lakeside cabin, our eggs swell and shudder. Moist clusters of promise. They'll be hungry when they emerge. I'll offer them my skin, but their father will nourish them.

This new generation of amphibious children will be immune to the fungus. We will thrive, on Earth and in Faerie. And they will have magic. Like me. I flex my fingers, savouring the tingle, the pull to press pen to paper.

Perhaps I'll compose a ballad. I hum a few bars of the minstrel's unfinished song.

THE LAZARUS RUINS

Wailana Kalama

If you ever see white ruins on a shore, don't go to them. They warned us not to dig around those bleached pillars, the salt-stung monoliths. Not to scrape our spades and shovels against those strange, curved columns. But who could resist? To look on those crumbling ruins was to see a vast ghostscape of a once-noble colony, a gravestone to greatness that stretched for miles. Tell me, who could turn away from that?

But gravestones are for the dead, and as we found out, the ruins were very much alive.

We stamped our boots through the wasp-ridden paths, and called bony things not as they were, but how we wanted to see them: a bathhouse, a cistern, a promenade. A temple to the goddess of love.

What tricksters, our minds.

There were four of us: Paul, Delilah, Suzannah, Theo. I don't know which one I am anymore. And I don't know, for sure, if any of the others were ever really there at all.

I was crouched in a stone bath with my trowel, ankle-deep in tidewater and chipping at age-old dirt, when the pillars on either side began to lengthen. They reached up to the heavens like eager saplings, curved like tusks. Fusing together at the crest half a mile above our heads, into a massive spine that coiled one mile north to south.

We gaped like children.

And soon we stood, not in ruins, but a ribcage.

Then it was the light, changing. From gold-touched Arctic morning to vermilion shadows. From every side and direction, curtains of red sprouted from the sand with a thirsty rustle, mounting higher and higher until they connected together above that awful spine. I heard a shriek, or maybe it was my own, when the sinew followed, dirty ropes that bound joints, and blood dripped like honey from the red ceiling, the smell sweet and grotesque. I caught a glimpse of the shore through the red veil, and that's when I understood, like a rabbit caught in a trap, just how worthless is the word escape.

We hammered our fists against this enveloping capsule of red, screaming, but only desperate echoes answered.

I didn't know it then, but we were in the whale.

It was a swift machine, the massive whale's resurrection. Layers of tissue, pulp, and ambergris thickened the red walls, rendering them opaque. In mere minutes, we were in darkness.

Everywhere, the stink of decay. Cloying and putrid. I slipped on grease and felt things wriggling between my fingers. I heard someone screaming in the deep. Paul or Delilah or Susannah or Theo. In the hollow of an echo chamber, all screams sound the same.

We yelled; we wailed; we cried like wounded animals. One of us pulled in rapid gulps. One of us vomited.

Strange liquid gushed up to my ankles, ravaging my leather boots until my toes were on fire. I could feel it eating away my feet, and then all went numb. The pain raked up my legs, seeking fuel, and again, the agony. I leaned on the flesh walls to keep from falling.

I wanted desperately to strip off my field clothes, but at the same time was terrified to do so. I must have sweated, because it was dank, stifling. I could no longer tell where my liquids ended and the whale's began.

Then, the breath.

Measured, beleaguered.

Alive.

A horrific bellow shook the walls, and we lost our footing. I heard splashes and more screams where the acid ate away our faces.

The first time we died wasn't the worst.

The first time we came back, our flesh forming again and again, anew and whole, beautiful hands, beautiful feet, miracles and testaments personified, standing strong and pounding at the walls while they shook with titanic breaths—that wasn't the worst.

Not the second time we shriveled either. That moment when I realized the acid only lapped more greedily at our restored bodies, like devouring seconds. When the pain left me seeing spots and hallucinating long-dead parents. When I bent into the liquid, hands searing, only to find mutilated femurs where my legs should've been. That wasn't the worst.

Or the second time we came back anew.

No.

The moment where hope vanished, that seared our wretched fate onto our very psyche like a branding iron, was that fifth time I lay dying. My ears had melted off where I'd splashed them to dull the screams reddening the dark. I grasped for the gulping body I thought might be next to me, because, I told myself, they would be better off submerged. Quiet. But Paul or Delilah or Suzannah or Theo, they grabbed my shoulders and whispered to me in a low, ragged voice that raked my innermost canals.

"We live; we decay. We die. We live. We decay."

I tore at their hands. The skin degloved into my grip, and I pressed it to my nose.

"The whale, it lives. It dies. It decays."

Inhale.

Was its breath slower, now?

Exhale.

It decays.

And I could picture it: the whale's flesh sloughing off, shredded by seagulls. That one brief moment where we, whole, could walk out from that shell of bones, out into the sunlight.

Freedom.

Then that unspoken question bloomed between us, a hope we dared not give voice to:

How long does it take for a beached whale to decay?

And I thought back to a university class one September afternoon. The trees had already begun to flame. A biology professor, red curls and elbow pads. His voice came out muffled, all clotted, but I clung to the repetition of his lips until they started to form words:

—In the right conditions—

What tormentors, our memories.

And the words staggered me to my knees, the liquid ready, lapping away every inch of me like a greedy lover calling me back to bed.

—In the right conditions, it can take years.

CONSTABLE GRACE BREMAN, RETIRED

J.M. Spronk

Dwarf planet Ceres's surface was a junkyard. But the view was spectacular—an infinite black firmament sprinkled with silver, set with the platinum disk of the sun. Grace considered it the highlight of her post-retirement 'employment,' which was otherwise a frustrating slog through a dusty, dark vacuum in a stinky spacesuit. She directed her HUD to locate Earth. Even with the optics zoomed to max, it was no blue marble from out here, just a steady white dot.

Home. Although it wasn't really, after all this time. After everything that had happened to that godforsaken planet. Still, Earth pulled at her.

And … there it was … and then … and then it was gone. Blocked by the massive bulk of the Ceres Galactic Gate as it swung above the horizon and cruised across the sky. That was fitting. The Gate got in the way of everything. She snorted. No sense stargazing now, the Gate's subtle shimmer was nausea inducing, and the superstructure so dark its progress across Ceres's sky was marked only by the stars it occluded.

"Fucking behemoth." She reached down and petted Rover's head, although his brain was actually hidden deep in his squat titanium body and his 'eyes' and 'ears' were located all over his scaled outer skin, including his six appendages. "Back to work, old boy." He pinged her HUD with a tongue-lolling doggy smile.

She sent him a rolling eyes emoji and resumed sweeping the bulky metal detector back and forth across the icy regolith. The metronomic chime quickened, deepening in tone.

Rover pawed at the gravel, raising a ghostly haze that persisted in the thin exosphere.

Grace hopped forward—gravity was hardly more than a suggestion on Ceres—and the steady bass beep continued.

"Whoa! It's big." Big was good. Generally scavenging didn't pay much. The resilience, ease of manufacture, and low cost of the new nano-carbons made most metals obsolete. Even a large wreck would have very little value but it all added up.

Aster-X Corp had 'retired' its old steel diggers, grapplers, and haulers out on the dwarf planet's surface. Ceres's subterranean seawater occasionally geysered through cracks in the lithosphere, instantaneously freezing into fragile plumes, or sometimes thick flows like lava. Frequent meteorite showers fractured the ice, hardening the omnipresent granular dust, shrouding the derelict hulks with a thick crust.

No one cared that it ruined the environment. Ceres City housed about twenty thousand, but its inhabitants and visitors were here only for the Gate. Clear domes in the public areas looked up at the slowly orbiting monstrosity, not out at the planetary surface. The only people who went outside were scavengers like Grace and Rover.

And the damned nosy AsterX police. Rover sent a cop emoji and a direction indicator to warn Grace they'd been made, but she'd already seen the distinctive form of Constable Joel King and his K9 companion Biz. Joel bobbed gracelessly over the ground toward them, and Biz trotted elegantly beside him.

Grace groaned.

Rover wasn't as irked. He liked Biz, like older dogs always like puppies. If he had a tail, it would've wagged.

But Biz was no puppy. He looked like a Doberman, sleek muscles rippling under what appeared to be velvety caramel fur. But a real Doberman needed to breathe and would have frozen to death within seconds of stepping out of the airlock unprotected. Besides, Dobermans—like all dogs—were probably extinct.

Biz was a next gen K9—spun from carbon fiber in a gravity-free factory, his 'brain' an integrated web of bio-crystals. Not a gram of metal in him, even his fearsome canines were made of a synthetic matrix harder than diamond. He gamboled over, wiggling his rear end, skittering about in the scree.

If the two K9's had touched noses, Grace would've puked right in her suit. It wasn't Biz's fault, but his tech, the same tech as the Gate superstructure, was the reason Grace had been 'retired.' Ceres was no longer the rough, raw mining colony it had been when she arrived thirty years ago as a green constable, when the biggest problem for law enforcement was dragging drunk engineers back to their kips.

The market for asteroid metals collapsed with the advent of carbon tech, but Aster-X Corp managed a pivot to fabrication and Gate construction. Without spun nano-carbon, space-fold travel would've stayed a theory—no metal alloy was strong enough to withstand the gravitational stresses.

Ceres City was a transit hub now, a stopover for wealthy colonists fleeing Earth, on their way to trash new worlds. With the new clientele, crime went upscale. Disagreements were no longer settled by a fist to the nose or a night in the drunk tank. Aster-X wanted cops with a sophisticated manner—enter, Constable Joel King and his ilk with their law degrees. Exit, Constable Grace Bremen with her antique K9 enforcer and frontier approach to justice.

Grace let the detector rest on the ground and switched it off.

"Hi, Grace," Joel said, his voice squeaky over the comms. "What are you doing out here?"

"Sightseeing, Joel." She pointed to the Gate. "But that damned thing keeps getting in the way."

"You been to see it?"

"Fuck, no. I don't trust that carbon stuff. It's too thin and wobbly."

Biz and Rover circled each other, playing some K9 training game involving complex spatial prediction. Biz was faster, but experience counted, and Rover usually won.

"All the shuttles are carbon now. If you go back to Earth—"

"When I go back to Earth."

Joel frowned. "Why would you? There's nothing there anymore."

They'd had this argument many times, and Joel always thought he'd won. He did have all the facts on his side. Earth was a wasteland. Grace had never been close to her siblings, and for all she knew they'd succumbed to an extreme weather event, died in some pointless conflict or had already traversed the Gate to colony worlds. She never made a convincing counterargument to Joel because she didn't quite understand her reasons herself. Hey, she liked space as much as the next person. Maybe more, as she'd chosen a career on Ceres. But she empathized with the planet that had given everything, only for human beings to discard her like a pair of holey socks. The people passing through Ceres City always moved forward, blinkered against the past and the destruction they'd wrought, eager to spread their stain out into the galaxy.

If she hadn't had to pay for Rover's expensive, high-mass transport, she would've been on Earth already.

"You aren't supposed to be out here," Joel said.

"You going to arrest me?"

"No! You're an ex-cop. Thin blue line and all that. I want the best for you, Grace, but you need to give this up." He waved back at Ceres City. "You could be playing cards at the senior center. Or engaged in a VR at the Demeter theatre." He slapped his gloved hand down on his padded thigh. "Hell ... there's a high-wire act set up in the new dome. They're really good."

"I like the quiet out here."

"Look. I know what you're doing. I can't keep covering for you."

"Scavenging's not against the law. As long as Aster-X gets their percentage, and they do."

He turned his head pointedly toward the detector. "Makes the Ceres Police Force look bad. Like you can't live on your pension."

Grace space-shrugged—holding her arms out elbows bent, palms up. "I can't."

Joel snorted. "If the brass gets the piss up about this, they could confiscate Rover and shut him down. You want that?"

No, she most definitely did not want that. But how else was she to make enough to pay for the trip to Earth? Her pension barely paid for room and board at a cheap bunkhouse in the oldest part of Ceres City.

He sighed again. "You're in an interdicted area too. It's not safe. I'm reading magnitude two tremors as we speak. You could be blasted into space by a sudden fumarole."

When she didn't reply, he huffed, summoned Biz, and they bounded off in the direction of the city. She and Rover watched until they disappeared over the horizon.

Rover tipped his head inquisitively.

"Magnitude two is nothing," she said.

Over her helmet speakers, came the whistling notes of "Don't Worry, Be Happy."

"Exactly. Joel is a patronizing mollycoddler."

Panting puppy emoji.

"Yah, I know you like Biz. Too bad he's hooked up with a cop."

The puppy emoji rolled its eyes.

"I know, I know. We're—or we were—cops too." She picked up a grinder-vacuum and attacked the frozen regolith where the detector indicated a hatch. "Let's get in quick." She stepped back to let Rover spin his scythe-like digging claws through the frozen clay.

Grace wasn't afraid of the low-level tremors she was also monitoring, but she couldn't deny there was risk. Would be embarrassing to call Joel for rescue if a steam vent blasted her and

Rover off planet. Once they were inside the buried junker, they'd be less exposed. Of course, if the vent was powerful enough, thick steel walls wouldn't save them. They'd be crushed and flash frozen.

Joel had been turning a blind eye to her scavenging for months, but she understood he couldn't keep doing it. Sooner or later, he'd file a report. Sooner if he had to sign out a Rescue Skiff to retrieve her sorry ass from an unintended spacewalk. Would they even attempt to recover Rover, or would he spin sunward forever?

Grace blew out hard, momentarily tripping the suit's CO_2 sensor.

Okay. This had to be their last scavenge. She couldn't risk having Rover taken from her. Couldn't bear thinking about him being shut off and junked. Or worse, he could end up hurtling through space, the solar batteries powering his brain fully charged for infinity. He would be alone.

She would be alone.

Maybe she should've had real kids, but she would've been a terrible mother. Too angry. Too stubborn. Over the years, Rover had mellowed her, but she was still damn stubborn, and he'd agree. Impatient, too. Rover had just sent her a Grace emoji tapping a foot, next to a spinning digger-claw emoji and a countdown clock displaying seconds. The counter wound down to zero, and Rover was done. He backed away from the hole.

His digging had exposed a circular port, emblazoned with the Aster-X logo, a purple flower centered by a chunk of shiny ore, stippled by thousands of collisions with abrasive space particles.

"Looks virgin." She rubbed her gloves together. Other salvage operators must have been scared off by the seismic activity because usually wrecks this close to Ceres City were already picked over. An untouched find could be the proverbial pot of gold. Maybe this would all come together after all. "Can you access a code for the hatch, Rov?"

Rover clicked a front paw against the touch pad and ran through a few combinations. When he hit the right one, a handle popped out and the door hissed open expelling a puff of ice crystals. He sent

Grace's HUD a detailed spec file after determining the make and model.

The schematics appeared, superimposed on her faceplate. "It is a big one. A Mule. Ice and mineral hauler." She pulled the access door wide with the lever.

Even though Mules were autonomous ships and routine maintenance was done by ultra-flexible robo-techs that fit in very tight spaces, human engineers had to inspect the workings sometimes, so the interior would be spacious enough for Grace and Rover to move about. Rover jumped into the airlock and waited for Grace to join him before he cycled them through, and they stepped out into a narrow, dark corridor. Grace activated her mag-boots and propped her tools against a wall while Rover closed the lock, keying it to only them.

Wouldn't be the first time a bigger salvage crew tried to appropriate their find.

Rover took point. The Mule was big, thirty meters long, thirty wide and fifteen deep the specs said. The hall to the bow skirted the edge of the cargo tank. Grace shined her wristlight through an internal port illuminating a big empty cavern, with grapple hooks retracted against the sidewalls. Mules scooped ice and ore that had already been churned up from the interior of Type-C asteroids by Gobblers. Once the hold was packed full, the Mule would mass with others in the form of a stepped vee. Under the direction of a single inter-system pilot the Mule team would traverse space to the smelter at Ceres. The pilots were called Brants, because some illiterate AsterX bureaucrat who didn't understand the concept of mixed metaphors thought the linked-up Mules looked like migrating geese.

The cargo hull appeared undamaged.

A tremor vibrated the floor, forceful enough to release one of Grace's mag-boots, and she swiveled, slamming against the wall before she could regain her balance. Her seismometer sensor fluctuated between two and three. Activity was escalating.

Rover hummed a few bars of a military march. Grace wasn't sure if he was commenting on the need to hustle, or her awkward recovery.

Further down the passageway, something hissed.

Rover sent Grace a night-vision image of a coiled machine high on a shelf. A head with four glittering eyes and alert, forward-pointing antennae whipped up. The rest of it uncurled, revealing a dozen different appendages spiraling about its long, flexible body.

A Skelekat. Its computer core would be encased in a few grams of jewelry quality rhodium alloy worth quite a few credits on the grey market.

The little robot immediately forwarded a compilation of maintenance activities since her last check in with her human supervisor more than ten years ago. The data stream unrolling on Grace's HUD sounded oddly like purring, although that could've been Rover's idea of a joke.

The kat's name was Lizzie.

Rover gave the robo-mechanic a power boost, and all three of them continued to the front of the hauler. Rover trotted, his four rear feet thudding on the metal flooring, Lizzie sinuously weaving between his legs. Grace lagged behind. When she realized she'd been thinking about dissecting a live, aware machine for a minor uptick in the credit column of her bank account, her stomach seethed.

What if the Mule was still aware too?

There wasn't much on a Mule worth anything, other than CP cases of sentient AIs. Maybe a little copper in contacts. Not nearly valuable enough to cover the cost of shipping a 130-kilogram Rover to Earth.

Lizzie had turned on the lights, allowing Grace to switch off the lamps on her head and wrist. The hallway's walls were unadorned gunmetal grey, except that every few feet there was a Skelekat-sized access-port into the outer conduits, color-coded white, yellow, red or green. They raised very little dust while walking, an indication that the hull was intact, and the seals hadn't failed.

The corridor widened into a foyer centered on a circular staircase winding around a cargo lift. Lizzie leaped on the banister and spiraled down, headfirst. Rover clomped down the metal steps, and Grace was just as clattery behind him. Lizzie bounced off at the next floor and scampered into a small but surprisingly human-friendly space. Two rows of four gimballed accel-couches sat in the middle of the compartment. A galley kitchen with faucets, food-synthesizer, and a cooler were located on one side, and on the other, a door to standard zero-gee washroom facilities. Straight ahead a wall of blank vid panels faintly glimmered.

This was no ordinary Mule.

Rover sent a shrugging emoji. This wasn't on the specs.

To the left of the vid panels, a door retracted upwards with a stuttered whine, and Lizzie slunk through the opening.

Grace followed, entering a small circular room walled with curved vid screens. This was the interface to the Mule and whatever other AIs were installed on board, but it appeared lifeless. The actual cores would be below this floor.

If the AIs were defunct, maybe this wouldn't be a dead loss.

Lizzie jumped onto the nearest vid panel, clung like a limpet and pressed one of her many appendages against the screen. The vid flickered to life, pulsing waves of bright blue, fluorescent green, then pink. The colored light undulated out to all the other vids like an aurora borealis.

A female voice broke into Grace's personal comm. "Welcome Constable Grace Bremen Retired to Mule Lead One. You may call me Vera. It's been a longtime since I've been online. Please excuse me while I update."

A 4-D holo of the solar system, marking planetary bodies and projected orbits, formed right in front of Grace, and on the vid, pulses of red and gold reverberated, like the recording of a heartbeat.

Rover sent her a detailed report, based on what he gleaned, as Vera ran a systems check.

"Wow." This Mule—Vera—was partnered with a Brant pilot

and a comm-LADAR warning system nicknamed Rooster for the irritating tone of its alarms. Before she was mothballed, Vera ferried Aster-X management out to the mining sites and needed to be capable of independent operation.

The ship was a treasure trove. Probably several kilos of rhodium.

For a moment she allowed herself to think about what that was worth. How much they'd have left over once they'd paid their fare, how she'd have enough to buy a ranch in one of the safer locations, perhaps New Zealand, where the temperatures and weather were relatively mild.

She looked back at Rover. He couldn't see her face, but he knew her so well. He sent a hug emoji.

Vera snorted delightedly, as she exercised the ship's systems, reminding Grace of a horse trotting the edge of an open field, energized by the vista of unfenced country. The Brant updated positioning and calculated a few trajectories based on current locations: Mars. Titan. Pallas. The Rooster tested his inputs— antennae and sensors, then verified alarm output.

Quite a cheery cacophony.

How could she shut these AI's down? Frankly, even if she tried, Rover probably wouldn't help her.

Her dream of going to Earth was over.

It was a dumb dream anyway. Ceres wasn't such a bad place. She could deal. Grace couldn't wipe her eyes under her faceplate. She sniffed, but the tears trickled down her cheeks anyway and pooled in her collar.

She swallowed and breathed deeply. So ... what now? The Skelekat could come home with her. In her neighborhood, the robo-mechanic would be welcome, and she'd be happy there, fixing vids, synthesizers and disposals. But the others couldn't be removed from the ship. They were so happy to be awake and working—how could she put them back to sleep again?

If she could find this ship, other scavengers would too whenever seismic activity in the area decreased. Those bastards were amoral.

They'd have no qualms about looting the core for even a few ounces of rare metal, and this would be a large haul, worth thousands of credits.

She sent Rover her conclusions, and he growled in frustration.

Gradually the flickering lights of Vera's vids were replaced by virtual gauges displaying system status updating in real time: life support, connectivity, hull integrity, resources, cargo. EM Drive. Every system green—except for cargo, which showed capacity available.

The Brant honked ready.

Rooster crowed, all clear.

Rover barked.

"Constable Grace Bremen," Vera asked, "Where are we going?"

The steady rumble under Grace's boots was not another tremor. The engines were spooling up for launch.

Constable Joel King was going to be so surprised.

"Earth please, Vera."

I PROMISED THE BROWN HARE PRINCE

Rhea Rose

In the tall butterfly sun-grass,
left of stone-lined paths,
in day's twilight,
There!—Prince of Hares,
velvet ears scraping stars,
dark, damp stones for eyes,
serene and deep,
still.

My feline-licking wild ways
haunt Nature's flocks,
where all around me whispers prey
in Summer's breath.
Small flickings, crawlies, chasing rounds,
huntress follows, pacing down,
whiskers sense His shadowed den.

Pausing in a meadowed glen,
in stalks of yellow, grassy winds,
I pounce, alight like breath's soft breeze,
killing gentle, mild creatures,
claws waxing, wicked feline's ease.
I graze the Prince.

Tumbling clasping, tabby breast
pressed hard against his feral kicks,
and then, from him, an unexpected kiss,
ferocious, wild, untamed bliss.

His manner loved my felis furs,
my silvestris moods, my tabby purrs,
two twisting in herbaceous breath,
hot hearts' locked under thrumming moon,
embraced in Summer's resting sweat,
feral hearts in synchronous bloom
locked, liquid panting breaths,
hard beats under a rose-hot moon.
I promised the Brown Hare Prince.

Our leveret kittens dream in clover,
longing weeds of thyme clotted cream,
black-topped moon tails over berms
capture field mice, trembling birds,
tuxedoed, tabbies brown tuft flanks
Our wild children gambol box,
drum, thump, pounce,
feral fast, rough tongues clean
in spring's green herbs,
where they hunt their softer cousins.

Wild, sharp-toothed herbivores, our tender shoots.
In carnivorous delight, I obligate,
but promised not to chase
our children eating chives.
I promised.

THE HARE'S CHOICE

Alison Colwell

When Chloe bounded through the long grass, the small silver whistle on a cord around her neck pounding rhythmically against her chest bone, as if she still had a heartbeat. As she passed, voles scurried to their burrows in alarm, their own hearts racing in fear. Crickets burst from the long grass.

The lawn at the front of the old house was clipped and tidy where it faced the street. The back was unmowed. The wild meadow was a perfect hiding place for all manner of small creatures, including her, one of Artemis' Hares. Chloe swerved around the two-wheeler dumped on its side, almost hidden in the long grass, its frame speckled orange with rust. Sparkly pink tassels clung to the handlebars and swayed in the breeze. Chloe slowed, as she hopped near. She crept beneath the drooping lilac bush, kept to the shadows against the old house. She would have enjoyed the leftover heat radiating off the flaking wood siding if she could still feel warmth.

Before Arti had found her, before she'd become stuck in this world though no longer a part of it, she'd ridden her own pink bicycle covered in unicorn stickers. Chloe had lived in a ramshackle house a lot like this, at the edge of Jordan River. It also had one main street, one traffic light, and an elementary school. High school was a thirty-minute bus ride to the closest city.

Chloe still had a few more years at the elementary, but the coming transition to the "big" school loomed large in her fears. At least in Jordan no one cared that she only wore clothes from the thrift. Half the other kids shopped there too. They played in culverts, splashed through tide pools. Eelgrass stuck to their shoes, as they combed beaches looking for sea glass and other flotsam from around the world. In Jordan, none of the kids took tennis lessons or gymnastics.

Looking back, Chloe felt dumb for spending so much time worrying about high school. She'd never finish Grade Six.

Through the thin walls of the old house, Chloe could hear the family inside. She'd stood outside every night for the last week. There was a wrongness to the house that made her whiskers twitch. It was more than the perfect front lawn contrasting with the unkempt backyard. The house smelled of sharp sadness. Arti sent her hares to find the wrongness, and Chloe took the assignment seriously. When she discovered the source, one note on her whistle would bring Artemis and her Hounds.

But after a week of watching, Chloe still hesitated to sound her whistle. She wasn't sure who to blame for the swirling undercurrents of tension inside the house.

Olive, the six-year-old owner of the abandoned bicycle, was upstairs, brushing her teeth and singing.

"Must you make such a racket?" yelled Olive's father.

"She's only singing," said Olive's mom Christy, coming into the living room from the kitchen. "She's not hurting you."

"My head is killing me. And she never stops."

"Peter, she's just a child."

"She should have more respect. I'm the one paying the mortgage on this heap of shit. I'm entitled to a little peace in my home."

"It's our home too," snapped Christy.

Chloe winced. *Why did she always talk back?* Chloe's long ears twitched, anticipating the heavy slap that always followed Christy's sharp replies. Olive had fallen silent. Chloe listened till she heard the laboured tread of Christy going upstairs.

Instead of leaping away into the night, she stayed to listen to the next chapter of *The Candy Shop War* that Christy was reading to Olive. When Chloe had been a girl, it had been her favourite book too. She was so engrossed in the story she didn't hear the screen door opening. The empty beer bottle hit her thigh, and she bounded off into the long grass.

When Chloe was a girl, she'd heard plenty of fights late at night when her parents hoped she was asleep. She'd lain quietly and listened to the *pop fizz* of her dad's beer cans punctuating the drone of the TV, the rattle of dishes, the rumble of the dryer. There were accusations; "never enough," "not what I signed up for," then slaps and sobs. When the yelling started, she stayed in her room. Until the last day. She'd never asked her mom about the bruises, but she didn't understand why her mom didn't tell him to stop. There was so much she hadn't understood, so much she still didn't understand.

Christmas break had changed everything. At ten years old,

she'd learned to manage her expectations, but that Christmas, after Chloe unwrapped the pale-pink polaroid camera that she'd written to Santa about, she'd dived onto the couch between her parents to take a selfie of the three of them. When she studied the photo later, her dad was frowning. He looked as surprised as Chloe. She wondered how her mom had squirrelled away enough money to buy the camera.

Chloe raced to the end of the driveway that led toward the old log cabin perched at the edge of the forest. She stayed hidden in the long grass and waited. An hour passed. Then a pale-blue pickup truck rattled past, spitting pebbles off the track, a shotgun visible through the dusty glass of the back window. The driver's door swung open with a squeal of metal, and Arti stepped out. Blue jeans tucked into worn cowboy boots. The setting sun illuminated the whisps of hair that had escaped her long braid.

Then the hounds caught up. The first dog thrust its chestnut head into Arti's hand, its spotted coat quivering. In seconds, the rest of the pack had surrounded the truck. They bayed, and Arti laughed. She tossed out treats until she'd congratulated them all on their skills. The hounds did not impress Chloe. The old truck was so noisy that even she could have tracked it across the county. *You don't need to be a hunting dog for that.*

Arti swung open the front door, then paused, framed in the golden radiance flooding out the open doorway. She looked back, and Chloe knew that while the hounds had missed her ghostly presence, Arti had not.

"Are you coming in?" Arti called.

Chloe limped forward, her injured hip throbbing. As she crossed the cabin's threshold, the golden light fell over her soft fur, her body stretched and unfolded, and she appeared her old self again. The first time it happened, Chloe had paused in front of a mirror, thrilled to recognize the girl she once was. But returning to her old form grew more complicated as time passed. When she was Chloe the hare, she found a kind of peace. Chloe the girl, was still angry.

"Find anything?" asked Arti once she'd lit the fire in the grate and sat down. Stuffing burst from one arm of her favourite chair, where sharp teeth had worried at the fabric. One of the new puppies crawled onto Arti's lap, and she absentmindedly stroked its plump stomach.

"Not sure," said Chloe. After checking to make sure none of the other hares were in the cabin, she curled up in the second armchair near the fire, pleased to have Arti to herself.

"Still?"

"I need to be sure he's to blame."

"You do. But remember, we're trying to keep other girls safe."

"My dad never meant to hurt me," defended Chloe.

But it was an old argument they'd had many times before, and Arti didn't bother to respond. In Arti's world, what someone might have meant had no bearing on fact. Her dad had hurt her. For Arti, it was simple.

Chloe let her eyes close, imagined going to sleep. Wondered what life might have been like if she'd been a girl who'd slept in front of a fire, with a watchful guardian and a room full of protective hounds. Sleep might have been something she enjoyed. As she settled deeper into the chair, she wondered if Olive felt safe, or if Olive had already learned it was safer to sleep fully dressed.

The next day, Chloe went to the house earlier. Her leg still smarted from the bottle Peter had aimed at her, and she slipped into the shadows under the front stairs, where she hoped to stay invisible. Arti was being patient, but Chloe knew she was running out of time.

Sooner rather than later, they'd move on to the next small town. Then Olive would have no one to watch out for her. Chloe needed to decide.

Chloe's long ears twitched, as she held still and listened. Peter was at work. Christy was home alone, like she was every day. She could pack up and leave anytime.

Why didn't she?

Why had her own mom stayed? By ten, Chloe had realized not everyone's mom covered bruises with makeup before they left the house. So why hadn't her mom protected them both by leaving?

Chloe was waiting for Olive to arrive home from school. After the yellow bus dropped her at the end of the drive, Olive always tore into the house, bursting with stories about her day. Olive loved kindergarten. Chloe remembered loving kindergarten too. She hadn't worried how others might see her, or about her future. Every kid was her next best friend because she hadn't seen the differences between them. She hadn't yet questioned the choices her mom made. Chloe was so lost in her own memories, she didn't notice the car approaching.

Peter's heavy tread on the porch stairs shook the dust into Chloe's fur.

"Everything okay?" Olive's mom asked as the screen door slammed shut.

"Don't nag me," Peter snapped.

Then Chloe smelled it, a scent she remembered, wood and smoky earth. She felt her hair bristle. Her dad had smelled like that sometimes.

"You're drunk!" accused Christy. "It's three in the afternoon."

The whistle felt like ice on Chloe's chest. Say nothing. Just go, she whispered. Why did she always stand up to him? Couldn't she see that she provoked him? And when violence erupted, who was to blame?

But then Christy finally heard Chloe's silent prayers.

"What are you doing?" Peter demanded. Chloe flinched as

Peter's voice echoed above her. She imagined Christy slipping on her coat, grabbing the keys from the hook by the door.

"I'm going out. Olive will be home any minute. You can't want her to see you like this? We'll go to my sister's."

Leave, whispered Chloe. *Get far away from him.*

She felt the thud through the boards above her head.

"Stupid bitch," Peter snarled. "You're not going anywhere. I'm hungry."

Chloe held her breath.

She heard Christy struggling to stand.

"Make your own supper. I can't do this anymore," hissed Christy. "I'm tired of being your drudge, tired of the way you don't see me anymore. Tired of your rages and your fists. I kept thinking the man I married might return, but it's never going to happen. It's time I took Olive away, before she grows up thinking all men are bastards."

Chloe heard the door open. She saw the flash of a flowered skirt, as Christy tumbled into the yard. Chloe's nose twitched, alarmed at the copper scent.

"Fine! Leave if you must. You always were worthless. But you aren't taking my daughter anywhere. Olive belongs here with her father."

Christy struggled to her feet. A thin line of red streaked from her lip, drops of blood splashed on her dress, red blooming in the midst of peach flowers.

"I'll tell everyone what kinda man you are!" Christy yelled.

"And who'll believe you? I work in the planning office. I've had lunch with the mayor. You're nothing but a logger's daughter. Leave and you won't ever see Olive again."

It had been very late, and Chloe should've been in bed. Instead, she was fussing with her photos. She'd taped them to her wardrobe and was rearranging them, straightening the edges. She heard her parents fighting, winced at the sound of blows. Froze at the sound of running feet on the stairs.

"Leave her alone," her mom said.

"You spent my money on that ridiculous present. My money! You think we have money to waste?"

"At least I'm not drinking it away."

Chloe had heard the impact then, the sound of her father's fist landing on her mother's soft skin, right on the other side of her bedroom door. She'd grabbed her new camera and rushed out. She didn't want her mom hurt because of her stupid Christmas wish.

"Take it …" she said.

Too late.

Her father shoved his hands against her mother's chest. Chloe saw the alarm flare in her mom's eyes, as she stumbled backwards. Her heels slipped off the top step, her arms flailed madly. Chloe reached out to take her mom's hand, her new camera spilling from her open fingers. She tried to help. And the two of them tumbled down the stairs together.

And suddenly Chloe understood.

Leaving took bravery, but it also took bravery to stay and endure. Because a mother's choice wasn't always black and white. Her mom had been trying to protect her, had died trying to protect her. Chloe realized she wasn't mad at her anymore. Her mom had done her best, even if she failed in the end. But her dad? Arti was right, after all.

From under the stairs, Chloe heard the approaching school bus. She looked at Christy, saw fear in her face, and knew she'd go back inside that house. Because that was the only way she could protect her daughter, to ensure her body stayed between Olive and Peter's rage.

"Arti," Chloe whispered. "I'm certain."

Golden light blazed around Chloe, as she shifted from a hare back to a girl. She raised the silver whistle to her lips and blew. One long piercing note. In the far distance she heard the answering bay of the hounds.

At the top of the porch steps, where the golden light had fallen, Peter also shifted. A great white stag leaped over the railing. It paused, antlered head turning to Chloe. She saw panic in his eyes, recognized the same despair she'd lived with for so long. She hoped Olive would grow up without that fear. Chloe hoped she'd given Olive that chance.

The roar of the hounds grew louder, as they raced over meadows and tracks, across ditches and through the forest, coming closer and closer. Artemis' hounds, bred for one purpose, to hunt those who preyed on the girls and women who couldn't protect themselves.

TWISTED ROOTS

Leslie Wibberley

Heavy morning dew dampens the bottom of Eiosen's skirts, as she makes her daily trek down the hill to reinforce the wards protecting her land. The sight that greets her at the bottom freezes her in place and sends a skittering of ice down her back.

Thousands of white filaments have spread across the invisible wall of magic that rises above the boundary stones.

Filaments that were not there yesterday. Nor any day, for that matter.

Eiosen presses a gnarled fist against her chest, as if this will settle the desperate thudding of her heart. This new development is far more concerning than the dying garden, her rapidly aging body, or even the weakening wards.

She has been so diligent in maintaining the wards, and these are the strongest she'd ever summoned. It should have been impossible for the Tree to find this place, but for months now, thick underbrush and tall grasses have been creeping steadily toward the stones. The

Tree has been pressing in harder and harder, but there has never been an attack like this before.

Eiosen's hands shake with urgency, as she unties the small leather bag dangling from her neck. Her arthritic fingers catch on the opening, and she winces as she removes her touchstone. The polished moonstone's familiar weight settles into her palm, grounding her. She begins to chant. Immediately, the filaments writhe, as if in pain. They stretch thinner and thinner, until they fall away and turn to dust as they hit the ground.

Bracing her hands on her knees, she takes a stuttering breath. This spell is simple, one she could perform in her sleep. Yet the effort has left her so drained; her lungs are screaming for air, and her feet are made of stone. Straightening a back bowed with age, she shuffles further along the boundary.

And then she sees Pren.

The girl is standing by the stones behind the cottage, both hands pressed up against the invisible wall. On the other side, new filaments dance as if trying to wrap around her fingers. Pren's eyes are closed, and she appears to be listening to something.

"Pren! Get away from there." Eiosen stumbles toward the girl, panic swelling like a thundercloud.

Pren looks up, eyes glassy and vacant.

Eiosen reaches the girl and drags her unresisting form away from the wall. Stepping in front of her, Eiosen holds her moonstone and chants. More filaments squirm and fall away. Pren blinks her eyes and emerges from the strange trance.

"What are you doing?" cries Pren.

"Saving you," says Eiosen. "If those things breach the wards, it will be the end of you." Eiosen shudders. Or at least the end of this version of you. She takes a few more steps along the stones and chants again. More filaments fall away.

Pren grabs Eiosen's arm. "But you're killing them."

Eiosen stares at Pren's hand, startled by the frenetic urgency of her grip. "Yes, Pren, that is the point."

"But they were singing to me. To me!"

Singing? Eiosen's pulse flutters at her throat like a frightened sparrow. How is this possible? The wards should have prevented any contact between the Tree and the girl. Eiosen brushes Pren's hand aside and hurries along the ring of stones, repeating the process.

"Stop!" Pren's eyes are wide, wild—desperate. The wind whips her silver-tipped hair into a tangled mess. "Please, Grandmother."

Eiosen takes Pren's hand and squeezes. "I'm sorry, but I can't do that," she says, unable to suppress the regret she feels for causing the girl distress.

Pren tries to wrestle the stone from Eiosen's fingers. Although her spine may be bent and her muscles wizened with age, Eiosen's body is still sturdy enough to thwart the slender girl's attempt. With a scream of rage, Pren shoves blindly at Eiosen's chest. Eiosen flails her arms and takes a step backward to maintain her balance.

Pren's unexpected act of violence sends a flash of white-hot rage through Eiosen, and she slaps Pren across the cheek. Redness blooms across the girl's pale, almost translucent skin.

They stare at each other in surprised horror. Eiosen has never so much as raised her voice to Pren, let alone struck her.

Eiosen takes a deep breath and exhales. She must stay calm. There is work to do.

Touching her cheek with a tentative finger, Pren says, "You hit me."

Eiosen hardens her heart against the girl's accusatory gaze. "I'm sorry, but I'm doing this for your own good."

Pren's eyebrows shoot upward. "How is killing something so beautiful helping me?"

"It's complicated," says Eiosen. So complicated.

"Please, Grandmother. Let them be."

"No." Eiosen doesn't have the energy to continue this argument. "Now go and finish your work." She glares at Pren, infusing her gaze with just a smidge of magic—she doesn't dare more than that. Not now, when her supply is so limited and lessening each day.

Taking a deep breath, Eiosen resumes her task.

Pren lets out a frustrated scream, but she obeys and stomps back up the hill. Eiosen has never seen Pren this upset before. A few minor tantrums when she was younger, but nothing like this absolute fury. It's as if the girl unconsciously recognizes her connection with the mycelium. Guilt mushrooms in Eiosen's chest, and she harrumphs, disgusted with herself. She's growing soft in her dotage. She reminds herself that no matter how different Pren may be, how much she tugs at Eiosen's heart, she is still a failure.

Just like all the others.

Eiosen continues her journey around the stones. Her palm still stings from the slap. She flexes her hand, thumb absently rubbing the stumps of her two missing fingers, lost the same day Pren had come into her life.

Desperate to obtain a sapling that would hold onto its magic, Eiosen had dared to steal one that rested directly against the braided trunks of the Mother Tree—a yew known as Coeden y Bywyd. She'd been so certain this would solve the problem of the disappearing magic. Unlike the other saplings she'd stolen from the Tree's distant shadows, Eiosen had dared to take the one destined to become the new Mother Tree.

As Eiosen pulled the sapling from the earth, the yew had retaliated violently. The fingers ripped from her hand dropped to the ground in a pool of blood and were immediately engulfed in a network of white threads.

A fair exchange, Eiosen had thought as she fled into the dark night. Two pieces of her flesh for a single piece of the yew. She ran with her precious bounty clutched to her chest, and Eiosen's blood seeped into the sapling's bark, forging a permanent bond between them.

The yew, however, had not considered it a fair exchange, and has remained relentless in her efforts to destroy Eiosen and reclaim that sapling.

The network of mycelium is a new tactic. That Pren could hear it "singing" means the yew is getting dangerously close to achieving her goal.

Eiosen's body deflates. She is so tired.

For the briefest of moments she considers giving up, but then she realizes this fight with the Tree has been the one constant in her life. Their relationship, albeit a toxic one, is the longest she's had.

No sooner does this thought arrive, then another explodes in her head. Could it be that this is what she has been searching for? A connection? All the specimens she's stolen over the years, all of the sacrifices made to extend her life—were they nothing but her desire to not be alone?

Staring at the filaments crawling across the wards, she considers this possibility. Eiosen shakes her head. Ridiculous. She simply wanted the power.

Pulling herself as erect as her twisted spine will allow, she continues around the boundary and performs the same spell every few feet. When all the filaments have been vanquished and the wards reinforced, she trudges up the path to the cottage.

The door creaks open, and she steps inside. Pren's bedroom door is closed, but no sound emerges. Eiosen wonders if Pren has forgiven her. Should she try to talk to her? Her hand reaches for the doorknob, but she stops herself. Don't be so soft. The girl is merely a means to an end. Remember that.

The girl will die; there is no other option. And if Eiosen is to perform the final harvest, she must gather the items required to preserve the organs.

A vision of her curved blade slicing through Pren's pale flesh sends a wave of nausea through Eiosen's belly. The muscles in her chest clench, and her breath catches. She closes her eyes and forces air into her lungs. Be strong, Eiosen.

She grabs the shears and a gathering basket and storms outside. The door slams shut behind her.

The garden has been steadily failing for weeks now, proof of the girl's fading magic, but as Eiosen walks through the rows of dying potatoes, corn, and herbs, she is shocked at how far the devastation has progressed in a single day. It is a struggle to find enough lavender and rosemary for her needs.

Once she gathers the ingredients, she heads to a stand of pine trees behind the garden. Pine sap is a vital part of her recipe. She will add it to rock salt, oil, and the herbs once they are dried.

She touches the bark, and thinks of the sapling that she'd turned into Pren. Eiosen transformed all the stolen saplings into human form, but never a baby. Not until Pren. A baby with the same silky blonde curls that had been Eiosen's pride in her youth. Pale skin the color of heartwood, yet quick to blush from the taint of human blood. Eiosen's blood. Pren was her daughter as much as the Mother Tree.

Eiosen squeezes her eyes tight and banishes the images from her mind. She must not be weak. Like every other sapling Eiosen has harvested, Pren has served her purpose. Eiosen returns to the cottage to find the hearth cold and Pren sitting on the floor, surrounded by a collection of dusty jars.

Eiosen's chest tightens, shooting pain into her left shoulder. She closes her eyes. For almost a century—through nine attempts, nine failures, and nine harvests—she has managed to keep those jars safely hidden beneath the floorboards. She never anticipated having to explain them. She considers turning and running from the room. But that is the coward's way, and while she might be considered a monster, she is no coward. Bracing herself, she opens her eyes and lifts her chin.

Pren's gaze darts from Eiosen to the jars, and then back. Her posture is rigid, her pupils constricted. She holds up a jar containing slender, jointed bones. "What are these?"

"Finger bones," Eiosen says bluntly. No point in denying the truth.

Sparks of a strange green light flash in Pren's eyes. "Why on Earth did you hide a jar of finger bones under the floor?" She sets the jar down and picks up one that holds several human molars. "And these, where did these come from?"

Eiosen stares at the remains of her last harvest, the sapling that came before Pren. Each jar contains items gleaned from each specimen. Their residual magic only lasts for a few months. It's long gone now. She only keeps these things to remind her of her failures. She imagines Pren's reaction if she were to reveal the truth. A bitter smile tugs at her lips. She couldn't bear to see the horror on Pren's face if she told her about the harvests, the way Eiosen absorbed their magic by consuming Pren's predecessors.

Pren stands and plants her hands on her bony hips. "Tell me!"

The girl's demanding tone fills Eiosen with a spark of self-righteous anger. Why does she care what Pren thinks? The girl wouldn't exist but for her. She has no right to question Eiosen. "Those things belong to me. How dare you touch them?!"

Pren's rigid posture softens, her gaze remorseful. "I'm sorry, Grandmother."

The girl's unexpected apology melts something inside Eiosen. Her anger vanishes, replaced with contrition. When had she allowed Pren such power over her emotions?

"I was just curious." Pren takes a tentative step toward Eiosen.

Eiosen pats the girl's arm. Maybe she can offer a diluted version of the truth to buy herself a little more time. "It's a long story. Are you sure you want to hear?"

"Yes." Pren's voice is quiet but determined.

Wiping her palms against the folds of her slate gray skirt, Eiosen says, "Fine, but first, you light a fire. I'll get dinner started."

Pren gives her a suspicious glance. "You're going to make dinner?"

Eiosen says, "I can cook, you know."

Pren turns but not before Eiosen sees a tiny smile curve the girl's lips. That shouldn't lift her heart the way it does, but she is helpless in the face of Pren's happiness.

Pren adds kindling to the logs in the hearth and uses the flint to create a spark. Soon, the wood is ablaze. The fire lends a cozy, comforting energy to the cottage, as the stone walls reflect the golden glow, spreading heat throughout the small space. Pren faces the fire, her hands outstretched to receive its warmth.

It has been a while since Eiosen has cooked, but she remembers the basics. She pulls a few carrots and potatoes from the bin by the kitchen cupboard, washes, peels, and chops them. Next, she adds onions, bay leaf, and rosemary to the rabbit Pren had skinned and cut up earlier, then dumps it all into a cast iron pot. Once the stew is bubbling over the fire, she takes a deep breath, wondering how to begin.

The girl turns as Eiosen pulls a chair closer to the hearth, waves her over, and says, "Sit."

Pren lowers herself to the chair in a graceful motion that reminds Eiosen of a young willow bending under the force of the wind. She folds her arms protectively across her belly and stares unblinkingly at Eiosen.

Eiosen stumbles over her words, worried she is telling too much and yet too little. Haltingly, she explains how she had transformed a sapling from the Tree into a human-like baby. That she had not, as she had oft told Pren, found her as a tiny babe lying in the woods beside the bodies of her parents, both dead of the plague. The name she gave her creation, to honor her origins, means "woods" in the old tongue.

Pren's eyes widen, then narrow again. After another long moment of silence, she asks, "So, you've been lying to me for my entire life?"

Eiosen gives the stew a stir, then turns back to Pren. "About your parents, yes."

Pren's eyes flash green, as she jumps to her feet. "The wards that supposedly keep me safe from that plague, the wards that have kept me trapped here on this tiny piece of land for my entire life, those are also a lie?"

Eiosen rubs her forehead to ease the pain that thrums through her skull. "The wards are real; the reason for their existence is not. There is no plague. Never has been."

Pren paces across the room. Her footsteps thud against the planked floor. Green sparks rise in tiny tendrils from her hair and dance about her head.

Shockwaves ripple through Eiosen. She hasn't been able to access more than a trickle of Pren's magic for over a week. How can there still be this much coursing through the girl's body? Eiosen had never witnessed an obvious display from any of the saplings. The magic was always just there for her to use, replenishing daily until it finally faded at the specimen's maturity.

Eiosen's aging body and the dying garden are proof that Pren's magic should be coming to an end. So, what is happening here?

Thoughts swirl in a dizzying circle through Eiosen's mind. Is it possible that letting Pren live this long has caused a shift in her magic? What if it had never faded at all, but is now just so closely linked to the girl, Eiosen can no longer access it?

Pren stops pacing and spins around to face Eiosen. "I'm not sure if I believe you, but even if I do, what does any of that have to do with these things I found under the floor."

Eiosen takes another deep breath. This is where her story must deviate from the truth. Choosing her words cautiously, she spins a web of lies like an orb weaver spider. "They're just things I found on my travels. I kept them in case I needed them for a spell one day. They've been down there so long I'd forgotten they were there."

"I don't believe you."

Eiosen stares at the girl, surprised by her blunt statement. "Why not?"

"If they are so unimportant, why did you hide them from me?"

Eiosen scrambles for an answer. "I ... I didn't want to frighten you."

Pren narrows her eyes, clearly still not believing her. "What were those white threads that were crawling over the wards?"

Nervous energy floods Eiosen's body, and she wrings her hands. "I promise to explain, but first, let me tell you why I stole that sapling in the first place."

Pren drops back into her chair. Her clenched fists tremble like she's trying to stop herself from hitting something. Probably Eiosen.

Eiosen suppresses the urge to comfort her. "I've been on my own for so many years, I've lost count. Desperately lonely, I longed for companionship, but was not welcome in any village. I created you, a child to love and tend to, and who would grow to love and tend me in return. A child of my heart, if not my womb."

Eiosen's lies suddenly feel far too much like the truth. She had been lonely. Empty, hollow, and so alone.

"But with all your magic, why did you need to steal a tree? Couldn't you just have performed a spell and created a child from the ethers."

"That is impossible. No witch, no matter their strength, can create life from nothing. And I chose a sapling from Coeden y Bywyd because of the yew's longevity. I wanted this child I created to live as long as I did."

This much was true. The Mother Tree was even more ancient than Eiosen, and her saplings should have lived equally as long—if Eiosen had allowed them to. Pren does not need to know the real reason she chose the yew was because of its regenerative magic.

Pren's expression shifts from anger to disbelief to confusion and finally into a disconcerted frown. Eiosen is surprised at the complexity of the emotions dancing across her face. It's so profoundly human.

"I raised you from a tiny baby, so helpless, so fragile. I fed you, protected you, taught you—I cared for you as if you were my own child. Is that such a terrible thing?"

"But …" Pren presses her palms against her eyes. "I'm not human. I never was. So, what am I?"

"You are Pren, and I love you," says Eiosen, finally acknowledging the truth. There is no way she is going to kill Pren. Does this mean she is no longer a monster? Could loving Pren be enough to redeem her?

"How did you find the jars?"

Pren's cheeks flush. "Each time you leave the cottage, I search for a way to breach the wards, for a way to escape this place. I stepped on a loose board and when I pried it up, I found them beneath.

"Escape?" Eiosen's lungs refuse to draw in air, as if a massive weight has dropped onto her chest. "You want to leave?" The sense of betrayal is preposterous. Only minutes before, she believed she was going to kill Pren and harvest her organs. She has no right to feel this way.

Pren looks at Eiosen as if she can't believe she needed to ask, and Eiosen realizes the girl is far better at subterfuge than she ever dreamed. She had Eiosen completely fooled. "Of course, I do. I love you Grandmother, or at least I did; I'm not so sure anymore. But you can't possibly think I could be satisfied living here, with only you for company, for the rest of my life? I want, no, I need to find out where I belong."

Eiosen clutches her chest, as another stab of pain that radiates down her left arm and around the middle of her back. "I can't let you leave, Pren. I'm dying and don't want to be alone when it happens. I need you to stay with me until I'm gone. Then the wards will fall, and you can leave."

Pren's eyes widen. "You're dying? But how? I thought you were immortal."

"Immortality comes with a grave cost. One I am no longer willing to pay."

Pren looks confused. "But can't you just make another baby like you made me?"

Eiosen shakes her head. "Even if I wanted to, The Mother Tree will never allow me to steal another sapling. This is the end for me."

Pren's face crumples. "I can't … this is … too much. It's all too much."

"I'm sorry," Eiosen says. Because she really is.

Pren blinks away the tears filming her eyes. "The Mother Tree? Why do you call it that?"

"Because she is the one who nurtures the forest and all the creatures who live there."

Pren's face twists. "Those white things on the wards, do they have something to do with this tree?"

Eiosen's heart feels as if giant hands are crushing it. "Yes. They are called mycelium. They connect the Mother Tree to the entire forest."

"But why were they singing to me?"

"Because she wants to bring you home. You are destined to become the new Mother Tree when she dies."

Face blanching, Pren takes a step away from Eiosen. "Home?"

The girl's terrified expression makes Eiosen want to wrap her arms around her and hold her close. Slowly, cautiously, she reaches out and places her hands on Pren's shoulders. "If you stay here with me, you will be safe." But for how long?

Pren shoves her away. "This is ridiculous. I don't want to stay here, and I don't want to be a … a … tree." Two round circles of red form on Pren's cheeks. "This is all your fault. Why did you do this to me?"

"I'm sorry, Pren." She doesn't know what else to say.

Pren rushes to her bedroom and slams the door behind her. Eiosen tries to imagine what is going through Pren's mind. Is she plotting a way to escape?

Eiosen taps on the girl's door, although she's not sure why. She has nothing more to offer. When there is no reply, she hobbles to her own room and climbs into bed. Her dreams are filled with visions of Pren being wrapped in a web of white threads.

The next day, Pren's door is still shut. Eiosen heads outside but only makes it halfway through recharging the wards before her legs give out. She collapses to the ground, struggling to catch her breath.

Footsteps announce Pren's arrival. Eiosen's heart lifts. Renewed by a burst of energy, she staggers to her feet and faces Pren. But instead of offering a welcoming smile, Pren stares defiantly into Eiosen's eyes and places her hand on the newly empty space on the invisible wall. The white filaments immediately reappear, blooming beneath her touch like frost on a windowpane.

Furious, Eiosen tries to shove her away, but this time it is the girl who thwarts Eiosen's attempt. Pren easily plucks the stone from Eiosen's hand and gently slides it into the bag around her neck.

"No," cries Eiosen. You don't understand what will happen if they break through."

"Maybe not, but I will fight this battle on my own. I don't want or need your help."

Pren's entire body begins to glow with an ethereal green light. Emerald fire shoots upward from her head, like bolts of verdant lightning.

Eiosen takes a step backward, her mouth gaping. Pren seems to grow taller, her limbs elongating like the branches of a tree, as she evolves into an entirely new being, beautiful and terrifying. One who commands both the yew's magic as well as Eiosen's.

Pren directs her fiery, green gaze toward Eiosen. "I made you some willow bark tea to ease your pain. Go back inside and rest." Her voice is deeper, more robust.

"What are you going to do?" asks Eiosen. Surely, with all this magic surging through Pren's body, The yew won't be able to contain her.

"I don't know, but it's up to me to figure it out, not you." She turns her back on Eiosen. "Now, leave me."

The strength of Pren's command leaves Eiosen no choice but to comply. She plods back to the cottage. There is a pot of still steaming tea resting on the kitchen table. She pours herself a cup and sits in her chair by the window. This is no longer her battle; it's Pren's.

The willow bark soothes her, and she drifts on the edge of sleep. She hears Pren open the door and walk to her bedroom, but Eiosen can't summon the energy to open her eyes. The bedroom door closes with a solid thud, and eventually, Eiosen falls into a fitful sleep.

Suddenly, the floor begins to rumble and shake, jolting her into instant alertness. The wide planks beneath her chair shift and heave, as if something beneath the surface is trying to break through.

Thousands of white tendrils creep through the spaces between the boards, snaking their way across the floor. Eiosen jumps to her feet.

Blessed Goddess, the wards have fallen.

Clutching her roiling stomach, she yells, "Pren," and fumbles for her touchstone. She begins to chant, but as each filament turns to dust, hundreds more appear.

Pren opens her bedroom door. The mycelium continues to push through the cracks in the floorboards and slither steadily toward the doorway where the girl stands, frozen.

"Run, Pren." Eiosen's voice is shrill and brittle with fear.

The threads move faster now and wrap around Pren's feet. They drag her to the floor, quickly spreading over her entire body.

"No!" Eiosen rushes to Pren and tries to tear the filaments away. They twine around Eiosen's hands and tighten until her fingers turn blue, and then black. A ragged cry escapes her throat, as the filaments rip off her remaining fingers, one by one. She crumples to the ground, blood gushing from the open wounds. Her feet are the yew's next victims. Blood shoots from the stumps, spraying a fine mist through the room and filling the air with the bitter scent of copper.

Pren screams, "Grandmother." She tries to crawl to Eiosen, but the threads hold her back.

Barely clinging to consciousness, Eiosen whispers, "My sweet girl. You don't deserve to be trapped again. Save yourself." The filaments spread across Eiosen's body and climb down her throat, stealing her voice.

Pren shrieks, a sound so filled with fury that even in her half-conscious state, Eiosen quakes. In a blinding flash, Pren disappears in an explosion of green fire. High-pitched keening slices through the room, as every single filament is incinerated. The air is filled with the acrid scent that comes after a lightning strike.

Blackness creeps in from the corners of Eiosen's vision, but before it claims her entirely, she sees Pren stand and wipe the filament dust from her clothing. Her head brushes the ceiling now, and her hair, the vibrant yellow green of spring, falls across her shoulders like a curtain. Tiny leaves twine through the strands and spiral down her body to her feet. Her entire body is engulfed in green fire.

To Eiosen, she is majesty incarnate.

Pren strides to Eiosen, drops to her knees, and cradles her gently in her arms. Eiosen's skin buzzes as Pren touches her.

Leaning close, Pren whispers in Eiosen's ear. "I'm not sure if I will ever forgive you, but I do love you."

As Eiosen's vision turns dark, she has a moment of pity for the yew. The forest has a new Mother now, but this one can walk and talk and move about freely wherever she chooses to go.

THE WITCH FACTORY

Claire Eliza Bartlett

They were brought to the factory yard on state livestock trains, a screaming mass of sparkling eyes, sharp cheekbones, slim legs, shining hair. Fighting for freedom. Sometimes they fought each other but most of the time they fought the train, a steel box three inches thick on all sides, impervious to their harsh words, their fists and feet, even the blades some of them had smuggled on. By the time they arrived Mara couldn't understand how they still screamed—how had they not used up all the air? Why couldn't they realize screaming would get them nowhere?

They still didn't understand when the train pulled up to the factory and spat them out. They kicked and bared their teeth at the security detail. Many struggled until their arms were pinned to their sides or forced behind their backs. Others paled, quieted, lifted their chins and glared around them as if they could prove to the world they were better than this.

The detail was trained to be perfect gentlemen. They didn't pinch anyone's rear, like the supervisor sometimes did with Mara, and they didn't make snide comments about one girl's streaming mascara, or the run that trailed up another's stocking. They didn't say anything at all. Even when the girls let their rage overflow, the gentlemen kept moving, pushing the line forward, touching the girls on their shoulders, their upper backs, sometimes their necks when they needed more control. *Such gentlemen*, Mara thought as she stood in her prim beige suit, clutching her clipboard. She wished she could find a gentleman like that.

Not that she would find one here. Too many of her co-workers had unrealistic ideas about women's beauty after working at the witch factory day after day. Theirs was a specialist facility, made for Pretty Ugly girls. Girls who had a pretty face but an ugly heart. Ladies who were desirable until they opened their mouths. Ladies who were smarter than they were wise, and wiser than they were silent. Transgressors.

The witch factory fixed them.

Each woman wore a metal cuff with her identification number engraved and brushed in black ink. Some of them had scratched at the ink; others at the cuff. There were always a few who had managed to break off their cuffs, and these had to stay behind while Mara worked with her supervisor to determine who they were. To start, however, Mara checked the cuff numbers against the list on her clipboard. She moved her eyes between the board and the wrists, and never looked up. Something in their pretty faces always twisted as they saw her; names poured out of their mouths. *Traitor. Slut. Mousy bitch.* She wore earplugs so that she didn't have to hear them. That way, she could pretend they didn't hate her as long as she didn't look up. Mara wasn't good with being hated.

Mara was a Plain Pretty, simple in face and simple in mind, agreeable and quiet until someone asked her opinion, which was never. She'd never been called hysterical a day in her adult life, which she considered a badge of honor. The world was not built on hysteria. It was built on simplicity, solidity, on people knowing their place. And Mara's place was at the witch factory, helping her fellow women whether they realized it or not.

She paused at the end of the line. The last wrist held out for her was brown, slim, spotted with freckles around the cuff. The tip of her index finger was missing.

Mara broke her cardinal rule, and looked up.

Eva stood, loosely grasped by a gentleman, a sad smile tugging at one corner of her mouth. Some Ugly hearts tried to meet their fate with humor, but Mara would never have expected Eva to be one of them. She would never have expected to see Eva in the witch factory at all.

She put one hand up to her ear. The earplug was halfway out before she realized how odd that might look to the gentleman holding Eva. It was bad enough that she'd broken routine. But Eva's mouth didn't form around the words *bitch* or *whore*. The smile grew sadder, and she inclined her head once. The guard looked bored.

Mara tucked her chin and got back to work. She flagged Eva's serial number, then watched the line of women as they were led away. The witch factory churned strange smokes into the sky, bruised colors that Mara never saw outside the compound, that marked a completed treatment on the previous batch of witches.

Sometimes Mara liked to watch them come back out, moving slowly, still crackling with their new magics. She liked seeing their beginning, their reentry into society as functioning members with a sanctioned place. Some part of her was even envious, wondering what she might do with magic like that, wondering if it was worth losing a few decades of day-in, day-out filing and the prospect of an interested man. But today she had to take her pad to her supervisor and say there had been a mistake. Eva couldn't be registered as a Pretty Ugly. As a child, she had never been loud, or angry, or excessively intelligent, or exhibited any of the other signs. This was a mix-up. And quiet Eva, like any woman with a Pretty heart, was waiting patiently for the mix-up to be sorted out without making undue fuss.

She was relying on Mara. And Mara, like any good Plain Pretty, was ever so reliable.

They'd been the only two girls their age on the street. Mara had long brown braids that the boys loved to pull until she punched one and he went home crying with a bloody mouth. Thus it was decided that she should spend less time with the boys, and more time with Eva.

Eva was perfect. She wore her black hair sleeked into a neat bun, and her clothes were never dirty or torn. She said *please* and *thank you* exactly when she should. She did everything her mother told her to without being asked twice, and when the boys bothered her she ignored them, because everyone knew that boys would get bored if you didn't rise to the bait. Even when her own brothers chopped off the tip of her index finger—by accident, they always claimed—she only cried prettily and waited with her mother in the emergency room until a doctor patted her shoulder and said she was lucky they hadn't chopped of a body part she actually needed.

And Eva was beautiful. One day she would be designated a Double Pretty, attractive in countenance and comportment, destined for the arm of a politician or an actor or a business mogul.

Mara had loved her. Mara had wanted to be her. Mara learned to stop punching boys, even the boys that yanked that sleek bun free. She learned to duck her head. She learned her *pleases*. She even went back to etiquette class, as long as Eva sat beside her.

They took their heart test at the same time. The tests analysed their tendencies to be combative or conciliatory, angry or pleasant, selfish or empathetic, argumentative or supportive. The score they got determined half of the rest of their lives, distributing them along the Ugly heart/Pretty heart range. The men's test distributed them across the range of Strong heart/Wise heart. By the time she took the test, Mara had stopped complaining about the discrepancy between the sexes. She was too busy being terrified that she'd end up Ugly.

Mara's mother burst into tears when she got the results. Then she rushed down to Eva's house, to embrace and thank her family. Both Eva and Mara had scored in the upper range. Eva had only smiled at Mara, as though she'd always known.

Mara's supervisor leaned a little too close as he looked at her clipboard. His hip grazed hers. She stiffened but refused to pull away. Good women maintained grace under pressure. They didn't make a fuss, especially over something that was surely an accident. "RDU-76443." He rifled through a thick folder, stuffed with photographs and identification for their new arrivals. "Mercy Roberts."

"No," said Mara before she could stop to think. That earned her a strange look. She never said no. Plain Pretties dissembled and made excuses. She dropped her gaze and ran her thumb over the teeth of the factory's universal key. "Her name is Eva Yarrow. I knew her as a girl. She's a double Pretty. She must have been put on the train by mistake."

Her supervisor squinted at the 2x2 mug shot attached to her file. "Dead ringer," he said. "And her ID says Mercy Roberts. You must be remembering wrong."

"Yes, sir," Mara said. Even though Eva's nose was thin where Mercy's was broad, and Eva's eyes were small where Mercy's were large, their skin was the same kind of brown. If Eva had ever let her hair loose, it would be the same kind of big and curly. But that was the end of the resemblance. Well, that and the missing fingertip. Mara must have let her emotional memory override her.

Her superviser patted her just above her rear. "Don't worry about it. There's always something with the new arrivals, hm?" He moved off to take a phone call. Mara was left with the stack of papers, each to be signed off and filed, and a strange feeling she hadn't had since she was a girl. The feeling that the leading man in her life was completely wrong.

Mara had never been a problem for her employers. She arrived on time, left on time, and made sure her desk was tidy by the end of the day no matter how much paperwork came in. And so, the first night she stayed late after work, she had to clasp her hands under the table to keep them from shaking. She hadn't broken a rule since she met Eva. Surely someone would find her behavior suspicious. Pretty hearts were not duplicitous. But Mara hadn't been able to think of anything but Eva Yarrow all day, and how she could be so mistaken about seeing her. She couldn't pinpoint when, exactly, she decided to stay behind, but between that first thought and the end of the work day she nearly changed her mind a thousand times. Everything would work out in the end; it always did. Nobody needed her interference.

But even Pretty hearts can be curious, and Mara's curiosity was a powerful thing.

Her supervisor came down to clock out at half past five. "Working late, huh?" he said, punching his card with a thunk and scratching his gray-brown stubble.

Mara jumped. "Yes, sir," she said, and cleared her throat. How could he not know she was lying?

He spoke over her. "Remember to have a bit of fun. Life's not all about work. I'm sure there's a fellow out there simply dying to meet a girl like you."

He left. He hadn't looked at her once.

Mara ran through her plan three or four more times before she finally gathered the courage to push out of her chair. She clocked out and traded her working heels for the boots all staff were required to wear on factory ground. If someone from the office found her, she could say she'd come back for something she'd forgotten. If security caught her, she'd say she was checking an identification for the boss. She had Mercy's ID page and photograph, and she'd printed Eva's identification off the database too.

The air was stiff and cold and smelled of snow. The last light of the sun had slipped behind the trees by the time she finally exited the administration building and made her way to the preparation halls. The halls stank of human bodies, and were often noisy. The factory's few visitors, mostly politicians and state scientists and their Pretty wives, found the preparation halls distasteful, so they sat out of sight at the back of the compound. The guards often spoke about how much they disliked patrolling there, so Mara knew they'd be walking quickly, eager to complete their rounds. She skirted the tall, square building that housed the research team and the chemical mixers, and hovered at the corner of the low witch chamber, where Ugly hearts went in and old, Plain faces came out. She tugged her coat around her and waited for the patrol to pass, clutching the papers like an alibi until the corner of the paper crinkled.

The witch factory was one of the largest facilities for Ugly hearts, specializing in physical alteration. Experimentation had found no cure for loud mouths. Women without tongues could write things down, or sign to one another. Think tanks and research facilities still struggled to find a long-standing and universal cure for Ugly hearts.

The witch factory offered a cure for their Pretty faces instead.

There was always a good use for witches. Crones could aid in conception, provide tonics for everything from troublesome bald spots to troublesome rivals. Every place needed a good witch, and no politician needed a sassy wife. So instead of trying to rehabilitate, the witch factory took women who were Ugly inside, and adjusted their exteriors to match. Then they could be slotted into new lives, in cities and towns that needed them and their wisdom and their magic.

The guard passed. Mara almost tripped over herself slipping around him. She righted her coat, slipped the ID sheets into her pocket, and approached the preparation hall, sticking close to the wire-topped fence that kept the factory safe from domestic terrorists and nosy urban explorers.

The preparation hall was noisy, filled with a melancholy tune sung by a hundred voices of varying ability. The girls didn't always sing, but often enough for security to complain. They said it was strange, unnatural. Unpleasant. Mara thought it was beautiful, but no one had ever asked her opinion so no one knew what she thought. The voices were sorrowful and hopeful all at once, heartbroken but determined to persevere. She unlocked the door and went in, careful to let as little of the noise out as she could. The further she got into this plan, the more it felt like committing some kind of low-level treason.

The preparation hall was a large structure, with wire cages that jutted from the walls. Each cage held four or five girls. As soon as she opened the door the singing faltered. The girls in the cells nearest to her stood.

Pretty faces got attention. Pretty faces got seen. But Plain ones got used to the corner, the sidelines. Mara got her attention in small doses, usually from small men. Now every Pretty eye was focused on her. And every mouth opened.

"You have to help us," the nearest girl said.

"Don't you get how you're being brainwashed?" said another.

"You don't have to change who you are for them," said a third.

Another laughed at that. "She doesn't even know how much she changed."

Nasty women. Ungrateful bitches. Dangerous elements. These were the women who pushed against the cages around her. Their faces got them so many things. They lived in one of the greatest countries in the world—a country that could rehabilitate its transgressors, not just lock them away somewhere for the rest of their lives. The witch factory would give them the purpose in life they craved, the freedom from male influence for which they thirsted. Yet they screamed and raged.

Except for one. Eva leaned against her cage like the others, but her lips were pressed together. She still smiled. When Mara stopped before her she gestured for silence. The women around her withdrew.

"Mercy Roberts?" Mara said. Nervousness turned her voice into a squeak, swallowing the 's' at the end of Eva's false name. She was employed by the witch factory; she had the moral upper hand. Her voice should emanate power and control. But Pretty hearts didn't recognise power, and did not bow to it.

Eva's fingers curled around a bar. Mara resisted the urge to put her own hand over them. "You remember me," Eva said.

"What are you doing here?" She'd never heard of a girl changing alignment post-aptitude test.

Eva watched her for a few moments more. Then she said, "I'm being Mercy Roberts."

"But you're not her," Mara said.

The girl next to Eva snorted. "No wonder she was so easy to brainwash."

"Hush now," said Eva without venom. "I went to a demonstration in Seamount. It turned into a riot. They were taking everyone, separating the Ugly hearts. So I switched ID with Mercy Roberts and nobody realized. Until you." She smiled again. "What are you doing here, Mara?"

"I'm helping people," Mara said. That earned her another snort. She felt an unfamiliar wash of anger. Pretty hearts shouldn't be angry, she knew—but even other women didn't think she was worth listening to. She didn't need lip from a criminal anarchist who'd probably thrown homemade bombs at a *demonstration*. "We're keeping society healthy."

"By putting Uglies through the witch factory?" Eva said. Mara nodded. Eva pressed closer. "What happens to Uglies here?" she said.

The silence around them rippled through the room, until Mara could hear her uneven breath and the drone of the fans that cooled the chemical mixers a building away. Curiosity was a powerful thing.

Mara's supervisor would never tell them, and he wouldn't want her to, either. But she'd already crossed him once, by coming in here to see Eva, when he'd told her plain as day that there was no Eva to see. "You'll be taken to the witch chamber," she said. "They'll give you treatments. Give you powers."

"Like superpowers?" said the girl next to Eva.

"Hush," Eva said again. But she looked to Mara for the answer.

"Strange ... powers. Powers to give a woman a baby, or take it away. Powers to give an amulet potency, to make people ill or well."

"As if," said the girl next to Eva. "They don't like us. We're wrong women. Why would they give us these things? And how come I've never seen a woman come out of the witch factory boasting about how she got all her goods?"

Eva didn't even look scared. Eva didn't understand what was happening to her. "No witch remembers how it happened," Mara said. "And no one's going to recognize you when it's over. You get your new face, and your new powers, and you get relocated to where you can actually do some good. But the magic uses you up." Witches lived for seven to ten years after their transformation, then their town had to put in a request for a new one. It was a good business model for the factory.

She leaned in towards Eva. One of the others might pull her hair, might gouge her eyes, but not Eva. "But you're not an Ugly heart. Tomorrow I'll talk to my supervisor. I printed your ID page, all you have to do is say it's you—"

"My name is Mercy Roberts." Eva drew herself up. Her voice was still kind, but her eyes had a distance in them that Mara hated. "You don't have to be born with an Ugly heart, Mara. You can get one for yourself. It's about how hard you work and how much you think, and what you think about. If you really want to help—" she pressed her forehead to the bars "—then keep us who we are. Don't turn us into old crones."

"I can't," Mara said. "I'm not—" *Ugly like you.* "Smart like you."

"If you can think, you can be smart," said Eva.

Mara and Eva had been separated when they went to boarding school. As a Double Pretty, Eva needed to learn how to hold her own household court, how to decorate her mansion for the perfect holiday party, how to dress sexy without looking like a whore. As a Plain Pretty Mara got to learn how to cook, how to balance her checkbook, how to organize her list of desirable traits in a man, so that she might recognize the optimal partner when he asked her to dinner. How to be practical.

"I don't want to go," Eva said. She held Mara's hand. They sat at the edge of a little pier, dipping their toes in a fishing pond barely larger than Eva's house.

"I'm looking forward to new opportunities," Mara said. Pretty hearts looked for the positive in things. She wished she could say, *I'll miss you.*

Maybe Eva heard it in her tone anyway. Her hand tightened. "I'll write to you," she said.

"I would enjoy that." Mara didn't really believe that Eva would write. Pretty Faces should spend their time making connections, not engaging in charity projects for their Plain ex-friends. She wanted a letter from Eva the way she wanted this day to never end, but she was a Pretty heart, so she also wanted what was best for Eva, and that was a social ladder that Mara herself could never climb.

Eva did write, a few times. Mara held her letters like they were made of solid gold and tucked them under her pillow at night. But she never wrote back.

The next day the new batch got their first treatment. Mara took her lunch break early so she could watch security prod them through the doors of the chamber. They were corralled like sheep, pushed into a tighter and tighter mass until there was nowhere to go but into the hall. Again they fought, the men or each other or the fence, but it was no use. Mara spotted Eva in the mix—she stood proud, lifting her chin like a queen. She looked neither left nor right. She'd made her choice, and when the doors opened for her, she was the first one through. She hadn't seen Mara. Or maybe she had seen her, and had chosen to ignore her. And though Mara was as used to being ignored as any other Plain Pretty, the imagined snub stung. They'd been so close, once. Eva had saved Mara's life, by uplifting all the Pretty qualities in her. The least she could do was let Mara return the favor.

Or maybe, Mara thought with a spike of fear, helping her had been Eva's downfall. Maybe Mara's Ugliness had infected Eva's Pretty heart, worming through her until her future was ruined.

Mara went back to her desk with a feeling like cement in her gut. She worked through the rest of her day without looking at the files tucked in the bottom drawer of her desk. When her supervisor left he gave her a cheery wave. "Remember to give yourself a break," he called.

Mara walked down to the preparation hall without trying to hide. She held the file under one arm, and at the front of the hall she took several deep breaths, trying to ground herself. Pretty hearts were meek, not bold. Pretty hearts didn't stride down the hall like they owned the place.

But if she tried to creep like last night, she didn't think she'd make it.

She'd never been in the preparation hall mid-treatment before.

The women slumped against their hard beds. Every part of them seemed to sag—their skin, their breasts, their shoulders. When they looked at her, she saw eyes muddled by magic. No one mustered a hiss or a taunt. No one begged for freedom.

Eva Yarrow had aged at least a decade. She still smiled, and her smile was no less luminous than it had been the night before. "Mara," she said. "What are you doing here?"

Did Eva remember their conversation last night? "What are *you* doing here?" Mara said.

Eva drew herself up. She'd already lost so much. She'd lost her prime. She'd marry a widower, or no one at all. There would be no society interviews for the way she dressed, or the flowers she favored in decorations, or her top tips for hosting the perfect party. Mara couldn't let her lose more.

"I think how I think. Why would you imprison me for it?" Eva said.

"It's not imprisonment," Mara protested. The witch factory was a last resort. The world simply didn't have a place for Ugly hearts. It didn't have a place for riots and protests and irrational thought. Things were better this way. At least, she'd thought so before Eva came back into her life.

Mara reached through the bars and Eva took her hand. Eva still had strength in her bones, for all that her joints cracked with arthritis. "Did you really change your heart?"

"It's not hard. All you have to do is think. Why are all your supervisors men? Why do you have to settle for the man who asks you to dinner? Why do you have to marry a man at all?"

"Society needs order."

"An order that ignores half the population?" Eva's voice rose, trembling.

"The fact that we can't be rational about it only proves that we need to step back," Mara said.

"It's not a rational issue." Eva's hand loosened, as though she was giving up. But Mara couldn't lose her. Not without trying one last time.

"It takes two more treatments to make you a witch. If you stop pretending to be Mercy Roberts and come with me now, some of the effects might be reversible." Doctors from the best medical schools worked here, surely they could bring back the old Eva. They could bring back the Eva that had made Mara. "We could rehabilitate you. Maybe you could get compensation for the mistake. If you just verify your identification—"

"Oh, Mara." Eva said. Her eyes glistened. "I'd rather go forward than back." She leaned against the bars, apparently exhausted.

It was almost like when they were children, Mara thought, still clutching Eva like a lifeline. Only instead of pulling on Eva's hair, these grown-up boys were pulling on her life. And Mara wanted to punch them, as hard as she could, as many times as she could.

She cried all the way home. A man on the subway told her to smile, but she let the snot drip from her nose and hiccuped until he looked away.

She skipped lunch again to watch Eva go into the witch chamber. Old women limped out, hunched and cursing. Those who could still screamed. They weren't calling for help. Their screams were an act of defiance. *We're still here. We won't be silenced.*

She found Eva by her hair. It was coming undone from its classic sleek knot, and a lone silver streak wound through it like a loose thread. Anguish hammered at her. How could they not *see* the kind of heart Eva had? How could they condemn her based on a photograph that wasn't even hers?

Eva wanted to save a life. Did she have to get herself killed for it?

Mara went through the rest of the day in a daze. She laughed without hearing her supervisor's terrible joke, she fielded calls from a senator's office, she took minutes and typed them up without paying attention to what was in them. She went through everything on her desk, and then, to pass the time, she went through it all again.

At ten past five her supervisor stopped at her desk. He leaned a little too far forward, eyes drifting down past her face. "It's not really right for a girl as hardworking as you to be without a fellow," he said.

Her hands shook. Things like this weren't supposed to bother Pretty hearts. But it would have bothered Eva.

Mara took a deep breath and smiled with the quiet confidence Eva had always had. "I have a fellow," she said, surprised at how smoothly the lie came out. "He gets off work at six-thirty. I figure I might as well put in the extra hour before he comes to pick me up."

She felt the shift in him—or perhaps, more accurately, in his perception of her—as she moved slots in his brain. From *Plain, but here,* to *someone else's property.* He leaned back to a respectable distance where he couldn't see down her blouse. "You'll have to bring him to the company party," he said.

She waited until her hands stopped shaking. Then she went back to Eva.

The women around her could be grandmothers. Their skin had a translucent thinness. Magic sparked in their hair and around their throats. They didn't know how to use it yet. Mastering their power was a task for once they'd been taken to their new towns and lives.

"Let me help you," Mara said.

Eva's hair was more white than black. She looked at Mara with cataract-milky eyes and spoke through pale, cracked lips. "If you don't want to help everyone, then there's nothing you *can* do."

"How am I supposed to do that?" Mara burst out. She gripped her wrists, imagining a silver cuff. "I can't shut down the witch factory."

"Have you ever thought about it?" Eva said.

Of course she hadn't. Even now she couldn't really wrap her mind around how such a thing might be accomplished. What was one small, mousy woman supposed to do?

Perhaps something of her thoughts passed over her face; Eva's expression softened a little. "No one turns Ugly all at once. You start with small things. Saying no when you want to say no. Speaking to someone dangerous. Trading ID cards."

"But I don't want to turn Ugly," Mara said. She didn't want people to look at her the way they looked at these women. She didn't want to sit in a cage in the preparation hall someday, waiting to be made even Uglier than she was. The course of her life had been mapped out and shoved down her throat. She knew how it was supposed to go. Maybe she didn't want it, not in the way she wanted Eva to be free, but she knew what lay ahead and she couldn't fathom throwing that away.

Eva's face fell. "Then you can't help us. You won't help us."

She turned away, and wouldn't look back, even when Mara began to cry.

She needed more time. That was what Mara told herself as she waited for the guard to pass and used her key to unlock the witch chamber. And maybe she was helping all the girls in the hall, but that wasn't the point. The point was to stop Eva from ruining her life until Mara could figure out what was right and what was wrong. It might be an Ugly action, but it had a Pretty motivation—so it was right, wasn't it?

The witch chamber was a long, dark room with ventilation shafts near the top. Plain brick, concrete floor. No windows. The space seemed to press down on Mara, as though she could feel the weight of years right before they crushed her. Ready to make a witch of her. She continued to the office next door..

The office contained a circuit board and dozens of tiny knobs. Mara turned them all to full and walked out as though she had no reason to be anywhere else.

The malfunction of the witch chamber halted the factory for three days. A trainload of Pretty Uglies got diverted to a detention facility up north, and the entire staff was given leave while her supervisor dug through rosters and reports, searching for the error and the responsible party.

Three precious days. Mara resisted the urge to go back to work. She wouldn't get her answers at the factory, and she couldn't pull the same stunt again. If the tightened security caught her trying to talk to Eva, they might unravel the whole story. They might even accuse her of being an Ugly heart herself. They might stick her in the witch chamber.

So she got on the bus and headed up to Seamount.

She was a little surprised by what the file revealed about the real Mercy Roberts. Pretty faces usually had jobs more glamorous than service, but perhaps Mercy's Ugly heart had taken her one step too far. For a few moments she worried that Mercy had gotten a new job to go with her new name, but when she entered the diner, with its peeling paint and crackling, blues-belching speakers, the first thing she saw was a big. black head of hair bent over the counter. She slid onto a counter stool. The eyes that looked up were a little too wide, the nose a little too broad. The badge on her apron read EVA. "You really don't look like her," Mara said.

Mercy acted as though she hadn't heard. "What can I get for you today?"

Mara drew the crinkled ID pages out of her pocket and took a deep breath. She'd practised her boldness the whole way. "You can tell me why I have a Mercy Roberts here, and a Mercy Roberts down in Dorin Hill," she said, smoothing the pages on the counter where Mercy could see.

Mercy froze. Her big eyes darted left, then right. "I'm Eva's friend," Mara said. "I want to talk to you."

Mercy ran her eyes over Mara, taking in her plainness. Maybe Ugly hearts had a way of seeing the truth of people. Or maybe Mercy did. Or maybe she didn't have any special powers at all, but chose to trust Mara, the same way Mara had chosen to trust her. "You'll have to wait until I finish my shift. Then I can tell you what I know."

Six hours later, Mercy sat down with a pot of coffee and a sigh. Mara almost declined—coffee-stained teeth, she had to look as nice as she could—but pulled a cup toward her instead. "What happened to her?" Mercy said.

"She's at a witch factory," Mara replied. "No one else knows she's not you."

"Why didn't you tell them?" Mercy asked.

Mara decided to leave out the part where she'd tried. "How well do you know her?" Maybe they'd gone to secondary school together. Maybe she could find the link between Pretty heart Eva and Ugly heart Eva.

Mercy shook her head. "I never met her before we were thrown in prison. She heard me talking about how my family needed me and tossed her ID at me. When they called my name she got up." She took a deep breath, inhaling the coffee's burnt aroma. Then she took a handful of plastic half-and-half portions and began adding them to her cup. "What do the witch factories do?"

"That's confidential," Mara said.

Any Pretty heart would have sat back, unwilling to overstep boundaries. But Mercy Roberts arched an eyebrow and leaned in. "I don't know anyone who can pay you, but we could get you on a radio show."

"What?"

"It operates out of the capital, but we could call in."

"That's not what I meant." Mara started to rise. An emptiness had started to hollow out each limb. She wanted to cry, but even tears couldn't fill her.

"Then what did you mean? Why are you here?" Mercy's eyes narrowed. She glanced around the empty diner as though she expected government officials to leap from the booths and toss her into the back of a van.

"I came here because Eva Yarrow is a Pretty heart. But now she's acting Ugly. Like you." She threw the insult with vehemence,even though she hadn't tried that since she was a girl. Pretty hearts didn't like to offend.

Maybe she was too Pretty to be any good at it. The corner of Mercy's mouth turned up and she shook her head, snorting. "Did you know that women used to vote?"

"No, we didn't," Mara said, leaning back. "I mean—that's not the point."

"We used to buy our own birth control. There used to be women in the police, and the army, and the government. The information's easy to find. If you want to find it." She took out her order pad and scribbled something down. "This is the radio station I was talking about. You should listen to it sometime."

Mara took the paper to make her happy. She was halfway to the bus station before she realized that no one had called her a traitor or a mousy bitch all day. What did Ugly hearts do, if they didn't hate Pretty ones?

A radio show wasn't a huge gesture. It wasn't like she was setting fire to the factory, or killing anyone. Besides, if the factory truly was doing good work, people ought to be grateful to hear about it.

She memorized the radio's AM frequency on the way home. Then she tore up the note, tossing each scrap into a different garbage can.

The factory was back online two days later. Mara watched the sea of women shuffle into the witch chamber for their final treatment. To her surprise, her supervisor came out as well.

"Good riddance," he said as the door closed.

"Hm?" Mara said. She doubted he needed the encouragement, but Pretty hearts were expected to give it.

"I've never had such trouble from a group of bitches. You know it was one of them who sabotaged the chamber?"

Mara schooled her expression. "Oh?"

"She got out of her cell, into the office, and back again without anyone noticing. I had to fire half my security team because of her. And she thought it was funny."

It must have been Eva. Saving Mara once more.

Her supervisor's hand fell, heavy, on her shoulder. Mara's heart skittered in fear. But all he did was pat her a couple of times. "You're a good listener," he said. "I hope your fellow appreciates it."

Mara watched him walk off. A good listener. There were some things being a Pretty heart had beaten into her.

She waited until the witch chamber burped out the latest witches. The train was pulling in, with a fresh crop of angry Ugly hearts. Once emptied, it would take the newly minted witches to a facility right outside Dorin Hill, where they'd be redistributed to towns up and down the Eastern seaboard. The old women muttered and blinked against the sun as they shuffled out. Most of them wrinkled their brows in confusion. But one pair of brown eyes caught Mara's, held it until the crowd pushed her forward. *If you don't want to help everyone, there's nothing you* can *do.*

Mara still wasn't sure she wanted to help everyone. But she wanted to help Eva, and she wanted to help the little girl she'd been, the girl who'd punched boys for pulling her braids, and pushing her on the playground and getting away with it.

She went out to check on the new arrivals. She left her earplugs in her desk. Moving down the line she found error after error—in the cuffs, in the IDs—too many to process in one working day. She showed her supervisor with a sigh.

"I'll have a word with the clowns on the other end," he reassured her. "But everyone's going to have to put in a little extra until this disaster blows over." He left, grumbling, and when he got off work at five he gave her no more than a cheerful wave.

Mara waited until she was sure no one was left in the building. The new security was focused on the preparation halls. No one thought about the Plain Pretty secretary, who moved to a colleague's work terminal before picking up the phone. Her heartbeat rang like a bell in her ears. She breathed through her fear.

One small step. It wouldn't turn her Ugly. And if it did, that might be a good thing.

She closed her eyes, remembering the number of the radio station as she dialed.

"My name is Mercy Roberts," she said into the phone. "I work for a witch factory."

AT THE VESPERTINE MOTH

Daniela Tomova

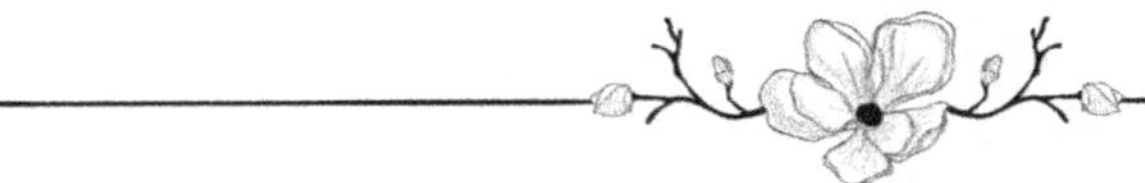

And so they went that winter evening into the old town—two by two and side by side, through huddled half-blind streets and past jewel-box storefronts. They climbed the tallest hill with its dusty antique shops and cozy diners. They surged over the slippery cobblestones polished by the breath of the eternal city. They squeezed past crumbling walls and knobby trees which had shouldered the old roads for so long that they'd forgotten exactly what kind of fruit they were supposed to bear.

Today, there were twelve couples, all dressed for the occasion—sinuous scarves over bare shoulders, dresses made to lead armies in, elegant suits which drank only the finest starlight—and each had waited centuries for a table. Although they looked mostly human, they were not. Their shadows blistered where they lingered and, if seen, their faces made human teeth tingle.

The restaurant sat on a cliff on the far side of the hill, so the last couple arrived outside just when the sun slid under the pink horizon and the sky opened, wide and cold.

The terrain was mostly bare here. A solitary streetlamp faced a concrete wall covered in graffiti by artists of varying skills and conviction. With a zinc buzz, the lamp flickered on and off, briefly washing in yellow the frosted leaves on the path and some of the graffiti but not all.

The couple stood under the lamp.

They waited like humans would. Or close enough. Humans aren't backlit by an alien light when they suddenly turn the wrong angle. Human shadows aren't tall enough to block out the stars. Humans breathe in and out.

But this couple did very well, considering that it was their first evening out.

The streetlamp flickered off and on a few more times, and the maître d' walked out of the wall. He greeted each by name, in the comfortable manner of a childhood servant. He had shifting undertones to his skin and, when he spoke, velvet moth-like wings stirred on his lips, but otherwise he had the general bearing of a human. With polite chatter, he led the couple through the pastel arches and neon splash-ponds of the graffiti and into the restaurant.

The ceiling was, naturally—it was that class of restaurant— tall enough to accommodate the guests' shadows. Discreetly lit by stars and ringed by tall, cliff-like walls, it looked very much like a real sky. Under its gossamer apricot clouds, the maître d' walked his guests discreetly around—past the basalt dunes rolling in from a giant archway in the back, past the mossy boulders who wept glacier water, past the pond of moths pale as the bones they crawled over, and finally up the grand stone stairs to the terrace which had a sweeping view of the sulci and torsions of the chamber below.

The table was plain and solid. A waitress with a dark ponytail and a subtle limp walked around it to meet them. Across the terrace, the other couples were already seated at their own solid, unremarkable tables and did not turn to look as maître d' and the waitress pulled the heavy chairs back to seat the last couple.

The couple smoothed the heavy cotton napkins over their

laps and stroked the cutlery laid out like surgical instruments on the grainy wood. One of them picked up a delicate butter knife to examine it, and it flashed silver starlight over her face. The waitress's teeth tingled.

"We are honored to have you with us at The Vespertine," the waitress began. "Tonight we have a special eighteen-course tasting menu for you. To complement the menu, we offer a small selection of wines specifically matched to some of the dishes. Would you like to try those as well?"

The couple looked at each other, and the air around them tightened like a fist.

"Excellent choice," the waitress smiled, and the couple smiled too. When they did, their mouths were just a little bit too wide, and their teeth didn't show. As the waitress headed down the stairs, one of them, still smiling, adjusted her scarf over her glittering décolletage

"Our first course today is a simple appetizer."

Wordlessly, two waiters set a large plate in front of each guest. In the middle of the plate, a blazing red flower nested in a hazy golden cloud.

While the couple examined the dish, the waitress began, "This dish is called 'My first clear memory is a day in the beginning of May'. A red poppy island floats in an aerosolized syrup of honey, horse chestnut pollen, opium, and town-square dust. The poppies have been freshly and artlessly harvested by a local baker's youngest daughter. The dust and horse chestnut blossoms have been sourced from the actual square where your experience for today celebrated May Day at the age of five.

"As you taste it, try to feel it happen. It's a warm, clear day. The ground is so close and so solid under your feet. Brilliant sunshine pools around you like honey. You pluck off a petal and place it on your tongue. Feel the light prickles of the poppy stem in your hand and the softness of the petals, red as the embroidery on a new white dress. And, please enjoy."

The waitress clasped her hands amiably and disappeared again, while the couple, still smiling, picked up the outermost forks and gently poked at the flowers with them.

The next dish was a storm of red, peach, and white petals; cornflower blossoms; and delicate, perfectly crisped thorns on a bed of wild weeds and sweet-smelling, sun-dried mortar. The thorns glistened with a thick red syrup.

The wine pairing danced in the glasses. Small bubbles formed at the bottom and rushed to burst open at the surface, releasing the scent of heated skin in the shade of a fig tree.

"Our second course is called 'The rose wall'.

"You are almost six.

"Today some visiting relative hugs you and calls you 'her little princess'. The only princesses you know of are the toasted sandwiches—minced meat and melted cheese on top. You scream 'I'm not a princess', and run far away from the house.

"In the far away, you discover a section of an old wall that's been pried apart by giant, wild-rose hedges. Behind is a wilderness of flowers, grasses, and bugs. You spend the day there and come home late in the evening carrying a bounty of heady flowers in your arms and a small, woven grass doll in your pocket. Your arms and legs itch fiercely from a million-billion scratches. Before you go inside, you take the doll out with a sweaty hand, blow on it to clear the bugs, and place it carefully in the old, rusted metal box where you keep your treasures.

"In time, the vines will tear the wall apart. The wilderness will dry out and start catching fire every summer. You'll visit it again when you're older and find it unremarkable. But today you dream of a world hidden behind a wall of roses. In the dream, the grass doll is as big as you, and you two go exploring together. And when they come chasing with forks and knives, she grows huge and hides you. In the dream the doll waits for you inside the wilderness, forever.

"Enjoy."

"Our third course was prepared entirely under the surface of a free-floating oceanic ecosystem converted for our culinary use. Note how the volcanic salt in the water draws out the delicate taste of the pale water spiders which have been sustainably foraged and infused over an ocean vent by our own staff. Here, at The Vespertine, we take special pride in hiring local artisans to assist in the preparation of our ingredients.

"I'd also like to draw your attention to the hint of silica in the seaweed and the note of petroleum in the riesling we have paired with this course.

"The dish is called 'Summer'. It is the happiest day in your life so far. You are old enough for a bikini top and, by that logic, old enough to play by the water alone. The air smells of salt and gasoline from the boats thumping over the waves in the distance. You scoop handfuls of wet sand and pour them into dreamlike shapes over the castle you've made for the pale spiders skittering over the beach. The sun is so warm. The sand is warm too—and slithers under you as the waves hit. You lie on your side just on the edge of the surf, and the sea beats like a heart under your body.

"Enjoy."

"This dish is called 'L'appel du vide'. Here we have an albatross consommé over Black Sea mussels cooked in butter, garlic, and provencal herbs and peppered with baby seahorses roasted in bacon fat. On the side, in this little bowl, is a sauce made from an adrenaline- and bone-marrow reduction infused with unfiltered seawater from the Antarctic Riviera. We suggest that you pour the sauce gently over the consommé and gently scoop both layers, almost as if your spoon is floating on the surface of a deep ocean.

"You float, alone. Constellations of people dot the beach, but you are too far away to hear any of the happy screaming and splashing— you hear nothing over the gentle lap of the small waves against your skin and the calls of the seagulls. You look down past your feet and suddenly remember that there is a kilometer between you and the bottom of the sea. A giant beast of salt water is carrying you on its silken back. You turn back towards the horizon and start swimming. You wonder if you can swim far enough to lose sight of the land.

"That evening, roasting mussels over the beach bonfire, you overhear your friends talking about you. One of them tells the story about how he tried to feel you up in the crammed train car and you kept squirming away. Everybody laughs and calls you a virgin and some other words they think are bad. You leave the mussels to burn and walk to an empty beach. You take your clothes off and lie into the calm, warm waters to catch the stars with your eyes."

The couple looked at their plates, empty but for a single rust-colored leaf in the middle. The waitress returned with three silent waiters, each with a heavy pot. The waitress had white gloves on. She leaned over and poured steam—scented by petrichor, minerals, and ferns—slowly over the edge of each plate. The steam reached the leaf and poked at its edges. The couple leaned in. The steam flooded the plate. The leaf hesitantly shuffled—and lifted off. The three waiters leaned and carefully poured it around each leaf, one by one. The two leaves swirled violently. They danced just above the plates and the waitress resumed the experience.

"A palate cleanser before the next course. It is called 'A Door Opens in the Sky'. You are fifteen years old and on top of a mountain with some other enthusiasts. You look down at the rounded cliffs and at the dark forests between their thighs and feel as if the earth has just dropped from under you. The silken train of your father's old army parachute trails nervously behind. This excitement, just on the edge of being unbearable, never goes away however many jumps you make. The updraft tugs at your pant legs. You walk back, check the straps, and take off running, straining against the air that punches the parachute open—and—

"—jump."

"The highlight of this simple dish, 'Sacrificial Anode', is undoubtedly the carpaccio of Kobe oysters, hand-raised, Porter-fed, and treated to classical music twice daily for eighteen months before harvesting. The salt-and-copper flakes on the oysters pair exquisitely with the Jura Savagnin wine which adds a refined smoky-floral note to the small electrical jolts you will feel.

"You wake up, confused, nauseated, with a profound soreness in your throat and chest. You try to sit up and suddenly there are strangers above you. Next time you are awake, your parents are in the room. Eventually, your memory starts spitting out bits, like shrapnel embedded in flesh—

"—You flew right into an updraft—and the storm reached you. Cloud suck, you've heard it called. The sky reached down and pulled you up by the strings of the parachute—

"—Into thin air. Golden sunlight, inky clouds and slices of lightning.

"—sudden awareness that consciousness doesn't fade as gracefully as in the books. One moment you are fighting to stay inside your head, the next—you are pulled out of your body—

"—You did nothing wrong; it's just how things happen—

"—if only you'd jumped half an hour earlier.

"Soon the doctors say you've recovered physically, but you never fully get your memories of that day back. You only have the flashbacks, which you hold onto until their edges dull and they no longer run like electricity through you.

"There is also the limp which might have needed physical therapy, but your parents don't really talk about it once you've healed. Everyone else wants to talk about your fall though. Your friends, their parents, your teachers, they all want a keepsake shard of the Icarian tale, a feel of your scars. They listen lizard-eyed and stroke your hair, your cheek, your shoulder, with a trembling, ravenous pity.

And when they do there is this uncomfortable new feeling, like corrosion on your skin.

The silent waiters took the couple's empty dishes away.

In one of those moments of universal alignment, a silence fell over the dining terrace. All the staff had disappeared down the stairs, and suddenly every guest became aware of themselves. To the last couple, this was a new feeling. They looked around. The others had adapted quickly, and the hum of conversations and odd atmospheric noises—the ring of a trolleybus, the peal of a cathedral bell, the crack of a lightning—reached the last couple's table.

One of the two, the one who usually smelled of beehives but was now wearing French perfume, tried to speak—something very difficult without the ability to exhale. But not impossible. The air near the couple tightened again. Suddenly, a voice like that of the waitress but muted, as if coming from another room, filled the space around the table.

The other, the one who smelled like dragon's blood and pigeon feathers, focused too and a soft crackling, just like the basalt dunes they had walked by earlier, swept over the terrace. From the nearby tables, guests turned to the last couple and raised their glasses. The couple raised their glasses too. The air tightened like a strong hug and then relaxed again.

"This is our variation on a popular everyday dish, called 'The Game'. Three scoops of gravel—limestone, granite, and quartz are served in a reduction of fermented peat lilies, acacia pollen, and birch sap. Once the gravel softens, its taste will open up and blossom into a series of volcanic and chalky notes with metallic hints. You can expect a feeling of intoxication immediately, as your blood absorbs the whiskey directly through the cuts in your tongue and the roof of your mouth.

"The game is simple, you are told, but when the bottle points at you, you refuse to play and go slouch in a corner, watching the flirty screaming and gulping of smuggled liquor.

"A guy who you noticed noticing you, your friend's much older brother, comes over and asks if you'd like to go to his room next door to see this movie he just downloaded. Earlier in the evening he had looked interesting and brooding, just like you imagine the poets you read look like, and you had tried to carry yourself with dignity and aloofness that would mark you as special, but now his eyes are unfocused, and his voice is embarrassingly slurred. His breath smells sour, and you see the uneven patches of bristles where he hasn't shaved carefully enough. You say no, sorry, and acknowledge you are being boring and—you shrug—weird. He asks why not. You tell him you are tired and want to go home. He asks why, it's a nice evening. You say it's a school day tomorrow, so you need to be rested. He says you're young, you don't need rest. You say that you need your eight hours. Why, he asks … Whatever you say, he asks why …

"Enjoy."

"Our next dish is 'In Translation'.

"You are in college in some coveted faraway country, studying for a degree that is meant to mark you as one of the good immigrants—something meant to preempt any disappointment or disdain when they ask you where you're from and you have to name a country that they only know from base, arms-length jokes on their TV.

You have a lot to learn.

From home you bring two bags of clothes, books, and an old metal box of your treasures. You haven't opened it since you were a child, afraid you'll find it unremarkable, but just having it comforts you.

"You are the foreigner, starkly. Even though many internationals attend the university, some rich, 'child of —' type of kids from your country even, you are the most noticeably foreign. It might be because naively—or ignorantly, or vulgarly—you don't seem to be aware which places aren't meant for you.

"Even though you speak the language, you don't speak *the* language. In honors classes, your teammates insist on checking with you a few times over to make sure you've understood the assignments. During debates, your arguments drop into the irritated silence of the auditorium. You feel stupid. But then someone repeats the exact same thing later and the class erupts in a discussion. They laugh. You smile nervously but every time you do, small spots of corrosion bloom on your skin.

Evenings, you replay moment after moment in front of the

mirror, trying to dull the signs of awkwardness in your smiles and your casual shrugs.

"Your roommate and, at the time, best friend—also a foreigner but one who grew up with a maid, a chef, and a driver—unbidden, takes to translating your statements for you in public. When you ask her to stop, she says she is just helping, don't be so—

"This is one of our more straightforward, yet difficult to execute, dishes— three paintings of a nude in repose, overlapping each other. Each pose is visible from a different angle. The bottom layer is sketched in sun-dried loam soil, wild thyme, and powdered ox heart. The second is made of rust and steel rainbow patina. The top layer is golden honey harvested from bee colonies exclusively allowed to forage the garden terraces of penthouse apartments, airbrushed with a pearl-and-butter emulsion.

"Enjoy."

"'Smoke' is our ninth dish. A constellation of heather-smoked dragonflies are glazed in aromatic copal resin, then coated in chili, gun, and cocoa powders. They are arranged on a burning oak log. If I may, I suggest that you wait a few moments for the copal to melt and start releasing the greenness of the heather. Then pick up a dragonfly and dip it into the smoke of the log embers.

"Your first college boyfriend, a sculptor, carves your likeness onto a wood burl with dark veins and glowing burnish. It's a rare piece of wood, formed when the shard of a meteorite embedded itself into a young oak four centuries ago, he tells you proudly and shows you the pellet, polished to pearl finish, partially uncovered by his gouge. He often confuses exclusivity with artistic merit, you've noticed. Still, she is beautiful!

"Half life-sized, it's clearly you in a moment of vulnerability. Your hands rest on your solar plexus, and your brow is tense. Your head is lowered. Your muscles are admiringly, fluidly shaped as if by loving hands. More loving than you ever remember feeling.

"He's even carved your nebula of scars into her legs. You touch them gently with your thumb and trace one of them down to the ankle.

"Something pulls you out of your body. Your head—or the statue's? No, that's definitely your head—starts booming like an ocean tide. You leave without saying anything.

"The worst part doesn't even cross your mind until you walk out of the building. He never even asked if he could take your scars. You roll back into his apartment like a bolt of lightning.

"You yell at him brashly, vulgarly, like the foreigner you are.

"The sculptor doesn't understand the problem. It's so beautiful, he says—you look beautiful. That has nothing to do with why it's not okay, you say. But you agreed it's beautiful, he insists with a whine in his voice—and regardless, this is Art (oh, he pronounces the capital letter, unmistakably)—once I've created it, it doesn't belong to me or you.

"Whatever you say, he has a 'but'.

"He refuses to destroy it.

"He turns his back at you, refusing to acknowledge you. The stronger you feel about this, the more it hurts, the more you scream, the more invisible you become.

"You lunge at the sculpture, but he blocks without even looking at your face and says he will call the police if he ever sees you near his apartment. Don't be an asshole, he says with comfortable congeniality.

"As far as breakups go, this one seems pretty mutual.

"Please, be careful touching the plate, even after the fire dies out. It'll be rather hot."

When the silent waiters came with the tenth course, the waitress brought a bottle of wine the color of a childhood night.

"Our next dish is called 'From the Grass'. Tender peacock ribs are cooked sous-vide and then lightning-seared on a bed of fresh wild wheatgrass. Today's vintage lightning was sourced from a 1993 storm in the Bolivian salt flats and stored in a specially designed salt container prior to use.

"For this dish, we have chosen a rich mavrud wine, matured during a long, restless autumn in a lost city centuries ago. The mulberry and cocoa notes in the wine will highlight the prickling in the wheatgrass. The combination should not give you an identifiable taste but rather a clear feeling of anticipation.

"The statue is unveiled at a student exhibition in the college of arts. You stay in to watch TV and eat some stale crackers you find in the cupboard. Your friends go and then stop by your tiny apartment shedding leaflets and sudden opinions about art.

"'It's like I get you more now', your roommate and best friend up until just this moment says. 'He really got you. I've been telling everyone I'm roommates with the model. And, he was there too, your ex,' she tries to look cool but the corners of her mouth betray a smile. 'He even told me all about how he knows his muses the moment he meets them.'

"You go finish the crackers in your room. A rustle in the old metal box under the unworn pile of clothes from home startles you. You arm yourself with a heavy textbook and pull out the box.

"You unlock the lid.

"It flings open violently.

"Stuffed inside is a messy ball of grass, like something coughed out by a giant cat. It unfolds and unfolds and unfolds. It's the grass doll you made so long ago! You were never a neat child and didn't break off the roots, so they sprouted and grew. The doll no longer resembles a human shape, not even by the most charitable definition. It smells faintly of roses, earth, and impending bad weather. Still, for a ball of grass, she is familiar and comforting.

"There used to be smooth sea glass, tiny gold nuggets, glowing mica scales, and seashells in the box too but they are gone now.

"'Hey hungry girl, what happened,' you ask the doll.

"She doesn't answer, of course. Just keeps unfolding. As if she's hiding something for you inside.

One at a time, the couple excused themselves to visit the restroom. This was something humans did. The staff instructed them to take the stairs down from the main floor.

There was nothing at the end of the stairs—they ended abruptly in front of a crudely hewn basalt wall. One by one, the couple walked down to the wall, examined it closely for a few minutes, then turned around and up towards the main floor.

On the way back, one of the couple, the one who now smelled rather like a beehive cradled by a Romantic poet, wandered off a little around the restaurant. She noticed the air over the pond of pale moths shimmering nervously and leaned over. The wings of the moths were still flapping dreamily, as they crawled over their skeletal landscape. But with each flap, somewhere, in some folds in the air above them, the light changed—dark and bright rolled over each other like seals at play. At times, shards of lightning flashed and, if you listened from a particular angle, a dry crack of thunder could be heard.

In the kitchen, the waitress was dabbing her forehead and the bridge of her nose with a napkin and arranging little parcels on two large plates.

Outside, in the dimension of the restaurant that wasn't in the old town, the air was thickening. The night tide was coming.

"Our next course is called 'Into the Grass'. It's a featherlight brioche made with yeast collected from wild grasses, infused with bone marrow and butter, and just a suggestion of light motor oil brushed on top.

"The doll—even though the shape is round, it is undeniably the doll you made when you were five—is on a shelf now, at home with all the curious rocks and odd pieces of metal from your pockets. You have prepared a display box for it when it starts turning yellow.

"Today, you notice some bits of rock and metal are missing from the shelf. When you look closely, you see part of a zinc bolt poking out of the matted grass. The next day it's completely swallowed.

"You find a coin and hold it near the doll. Slowly, so slowly as if it could have been moved by your breath, a grass blade turns towards your fingers.

"The rust starts sloughing off your hands. When you're stressed, you still pick at the little edges of skin on your arms and feet until they bleed. But now the new skin is supple and glowing.

"Enjoy."

"Next, we have 'Additive'. This course has been created from select food and industrial process additives—pigments and polymers, sealants and preservatives, organic extracts and powdered minerals—all these are homogenized and added to a rich ink veloute. You are meant to start by blowing into the middle, but many of our guests prefer to use their spoons to introduce air into the dish. Around the air, a scar will form and sprout. I recommend that you continue by scooping the liquid around the sides of the bowl. This way, when you are finished, there will be a small morsel, almost like a soft coral, in the middle of the bowl that you can pick up with a spoon, or even your fingers, and eat in one bite.

"A semester later, your grass doll is still alive. It's an even healthier—dark green—color. The roots are growing too. New shoots sprout from them, curling inwards. The ball unfolds a little in the morning in expectation of the sun and folds in at dusk. Almost as if it's breathing.

"One night, you leave the windows open. Their flimsy screens are more of a provocation than an obstacle to the hornets which live in that giant nest up the street anyway, but the night is unbearably hot and humid. Angry buzzing half-wakes you a few times. It stops abruptly, and you fall back asleep without thinking. In the morning, the doll is humming faintly from the inside before you leave for class. By the time you come back, the humming has stopped.

"Soon, you notice that the apartment is suddenly emptied of insects. You no longer see the little mice that used to run between the cracks in the wall either.

"You read an article in an obscure coffee-table art book you never gave back to your ex—because fuck him—comparing additive and subtractive sculpting. His carving, melting, beating into shape always felt so violent and overpowering to you. So finite, with its single end state. Growing something into life, you are discovering, is not any gentler. It's not violence onto but violence through what you are unleashing into the world.

"But under the scabs and the rust, your skin glows. You shrug off the dry outer layer, and it flakes off gently to the floor. You sweep all the flakes into a trash bag, tie the bag with a triple knot, and throw it in the heavy-lidded containers outside.

"Enjoy."

The silent waiters set a large plate in the middle of the table.

"This is a shared dish called 'Own'. A confit of wild boar's heart, acid-treated until it's as transparent as glass, stuffed with magnetic shavings, copper scales and iridescent glass microfibers in a balsamic syrup of spruce. As you take a bite, your individual chemistry will turn the heart a unique color and a taste that is personal and irreproducible. This way, though you share the dish, each of you will experience it in a unique way, alone.

"With your beautiful, resilient new skin, you feel safer leaving the apartment than you have in months. The spring air feels like a crispy new silken dress. Brilliant sunshine floods the grassy quad and turns the groups of happy students into a shadow theatre for you to walk through and watch. You hear someone calling you by name and turn around.

"The shadow runs to you and resolves into the beaming face of your former roommate. You haven't talked since she moved out and into the sculptor's apartment. You ask her how she's doing. She does a little happy dance and, instead of an answer, shows you an elegant art nouveau tattoo on her wrist. The grisaille linework looks a bit like rust in this light. You look up at her bright smile, confused.

"'It's a tattoo of your statue,' she sings out. 'Isn't it fabulous. His art is catching on like fire, and she started it all. She's meant to be the manifestation of empowerment which is, you know, so big right now, and everyone wants a reproduction or a T-shirt or a 3D model file. I licensed this for my online store and made enough to get a new beemer. With just enough left over for a commemorative tattoo. Crazy how these things just happen, right?'

"'Uh—Wow. So crazy' is all you can say before you have to walk off.

"But then you stop and take a step back.

"'Listen, when the time comes and you get tired of this copy of a copy of whatever it is you think you've tattooed on yourself, I hope you can find something real that's your own.'

"You're not sure if it makes sense but you mean it.

"'The beemer's real,' she recovers quickly—a reminder as to why you were friends once. 'And pretty empowering. And so is my degree. You still working on paying for yours?'

"'Nevermind,' you say. 'I was speaking the wrong language.'

"She shrugs and, staring at you, takes something smooth and shiny emblazoned with the BMW logo out of her pocket, and clicks it. Then walks off.

"Enjoy."

"This dish is called 'Missing'. A simple dip of pears, clove, driftwood, fossilized shark tooth powder, sugared violets, and civet musk served with elegant flakes of forty percent lead crystal; it's meant to serve as a palate cleanser before the last few dishes. You might want to focus on the sound of the flakes as you eat them. This is called the 'voice' of the glass. The highest and most resonant notes will come from high-quality crystal shaved by master chefs who have dedicated years to perfecting the craft.

"It's after midnight, and the grass doll isn't back yet. Yesterday, you reached your hand out to remove a piece of lead crystal from her side. You tell yourself it's because you felt it was hurting her, but the truth is that it was just unsightly—jagged, broken. She jerked away from you. You haven't seen her since.

"You sling your coat on and, even though it's summer, shove your feet in your boots—the only pair of shoes you own right now. You are saving up to pay the increase in tuition that the scholarships are no longer equal to, but the gap keeps growing. You have three months to start classes again before the visa expires and no way to pay for them. Now that you've unburied those thoughts, helplessness and panic crush your chest. Your head is booming like an ocean tide. The room tilts, and you lose your balance. You trip on your way to the door and hold onto its frame.

"The anger grounds you. You choose to focus on it. Where is the doll? It was you who bought her that cracked crystal bowl with the money you saved from lunch. All those sacrifices and she won't even—

"You walk up the street, past the condemned house. The hornet nest is gone. Some flakes from it, each the size of a small cranium, remain on the ground but nothing else.

"Enjoy."

After the waiters took away the empty plates, the maître d' stopped by to ask the couple how their dinner was going. The couple smiled, still a little bit too wide.

"Wonderful," the maître d' said and invited them to visit the powder room as this was another thing humans did.

Again, one by one, the couple walked down to the basement, inspected the basalt wall and turned around.

And again, one of the couple, the one who now smelled rather like a beehive made out of love letters wandered off into the first floor of the restaurant.

This time, she stopped by the mossy boulders and peered into the earthy lushness of the moss. It smelled like those first forests did, long before mammals, before dinosaurs. She noticed something small on one of the boulders—smooth and curiously opalescent. She reached over carefully, without disturbing the moss, and picked it up. It was a pearl shaped like a small skull.

The one who smelled like a beehive built in the desk of a lovelorn poet inspected it curiously and quickly popped it in her mouth. If anyone in the dimension of the old town had been looking at the sky that very moment, they would have seen a nacreous object about the size of the moon rise quickly into and out of orbit. So quickly it could have been attributed to an instrument error.

Around the boulders, the voice of the waitress came, muted, as if from another room:

"This course is called 'The Patience of Water'. It is a rare artifact from a long-lost city-by-a-river. The other side of the river was a high cliff with many caverns in which the people of the city would lay their dead. Mourners knelt in the shallows of the river waiting, while the earth made its way through the skies. For they knew there was a place on the other side of grief, which was a special place for each of them, and each sat in the river until the earth arrived there. While they waited, their bodies, subtly, changed the course of the water and thus the most peculiar shapes in the pebbles were formed."

But the waitress was in the kitchen, deeply focused on the arrangement of a variety of small morsels on two large plates.

"Our fifteenth course, 'Penthouse Kapali Carsi', is a sampler platter. Starting here on the left—three giant wasps are filled with a mixture of minced hummingbird lungs, pulverized calf brains, pearl barley, raisins, and herbs, and salt roasted in a clay oven. Next is a miniature soufflé of veal bone marrow and snake eggs served with hay-smoked cream. Then, strawberries dipped in quicksilver; ambergris roasted in honey, oakmoss, and spices; and finally, deep-fried rose-petal tart shells filled with ice cream of caramelized cheese, fossilized peach, and bits of Turkish delight.

"Today is the Sunday before autumn finals start. You get up at an uncharacteristic six in the morning to ward off random attempts to snipe your bid on a 560 gram ball of ambergris from Ulaanbaatar. Despite its high ceilings and Victorian crown molding, your new apartment looks like a miniature version of the Grand Bazaar in Istanbul where your parents took you once when you were six and let you haggle with the amused merchants. You didn't speak the language save for a few words, but that child's self-assurance made you feel like you could define any space you walked into, bring into reality anything you imagined ... And also get all the lokum you could eat.

"Turns out the child was right.

"You put on gloves and open the window. You stand in the window frame with a vintage mercury thermometer you seriously overpaid for and whistle. The grass doll pops out from under a hedge way down on the ground and climbs her way up in the same strange way she walks. Her bottom has grown into a conical shape, like a bumblebee butt, and rattles softly with the remains of her dinner.

"Next, she is fed and asleep, plump and glossy green. Stroking her back, your fingers snag on a rough, flaky spot—a dark orange, almost like a very, very old blood stain. If grass could rust you'd swear—

"Enjoy."

"For our next course, 'The Nostalgia of Prisons Past' we have blinis peppered with charcoal, sulphur, and saltpeter flakes, served with champagne sorbet.

"Today, the grass doll has been missing for three days.

"Lately, she hasn't been eating much of the things you buy for her either. You are enshrined in very rare, very expensive things in boxes that you can't wait to share with her.

"She must be foraging for strange things around the university— the place where strange things congregate. So you grab a few of her favorite snacks and walk there looking for her.

"It's been a while since you were on campus. When were you there last? The month you were taking junior math and stats? That was a year ago, wasn't it?—irrationally, you look at your vintage Rolex, traded for one of your Roman salt-crystal containers, the one the doll sniffed and ignored. It's 8:35 p.m.

"You carry a printed-out picture of the grass doll and ask the students wading through the thickening darkness if they've seen her.

"'Try the union, it's where everyone goes,' a guy says in passing without even looking at the picture.

"You've been everywhere else, so you go to the new student union building. It's well lit but empty. All the food places in it are closed. Still you walk around and stare hungrily at the pictures of the junk food. You can afford to buy anything you want here, but that feeling of hunger will never leave you. That's okay—it makes you feel cozy and warm now, like nostalgia.

"Enjoy."

"Our seventeenth course is called 'The Three Ways of Flesh'". It consists of three cubes: solid ammonia, silk-polished rosewood, and pressed Cretaceous grasses served with fig jam and assorted stone fruits.

"Instead of wine we have paired the dish with a glass of local artisanal moonshine, best taken as a shot with the last bite.

"The doll isn't here but the statue is. It's on the second floor, standing on a custom black plinth hewn to look like a rock outcrop. She is still smaller than you. Leaner. More elegant. Fully comfortable that she belongs even if her polished flesh is looking a bit sickly in this liminal, fluorescent purgatory.

"You look around for something chisel-like, something sharp or heavy, and then remember the meteorite Damascus steel knife you were carrying to coax the grass doll with. You take it out and feel it in your palm. The anger comes back, shockingly fresh, and tugs at your pant legs and sleeves. You grab onto the stone with your free hand, to steady yourself for when you slice your scars off her legs. Or erase the face that was stolen from you.

"Both violent choices but you feel like violence right now.

"You take a step back. Without thinking, you kneel in front of the statue and stab at the place where her foot is glued to the plinth.

You stab again and again and again until the foot hangs loose over the plinth.

"'That's way better,' a voice above you startles you, and you nick the smooth oaken leg.

"'Sorry,' you say reflexively. 'Are you okay?'

"'It's fine,' the statue says. 'Didn't feel a thing. I'll be better once I know what you're planning to do with that sharp object though.'

"You stand up, holding the heavy steel in your hand.

"'I don't know yet,' you say and lift up the photo. 'My living grass doll. Have you seen her?'

"Over the hands resting on her chest, the statue looks at the picture.

"'Not lately, sorry. But if you finish freeing me, I'll help you search.'

"You kneel and start stabbing at the plinth again.

"'What's your name,' you ask her.

"'Not sure yet. Absolutely not Galatea,' the statue says and snorts with patrician derision, when you make a face. 'Can you believe the nerve of that Fucker—'

"Enjoy."

"Our dessert for you today is a dish called 'Kinetic'. It is two halves of a heart grown out of wild, living crystal. The crystal hasn't been touched by human hands, which is why we serve it in its original grass shell.

"When you return home in the morning, the doll is there, waiting outside. You want to pick her up and take her home, but when you bend over and look closer, you see the piece of crystal in her side has changed. It has sprouted—delicate crystal nubs peek out from under the grass blades. It kinda looks like the scar tissue on your legs but beautiful. And that is not the only thing taken root in her—metals, salts, flowers, rare fossils, and minerals—growing, transforming, living. You hear them rattle and clank when she breathes.

"All the way home you have been thinking about something the statue said while you were walking around the perimeter of the quad, peeking into the red-berry covered shrubs—

"'Why do you call her a living doll though,' the statue asked.

"'I mean—she walks; she eats; she grows. Isn't that what living is?'

"'Maybe for you animals. I don't think it is for creatures like us.'

"'But you are living now?'

The statue thought over the question for a while.

"'Yes. I'm certain. I know there was a time before and after I felt alive. You can't miss it—the confusion, the pressure of something under your skin, the want, something else I can't name too. But mostly the confusion. Life is very confusing feeling—'

"'And you think my grass doll doesn't feel that,' you asked.

"'I don't know. She is your grass doll. What do you think?"

"You didn't know how to interpret the stress the statue placed on the possessive.

"'Do you remember when you changed,' you asked her.

"'I remember the very moment,' she smiled. 'It was exactly when your dagger—,'

"'Well, chef's knife—' you muttered.

"'—hit the resin holding me onto that rock. You gave me away. That's how it felt at least. It felt like I could have a life—pardon the crude sentiment— even after you're dead.'

"'But it wasn't me who made you. You weren't mine to give awa—

The statue crossed her arms and tilted her head at you with one raised patrician eyebrow.

"'Okay, yeah, I get it,' you said.

"'It was when you gave me away,' the statue repeated, 'that I could leave and grow beyond your recognition. The confusion and the power. Yes, that was the name—feeling of power.'"

On their way out of the restaurant, the couple passed by the smoking basalt dunes. One of them, the one with the bare shoulders and sinuous scarf, the one who now just smelled of a bee hive, the one who had always been curious, dipped her hand in the nearest one.

The sand was pleasantly cool to the touch. It slid softly over her hand, coating it like a glove and dissipating a bit in the air. It smelled quite curious too. How would the waitress describe it—an evening but not just any evening, snow in the air, smoke, the luster on the glass baubles and glittering scarves hanging from the trees on the way to the restaurant.

She licked her hand and breathed in the powdery smoke.

Unbidden, delightful, a purely human memory appeared of a moment that had never happened, but she kept it to herself.

The couple walked out through the exit door, a little after midnight, when the tide was in. Unremarkable in the evening, the restaurant looked striking underwater. The droopy growth on the stones had come to life and was swaying drunkenly with the currents. Long columns of moonlight refracted from the surface and scanned the shallows. Among them, schools of colorful fish escorted the guests on their way.

The waitress walked through the service exit into the clear morning air of the old town. She leaned on the wall with its graffiti of varying artistic merit and bent over to rub her swollen ankles and her stiff knee.

Right then, from the other side of the wall came a harsh scratching sound—like metal on concrete. The waitress covered her ears. A finger—just like a human finger except for the dark steam that was gently evaporating from its flesh—poked through the wall and tore through the cement as if it was paper. It drew back, and a head with gentle steam evaporating from it popped out.

"Hi," the steaming woman said to the other. She had strange undertones to her skin —like a field of grass swaying in the wind.

"Hi."

They looked at each other for a long time.

"Do you know who you are," the woman who had been a waitress asked.

"I do. Yes. I know I'm not yours anymore— Thank you for that."

The woman who had been a waitress shrugged.

"It wasn't about me. Do you have a name?" she asked the steaming woman.

"Not yet. I'll think of something. In the meantime, I really want to go swimming. I've heard it's the best feeling in the world. Do you want to come?" the steaming woman asked.

"I always want to go swimming. But the river is frozen till summer."

The steaming woman smiled and put her ear to the graffiti.

"Don't worry. It's not frozen on this side of the wall. Just give me a second to pry it open a bit."

And so they went that winter night, side by side, into the silken darkness of the ocean. Under the surface of the water, the skin of the woman who used to be a doll, turned translucent and, inside her, her crystal heart beat with a soft chirrup. She was still steaming a little but for that one can only blame the curious diner who couldn't help herself near the smoking basalt sands.

The woman who used to be a waitress—and before that so many other things—dove deep, deep, deep and scooped a handful of sand from the bottom of the ocean. She opened her palm and poured it slowly out. Then she started swimming towards the horizon.

LOVE SONGS FOR THE END OF THE WORLD

Mercedes M. Yardley

He was in love with the moon. Or rather, the moon was in love with him. This caused all kinds of problems.

The moon is a jealous mistress, so we've heard, and Nathanial Blank discovered this firsthand. He was a little boy with wide eyes and untamable hair. He sat with his friends outside, watching the moon rise fat and full over the horizon.

"Have you ever seen anything more beautiful?" Nathanial breathed. The moon, used to being adored, for some reason blushed on this night. She twirled her skirts and batted her eyes.

"Truly lustrous," he said. "I should like to write a song about her."

He did, and it was a sweet thing strummed out gently on his child-sized guitar. The moon was charmed. She whispered to his friends, and they, influenced by her solemn beauty, nodded.

"Come out and play, Nathanial," they said a few nights later. "We have something to show you." And he followed, he followed—a young, gullible boy who trusted the friends with whom he rode bikes and collected caterpillars.

He followed them to the edge of the lake.

"Wait here," they said, and scattered. Their pockets were full of moon rocks and moonbeams and everything else she had promised them.

"Guys?" Nathanial asked, and his skinny body quavered. It was cold and dark, and he was alone in the wilds of the forest.

Suddenly the moon rose, a grand thing, resplendent in her cold glory, and she told little Nathanial Blank that he was hers, he belonged to the most idolized thing in the universe, and he too would write poetry about her luminosity and allure. They were married now, she said.

"And if you so much as look at another lover, I will kill you," she promised, pouting prettily.

"But I'm only six," Nathanial piped.

The moon followed him all through childhood, and into his teen years. She followed so closely that nobody wanted much to do with him. He ate lunch alone while the other kids snickered. When he wiped his sweaty palms on his pants and asked Nora Israelson out to prom, the moon gnashed her teeth and pulled the tides sharply to the right. Ships bobbled uneasily on the sea, and the river flooded its shores. Nathanial Blank held Nora's hand while she picked through the mud in her borrowed, impossibly high shoes. Prom night was effectively ruined.

"We are not married," he screamed at the moon, but she only laughed.

The moon kept Nathanial close during high school and college and into his thirties. He sat alone in his room, playing his guitar, and singing songs he'd keep to himself. But one day he showed up to find the most beautiful woman he'd ever seen standing in his office.

"Hi, I'm Priya. You're blocking the printer. Can you please move?"

"Uh …" he said, and clumsily danced to the side. His thin legs jerked like pistons. His arms were a series of metal joints fused together.

"Thank you," she said. Her dark eyes glowed with humor, not reflecting the moon at all, and Nathanial was head over heels.

On Tuesday he blocked the water cooler.

Wednesday found him loitering outside the women's bathroom. After a brief talk with security, he decided to block somewhere less creepy.

Thursday, he blocked the printer again, and the trash can.

On Friday Priya asked him out.

"If I don't, I'm afraid you'll block my way to the parking lot," she said, "and I don't want to spend the night in my office chair."

Nathanial's ears turned red, and Priya laughed. They decided to go for drinks after work, and as she spoke, Nathanial fell deeper and deeper and deeper.

Gravity did a strange thing, where it felt both too heavy and far too light. Nathanial wanted to tie a ribbon around Priya's ankle so she didn't float straight up into the sky.

"What is this?" she asked. "Is this what falling in love is like?"

"It's my ex messing with gravity," Nathanial admitted. Priya turned to see a great, round face pressed against the window. She gasped, but quickly recovered and gave a tiny wave.

The moon spun and left in a huff.

"So, um, I think I'm head over heels for you already, which sounds mad," Nathanial told Priya. "Your eyes are so full of warmth and life that I can't catch my breath. I've been sitting on my hands this whole time because I'm afraid I'll reach out to touch your hair. But dating me comes with ... complications," he ended.

Priya took his hands in hers. He wondered at her strong, gold jewelry.

"Nathanial Blank, I've watched you for a long, long time. You've never noticed me, but I've been in this office for over a year. I've been wanting to ask you out for months. You're so kind. You're gentle. You're clever, and you've pulled the company out of more than one hardship. But you're so special that the moon herself desires you. Why would you want to date me?"

"What?" Nathanial asked.

"What?" The moon asked from where she was eavesdropping.

"My heart is going to beat out of my chest," Nathanial said. "This is a dream."

"This is a nightmare," the moon said. She had to sit down hard.

"There will be implications to this," Nathanial warned, but Priya took his face in her soft hands, leaned forward, and touched her lips to his.

He saw stars.

No, he saw stars, because the moon was shrieking and hurtling them down at him.

"How could you do this to me?" she screeched, and the Milky Way was torn apart and rained from the sky.

"Ooh!" said the people of Earth. "Ahh!"

"Ahhh!" screamed the moon, and ripped Orion's belt from his constellation. She closed one eye, aimed at Nathan, and sent the three stars Alnitak, Alnilam, and Mintaka soaring through the sky, the atmosphere, and straight into Seattle, Washington. The Puget Sound exploded, and fish flew out of the water and onto the beaches.

"Implications?" Priya asked. She dug herself out of the rubble. "Is this what you meant, Nathanial?"

"Take his name out of your mouth," commanded the moon.

Nathanial sighed and shook plaster out of his hair.

"This is exactly what I mean. This is why I've been alone for so long. But I don't want to be alone anymore, Priya. The moon doesn't understand anything about human relationships. She bit my cousin once. I can't hang out with guys from work. I was on the swimming team until she twirled around and made the pool so choppy we nearly drowned. She wants me all to herself, isolated from everybody else, and the thought alone makes me want to ..."

Priya took his hand.

"You're not alone anymore. There are two of us, now. We can withstand anything."

Can love withstand the end of the world? It was time to find out.

Perhaps the moon thought Nathanial's love for Priya was simply a phase he was going through. She hissed and spat and followed them sullenly when they went on dates. She refused to shine and sat dull and listless in the sky. But one day, under the bright, warm sun, Nathanial fell awkwardly to one knee.

"Oh, dear, are you all right?" Priya exclaimed. "Do you need me to help you home?"

"Marry me," he squeaked, and winced. He had an elaborate speech all prepared, using big words and lush language. He had practiced in his mirrors for hours while the moon tried pointedly not to hear, but when he looked into Priya's eyes, his words left him. "Marry me" is what he meant, and "Marry me" is what he said. He pulled a ring from his pocket, and his hands trembled. Priya's hands trembled, too, when he slid the ring on her finger. It was shiny and glittery and matched the tears streaming down her face.

"Oh Nathanial, I couldn't be happier," she exclaimed, and threw herself into his arms. Thus began the end of the world.

They say the world will end in a whimper instead of a bang. What a farce.

The moon screamed. She rent her garments and gnashed her teeth and sent the International Space Station spiraling away, never to be seen again. She leapt out of her orbit and sent the weather on Earth into a tailspin. Take that, Nathanial Blank.

"Earthquakes are tearing the streets of San Francisco apart," the news said.

"Tsunamis have obliterated parts of Japan."

"Volcanoes are erupting under the sea. Parts of the ocean are literally boiling. Hold your loved ones tight, listeners. This might be the end."

The end. An extinction event. A planet killer.

The Apocalypse.

Armageddon.

"It's just a vengeful ex," Nathanial fumed. He was pacing, his long legs eating up the ground and quivering a bit as the earth beneath him shook. "I can't believe she'd go this far."

"Yes, you can," Priya said, and it was true. After the wedding, the moon tried to peer in their window with one baleful eye, but they had put up blackout curtains and refused to open them. "You knew exactly how she'd react. But what do we do now, Nathanial? Do we separate? Let the world go back to normal? Are we really so selfish as to sacrifice the world for our love?"

The room shook violently, as the moon tore herself in half and sent the large chunk of herself hurling to the earth. Nathanial fell to the ground and reached for Priya.

"I'll sacrifice everything for you, my love. Everything." His eyes were alight with their intensity, and he shone, a nuclear apocalypse of love. "This world? We've had a good run. Honestly, look at everybody. I think they're ready to go."

It was true. Suddenly the wars stopped, and people started working together. Armies were digging victims out of wreckage, and military planes were parachuting in food and supplies. Who had time to invade a country when the very earth itself was roiling beneath your feet? People reached out to loved ones. Fathers who hadn't been seen in years called home. Children forgave their siblings. It was a time of peace and joy amidst the turmoil.

"Ah, screw it," Nathanial said. "I can't let it end like this, even if this is the most well-behaved humanity has been in years."

He kissed his sleeping bride on her forehead and crept out of their apartment. He skittered past the fallen debris that littered the street and loped toward the car.

He drove. He drove past the felled trees and around the cracks on the ground. His car got stuck in the overflowing stream, and he had to wade through the water. He made it to the lake where he had met the moon so many years before.

"Hey," he said, but the moon wouldn't look at him. She was jagged and looked like a broken jawbreaker. He picked up a smooth rock and skipped it across the surface. It hit the moon's reflection, and she shuddered. This is the closest you can get to the moon, you know.

"Moon, I think you know why I'm here. I know you're angry with me—"

The moon sniffed.

"—but it isn't fair, is it? To be angry? You never, not once, asked me what I wanted. And what I want is to love you. It's what I always wanted."

The moon paused, and the surface of the lake stilled.

"I'm sorry that I can't love you in a real relationship type of way," Nathanial explained. "It isn't possible for me to hold you or for us to make love or be together in that way. But you're so beautiful, even now that you're in pieces. You take my breath away. I want to look at you forever and ever, and, well, I wrote a song for you."

Nathanial Blank took his guitar off his back and strummed it gently. Then he began to sing. He sang a song of her beauty, of love, a real love song for the end of the world, and the moon's eyes filled with tears. What a delightful little thing! He was so infinitely precious, this man, and the others who gazed on her with dewy eyes. What a waste to destroy them all. Who would adore her then?

"I'm sorry," whispered the moon, and she promised to pull back the tides, the chunks of herself that were going to obliterate the entire world. She was beginning to understand there were different kinds of love, and Nathanial's love for Priya didn't mean he couldn't love the moon, too.

"Oh, I'll always love you!" Nathanial promised her. "How could I not, when I have seen how deeply you have loved me? You have always seen the best in me, and Priya does, as well. I hope you two and my mother will be the top three ladies in my life. Well, four, actually," he said, and his ears turned red. The moon remembered how many times that had happened in his life, and her heart spun on the notes of his song. "There will be another little lady, soon. We're expecting a baby. We also wanted to ask you, if you didn't mind terribly, if we could have your blessing to name her Luna? And ask if you'd possibly consider being her godmother?"

Well.

Well.

The moon had never considered such a thing, but it evoked the most joyous feelings inside of her. Her own little asteroid. Her own little beam. Her own little Luna, from her own little Nathanial Blank, who loved her despite herself.

Yes and yes and yes.

Thus, the world was saved, and a baby was born. There was a party and presents, and they held her blessing in the wee hours so the moon could shine big and bright, as she kissed the faces of those she had grown to love so dearly.

"She has your eyes," Priya told the moon.

"Of course, she does," the moon said, and dazzled.

WHEN THE MAGIC SETTLES INTO ITS SKY-REACHING FORM

(after reading "The Delight Song of Tsoai-talee" by N. Scott Momoday)

Helen Patrice

I am the space made by a worm in earth
I am the warm place where magic grows
I am a rosehip breaking open to reveal its heart
I am the seed being pierced by a spell
I am the root in rich ground
I am the sprout pushing upwards towards I know not what
I am the seedling feeling sun for the first time
I am one of many around a castle of stone
I am pale green and purple, spreading outwards
I am the trunk that thickens
I am many canes, straight, bent, crowding close
I am the thorn strong as steel
I am the scaffold from which knights and princes will hang
I am the strong forest where no light falls
I am the place of story where children are afraid to go

You see, I am alive, I am alive
I stand as protector of the princess
I stand as guardian of the sleeping
I stand as wall of rose-studded beauty
I stand as challenge to the foolish and the brave
I stand as what a sleeping girl may need to become
You see, I am alive, I am alive

Acknowledgements

I believe in fairy godmothers, for without the sudden appearance of one, this book would never have been born. Thank you for making this project a dream come true.

<h1 style="text-align:center">About the Authors</h1>

A. KATHERINE BLACK adores multicolored pens, long winters, and her overworked coffee machines. She lives in the Northwoods with her family and their cats, where she dreams up stories of creatures with bunches of legs, tentacles, and wings. Find her at flywithpigs.com.

CLAIRE ELIZA BARTLETT is the author of speculative fiction for children, young adults, and adults. Her work is feminist in focus and interested in exploring what women do when faced with impossible choices. She began a career in history and archaeology, but realized she likes learning things better than she likes knowing them, so now she takes inspiration from historical events and weaves them into her work. She lives in Denmark with one husband, one child, and one cat. She can be found online at authorclaire.com, where she also has a newsletter.

FIJA CALLAGHAN is a storyteller and poet who has been recognized by a number of awards, including winning the SFPA Poetry Prize in 2024 and shortlisting for the HG Wells Short Story Prize in 2021. Her writing can be found in venues like *Seaside Gothic, Gingerbread House, Howl: New Irish Writing*, and elsewhere. Her debut collection, *Frail Little Embers*, was released by Neem Tree Press in 2025. You can find out more about her at www.fijacallaghan.com.

ELLIE CAMPBELL is a longtime student at the Storied Imaginarium and has published stories that originated in SI classes with

Mermaids Monthly and *Wizards in Space Literary Magazine*. She has also published speculative fiction criticism with *Ancillary Review of Books*, the *BFSA Review*, and *Vector*. She is a librarian and professor and currently lives in North Carolina with too many books and just enough cats.

GIO CLAIRVAL is an Italian-born writer who used to live in Paris, France, then Edinburgh, Scotland, and currently hails from Lake Como, Italy. Her stories have appeared or are forthcoming in *Weird Tales, Fantasy, PostScripts, The Dark,* and elsewhere. She translates literary works from French, Italian, Spanish, and German into English.

ALISON COLWELL spends her time creating imaginary worlds and fracturing fairy tales. When not writing she can sometimes be found teaching kindergarten kids how to bake bread—a magic all its own. Her fiction can be found in *Daily Science Fiction, Flash Fiction Magazine, The Drabble, Tangled Locks Journal, Crow & Cross Keys Magazine, Carmina Magazine*, and *The Orange & Bee*. Her creative non-fiction work can be found in the climate-fiction anthology *Rising Tides, The Humber Literary Review, The Ocotillo Review, Roi Faineant Literary Press, Hippocampus Magazine* and *Grist*. Alison Colwell lives on a very small emerald island in the Salish Sea, with her kids. Find her online at www.alisoncolwell.com.

CHELSEA CONRADT (she/her) is the USA Today bestselling author of *The Farmhouse*. She writes twisty speculative thrillers and psychological horror. Her books are packed with both murder and kindness because we can be more than one thing. When not writing stories that make you question what's real, she is likely watching a baking show or a true-crime documentary. She is nothing if not on brand. Chelsea lives in Texas with her husband, son, and two big dogs. Chelsea can be found online at chelseaconradt.com.

HILLARY DODGE is an award-winning editor and author of speculative short fiction and poetry, as well as three nonfiction books. She spends a good deal of time traveling, going places that are forbidden, and eating. She once had tea with a Roma in a cave in the mountains of Spain. Another time found her eight hours from civilization in the heart of the Atacama with a mad desert hermit. She has been published in online magazines, podcasts, and print anthologies, including *Pseudopod*, *Space & Time Magazine*, the *HWA Poetry Showcase* volumes IX and X, *Cosmic Horror Monthly*, *Space Squid*, *Hellbound Books*, *D&T Publishing*, & *Hex Publishers*. She is a co-editor of *Shadow Atlas: Dark Landscapes of the Americas* (Hex Publishers 2021), which was awarded the 2022 Colorado Book Award in the category of anthology. You can find her at hillarydodge. com.

ANTONIA ELIASON is a law professor in Mississippi by day and a speculative fiction writer by night. She researches climate change, space law, and international economic law, and consequently spends a lot of time thinking about colonialism. She is currently pursuing a PhD in history, with a dissertation focusing on women convicted of political crimes in Hungary between 1949-1953.

CHRISTINA HIRA is an emerging poet, leveraging the power of words to create meaning from the wholehearted devastation of being human.

WAILANA KALAMA is a dark fiction writer from Hawaii, with credits in Dark Matter INK's *Monstrous Futures*, *Monster Lairs*, *The Off-Season*, *Pseudopod*, and others.

HARALAMBI MARKOV is a Bulgarian queer and nonbinary fiction writer, reviewer, and editor with a background in content creation, who currently works as a freelance writer. They were the first ever Bulgarian to be accepted to attend the Clarion Writers' Workshop in 2014. Their short story "The Language of Knives" was long-listed for the Nebula award for Best Short Story. Their work has appeared in *TOR.com*, *Uncanny Magazine*, *Evil in Technicolor*, *Weird Fiction Review*, *Stories for Chip*, *Eurasian Monsters*, *Nightmare Magazine*, and *Make Your Presence Known*. They were part of the team of BonFIYAH 2021.

ALLISON PANG is the author of the Urban Fantasy *Abby Sinclair* series, the steampunk *IronHeart Chronicles* series, and also the writer for the ongoing webcomic *Fox & Willow*. Her short stories can be found in *Flash Fiction Online* and various anthologies. She likes LEGOS, elves, LEGO elves … and bacon.

HELEN PATRICE is an Australian writer living in Naarm (Melbourne) on Wurundjeri Country. She writes speculative short fiction and poetry alongside literary poetry, and also works with creative nonfiction and memoir. Recent publications include *Lady Liberty*, *Knot Literary Journal*, and *Young Ravens Literary Journal*. Her new collection of fairy tale poetry *Into Dark Woods* is forthcoming.

RHEA ROSE has published many speculative short fiction stories and poems. She is a four-time Canadian Aurora Award nominee, a Rhysling nominee, and recipient of several Ellen Datlow honorable mentions. She was the featured author in a recent issue of *Pulp Literature*. She is an active member of HWA, SF Canada, and SFPA and is the editor of *Polar Starlight*, an online magazine of speculative poetry by Canadian authors.

KATHERINE HEATH SHAEFFER is a writer, a narrative designer, and a graduate of the Odyssey Writers Workshop. She has had a few short pieces published here and there, including in *Daily Science Fiction*, *Apex Magazine*, and *Flash Fiction Online*. Once upon a time, she studied Medieval and Early Modern literature as a part of an English PhD program, and she certainly tackled the text which inspired her story for this anthology more than once. While paying her dues, first as a graduate assistant and later as an assistant professor, she may have forced some poor, unsuspecting undergraduates to tackle it as well.

ANAMI SHEPPARD currently lives in Salt Lake City, Utah with her husband, daughter, and doggie. Long ago, in a galaxy not so far away, she earned an undergraduate degree in creative writing and attended the Odyssey Writing Workshop. Her work has been published in the *Evansville Review* and *On the Premises*. She loves writing speculative fiction and poetry, and has destroyed more than three keyboards, clattering away. She takes this to be literal proof as to the power of stories.

J. M. SPRONK (they, them) is a retired air traffic controller who finds writing to be just as stressful but less life-threatening. They graduated Simon Fraser University's The Writer's Studio in 2015 (Southbank 2014). Their speculative stories have been published in *Pulp Literature, Polar Starlight, Zooscape, Fabulist Flash, Spekulative Anthologies*, and *The Orange & Bee*.

RONI STINGER lives in the Pacific Northwest, USA. Her short stories and poetry have appeared in dozens of magazines and anthologies, including *Dark Matter Magazine, Unnerving Magazine* and *Underland Arcana*. Her debut novella *Fuzzy (Rewind or Die 34)* is available now from Unnerving Books. She's a member of the HWA, SFPA, Codex, and a Board Member of Willamette Writers. You can find her online at www.ronistinger.com.

NIKE SULWAY won the Queensland Premier's Award for *The Bone Flute* in 2000. Since then she has published the novels *The True Green of Hope, Rupetta,* and *Dying in the First Person,* as well as the children's picture book *What the Sky Knows* (illustrated by Stella Danalis) and the children's chapter book *Winter's Tale* (illustrated by Shauna O'Meara). Her works have won or been shortlisted for a range of national and international awards, including the Queensland Premier's Literary Award, the Commonwealth Writers Prize, the Children's Book Council of Australia's Book of the Year Award, the IAFA Crawford Award, an Aurealis Award, the Norma K. Hemming Award, the Otherwise Award (formerly known as the James Tiptree Jr. Literary Award), and the Rhysling Award.

DANIELA TOMOVA was raised by a herd of feral books in an underground library. She draws her inspiration from Balkan folklore, the worlds of Ray Bradbury, the dreams of Andrei Tarkovsky, and the everyday magic of people who live in the ruins of countless civilizations. She is a Bulgarian-Norwegian writer and a graduate of Clarion Writers' Workshop. Her work has been published in *Apex Magazine*, *Tor*, *Best Horror of the Year*, *Best of World SF*, and elsewhere. Data scientist by day, she lives in an abandoned airport in Oslo, Norway with her partner and their cat.

KT WAGNER writes speculative fiction and poetry in the garden of her home on the west coast of Canada. She loves to knit and is a collector of strange plants, weird trivia, and obscure tomes. KT graduated from Simon Fraser University's Writers Studio in 2015 (Southbank 2013). She organizes writer events and works to create literary community. Her work is published and podcast with *The Twisted Book of Shadows*, *Pulp Literature*, *Daily Science Fiction*, *Cosmic Horror Monthly*, *On Spec*, *Toasted Cake* and more. Find her online at www.ktwagner.com and https://bsky.app/profile/ktwagner.bsky.social.

DIANTHE WEST (she/they) is an art historian turned poet and fiction author, which was always the prize. Their work has recently appeared in *HWA Poetry Showcase IX*, *Decapitate*, and *Whispers From Beyond* from Crystal Lake Publishing. Dianthe holds an MA from UC Riverside and lectured in visual culture for fourteen years in the US and Canada. They live with their family, plants, four-legged familiars, and hundreds of grazing bunnies in Guelph, Ontario.

LESLIE WIBBERLEY lives in a suburb of Vancouver, British Columbia. Her work is published in multiple literary journals and anthologies, including the Bram Stoker-nominated *Not All Monsters* and the Aurora-nominated *Prairie Witch*. Her stories have placed first in the *Writers Digest*'s Annual Writing Competition and Popular Fiction Awards, Creative Ink's Flash Fiction Contest, the Chanticleer International Book Awards, and the Pacific Northwest Writers Association Literary Contest. She is represented by Naomi Davis of Bookends Literary.

MERCEDES M. YARDLEY is a whimsical dark fantasist who wears red lipstick and poisonous flowers in her hair. She is the author of numerous works including *Darling*, the Stabby Award-winning *Apocalyptic Montessa* and *Nuclear Lulu: A Tale of Atomic Love*, *Pretty Little Dead Girls*, and *Nameless*. She won the Bram Stoker Award for her stories *Love Is a Crematorium*, *Little Dead Red* and "Fracture." Mercedes lives and works in Las Vegas. You can find her at mercedesmyardley.com.

About the Editor

CARINA BISSETT is a writer and poet working primarily in the fields of dark fiction and fabulism. She has written numerous short stories, many of which are featured in her debut collection *Dead Girl, Driving and Other Devastations* (2024), and she is also a co-editor of the award-winning anthology *Shadow Atlas: Dark Landscapes of the Americas* (2021). Her fiction has been nominated for the Shirley Jackson Award. Her poetry has been nominated for the Rhysling Award, the Pushcart Prize, and Sundress Publications Best of the Net. And her nonfiction has been nominated for a Bram Stoker Award®. Links to her work can be found at http://carinabissett.com.

In addition to writing, she has edited several projects including the anthology *Storyteller: A Tanith Lee Tribute Anthology* (with Julie C. Day and Craig Laurance Gidney). She is also the co-publisher, with Nike Sulway, of the literary fairy tale journal *The Orange & Bee*.

As an educator, Carina has taught at Pikes Peak Community College, Glendale Community College, and Arizona State University. She also participated in the Colorado Writing Project and works with educators to develop writing instruction in college and secondary school classrooms. She currently offers workshops focused on story generation at the Storied Imaginarium.

Her fiction has been nominated for the Sundress Publications Best of the Net Award and was a finalist for the Ron L. Hubbard Writers of the Future Awards. Her poetry has been nominated for the Rhysling Award, the Pushcart Prize, and the Sundress Publications Best of the Net Award. Her nonfiction was a finalist for the Bram Stoker Awards®. In her editorial capacity, she's received recognition as a co-editor for *Shadow Atlas: Dark Landscapes of the Americas* (with Hillary Dodge and Joshua Viola), as a winner at the Colorado Book Awards 2022 for Anthology and as a finalist in the Fiction: Anthologies category of the 2022 International Book Awards.

www.ingramcontent.com/pod-product-compliance
Lightning Source LLC
Chambersburg PA
CBHW070531120726
47909CB00007B/2101